Jamaica Rush

By

Jef Huntsman

Belray Books, LLC

This book, and all characters contained herein are fiction.
Any resemblance to actual people or real events is
unintended. The places found in these pages are real with
some adjustment to make them fit within the story. Any
liberties taken are those from the author.

Jamaica Rush / Jef Huntsman – First Edition
ISBN # 978-0997574821 (pb)
ISBN # 978-0997574838 (ebook)

Cover designed by Harry Baldwin

Dedication

This thriller novel is dedicated to all those shelves of books and volumes of e-books which have stirred a creative curiosity in me, and to all the people who, even unknowingly, left tiny crumbs of themselves for me to gather and put together as a character or event. And to my best friend, the lady who keeps my heart ever thumping, Diana Huntsman.

**Also by the Author
Jef Huntsman:**

Heart Attack, Yak, Yak

Tattered Portrait

*Bald Cats and Deaf Elephants
(A Book of Poetry)*

Coming in the Fall, 2018

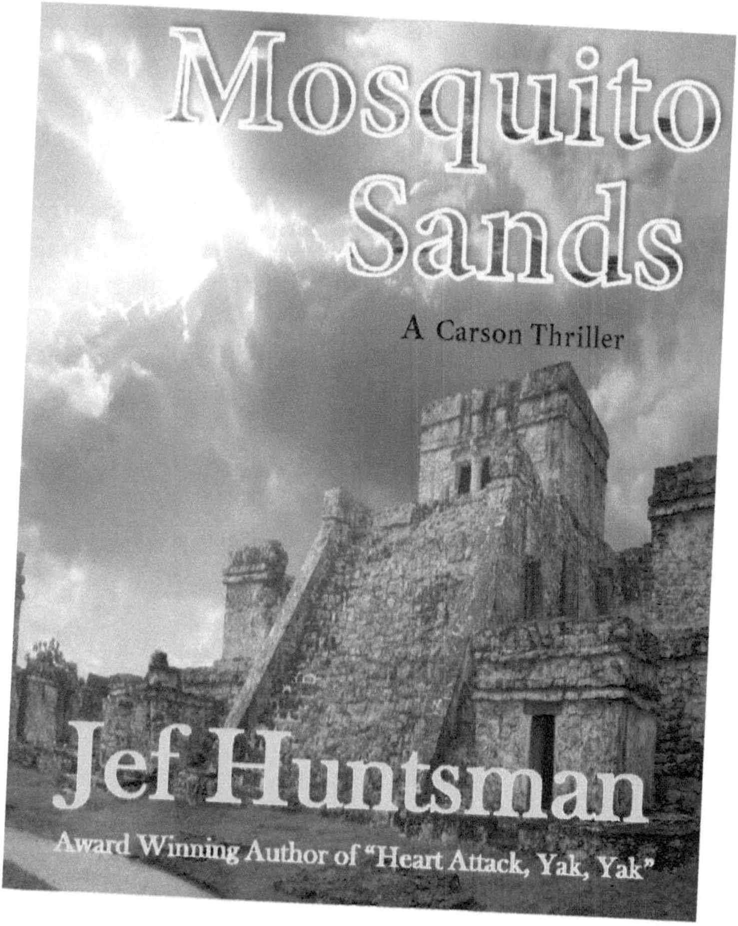

Mosquito Sands

A Carson Thriller

Jef Huntsman

Award Winning Author of "Heart Attack, Yak, Yak"

A Carson Thriller

Belray Books, LLC

Acknowledgments

To Belray Books who saw my vision and thanks to my incredible writer friends. Big thanks to Nolyn Starbuck who has that musical gift of language. Jae Dansie for her never ending red marker. A tip of my ballcap to Kathy Goodman for her insight into poetry and prose. Thank you, Kevin Shannon, whose understanding of odd and timely words would put Webster to shame. And to Cindy Hung, the girl who fully understands what a novel should look like. To Gene Springsteel for making the water flow in each chapter. And to the wonderful spirit of writing that Heidi Voss shares. A special gratitude to Rachel Jensen for throwing punctuation hither and yon.

As always, teary appreciation toward the sky to my dear mother who taught me the privilege of reading. And to a God who has allowed me to have an abundance of fun and laughter in my life.

Jamaica Rush

By

Jef Huntsman

Jamaica Rush

1

Carson

The car billowed clay dust in a hurried tail half a mile long, coating the cedars. I sat lazily in my *office*, with both feet propped up on the edge of an outdoor fire pit. Even with the blurred shape, I could tell it was a newer vehicle meant for roads with stoplights and street sweepers. Where else could they be heading but right here. I wondered if they'd lose it over the cattle guard. A short sideways slide and the car found a furrow and locked in. The front end bounced out over the ridge, the driver overcompensating as sage brush scratched new paint. My cheeks puffed as a smile pasted upon my face. *City.* I turned and marked my place in this month's *Psychology Today* with a Twix wrapper.

The shadows were lengthening off the Chinese elms and thick desert cedar clumps. The late afternoon was calm in every direction but west. The car slid as it rounded the corner, bottomed the shocks over the culvert, forced its way down my rutted lane, and passed through the open gate.

Rocks spit from the tires. I imagined rabbits and lizards scurrying from the sound and coughing in the upheaval. The once shiny gold Lexus stopped with a crunch of gravel and the settling of fine dirt on its professionally detailed surface. The car gasped twice before shutting down. A dry earthy taste filled my mouth.

Tan legs with chiseled calves stepped out of the car. My appreciation followed them. As I looked upward, I watched a tight face accentuated by black hair pulled back into a French braid. She seemed annoyed as she squinted down a thin nose. Her delicate hand snatched a tissue off the dash board. Glancing around, she stood lost for a second, waving the tissue. Back in the car it went. A displeased tightening of her mouth followed her strained neck as she inspected the property.

"You Carson?" Her voice was demanding but still soft. Feminine. Her eyes rolled over me as if I were green meat found hidden in the back of her fridge.

"Yes, ma'am." My hands grabbed the back of relaxed neck muscles, elbows out, as I stared up at the cloudless sky.

A canyon breeze torqued up and rippled her flowered skirt. Plump hips made her waist appear thinner than it was. "A Mister Calvin told me you could help me."

"The DA up in Salt Lake?" I asked. A squirrel ran up on the log pile, his head rotating in a jerky motion.

She eyed me with suspicion, keeping her distance as if a disease might strike her down. I ran my long fingers through matted blonde hair, watching powdered dirt feather out. I'd forgotten about chasing Ernie's sheep that hid huddled inside my outhouse this morning. Those three damn ewes think the head is their bedroom. They snuggled so close last week they broke the mirror off the short wall.

"Yes, Roger Calvin. He's married to a friend of mine from college." She pulled her expensive, pre-frayed, denim jacket closed.

I waited.

Her hands went to her sides as she looked me over, shifting her weight from one leg to another. She didn't seem all that impressed with me. Maybe she wasn't all that perceptive, hadn't noticed my six-foot two-inch height or my BMI. I thought about standing up and flexing a few times but thought better of it. A brief chortle erupted between my lips.

She raised her eyes. I'm pretty sure she was thinking of leaving. I tried smiling.

With puffed lips, she blew out air. "Well, can you help me?"

"What's your name?"

"My name?" Two deep pressed lines formed between her

eyebrows. She stood her ground for a moment, then with a loud exhale she dropped her shoulders slightly. "Annabelle Christina Linford. I go by Annie."

I nodded. I assumed she wanted me to stand at attention in recognition of her name. My grin seemed to have no effect on her.

Her throat cleared as if hearing was a problem for me. Waiting exasperated her and gave me a little pleasure. "Can you please help me?" she repeated.

"Depends."

"Depends?"

I nodded my head and threw a log on the fire. It wasn't cold enough or dark enough for a campfire. I just liked the peacefulness it brought. "What is it you need help with?"

She looked at her heels covered in dust. "Is there somewhere we could talk?" Her eyes narrowed, glancing toward the cabin and then her feet. I think she planned to buy new shoes shortly after this encounter.

"Sure, grab one of the camp chairs and have a seat." I pointed at a couple of Cabela's chairs folded and leaning against the picnic table.

She scrunched up her nose and coughed as if having a hard time breathing.

Trying to be cordial, I stood up slowly, walked over, grabbed a chair, and unfolded it next to mine.

Annie brushed off the seat with a Wet Wipe from her brown leather purse and sat down. I watched her stare into the fire, perhaps organizing her thoughts. Maybe wishing she could push me into it. The sun was about halfway dissolved into the Pavant mountain range, as the moon watched between clouds on the other side. She turned in the chair and glowered at my property.

"My closest neighbor is three miles to the southeast and unless you're afraid of a critter listening, you're probably safe telling me what you're here for."

Her face reddened. "Who the hell do you think you are?"

"I'm the one without a problem," I said. "I assume I'm not what you expected." Her red lips tightened together. "You know, handsome, brilliant, and the owner of all this." I held my arms out, then swiped at some soot on my pant leg.

Her face softened, and she let out a sound that could be

construed as a chuckle.

"Well, you're not what I expected either," I said. "Especially since I wasn't expecting any visitors today. You were a bonus. A pretty city girl driving all this way just to see me makes me wonder about all the ones that don't make it this far."

"Don't flatter yourself," she said. "Didn't Roger Calvin call you? He promised me he'd tell you I was coming." A breeze kicked up, pushing the smoke south and into her face. She leaned to the left, then the right, trying to get out of it. Her hand fanned in front of her as she glared at me.

I ignored her obvious annoyance. "Roger could have left a message. I haven't checked my messages for a couple of days."

"This was a week ago."

"It's probably good you reminded me. I'll get to that tonight."

"Do you even have a cell phone?" She scrunched her nose again.

"Of course I have a cell phone. A good one. It's on the charger or in my glove box." I couldn't remember where I'd left it.

"What if I wanted to call you?" She was still leaning to the right as the smoke shifted.

"Just let me know when and I'll have it with me."

"That's preposterous. What if I hired you and wanted to get a hold of you?"

I gritted my teeth and took in a slow breath. "If I'm on a job, I carry the cell with me at all times. We are on my time now, so there's little need." My eyes had narrowed unconsciously.

"But . . . Oh, never mind."

"Okay Annabelle Christina, what did you travel all this way for? I assume Roger told you I have a fairly good rep for tracking people and I'm not a licensed PI." I tossed a couple more logs on the fire. She leaned way back in the chair as the smoke and ash billowed out. I folded my arms and waited.

"My sister . . . she's missing." She closed her eyes, and I watched a single tear flow over her cheekbone.

The word "sister" stilled me like a heavy net. I had lost my sister in my mid-teens after she'd disappeared while jogging with Lucy, the corgi Nan had bought me. The police found Lucy hung in a tree, but no trace of my sister. Years have passed but that word still tightened up every muscle in my body. I shook my head to erase my thoughts.

My focus centered in on Annabelle. I waited. I expected more and raised my eyebrows. She stared off into the valley below. This had become hard for her. I watched the muscles in her throat roll up and down. Women nail me with emotions I'm unfamiliar with. I tried coaching, "How long has it been?"

She kept her gaze at nothingness. "Over a month now. The police think she took off with her boyfriend. He's missing too, as if anyone cared." She spat out his name like a bad taste, "Tyrell. Tyrell Chandry, but I think it's a fake name. He dresses like trailer trash and talks as though he's selling you a used car. He wears wide lapels on second hand jackets and T-shirts with rock band photos." She looked straight at me suddenly. Her nose gently flared and her cheeks flushed. With a long glance, I could see the wetness held in by eyelids. "Can you believe Tia could be in love with something like that?"

It was rhetorical, but I shook my head anyway.

"I only met him twice. I'd hoped he would scurry back to his hole. Every time I called he answered her phone." Her hands were gripping the fabric of the camp chair. "Her phone! Like, he was monitoring her calls or something. He even texted me back a few times."

She sucked in a hard breath. Her eyelids tightened, forming two folds that mountained up between well-maintained eye brows. Veins were beginning to show at her temples.

I wondered if she would bend the aluminum piping on the camp chairs. "You want a glass of wine or a soda?" I asked.

Annabelle turned a steely face toward me. Irritation crossed her face, and she kicked dust from her once shiny shoes toward me. It wasn't intentional, just frustration.

I held up my hands and feigned a cough. "Or we can talk about Tyrell some more?"

She had a nice grin. It seemed forced but nice. Her lips elevated on the right side and expensive dental work glistened back. "You have herbal tea?" she asked.

"Chamomile."

She consented and followed me into the cabin. She had been here a while, but I still knew nothing about her sister except she had fallen for a loser named Tyrell, and she was missing or had taken off.

I find people come to me in two ways. One, they just blurt their stories out and want me to get on it yesterday. Two, like Annie, they take their time and aren't real sure why they're asking a total stranger for help. I prefer the latter. Expectations are more genuine and realistic.

Annie watched me as I slipped off my shoes, set them by the door, and walked in. I turned my head slightly to study her peripherally. She hesitated, then lifted one toned leg after the other, setting her shoes neatly behind mine. The gentleman in me came out, and I held the door for her and her manicured, peach toenails.

In an admiring motion, she checked out the main room of the cabin. I watched her silently. Outside the sun crested over the mountains and the full moon created a bluish cast. Instinctively, my finger hit the light switch. Her eyes glanced back at me and she shook her head a couple of times. I thought I heard a slight giggle which was odd. An air of hidden fear was held stoically within her actions, a rubbing of her palms and curt breaths.

"You are nothing like I imagined. This is nothing like I imagined." Her hands waved in front of her. "I hope I'm not being condescending, but this little cabin is cute and immaculate. Even the damn bear rug draped over the upstairs railing looks vacuumed and shampooed. You either have a maid, you sleep and eat outside, or you are the most meticulous man I've ever met; and we need to be out buying rings."

I laughed.

She smiled briefly.

Her face became serious. "You are this big husky man who lives out in this godforsaken place." Silence filled the cabin long enough to make me uncomfortable. She wobbled slightly, as if her legs couldn't hold her up anymore. Her focus went down to her bare feet. A high-pitched voice asked, "Can you really find Tia?"

"Let me be frank. I'm somewhat selfish. I only do what I want to. I don't accept a job unless my heart is in it. If I decide to take this on, I will find her. I need more information to make that decision." I was having a hard time looking her square on as tears had started to roll down her cheeks.

"Wow." She wiped the moisture from her eyes. A black

streak crossed her cheek. "Okay, may I have that tea and sit? Roger told me you make money selling charts or posters to hospitals and that you were some specialized psychologist? He also said that in the Marines you had these 'divine skills' for ferreting out missing soldiers and terrorists that the government wanted to interrogate?"

I deflected her questions and pointed at the futon. "Something like that."

The "charts," as she described them, are the reason I have a sizeable bank account and time to do as I please. What started out as a wall chart for doctors' offices developed into online guides for psychiatrists, physicians, nurses, and hospitals. I had no idea they would go worldwide.

She sat as I heated water and pulled out two coffee cups. I poured myself the last of some Sauvignon Blanc that I'd picked up in Sonoma Valley last summer and dropped a tea bag in the other cup. Bending over to look out the window, I could smell the settling pleasance of cedar smoke on my shirt. Turning and sitting on a stool, my head swayed between Annie and the teapot. She stared absently at her hands and adjusted her skirt a couple times. She seemed content with quiet. Annie and I had that in common. We listened as the early crickets started up. Silence bothers most people. Maybe we weren't as different as I first thought.

After a couple sips of hot tea, her head rose, her eyes staring just above my hair. "She used to call me every night at eight o'clock and text me most mornings. We would talk about silliness and nothing for almost an hour. She was a Facebook fanatic; she posted pictures and sayings several times a day. I'm surprised she didn't get fired, probably helps she's a whiz at her job. Since Tia was born, we have been inseparable."

Her speech rhythm quickened as she talked about her sister and her hand animation was all over the place. "We were both mistakes, born eleven years apart. I was her mother before I was her sister. My parents were stone heads, worked crappy jobs. Our mom was a breakfast waitress and Dad did janitorial. They were the hippies who never graduated into the system."

Annie slapped her cheeks and shook her head as the memories raced through her brain. It took her a minute to come back to the present.

"One day, Tia quit calling. I must've dialed her number a

thousand times for like three days. I texted her and finally went to her apartment. The manager knew me so she let me in, but her place wasn't locked anyway. All her stuff was still there. Her makeup and hair dryer lay on the bathroom counter, and her suitcases were in the back of her closet. A broken glass vase was on the kitchen floor." Her fists tightened.

"Any other signs of a struggle?"

She bit her lip, "No, it was as if she just ran to the store."

"Her car was gone?"

"Yeah, that was the weird thing. Her car had disappeared, but her keys with the furry bunny were on the kitchen table." Her head turned slightly and her eyes brightened. "I didn't see her purse. Wow, how come I didn't think of that before?"

"She have a spare set of keys?"

"Probably . . . I don't know . . . Doesn't everyone?"

She hadn't touched her tea since the first couple of sips. She held the mug in one hand with enough grip to crush a tin can.

"You said Tia has been missing for over a month?"

"A month and three days." She let all the air in her lungs out slowly through gritted teeth.

"What have the police found?"

"The police? Nothing. They turned me over to a Detective Brower, who seems to be busy whenever I call lately. He keeps telling me she'll turn up. They haven't even found her car. Those morons think she went on a trip with Tyrell. For thirty-four days? I hired a PI and $2,500 later, I know where Tyrell went to school and that his parents haven't seen him in ten years. They weren't concerned. He's spent forty-three days in jail on unpaid tickets, has a revoked license, and an impounded car. Oh, and he barely finished tenth grade; no surprise there."

Annie set the coffee cup down and fumbled in her purse. She began laying things on the futon by her side. She picked out a piece of paper from her bag and stretched toward me.

"Here's the PI's name and number."

Setting it down on the counter without looking at it, I asked, "You have a picture?"

She unzipped a pocket on her purse and pulled out a folded 5 x 7.

A pretty twenty-something bleached blonde stared back at

me with wide, energetic eyes. I studied it for a bit. There was a familial resemblance, though not a striking one. Same cheekbones but softer in the neck and shoulders. The smile was lopsided like her sister's. It was a nice face full of promise and adventure. I handed it back carefully.

"Let's go back outside. I think better out there."

The fire was more coals and smoke than flame. A few red embers glowed as a mountain breeze kicked up. I got up and grabbed a handful of cut wood from my pile and dropped it next to my chair. Stirring with a denuded, grey branch, I pushed a couple of bigger twigs into the smoke. Annie appeared uncomfortable. Her eyes scanned her shoes.

I wasn't sure I wanted to get involved in this. It didn't sound like it was going to turn out well for either sister; but if it did, now that would be five steps of delightful. Sure, Annie has all those traits I like and despise: spicy, sturdy, womanly, a cleanliness freak, with a sharp intellect, who wasn't one to take any crap. I had a hunch her sister didn't have the street smarts or the adulthood Annie had. Tia sounded young and susceptible to guys with big ideas and small brain mass. Did I want anything to do with this?

Our eyes never left the fire. It was slowly building up, throwing dancing shadows around us. Annie's face said she wanted to talk and ask questions, but she held out, fidgeting in her chair. A big, white owl flew overhead and banked left toward the field, looking for nocturnal rodents. Annie gasped, her head following the bird's path.

I turned toward her and she grabbed my hand. That I didn't expect.

"Oh, my God, that had to be a sign." Her face lit up. "You're going to help me, aren't you?"

"The bird." My whole body remained motionless. My mind always seemed to swirl and tear through my whole life when making these decisions. The faint aroma of good perfume cut through the smoke. My life was so content right now, but for some reason I wanted to help Annie. I guess I had fewer reasons not to— nothing major going on. I smiled and nodded.

She stood up and wrapped her arms around my forehead and began jumping up and down. My scalp was pulled every which way.

I think my face reddened. Nah, I must've moved up too fast.

She stepped a short distance back but began patting my shoulder with a grin that made me uncomfortable. Suddenly, she stopped, then pulled her emotions back in and stepped away a couple of steps. Her head bowed and her face tightened. The business woman took back over.

"Let me tell you the downside. I have no idea how long this could take. It might be a couple of days or six months. My clients pay all expenses plus my fee. If I decide I will never find your sister, any leftover retainer is returned."

"I heard you've always found whoever you've searched for." Her narrowed eyes bore into mine.

I ignored her. "Also, if your sister doesn't want to come back, I won't make her. When I'm out . . ."

Annie's face was turning red again. She backed up with clenched fists at her side. "Why wouldn't my sister want to come back?"

"Things happen."

"Things happen? That's your big answer? What if she was in danger?"

"Then I guess I'd make a decision about that." When I held up my finger, she closed her mouth. "I'm not saying she would. I just want you to understand the possibilities. Your sister is an adult, and we should treat her like that. But, I wouldn't leave her in jeopardy, and I'd probably call you if possible to get your opinion. Does that work for you?"

Her rage ebbed. Shoulders slumped. With a deep breath and a long exhale, she started to softly mumble something. The sounds didn't really form words, and I watched as her mind rustled through inner thoughts. She was slack. Defeated.

I gave her time to find her voice.

In a hushed tone, with her eyes finding mine, she said, "I can't decide if you're a pompous ass, or the guy that might find my sister." She had used a matter-of-fact voice with listless emotion.

She seemed broken enough to need a hug and reassurance. That wasn't quite my style.

"Couldn't I be both?" I asked with a grin.

She gazed up at me in an irritated but pathetic way. A spate of tears and spasms began. She sat. Her arms wrapped around her knees. She held on while uncontrollable explosions welled up and out from her chest. Her voice quivered and she talked to the fire, "She's in trouble and you know it."

Hugs were out of the question, but there was an anxiety building in me. I held my sympathy down deep even though every fiber was trying to go to her and wrap my arms around her blubbering body. I could use Maria right now. But she was at work. After watching for an eternity, I stood, walked up to the cabin, and reheated water for tea. It was the only thing I could think of to do. The convulsions anchored back as her swollen eyes raised, and she took a cup of chamomile, holding it close to her abdomen. Lips parted, "She's my only sister, my only real friend." She said it more to herself than anyone else.

Completely unsure of myself, I patted her shoulder as if touching a lit burner on a stove. She didn't even notice. Relief swelled as I backed up a step. I'm reserved when it comes to physical contact with anyone I don't know. Don't even like to shake hands. My greeting is more of a nod of the head. It comes from my history of foreign lands and unscrupulous people.

I hadn't noticed Annie was standing up now, staring at me.

"I need to know about my sister."

I love my peaceful cabin life. Few friends, soundless nights with short breaks of scurrying nocturnal feet, campfires, visits from Maria, and lost cell phones. "Okay," I said.

2

Tia

A turbulent shift racked my spine as wheels banked from asphalt to shoulder and back. I rolled, half-conscious, scraping through layers of soft skin. My skull bounced off rough plywood, kicking me fully awake as slivers penetrated my bruised cheek. I heard a muffled scream to my left. Frantic sobbing, perhaps in the next room, came in stuttered and suppressed resonance. My head throbbed, my body slipped weighted with lead. All around was darkness and a hard floor. I leaned toward the weeping, but my legs caught on something. A numbing pain shot up my calf. With fading stamina, I kicked haphazardly, to no avail.

The smell of new pine and diesel fuel surrounded me. My hands reached to untangle my ankles; there was a tug and slight burn on my wrists. Panic struck me and I clasped my arms violently to my chest. Except for loose, men's boxers, a sweat-filled bra, and one sock, I was naked. Sitting, even partially up, caused nausea to rise in my throat, and my head pounded from inside. A burning gulp of bile rose and fell. I rolled my tongue to find saliva. My parched throat had the texture of pumice. A need for liquid panicked me. My tongue darted around the inside of my teeth. I wished for water and a couple of aspirin between the throbbing and the desert thirst.

A burdening fatigue overwhelmed me, and I lay back down on the rough floor. I started to curl up, but my ankles were gripped. Movement added to the other pains. Tears rolled down my cheekbones, dripping into the salty sweat between my breasts.

I wondered if I had the flu and tried to think of yesterday, but the memory wasn't there. I could feel the hum and rhythm of travel. Dizziness enveloped me. A jolt tossed me again. My ears caught the grinding hum of a truck. Fear shot through my body in waves sucking away any strength I had left. Everything dimmed to black.

I knew time had passed, but was it minutes or days? My eyes opened first to slits, then a touch wider. My irises had adjusted to pitch blackness, without much help. There was a jostling, like traveling on a train. As I began to sit up, a biting kink stung my neck and speared up through my skull. Sliding my hair to one side, I reached to rub sore muscles. Something bound my wrists. I yanked and twisted with all my might—exhaustion and dread followed. Fear blanched through my body. My heart was going to explode. There was a faint memory of this happening before. I inhaled long breaths. *Calm, please, calm.*

When my heart slowed, I moved my left hand with careful apprehension; my right hand was pulled and followed about a foot behind. My fingers traced the thin, leather wrap that enslaved each wrist and strapped them together with a metal clamp. I tried yanking them apart again, but their strength was greater than mine. Screams rattled in echoes between the metal walls of the semi.

Claustrophobia struck. I couldn't help it; I screeched and tried biting through the bindings like a wild dog on a leash. The screaming and gnawing turned to heavy sobs. My ankles were bound to the floor. A wail so deep it frightened me, spurted from my dry lips. I heard echoes of others.

I stretched out with arms and legs as far as the binds would allow. In burning agony, my surroundings formed from touch to mind. I was in a box. Wooden. Maybe large enough to ship a soft chair. Tears welled up and my mouth quivered. I laid back at the edge of shock. My mind shifted between comfort and shivers as bellowed agony murmured in echoes. I felt the cries around me as much as I heard them, other girls moaning in fear, like me, like cornered prey.

e

3

Carson

Interstate 15 was a maze of cement barricades, shifting lanes, and groups of hardhats chatting while leaning on monstrous, million-dollar machines which sat idling carbons into the spring morning. I hadn't been to the big city for months. Nothing had changed. Traffic was inching like a neurotic caterpillar over the point of the mountain. Salt Lake greeted me as I finally crested the hill. A sea of smog blanketed the valley, holding distant landmarks captive. The southern gateway to the city was entered through an outdated prison on my left and a mountain hollowed out by a gravel pit on the right. I wondered about having my window down.

My plan was to meet Annie for lunch at Einstein Brother's Bagels near her sister's apartment, so she could let me in. First though, I had scheduled a meeting for ten o'clock with her private detective at his office. My eyes drifted to the car clock. It was 9:28 and my stomach kept mentioning hunger. I'd had a coffee and an apple before I left the cabin this morning. That wasn't enough to sustain a male with enough working cells to tip the scales at 205. With eyes on the road, my hand checked the glove box and seat for edibles. An empty sack of chips and a crushed paper cup certainly weren't rations. I turned on the radio as if that might help. Nah, I was still famished. I doubled up at an In-n-Out Burger and headed to the PI's.

The office of Moon Investigations was in a commercial six-plex. A catalpa tree hid most of his sign. Very covert. My nose scrunched up involuntarily as the smell of burnt coffee followed swamp cooler air out the front door. No receptionist greeted me at the front desk, though the pencils looked sharpened. With both simian hands curled, I tapped my knuckles on the quartz countertop. I heard a voice mumble something from the back.

Tory Moon came through the door and glared at the empty seat behind the desk. He looked just like the picture on his card, other than the scowl. He ripped a sticky note off the computer screen then glanced up at me.

"Sorry, looks like Bernadette's at lunch . . . again." He gazed at the wall clock. 10:02. "Hope you didn't wait long." He brushed what little hair he had back off his ear.

"Not a problem. I'm Carson. I believe Annabelle Linford called you about me? We have an appointment."

"Yeah, sure, come on back."

The hallway consisted of four feet of worn carpet and a door on either side. No nameplates. Tory sat behind a huge wooden desk, motioning me into one of two client chairs. He leaned back and crossed his arms. I waited.

"You a PI? 'Cause I want you to know I searched hell and high water for the sister and everything leans toward her and that Tyrell fella taking off together. Probably in a rental car under fake names. Her boyfriend left a lot of people wanting money." His eyes narrowed.

"No, I'm not a PI. I'm just checking a few things for Annie."

He leaned forward on his desk. "Oh, so you're friends?"

"Just met her yesterday."

He waited for me to explain.

"Why do you think she would have gone with him?" I asked.

Tory cocked his head and stared at me for a time. "Love. People get stupid with love. You been in love before?" His arms uncrossed and he purposely smacked himself in the forehead. "My wife of 32 years, she falls in love with the guy I paid to add an addition to the back of our house. The love of my life. They went on a honeymoon with the money from the court settlement. It simply makes people stupid."

I nodded. "Anything else you find besides love?"

"He was in big debt. Had three checking accounts with negative balances. He had terrible luck at gambling, but they kept letting him play. He owes some pretty rough people."

"Now Tia, on the other hand, paid her bills, never missed work, was a good neighbor, and had lots of friends. At least, until she met Tyrell. He was spending her money, and he had done it before with several previous girlfriends. I'll give you my notes on what they had to say. I left out the foul language, or I would've needed three note pads."

"Did you check Tia's apartment?"

His eyes raised, "Of course I checked her apartment."

"And . . ."

"Looked like they were coming back. I figure something else came up. A lucrative job. Maybe he had a stash somewhere. Maybe they're enjoying the beach in Belize. Hell, all I hit were dead ends." His secretary walked in with a paper tray. Moon glared and bit his lip. She smiled.

I watched him closely. For $2,500 he should have more. Maybe he was holding out, but I doubted it. After a few more questions, I realized he had nothing to offer. Tory handed me a manila folder with less than a quarter inch of paper inside. On the way out, I nodded at Bernadette. A large latte and a muffin sat on her desk, centered within a ring of crumbs. She gave me a potential-client smile and sipped her coffee.

I picked up Annie. She was subdued but wanted to help. Her shoulders slumped, and she stared at nothing through the car window. The silence solidified as we headed to Tia's apartment.

The complex was one of those quaint, pseudo-getaway rentals with fountains, pool, tennis courts, and hills and greenery keeping full-time gardeners busy. Tia's was in building G, number 7, on the ground floor. Annie had mentioned at Einstein's that she had been paying the rent and utilities on the place.

Tia's home had that quiet, dim appearance of abandonment. No one had stirred up the dust that waited silently on tables and counters. Annie had emptied the fridge and garbage cans of anything that might smell or give clues, some time back. "Other than that," she said, "I left it the way it was."

Annie was uneasy. Her hair was slightly tousled from a twirling finger on the way over. She stood barely inside the doorway, uneasily rubbing her hands and squinting back tears.

I strolled through, listening and smelling nothing in particular as I flipped on lights. Searching for anything, twenty-five days later, boiled down to nearly zero. Checking the back of cupboards and drawers mostly made a mess. You could tell someone had done it before me. Nothing was folded or straight.

I noticed three empty shoe boxes on the upper shelf in her closet. The fourth one on the far end had boots in it, sadly in need of new soles and heels. Inside one boot I found a roll of cash. Five $100 bills held together by a yellow hair tie. Tia didn't let Tyrell know about all her money. She also hadn't taken it with her. Wouldn't that have come in handy?

I walked out of the room and tossed the cash to Annie. Her face went blank.

"She left that in a boot."

"Why," she asked, "didn't she take it with her when she left? He kidnapped her. Didn't he?" Annie's cheeks flushed and the tendons in her neck tightened.

"Annie, it could mean lots of things or it might mean nothing. She may have forgotten it. Maybe she didn't need it at the time. We need more information." This wasn't calming her down, so I let the water in the sink run and got her a cold glass and handed it to her. Grabbing her by the arm, I settled her into a chair, then went back to search the bathroom and the extra bedroom. Her lost look burned in my brain.

Shuffling through a pile of mail in the center of a card table covered with a flowered bed sheet, I found nothing substantial. Mostly, it was a mound of throwaways—ads for gym memberships, offers for credit cards, single sheet discounts to shoe and dress shops, and a stack of insurance companies each offering 50% off. Her old electric bill was so inconsequential the amount couldn't have run a 100-watt bulb for a month. I couldn't locate any loan payments or rental receipts in the fan folder under the table. I'd have to ask Annie if everything was paperless. The closet in the room had winter clothes and two boxes of old memorabilia—prom corsage, yearbook, an inch of elementary school drawings, a purple rabbit's foot. I heard a murmur.

Annie leaned into the door frame. Her cheeks were rubbed red, her eyes distant. At some point, she had run a brush through her hair. I decided to put her to work. People who are busy don't have time to reminisce. "Can you help me get into her computer?"

"Sure . . . sure," she replied with a faint echo.

She sat on the folding chair and sorted the papers onto the floor. With finger and thumb she yanked the computer closer then hit the on button. We waited. Nothing happened. She poked the button again. Nothing. She slapped the keyboard.

"Maybe it's not plugged in?" I lifted the sheet on the table and peered under. The cord and the plug were unhooked. As I was inching back out, I noticed an olive envelope taped under the card table. Snatching it, I rose to show Annie.

She was grinning and snapping her fingers as the laptop came to life. With a twist of her neck, a puzzled face stopped on the envelope in my hand. By the thickness, we both knew what it held. She grabbed it, slicing the end open with her extended nail. She thumbed several hundreds out onto the keyboard. There were nine $100 bills and two fifties.

"Tia doesn't believe in banks? I like that. I've never trusted the fee raisers either."

"She has never been a saver. This is crazy."

"So, this isn't your sister's?"

"No, it's not that. All our life she has gotten her paycheck and spent it within a couple days, then she complains that she's broke. This doesn't make sense."

"So, the $1,500 cash is someone else's, or she found a reason to save and hide cash."

Annie rubbed her temples. I'd noticed that before, at my cabin, when she was trying to make things congruent in her mind. Even with red blotchy cheeks, the business woman face came through.

"Tyrell, she was hiding money from Tyrell. That's got to be it."

"Or, it's Tyrell's money."

She turned in the chair abruptly—eyes burning. With tight pink lips, she said, "No way."

"Just thinking possibilities here. I also realize her boyfriend wouldn't hide cash in her shoe or under her table. Sometimes the most obvious is the right answer, and sometimes it's not."

"But, it's her apartment and her money."

"There are other angles. A person is not just one thing. An

accountant can be a husband, a tennis player, and a John arrested for solicitation. People are the things we know, and they have those things they do that are a total mystery to their closest acquaintances."

Hands on hips, jaw out. "You're saying my sister is a prostitute?"

With a deep breath and a shake of my head, I said, "No. I'm saying Tia is all the things you know about and some that you don't. They are not always bad. She could be saving money to give to a child with a brain tumor, or she might sing for centurions on Sunday. I haven't the slightest idea what your sister might keep from you."

Her face was so tight I thought she might have an aneurysm. She finally began breathing again. "Let's check out the computer," I said.

"Let's."

Tia's bills were all paid up at the time she disappeared. Her final payment on a six-year-old car had been made. She had joined an online dating service a year ago. Nothing showed that she had gone out with any of the smiling creatures we viewed. We couldn't get into her emails, but Annie had a friend that could. She'd let me know.

With her mind off her sister as a streetwalker, we settled into opposite ends of the couch in the front room. I told her about the info I'd received from Tory Moon, PI. She gave me a list of Tia's friends and the address of where she worked. Annie had a business appointment she was late for, so we parted, after I dropped her off at her car.

I sat with the car idling at the curb, realizing how little I knew about Tia.

4

Carson

The day was clouding up, the asphalt darkening. And the smell, just before a hard rain, wasn't helping the foul mood closing in on me. Sitting in the car reading Tory Moon's report, I realized he'd done little more than I assumed the police had. Some futile surveillance, credit checks, listless phone calls. Looked like he spent more time on the report and billing than on searching for Tia. I made a few appointments with Tia's girlfriends, then headed to Tia's work.

In a two-story office building, I checked the office roster. There was no main receptionist, only an expanse of lime green tile and a gaudy chandelier. Polk and Gadley was on the second floor, near a silver water fountain. I tried to glance through the window to the left of the door, but all I could see was a forest of large potted plants, live, I think. As I entered, the sound of a copy machine whooshed in the back room. The secretary glanced over the top of her glasses, eyebrows raised. I waited a few seconds for a greeting. The glance was it.

Resting both elbows on the counter, I leaned forward enough that she startled and straightened up. "Good afternoon." A wholesome smile lifted my cheeks up. It didn't appear to disarm her. "I understand a Miss Tia Linford worked here?"

"And what is this pertaining to?" Her lips didn't move and the voice was a bit nasal. I thought of old TV ventriloquists but could not recall any names. Chuckling to myself, I imagined her with a puppet.

"Trying to gain information about her disappearance. Did you know her well?"

"We ate lunch together sometimes. Had a couple of drinks

after work with friends. Wait, you have a badge or something?"

"Nothing I can really show you. But, I could probably give you a glance at my library card. Did you two do anything just prior to her not showing up for work?"

She appeared stumped for a second or two, then forgot about any badge. "Yeah, we went to lunch at Bigby's Deli the day before. She had turkey on rye, I remember 'cause she spilled her cola all over her plate. The bread was wet and black. She giggled and ate it anyway. She had to use a fork."

"Anything seem peculiar or bothering her?" I raised my elbows off the counter and straightened up. She leaned forward. That was a good sign.

Her lips were in full motion now. Her attitude changed. I think she enjoyed talking to someone. I'm not sure she had many clients that stopped in. "She was breaking up with that leech boyfriend."

"Tyrell?"

"Yeah, that's him. I never could understand what she saw in him. He was good looking enough, but he talked so fast, you knew he was a player. And slippery like a weasel."

"Player?"

"He even came on to me, here, when she was in the bathroom. What a creep."

She kept glancing at her desk phone as if wishing it would ring, or perhaps happy it stayed silent.

"You know where he might hang out?" Something way in the back of my mind was bothering me, but I couldn't seem to grab hold of it.

She twirled her hair with one finger, squinting her eyes. "I think he spends some time at the Grotto on Main and 33rd South."

"Anything else you could tell me?"

She pouted her lips and shook her head. "You wanna talk to Susan Gadley? She's in her office in the back. She's always at her desk." She glanced behind her. "She works more hours than father death. Ms. Polk is on vacation. She's the nice one."

I figured her boss would know little about Tia's life outside work. "Anyone else work here?"

"Larry, and Tia's replacement, Lindy. They're both out working."

"What did Tia do?"

"She was our best insurance adjustor. She comes across kind of dizzy, you know, but with math and appraisals she's amazing. Susan loves her work even though she'd never tell her."

"Car or Home?"

"She did business and industrial. Mostly fire. She really knew her stuff. I don't think Lindy will ever get it."

"Thank you for your help. I might check back later with your bosses."

There was a moment of silence between us. Her head tilted. "Are you like undercover?"

"I can't divulge that."

The look in her eyes told me she couldn't wait to tell her friends about her visit from an undercover cop. I left it at that.

Traffic had tied itself in knots at each intersection. Beet red faces peered around like those funny dolls in rear windows. Bobbing and swaying. Heat reflected off building windows, swirling back and forth with increasing convection. A few horns, several middle digits waved, and I inched closer to my destination. I wasn't in the hurry everyone else seemed to dwell in, my time was spent thinking about questions for Tia's friends and where I might find Tyrell.

Tyrell's old girlfriends I could skip. Tanji was first on Moon's list. She, and two other girls were in his scribbled notes, but it didn't appear he ever talked to any of them. Friends—Tanji, Toni, Pauline. Moon had scrawled three question marks at the end.

Pulling over to the curb, I noticed all the houses boasting their grandeur. Tanji's parents' was no different. Green lawns, shrubs and trees framing the doorways and windows. Potted flowers and eight-foot doors.

A sturdy bleach blonde answered the tall door. I recognized her from a picture Annie had shown me. Her feet were too big for her shoes and too small for her frame. I guessed six feet.

"Mister Carson?"

"Carson's the first name. You must be Tanji. Is there a place we can talk?"

She looked hesitantly back into the open doorway, then grabbed me by the arm and escorted me across concrete stones embedded into plush lawn, around to the side of the house. Within a hedged garden sat two wrought-iron benches facing a common area of more flat stones. She nodded to the bench on our right. We sat. A potpourri of flowers and moist earth filled my nostrils. As Tanji turned, I caught a hint of girl soap.

"My mom's in the house and the baby's asleep. Mom has ears as sharp as a bat. I wouldn't want her giving me any more crap about Tia. She thinks she's a skank just because she's so pretty. But Tia didn't really hook up all that much. She . . ."

We stared at each other for a moment.

"Annabelle told me to speak freely with you. I really hope you find her. You know about Tyrell. Right?"

"Yes. But I could use any information you might have, no matter how insignificant."

She was a lip biter, chewing between sentences. "Tyrell is a taker. Lived off her, drove her car while she worked, and filled her head with promises. Amber and I kept telling her, and she wouldn't listen. 'You guys just wait,' she would say."

"Then, just before she disappeared, like the week before, she talked about dumping him. We were relieved. But now, I'm scared he did something."

"He ever hit her, or anything like that?"

"One time, he shoved her when she sank the eight ball and beat him at pool. She was dancing around and feeling good, and he elbowed her into the table. She had to have a bruise the size of Texas." Tanji shook her head and raised her shoulders. "He had those mad eyes and tight face, like 'don't ever do that again.' She nuzzled up to him, and they went over to a corner to talk. They came back holding hands like nothing happened. I wouldn't have put up with that, I'll tell you."

"Did he work?"

"Not that I know of. He talked about all these big schemes that were coming up. Said he had people to back him, but nothing ever happened."

"Did he have any friends or names he talked about?"

She gazed over at the corner of the house as a tan, feral cat ran by. It momentarily stopped her from nibbling the reddish skin below her mouth. She began again. I looked at the ground, slightly worried a tooth might come through.

"I never saw him with anyone, but he mentioned a guy named Himan or Lyman, something like that."

"Do you know anything else about this Himan/Lyman guy?"

"He just said he needed to drop something off to him, and I remember he looked worried."

"Worried?"

She rubbed her brow for a second, then pushed back her short bangs. "Yeah, like he was short on paying a gambling debt or something."

I thought about that for a minute. From the information I had so far, I assumed Tyrell probably had a lot of people he owed money. More than his funds or his willingness could fathom. Himan/Lyman must have been a priority. "Anyone else I should talk to?"

"Our friend Toni. Maybe. She kind of pays more attention to herself, if you know what I mean."

"I'm talking to her next," I stood. She walked with me back to the front. I handed her my card, simple white stock with one name, Carson, and a phone number, both in a small font. "Call me if she gets ahold of you or something important pops up."

She grinned.

A tiny woman opened the door saying, "Amy's awake."

"I better check on her." She turned back to me. "I hope you find her." Her eyes were wet.

After about twenty minutes, I found the mall and the upscale boutique, with music blaring, where Toni worked. Her hair was red, real red, not the orange of most natural redheads. Her face was thin, her arms and legs boney, and she talked in breathy tones. She took a break and we headed for the food court. I had coffee and a scone. She picked a corn dog and coffee. I watched her pour five packets of sugar into an eight-ounce cup, the coffee cresting the edge.

Half an hour later, after buying her another corn dog, I found out she knew less about Tia than I. On the other hand, I now knew Toni owned twenty-seven pairs of shoes, had a cat named Theodore, refused to pay all those stupid parking tickets, and owned a new Miata her divorced Dad had bought her to piss her mom off. I didn't leave her one of my high-profile cards.

In the mall parking lot, I searched on the GPS for the address Moon had given me for Tyrell's parents. Two teens gazed at me with disinterest as they chatted, cells in one hand, and fancy sacks in the other. The parents were in Grantsville, a small town about forty minutes away. I sighed, thought about just calling them. But a face-to-face was always more fruitful. With a deep breath, I started the car. My cell played the tune *Highway to Hell.* It was a joke my on-again, off-again girlfriend, Maria, had put in.

I think we were in the on-again status this month. She has long, pitch-black hair, brown eyes that melt my heart, and either a voice of soft tenderness or one that raises to an octave that fissures my bones. Mostly, she's gracious and indulgent of my imperfections.

My thoughts were on Maria when the chorus came again. I slid the arrow over.

"Hello?"

"Carson, I thought of something," came Tanji's voice. "Tia went with Pauline and Amber to a bar the night she disappeared. I assumed you knew about it, but then I thought, maybe you didn't. Did you know that already?"

"No. Do you know where they went?" Thinking back, there wasn't anything about an Amber in Moon's notes or on the police report he had included.

"My mind jerks from one thing to another sometimes and any kind of recent memory seems to fall out when I least expect it. My last girlfriend called me dizzy, but my friend Lisa says I process things differently. Tia texted me that night, and when I got to texting this afternoon, I remembered it."

"Tanji . . . Tanji, do you have any idea where they went?"

"Oh, let me look at the text again."

I listened to what sounded like her clacking her teeth. Then she mumbled to herself a few seconds.

"No. It only says they are going out. I assume they were going to the Star or Brother Zak's. I could call Amber. Me and Pauline don't really get along."

"No, don't call. If you wouldn't mind, how about I visit them. You have addresses and phone numbers?"

They were roommates in an apartment not far from the

mall. Tanji gave me their work and cell numbers. I called. Pauline was home and could see me, but she had a dentist appointment at 4:15. It was now 3:10.

The area was an expanse of thirty-year-old apartments, nestled between a fancy shopping center and a row of franchise restaurants. As I turned off Van Winkle, the taste and aroma of wet cut grass and lawnmower exhaust came at me, prior to the buzzing sound of the mower. Pauline had said third floor, fourth building on my right. I gazed over the rail before knocking. A view of a plastic-lined lake with ducks and their green-and-white excrement spotted the shore and walkways. The trees blocked a major part of the landscape.

My pulse increased as I knocked firmly on the six-panel door. I had the hope Pauline might solve the whole mess and was curious why the police or Moon hadn't written anything down about these two girls.

A sad-eyed girl in a T-shirt and jeans answered. She was holding her left cheek, intently. Bare feet, chipped nail polish, skinny ankles.

"You another cop?" She grimaced as if it were painful to speak.

"I'm a friend of Annabelle Linford, Tia's sister."

"Ain't seen Tia in weeks. Heard she left with her boyfriend."

"Could we sit and talk?" I softened my face and braced a smile in her direction. Her rigid stance ended and she dropped her shoulders slightly.

She squinted and peered out the door. "You look rough enough to push your way in if you wanted. You a rapist?"

"Never have been. You?"

She laughed. It was a pitiful laugh. Her hand pressed deeper into her cheek and she backed up. With the motion of her arm, she welcomed me in. I thought that was a little too easy.

The main area was kitchen and front room in one. A counter filled with polystyrene carry-outs and a well-spotted carpet greeted me. The smell of marijuana and cheap air freshener filled the room, overpowering any smells of misplaced leftovers. I glanced at the love seat and something that had once resembled an ottoman, picked up an empty carton from a barstool, placed it on top of a pizza box, topping off an unmaintained trash container, and sat down. Pauline gave me a sour grin.

"You've been waiting to get to the dentist for a while?"

"This is the third day. I've been trying to find one that takes my crappy insurance and doesn't need $200 just to sit in his chair with my mouth open. Found one that only needs fifty, so I figure after he's done, he'll take the twenty I have." With a well-cultivated bat of the eyes, she asked, "So, you're sure you're not a cop?"

"How well do you know Tia?"

"We used to hang once in a while. She was mostly the friend of my old roommate. She was a little fake to me. Way too sweet and chummy, but she was nice enough."

"Old roommate? You mean Amber moved out?"

"Oh, I thought you knew. That was a blow. Amber was found off I-15 in a ravine about five miles past Park City. She was naked, wrapped in a blue tarp." She stuck out her tongue in distaste. "Detectives were all over here two weeks ago. Scared the shit out of me. They tore this place apart, found a little weed, but didn't press it with me. Her funeral was in Boston. That's where she was from. Parents came and got her stuff, eyeballed me like I was trash." Pauline gave a huff of air and raised her brow.

A sick feeling gurgled in my stomach. "Did they say how long she was there or what she died from?"

"I overheard them saying something about stab wounds from a screwdriver. Boy, there are some sickos out there."

"When was the last time you saw her?"

"On the fifth. I remember that 'cause it was the day we paid the rent. One more day and that witch over in the office charges you a $60 late fee. It was the same night the three of us went out."

"When you and Amber and Tia went out?" I leaned forward enough on the bar stool, I almost toppled over. Scooting back, I waited for her reply.

"It's about time for the dentist, and I still have to comb my hair and catch the bus." Standing up, she winced and shoved her knuckles into her cheek again.

"It was the same night all three of you went out?"

"Yeah, yeah, but look, I'm in a ton of pain and I gotta go." She walked to the door and opened it.

I started to walk out but stopped short of the door and turned. "Pauline, how about you go get ready and I'll drive you over? Save you some bus fare."

The ball of her palm made tiny concentric circles deep into her cheek. She stood thinking.

My fingers dove into my pant pocket and I pulled out my money clip. Yanking out three twenties, I said, "I'll pay for the dentist, plus ten, if you'll answer a few more questions on the way over."

She forgot her tooth, grabbed the cash so quickly I had the feel of paper still in my fingers, and she scuttled off to the bathroom. Ten minutes later, she came out. Her hair was still uncombed, the bath fan was roaring, and the fragrance of weed followed her.

5

Carson

The next day was stormy, the sun darting through fragmented dark clouds. I found 1715 Simon Street. The house stood, insignificant, in an acre of weeds and discarded cars. Probably less than 800 square feet. As I turned off the key, a hard rain began pelting my windshield. The mailbox leaned to one side, flag up. I wondered if the storm would knock it to the ground. I opened the car door. A wild-eyed dog with stained, spiked hair rammed into a chain link pen, mouth open, baring a sharp set of teeth.

I put my hand above my eyes as a canopy to see through the downpour.

A large-headed woman sitting on the porch yelled, "Cougar, shut up," several times. Cougar barked, then began pacing his cage and growling in a low rumble.

"Mrs. Chandry."

She nodded and raised one of those twenty-ounce cups from a convenience store.

I ran to her porch. Running didn't help; I was sopping wet.

"You the fella looking for Tyrell?"

"I'm Carson." I reached down to shake her hand. She smelled like beef jerky and that imitation powdered cheese they put on chips. She brushed my hand away.

"He owes you money? Or what?"

"Like I said on the phone, I'm trying to locate his girlfriend, Tia. They just came up missing at the same time. Have you talked to him?"

"I don't know about no Tia. Ain't heard from him since Christmas, except for that email a month ago. He wanted money."

The rain stopped suddenly, and we both turned to watch the sun search through black clouds.

"Did you send him any?"

"You crazy? I'm on Sosh. Can't hardly pay the bills I have now."

I leaned on the rail. It bent more than it should have. I stood back straight again.

"A thousand bucks? Like I'm just stuffing my mattress for a rainy day. Ty's always got big ideas. He never wants to work for it. No money, no skills, and big ambitions, that's Ty."

"Did he tell you where he might be?"

She tightened her lips and eyed me in deep thought. "You got a picture of this girl you're searching for?"

I reached in the notepad I was carrying and pulled out the one Annie had given me and handed it to her. Hearing a couple of sharp barks, I turned toward Cougar. He was still pacing with one yellow eye on me.

"She's a little too wholesome for Ty. That's one pretty dress. I bet she even has a steady job."

I waited.

"You aren't going to hurt him, are ya?"

"Just want to make sure Tia is safe."

She examined me in a blatant, obvious way. My wet clothes seemed to dry under her stare. A full minute passed, then she said, "I'm not sure why, but I trust ya." Her body rocked back and forth on the chair, then with the right momentum she stood up. She adjusted her feet a bit and then proceeded into the front door.

I followed. Her house was decorated in old cheap furniture, but it was spotless and organized. I was surprised. "You have a nice house."

She stopped and sort of sneered. "It's crap, and the outside is complete shit. I don't need no sweet talk."

Mrs. Chandry mumbled something else, then sort of fell onto one end of the couch. Reaching to the side, she pulled out a laptop, one of the older thick ones. "Mr. Pickett, my neighbor, gave me this last year and showed me how to use it. He comes over whenever I screw it up," she grinned, "which is often." She patted the cushion next to her, and I sat down.

The computer made a whirring noise. I watched as the

screen flickered and chugged forward.

"This machine teaches me patience, even though I've got nothing but time. You want a cola?"

I was thirsty but knew getting up and down wasn't her strong point. I stood. "I could use a glass of water. You want me to get you a cola?"

"Second shelf in the fridge," she said, glaring at the screen. "Cups are in the dish drainer."

When I returned, she was searching through her emails. She set the cup down on a corner table next to her. Her concentration was locked on the computer. Finally, she slid the laptop over to me.

"There it is."

Mom, I'm in Idaho. Could you send $1000 to me? I got a big deal going. I could pay you back in two weeks, but I gotta have it quick. I may even be buying you a new house this year. This is big, mom. My address is 1642 Tamarak Way, Hayden Idaho 83835

Thanks, Ty

Disappointment crossed her face. She looked away. "He's a good boy. He just forgets to ask how I am." Her shoulders drooped. "He's a good boy."

6

Carson

Annie had given me more reasons than I cared to hear. And here she was in the seat next to me, buckled up as we landed at the Spokane airport. I was more disgruntled than I should have been, sitting next to a pretty lady who smelled nice. She kept that smirk on her face that said, *I won*, during most of the flight. It was lovely and annoying at the same time.

Maria called me just as we landed. She thought I'd be back home tonight but understood when I explained. She asked if Annie was gorgeous or homely. I didn't answer. She even made me hand the cell to Annie. Maria told her I'd find her sister and not to worry.

"I'll let you drive," Annie said as we found the rental car in space 68 as promised by the clerk, who pushed more options and add-ons than a Toyota dealer.

I crinkled my forehead as I jiggled the keys in front of her. "Remember your promise to be a bystander and not get involved."

"I'll be good."

"Annie, this could get rough and ugly. I'll make the decisions about whether you stay in the hotel, or car, or go with me to check things out—"

"Yes, you mentioned that last night and this morning. You're in charge. Can we get in the car now?"

A couple of swear words mumbled through my tight lips and I beeped the locks. As I adjusted my seat, she said in the sweetest fake voice, "I'm sorry, what was that?"

"Buckle up."

The only car they had available was a cherry-red Ford Explorer, the size of a battleship, with extra seats in case we had to haul a platoon of leathernecks. Inconspicuous as hell.

Twenty minutes of road numbing silence later, Annie asked, "What's our plan?"

"*Our* plan is to drop you off at the hotel, and for me to drive by the place and see what shakes."

She turned a darker shade of pink, then blew air through her fingers. I straightened and watched the road. The air conditioner didn't seem to be working well enough.

The back of her hand patted my bicep. "Wouldn't four eyes be better than two? I might catch something that you miss." She used that tone of a five-year-old girl—pleading, lost, and innocent.

I tightened my grip on the wheel and remained silent, watching our exit roll by without any realization.

"Ignoring me is not going to solve anything. By the way, you just passed our exit." She stifled a giggle but not well.

"This is exactly why I didn't want you coming."

"So, you could miss the exit on your own?"

Adrenalin swelled through my veins as irritation increased. I pulled off the next exit and turned back the other way, powdering tread marks on the shoulder. I liked to work alone. That's the way I did it overseas and it always worked for me. I normally stayed calm. Annie being here tightened all the veins in my body.

As the road cut through thick pines, I took in three long breaths. I felt the flush pass. The humor of my anger made me smile. My stupidity did not. A mile and a half later, I exited onto the right road.

Annie leaned forward to catch my eye. She grinned softly.

"Maybe I was checking to see if anyone was following. Did you think of that?"

"No, and you didn't either."

"The hotel should be just up the road on the right. Let's try using our *four eyes* to find it."

We dropped our bags off at units seven and eight. I kicked the obnoxious air conditioners on and crossed my fingers that the stale heat would evaporate. It didn't seem likely.

"Yeech. Did you book a single star to impress me?" asked Annie. She stood outside, gazing in through the open door. Her thumb and forefinger pinched her nose.

"You've never been in a three-star hotel before? Figures."

"Sorry, but I'm not used to sleeping where they birth cattle."

"Funny. Okay, silver spoon, you wait here."

She walked back to the car, opened the passenger door and hopped in. Her arms crossed as she peered straight ahead.

This is such a bad idea. I climbed in, gave her a growl and started the car. "You will stay in the car," I said, mostly to myself.

The house was set off the road about 30 yards. It was small and hidden behind pines and well-trimmed bushes. There was a double-door garage to the left of the house, with three males inside talking. I couldn't make out if one was Tyrell or not.

"Are you going to check it out?"

I noticed the way she hadn't used *we*. A grin crossed my face. After three passes, I pulled over on the opposite side of the road and parked fifty feet away. "There are binoculars on the back seat. Will you grab them?"

She put them to her eyes and stretched over to my window. Slightly perturbed, I grabbed her shoulder and slid her back. An astonished face glared back at me. I put my other hand out with the palm up; she bellowed an exasperated sigh and dropped the binoculars hard into my lap.

"Oh." Traffic was nonexistent and it seemed so peaceful here. Focusing on the group, I found Tyrell, beer in hand and mouth jabbering. The other two laughed.

"Stay."

"I'm not a pet." Her eyes burned through me as I opened the door.

"Nevertheless, stay put."

Her arms crossed tightly under her breasts, and she stuck her tongue out at me. I shook my head and turned, tossing the binoculars to her. That seemed to placate her.

About twenty feet out from the garage, they noticed me. A raw, feral regard came from all eyes. Their stance adjusted. They whispered back and forth. Tyrell moved slightly to his left.

"Hi, all, I'm trying to find Culver Street. Can you boys help me?" With my southern drawl and powerful smile, I wondered if my cheeks would rip. I was hoping they didn't have guns. I slowed my pace. Their movements told me they thought I was someone else. Someone they expected but would teach a lesson to.

The big one on the right reached behind the door and came at me fast with a short length of two-by-four. He moved well.

Tyrell shouted, "Captain, clobber that prick."

He swung it like a bat. I arched my back, feeling the air of that square piece of wood whoosh by. I dropped and put my heel into a once-solid knee cap. There was a blaring moan and Captain dropped in sweaty agony. Hands grabbed the splinters of bone and blood. His pants began spotting with blood.

I up-ended myself, keeping my eyes on the other two. Shock filled their faces as they watched their friend squirm and squeal on the dirt path. Their heads raised with an anger so thick, I could smell it. I watched their eyes darting for weapons.

Thank God they didn't have guns. Who did they think I was?

They circled, keeping dark, mean faces trained on me. Tyrell grabbed a pitch fork. His friend yanked off his belt. A menacing buckle caught sunlight through the trees.

Adrenaline seeped through my pores. I felt my muscles tighten. My mind raced.

They both came at me at once. Their mistake. I crab-walked to the right as I scooped up a fistful of gravel and dirt. I tossed it into Tyrell's face. He howled as he swung the pitch fork blindly in an arc. The back of the tool clipped my shoulder, shooting numbing tingles down my arm. I rolled in the direction of the swing, narrowing the gap between me and his friend. He wind-milled the belt, moving it closer and closer. I glanced over at Tyrell. He roared like a bear and took another swing. Ducking at the last second, I watched his powerful follow through as the tool cracked bone and split flesh in his partner's jaw. Teeth and blood flew into the air. His friend's eyes rolled, his body went limp, and he collapsed backwards.

Dread washed over Tyrell's face. He stood motionless. The pitchfork angled outward from his loose grip. Red dripped from the tines. "Mooney," he mumbled.

I moved behind him, watching the muscles of his hand, I lessened the distance. Tyrell's head twisted, and he stared at where I had been. Veins popped and skin tightened around his knuckles. He began to turn. I tackled him hard from behind, knocking the air from his lungs. I heard ribs break as his chest hit the rocky ground.

The handle lay pinned under him.

I winced as I sat up slowly, shoving my knees deep into his back. Glancing over, I noticed that his friends were lying still. I shifted, peeking over my shoulder. My shirt was ripped and a red blood spot the size and shape of an iron was slowly expanding.

"Tyrell . . . Tyrell . . . Don't move."

"What the hell did ya do that for? I think you broke my rib." His cheeks puffed as he tried to catch his breath. Eyes wide.

"Probably no more than two of them. Don't worry. They'll heal."

I heard footsteps on the gravel to my left and caught Annie's beige pant suit out of the corner of my eye. She stumbled on the rocks. Her perfume cut through the sweat.

"What was that?" she asked.

I started to turn, then thought better of it. "Annie, you were to wait in the car. I'll be with you in a minute." My voice was void of emotion.

Tyrell's head turned. "It's you." He spat dust. "You bitch."

"I've never seen anything like that Carson. Who does that?" She ignored him.

I drew a long breath. "Annie, please go to the car. I need to talk to Tyrell. Please."

"That's the loser. You hurt him, didn't you?" A menacing grin widened across her face. She leaned closer and glared down with hateful eyes. She turned as if to walk, then stopped. With eyes narrowed, she twisted her knee slightly, pressing her spiked heel deep into his neck.

"Where's my sister? Huh? Creep." Her calves tightened, and he squirmed as if trying to press through the earth, his arms caught under him.

"Ahhhhh. Back the bitch off, asshole," screamed Tyrell. Fear crossed his face.

"Sorry, I wouldn't tangle with this crazy woman. I'm staying out of it. Probably be good to answer her questions."

He tried to move. Annie pushed his face into the gravel with her toes, then put her sharp heal back on his neck. He grimaced.

"I haven't seen Tia in months." His voice sucked in air, in-between words. "I dumped her. I didn't deserve a crazy bitch like that."

His friends were starting to move. *I'd better do something.* "Tyrell, don't move." I turned to Annie. "If he even breaths wrong, press that spike right through to his Adam's apple."

His eyes showed worry, and I watched as new sweat lines appeared. Chest pain tightened his face.

I stood up, nodded to Annie, and walked over to the big guy. Finding a length of flexible hose, I bound his feet to his hands. He struggled a bit but didn't have much in him. He smelled like beer and sausage.

I thanked Mooney for holding the belt for me. He started to get up, so I backhanded the gash on his chin. He still had more in him. His foot swung around, trying to trip me. He could have, if his face hadn't given it away. I dove and landed with a hard elbow to his calf. He screamed. There was still too much venom in his eyes. Reaching over, I cranked his neck just enough to make him lose consciousness for a while. I certainly didn't want to kill him. With the belt wrapped tight around his arms, I yanked his worn boots off. Any movement on gravel would be hard on him.

I rechecked Tyrell and Annie a few feet away. Fear and hate blazed from his half-shut eyes. His smell stopped me for an instant. It was like entering a boy's locker room, mixed with the fragrance of trees and cars. He was still sure Annie would send that heel into his windpipe. *She wouldn't, would she?*

"Where's Tia, you bastard?"

His face grimaced as she pressed a bit deeper.

"It's okay. Let me talk to him."

She lifted her foot, backed up a step, and kicked him in the side. "Loser!"

Tiny gravel fell off his face, leaving red blotches as I lifted him up. A drop of blood rolled down his back from where the heel had embedded a tiny circle.

Tyrell gazed over at the big guy, hog-tied on the ground. He watched with hate-filled eyes. "You couldn't hurt him. Captain's going to kill ya when he gets out. You're lucky he was half drunk." He turned and rubbed his neck. "Stupid bitch."

I clubbed him with the palm of my hand. He winced and shook his head, waiting for the pain to pass. When he finally glanced over at me, I could tell he was spent. He didn't have much to begin with and the little he had, sloughed off. He stared at the ground.

Annie began to say something and I held my hand up. Anger rolled across her face, and she gritted her teeth.

I grabbed Tyrell by the shirt. A button popped, then two more, as I hauled him the twenty or so yards to the porch. The house was tiny, probably two rooms. It needed paint and some of the slats were missing or ready to fall. With little force, he dropped like a sack into a blue metal chair. A 5-gallon bucket sat close by, a cereal bowl filled with cigarette butts on top. Tossing the bowl into the yard, I slid the plastic bucket over and sat, my face inches from his.

I took a quick peek at Annie. She leaned against a corner rail. A mist of ashes still lingered in the air. Few things worse than the smell of an ashtray. I let it pass.

"Tyrell, where's Tia?" I said in a near-whisper.

He closed his eyes and dropped his forehead.

"Tyrell, look in my eyes. Peer way in. You see in there what I'm capable of?" My voice was soft but not soothing.

He blinked and a tear slid down his cheek.

"I don't care about anything you've got going here. I don't care if I have to dig three graves out there by that wooded area." My chin pointed to the left. "Tyrell, do you see that?" I asked in the same calm voice.

He began bawling. His hands rubbed fiercely into wet sockets.

In a slow rhythm, I demanded, "Tyrell, you look hard into these eyes. Now, drop those hands." I tapped each one.

He did as he was told.

"Good, good boy. Now tell me about Tia."

His whole body was shaking like a chill he couldn't warm. Through quivering lips, he began. "Tia dumped me. It was out of nowhere. She had all my stuff on the power box just outside our place." He kept gulping in breaths as he spoke. "The bitch even changed the locks. She planned it. She kept yelling at me through the door, wouldn't even open it." He paused. "Hell, I loved her."

A scared, hurried voice behind me said, "Carson, that guy, Mooney, got the belt off. He's untying the big one. Carson!" She tugged at my shirt.

I ignored her as I stared at Tyrell.

"She said it was over. She said some mean shit. I've never seen her so mad. I'd only used her car for a couple of things that I needed. I told her I'd pay her back."

"Carson . . . Carson, they both keep checking over here. We need to go."

"Tyrell, did Tia meet someone new? Any suspicions of that?"

He waited a minute while his bottom lip quivered. "No, I don't think that was it. Her girlfriends always talked trash about me. They poisoned her. They're all bitches." He began crying hard and rocking back and forth. Blood dripped from his open mouth.

"Which girlfriends? Give me names." I remained focused on him. Just getting information. No hurry.

"Carson, dammit, those two just snuck behind the house." She shook my shoulder. "I think the big one's hurt. Are you even listening? Carson, something bad is happening. Let's go." Her voice was pleading. She began pacing the edge of the rail and watching the front door.

"Names? There was a Kathy, maybe it was Katy, Amber, that super-bitch Tanji, and Pauline. Oh, and sometimes she went with Allie Fieldhouse to things like movies and piano stuff."

"When exactly did you two separate?"

"Separate? That's a good one. You mean when did she kick my ass out? I didn't do anything. She had a good thing with me."

"When?" I patted his cheek slightly.

He appeared physically and mentally exhausted. He stared at his shoes. "I really don't know any date." He rubbed the mark on his neck. "It was the day after the White Sox beat the Cubs."

I stood up, reached in my back pocket, and pulled out a card. There was only a phone number on it, in bold print, no name. I put it in his sweaty palm and folded his fingers around it. "Call me if you hear from her or think of anything that would help me find her. It's important. Don't make me come back here."

Tyrell glanced up.

He would call if anything turned up in a few days, maybe two. After that, his bravado would return.

Turning to Annie, I asked, "You ready?" She seemed to fly to my side. We walked down the steps, obviously not fast enough for Annie. She pulled me by the hand. Her high heels caught on the sparse grass. She went bow legged for a few seconds.

An old, faded-blue Buick appeared from the side of the house. It spat gravel as it sailed out to the main road and took a left.

As we crossed the lawn, Annie leaned in. "You knew they would take off?"

"Heard them trying to start that car out back. They had trouble keeping it running. Something must have finally worked."

"Why'd you call me crazy back there?"

"I figured it'd get his attention. Seemed to work."

7

Carson

Clicking the doors open, I tossed the keys to Annie, "You drive."

"Okay." She missed the catch, scrunched up her nose, and picked them off the pavement. "You tired after all that with Tyrell and his running-scared friends?"

"Hardly, I just need to make some phone calls." I glanced back at the house. Tyrell was still sitting in the chair, watching. The house looked smaller, as did he. Annie dabbed a cut above my eye with a tissue. She was trying to figure out how to put the seat forward. I leaned over and pushed a button. With a whirring sound from the driver's seat, her outstretched feet hit the pedals.

She cranked her neck around and peered in the back. "I feel like a soccer mom. There's way too much space in here. I don't think I could ever be that woman—lunches, spills, diapers, butt rash, vehicles like this, rows of car seats, screaming, and more screaming. I've watched my friends. Their hair loses all the glow. Gravity seems to pull at their shoulders."

"Where's the love?"

"I don't know. Maybe that happens when those short humans gain height and move out."

I nodded. "Well, let me know when it happens to you—I'll get you one of those stickers with the descending stick figures for your back window."

She scowled at me, then turned her concentration back to the road and headed the Explorer toward town. The silence felt as heavy as gravity. "I was married once," she said, "bridesmaids, the white flowing dress, layered cake with those stupid dolls on top, outdoors in spring, flowers down the aisle, a priest, the whole ridiculous thing. Jason loved the wedding night. He loved it so much, he had one with every girl in his office. His hotel bills were higher than the cloud he hung on. In the divorce decree, I somehow got stuck paying our VISA for food service, expensive wine, and clean sheets for him. Ironic, isn't it?"

I stayed silent.

"Guess my sister and I aren't that different."

We listened to road noise for a while. Finally, I remembered why she was driving and grabbed my cell out of my backpack. I found his picture and punched the phone icon.

A recognizable voice answered, "I knew you were going to call."

"I did call," I said.

"I knew it twenty minutes ago." I heard a click from his tongue. "Premonition, man, from the system. I've been eating these mangoes that Sarah Rule sent me from Brazil. My mind's overloaded with psychic understanding. Waves so thick I can taste them. You remember Sarah from that thing when she lived in Vallarta? She always wears orange and has that hair rolling down her back like blonde water. I'm telling you, you have to try these . . ."

"Hub! Enough with the mangoes," I interjected.

"But, I'm telling you; they have a life force. I knew the instant the phone would ring. And I knew you were going to call. The energy was swirling."

"You realize it's not very believable when you tell me things like that after the fact." The car bounced over a gutter and I scrambled for my cell. "Hub?"

"Carson?"

"Sorry, I thought I lost you. I need you to find out some information on an Allie Fieldhouse—she likes piano music, and I assume lives in Salt Lake. We'll be flying back as soon as I can book a flight."

"We'll, as in 'we will'?"

"Annabelle Linford and I. She's the client who wants to know where her sister is. Anyway, get back to me as soon as you can."

"Shouldn't take long. At least this time you have a full name. Last time all I had was male, thirty-ish, initials, Camel filter cigarettes, and his high school, no year. That took me two weeks and 13 bottles of cheap shiraz."

I pressed the end button and glanced over at Annie. She was shaking her head.

"Hub believes he's a Shaman."

"What do you believe?" asked Annie.

"I think he believes he's a Shaman, and he has enough followers he could make a heck of a show in the popular vote for president. I have no doubt that he comes up with a lot of things I can't fully explain. He's a phenomenon."

"You believe he's a Shaman?"

I gave her a smirk and tapped my chin with my index. "Not really."

Annie pulled the car into the hotel parking lot. "So, what is he?"

"He's a friend who is incredibly intelligent and clever. Computer whiz. He knows things. He figures out things. Once you get through all his wacky babble, mushroom use, and embarrassing uninvited visits, he's just a good man. My best friend."

Her right fingers drummed on the dash. She gazed straight ahead. "You two are opposites. It seems . . ."

I watched a mangy dog walk down the sidewalk from side-to-side, sniffing everything. "We understand each other's occupation, for lack of a better word. We *get* what each other does even if we don't want the same thing or live the same lifestyles."

"Much the same as opposites attract, like that old Paula Abdul song?"

The dog stopped, lifted a leg, and watered a telephone pole. A pale lady in a paisley dress pulled her husband on an arc away from the mutt, disgusted. The dog followed. Their step increased.

"No, that's not it. We're completely different, but we are ever aware of those differences, and it doesn't matter. We can count on each other if needed. Plus, he likes my wine reserves."

We left the car and went into our rooms to repack. I had previously called the airline and had a flight on Air Alaska in four hours. Enough time to rest, pack, grab a bite to eat and get to the Spokane airport. I lay down on the made bed, thought about an article comparing hotel bedspread cleaning to sleeping on a stray dog in Chicago, and tossed the covers back. The nap took about twenty minutes, five more and I might have been snoring. The phone rang. Hubbard again.

"Allie Fieldhouse, or rather Allison, is heavy into Facebook. She's a Capricorn. She complains about everything. She has thirteen-hundred friends. She's a selfie addict. Her hair seems to change style every tenth entry. She's friends with Tia and has a Rubenesque figure. She needs one of her followers to tell her to go easy on the mascara."

"Hub. Slow down. Did you get an address?"

"Of course, but I've got a lot more."

I heard Annie's voice and a knock on the door. I bounced off the bed and opened the door. Motioned her with a tilt of my head to take a seat. She chose to lean against the dresser. I mouthed "Hub."

"Great, I want it all, but I'm about to jump on a plane, and I just wanted to make sure Allison is in Salt Lake."

"I tried to get a take on that when I called her. She's like anti-metaphysical. I think her neurons are spongy. They don't let anything come back out. She speaks with this high-pitched, fast-talking drone of a voice. She's heavy on the first syllable. Anything after that is packed babble. I've never had to listen to anyone so intently. It took two glasses of some merlot you had on the counter for me to calm enough to decipher it."

"Are you at my house?" I said, a bit annoyed. Then I thought better of it. "Is this leading to her address somewhere?"

"Oh, oh yeah, she's at the Tarragon apartments in Midvale, C-12."

"You're the best. Did she actually give you her address?"

"No. I picked up most of the info off Facebook. She had a picture of her, next to her late model LeBaron. I scoped in on the license plate, then called my friend Julie at the DMV. You owe her a lobster dinner."

"Thanks," I said. "That merlot was a present for Dana and Kit's wedding, by the way."

"I wondered about the bow. My info, your merlot. Besides, champagne is for weddings."

I rolled my eyes. "I'll call later. Email me everything you found that's pertinent." In my mind, I knew he'd send everything. I hung up and groaned.

Annie giggled.

8

Tia

My mind groggy and spent, I awoke in abated strokes of imaginary sand and dense smoke. My hands and legs were swimming with lethargic panic. I shuddered as a full inhale shocked my whole body. The smell caused tears to tumble, and a fear of breathing washed over me.

It was the scent of death, decomposing flesh. I tried to shut my nostrils down—the smell through my open mouth was just as bad. The ghastly aroma of animal death—human death. The aroma of recent-cut pine only added to its presence.

I gagged and dry heaved into the dark void, my stomach so empty it felt as if the lining was turned inside-out and blocked my airway. Pressing my palms deep into my gut gave little relief. My body involuntarily curled into a ball and I huddled there, breathing in short gasps.

I almost hated that the drugs had worn off. I cupped my hands over my nose to abate the odor that surrounded me. It didn't work. I had cried so long, tears wouldn't flow, though I felt the wetness on my cheeks. A spasm ran through my torso and down my arms. I rocked back and forth in an uncontrollable mantra.

Somewhere in that time with no end, I caught the cries and moaning screams surrounding me. I recalled panic and high-pitched voices from before. A faint memory huddled with me from some recent past. I knew my mouth had the same taste imbedded and the same dry tongue. I must have been awake, before, until shock and drugs had pulled me to a safe place. I had tried party drugs. I knew the after-effects and the depression that filled the body, asking for just a touch more, some relief.

A terrible wailing and banging shook me from my

thoughts. It was close and echoed in a metallic way. I tried to utter words of empathy, but my jaw and throat were unable to speak. One girl's horrifying sound could be heard above all others. One by one, the other girls faded as if they were listening also.

I remembered the water bottle, or maybe it was two, from whenever that time before was. My hands and feet scrambled along the edges of the crate searching with purpose. My knee kicked something round and hard. Pain shot out from under the kneecap. My hand fumbled until it found something to grasp, an I-bolt that held the binds for my legs. That was not it.

Finally, I found it. Passing the plastic bottle from feet to hand, I twisted the cap and lifted it up to my mouth. My swig was too hurried, and I coughed and choked for several seconds. Taking a second drink slowly and letting the wetness rest in my mouth, I closed my eyes. My body limbered and my breath came to me in slow meaningful slurps.

Taking a frantic moment, I felt my surroundings as far as the leather binds would allow. The sides were rough boards with no gaps between them. The ties allowed me to barely reach to the top, so I assumed I was in an almost square crate. Maybe, 4 feet.

My nose cringed. The odor of death had diminished, sweat and pine covering some.

My neck twisted to the left as shrieking bounced off walls in an earie echo. I felt my heart exploding out through my chest. There was no escaping these horrid smells and sounds as I writhed in my binds. Screams. Lots of high-pitched screams.

I mentally counted to slow my heart and breathing. It took forever. Over time, my body loosened. It was a trick my dad had taught me when my homework gave me anxiety. Oh, I miss him. He would know what to do.

I called out to the howling frantic girls, "It's okay. There are others here."

"Where's here?" another voice yelled.

A girl wailed without end. She moaned slow and loud. Her voice raced in short mutterings, going quickly up in scale, then dropping down in volume as if moving farther away, and then she would start all over again.

Something reshuffled and moved to the front of my mind. *The smell? Where was it?* Sniffing the air, I puzzled over the loss of a working nose. The brain in its autonomic wisdom had shut down the sense of smell. I sniffed again. Nothing, not even the sweet smell of pine sap, nor the sweat that drenched our bodies.

The shrill sound continued—another voice followed suit. I covered my ears with pressured hands and tightened my eyelids enough that my forehead hurt. Any bravery I had before was lost. Sobbing and moaning seemed to reverberate inside my skull. I felt myself headed closer and closer into the depths of shock. Something inside me screamed.

Other voices yelled the same thing. Fear boiled. I felt a comradery in this dark terror of a place. My mouth dry, my throat sore—I screamed louder. Just then, the bottom came out from under me and my body was thrown around in the box. The ties bit and ripped at my wrists and ankles as the crate slid into another. Screeching came from outside tires and the inside walls of the truck as if battling each other. I landed with a thud. Instant pain shot out my elbow and tailbone. I let out a horrifying cry that filled the hollows around my sister prisoners.

Sobbing uncontrollably, my body battered, I lay still, feeling the truck bounce steadily over rough terrain. I knew from the previous vibrations and jarring that we were in a truck, a semi-truck, probably.

The brakes squealed, and a sharp forward jolt tossed me to the ends of my bindings like a puppet. My chest heaved, gasping for air. Somehow, my knees had jammed into my chest. My breasts burned and throbbed.

Exhausted and terrified, I touched a gash that had opened above my eye. I followed the trail of blood with my finger, tracing down the side of my nose. The wetness tickled my nostril.

The motor stopped, and I listened in the stillness. Faint sobs passed softly through the deathlike quiet. A door slammed, and I heard a startled catch in my hushed breathing. My nose scrunched up as the dead animal smell wafted through my crate. Unsettling, horrid.

Twigs crackled. The sound moved closer with each snap. Bile had risen in my throat; I was too scared to fully acknowledge the taste of the caustic acid. I had also peed on myself, my calves wet and warm. My breath was so shallow, I wondered if I might pass out from lack of oxygen.

I heard something resembling the clank of hardware and a metal door rolling up. The noise was straight in front of me. I tried to swallow, keeping perfectly still.

"Ohhhh damn, we have another one. Damn! Get me a rag and the can of gas by the tool bin behind the cab. Hurry."

"Hold your horses, I've gotta empty some of that beer." There was rustling in the bushes.

My eyes closed, even though I was in total darkness as I listened. There were traffic sounds far to the left. The screech of an owl had broken through the incessant crickets. I thought I heard a river but wasn't completely sure. Even if the calming rush of water was a fantasy, my pounding heartbeat dropped and my chest slowed its rapid billows. I knew it wouldn't last.

"Cedee, you parked so close to the trees, I can barely get the damn door open. Where's the flashlight?"

"It's in the glove box—rags are under the seat. Are you stupid or what?"

"Quit calling me that." Thirty seconds passed. "Ahhhh . . . shit!"

"Now what?"

There was a litany of swearing and more branches being cracked. "That damn gear shift almost poked my eye out."

Laughing ensued. "Gotta hate it when it does that. Damn, you do the dumbest things."

It sounded like he ran into every tree in the forest as he made his way toward the back of the truck.

A light. I could see a light. Twinkling. There were four holes the size of a peanut drilled into the side of the crate. Carefully, I cranked my neck to get a better view. I could see the two men as they shifted and the open door. Not faces, but silhouettes. One was tall with a big head, short neck and protruding belly. The other was half a foot shorter and kept rubbing his eye socket with the palm of his small hands. There was another pine box to my left; I could see a corner of it and others in front of that.

"Tony, lay the rags over that downed tree there and hold the flashlight, while I pour a little gas on 'em. Put out that cigarette and quit playin' with your eye."

"It hurts."

"The other one's going to hurt in a minute. A rig off the

highway here might look suspicious. We gotta move fast."

I watched the silhouette called Tony drop the rags over something to the left. His flashlight clipped under his armpit.

"I may need a hospital or something. Everything's blurry."

The big one shined his light back toward Tony. I watched the light somersault. He tapped the back end of the flashlight hard into his partner's receding hairline. "Watch yourself, or this young thing won't be the only body out between the trees."

Tony lifted his hands up in surrender.

"You okay?"

"I'm good." He stared at the big one's feet.

"Git back to work then."

I could see his eye clamped shut just above a beak of a nose. These truckers had a total IQ that would barely add up to a warm spring day. I wanted to giggle but shuddered instead.

Within a few moments both men lifted themselves up into the truck. I tucked myself away from the light coming through the holes. There were footsteps moving around and checking. One hummed softly, a tune from a movie I recognized, Frozen.

"This is the one. She's ripe," said Cedee. "Tony jump over here and help me. C'mon; move yer ass and grab the pry bar by the door. This gas isn't doing shit."

I listened without breathing, there was sliding and panting, and then a sharp crack. And more wood splintering. My heart wailed against my ribs, and I took in slow breaths through an open mouth. All the crying and screaming from before had ceased. The air was dripping with fear. I wished for my drugged state to return. One of the men was wheezing; the other grunted. I strained to hear as the box scraped on the floor as they moved it slightly. They lifted a limp body out of the box, eyed it carefully, and slapped the face. The light glimmered through drooping blonde hair. The big guy dropped her back in. The sound of the crate being thumped on the ground raised tears through my lashes.

"Cedee, J.B.'s going to kill us. This is two."

"Well, he ain't going to be no happy camper, but he needs us. Don't worry. This ain't our fault. We're just the haulers. He won't do anything." There was worry in his voice.

"He scares the crap out of me," said Tony.

I peeked through one of the holes and saw the flashlights

sitting on the truck bed by the door. Their beams lit the two figures better this time. The big guy had a scruffy beard and a three-inch white scar across his cheek bone. A doughy face and lips made him appear almost adolescent. His arms, like tree trunks, lifted the body out of the crate and dragged it by the arms into the woods. The thinner one, Tony, followed dutifully with a shovel.

"Hey, dummy. Grab a light, I'm in the dark here."

Tony walked back, grabbed one of the lights and shined it into the trees. A few minutes passed. The sounds of broken twigs and shoveled dirt cut through the night. One of the girls whispered, "Are they gone?"

Another said, "Quiet, they'll be back. Better if they think we're all in La La land."

The first girl said, "My name's Lisa—Lisa Rundle. Some bastard with blue eyes . . ."

"Wait 'til they close the door; we'll talk," I hissed. "These guys may seem kind of dumb, but they're mean and without conscience." With my dry mouth, my words sounded as if my cheeks were filled with chalk.

"You saw them?" another voice asked.

"Shhhhh."

The better part of a century passed before I heard talking in the distance. As it came closer, the hair on my arms stood on end, even with sweat dripping from each body pore. I ached for a sip of water but thought better of it. My hands comforted the plastic bottle. With my mind racing over our vulnerability, my lip quivered involuntarily. I slumped down like a pile of dirty laundry. The binds tugged at my wrists.

"Should we check the crates?" asked one of them as they approached.

"We need to get out of here. I know a place about forty-five minutes further on where we can hide the truck, eat, and sleep for a while. It'll be daylight soon." It was the big one's voice—Cedee. I slumped further, willing the semi-truck door to close.

Through my closed eyelids, I could make out flickers of the flashlight as Tony undid latches and glanced in each crate. He seemed to linger as the light shone through cracks in the wood on my box. Inside, my organs twisted; my mind screamed. Outside, I forced my body to lie flaccid, a sliver of pine pressing into my thigh. He finally moved on.

I heard a thump. "This one's awake. She looks shell-shocked, like those street kids in Qatar. You better git up here." A shattering shriek filled the bed of the truck. Someone screamed endlessly. There was a gagging sound as they forced something down her throat. A slap rippled through the trailer. Silence.

The sound of the door closing felt safe—frighteningly safe.

9

Carson

Allie Fieldhouse had a long face and a crooked smile. I stared at the picture on my cell wondering what kind of person she was. Under her burden of makeup, she was pale. She wore only a Raiders' shirt that accentuated her twig-like arms and legs, hanging loose in one photo. As I scrolled though Hub's uploads, I noticed she had buttered herself in rub-on tan in all but two pictures. She had an attitude on Facebook that I doubted passed over into her real life.

I'd been sitting in my car for six hours now. She might not show up today at all. Her cell went quickly to voice mail, and I didn't leave a message. I had talked to her roommate, when he had arrived a couple of hours ago; he was one of those flaunting gays that just wanted to talk about himself—all body language and smiles. I learned nothing helpful from him, except that she wasn't home and might arrive sometime between now and a week from now. He had no idea where she was. "We run in different circles," he'd said.

With the Danish gone and the thermos of coffee empty, I began talking back to my stomach growls. The cell rang and my spirits brightened.

"Here."

"Carson? Any news? What have you found?" asked Annie.

"Mostly that breakfast was a long time ago."

"What?"

"Allie hasn't shown up since we talked. It's been two hours. I'm still at the apartment, but I've got to go get something in my belly in a few minutes, plus my bladder is eyeing the snowball bushes with evil intent."

"Guys like you think you're so funny," a half-amused tone filled her voice.

"Guys like me?"

"Yeah, you know, healthy, outdoorsy, and all that solidness," she paused. "I want my sister. Something has to be done."

"I'll find her. I know this is hard on you, but just give me time to do my job." My belly felt hollow, and I was getting lightheaded. I needed fuel. A milkshake sounded good, and a plate of lasagna, and a roast beef sandwich. Maybe a buffet.

"Should I come over and watch the place while you eat?"

Alarms went off in my brain. "No! That's not a good idea. Aren't you working?"

"Yes, I'm working. But I can't get all these morbid thoughts out of my mind."

"First thing, she's not dead. Stay away from those thoughts or you'll end up babbling into a plastic cup at a state facility. Try to keep positive. Something will shift, and I'll find her. Give it time."

"Does she have time?"

I didn't answer.

"Okay, I'll try to work. Please call me with anything, and I'll try to let you do your job. I trust you though I'm not sure why."

Halfway through a meatloaf sandwich, I had a thought. I mulled over the consequences and finished my salad and the rest of the sandwich. Then I ordered a chicken salad sandwich to go, chips, orange juice, and a full thermos, black, and leaned back in the booth, hands behind my head. I thought about alternative plans. I shook my head at one, but it kept coming back to me. The waitress dropped off a sack, my bill, and a full thermos on the table. I watched her tip-smile fold back into her face as she walked away.

I sat in the car and talked to myself for a bit in front of the restaurant. A Land Cruiser with an irritated lady driver waited for my parking space. I ignored her. Finally, she honked and sped away. Twenty minutes passed; in that time, I decided it might be a small enough favor to limit my obligation. I knew he would want more than he gave. How much more? That was the problem. Should your past stay in the past? He had access to information.

Pulling up to the curb at Allie's, I noticed a used-to-be-red Chrysler Le Baron parked in front. The ragtop was worn and duct taped in enough places to make it look like a horrid quilt. The rear window was a brownish, cracked vinyl that would disappear with a good sneeze. License plate—2gud2btru. It was hers.

She had plastered pictures of the Le Baron on Facebook as if it were a new Mercedes. Her roommate's car was back, just to the south of hers. I sat for twenty more minutes to see if anything changed. It didn't.

Pulling the Walther out of the glove box, I eased it under my waist band. I normally didn't pack, but this girl might be on the far side of crazy, and I didn't know who else was in there. And, when I visited earlier, I noticed there were two bullet holes in the main window. As I stood out of the car, I loosened my shirt. The tail slid over the nine-millimeter.

The roommate answered the door. "Hey Al, that guy with the face is here." He turned to me, "I knew you'd be back. I told her all about you." I wasn't sure what that meant, but it made me uneasy. A minute later, Allie came around the corner, peeling a mandarin orange. She stared at me and scrunched up her nose.

"I've never seen you before," she stated. "Do I know you?"

"Carson, I'm Carson." I took a step in the house. The roommate tried to stay his ground but gave up. "I'm trying to find a friend of yours, Tia Linford."

She took a slice of orange and popped it in her mouth. Hub was right; she highlighted her eyes with more makeup than any four girls together. She wore low cut jeans and one of those see-through blouses to show off fancy bras. Hers was standard Walmart.

"You a cop?"

"Just a friend of a friend." Her roommate sat on the couch and gazed at me with a grin.

"You don't look like a friend." She tilted her head. "Take a seat."

There was an overpainted wood rocker by the door. I sat and waited for her to say something. She perched her left thigh on the soft arm of the couch, her right foot on the couch, and leaned forward. "What da ya wanna know?"

"She's missing, but I think you know that," I said.

"Heard she'd taken off with her Ty."

Allie gazed at the ground when she spoke. Her hands fiddled with a cheap necklace. Every word she said to do with Tia was slow and deliberate. She was a terrible liar.

"So, you didn't see her at Brother Zac's bar after her other friends left? I was told you came late." I didn't really know; I was just fishing.

"Guess you were told wrong. Who said that?"

Her roommate peeked over at her, then quickly back. His left leg was thumping like a rabbit.

She was there. I just had to find a way for her to admit it. "The bartender and that guy that always wears T-shirts."

"You mean Dan?" her roommate asked.

She turned like a rattler about to strike. "Shut up."

Allie's eyes found mine and the meanness faded. "I've only been there a couple of times, and who the hell remembers what they did weeks ago." I watched her fidget and stand up. "I could've been there, but I don't remember seeing Tia. Last time I saw her, we went to a movie." She sat back down as I stepped forward.

I moved over closer and leaned down in her face, my arms braced against bent knees. "I wonder why someone would say you were there talking to her?"

Her roommate started to get up. My glare caught his eyes, and I signaled for him to sit down. He did. With his hands tight between his legs, he watched the carpet.

My forehead nearly touched hers. She froze. "Well?" I asked. Her black eyes slowly glanced up at mine, then quickly away. Eyelash makeup flicked into my face. Her face flushed.

After another 45 minutes of prying and watching her makeup bleed down her cheeks, I had all the information she was going to give. Her roommate helped in a few stops. She was scared, not just of me but of something else. I could feel it. There was more hidden deep behind her dark green eyes.

I drove away with more puzzle than pieces. I stopped at a coffee shop, my cell rang. I listened to silence on the other end for thirty seconds or so. The call was blocked. I knew exactly who it was. My pulse quickened as I waited, decided against coffee and pulled into traffic.

"I cannot believe you begging for help, like a little lost

school girl," the rumbly voice finally said. Bear is someone from my pseudo-military past. I've never liked him, but he was one hell of a covert, and he still had contacts. Ones I've dissolved.

"Begging . . . is a strong word," I said.

"Sounded like on-your-knees pleading to me."

"A simple request between old friends. So, when can I pick it up?" I knew what would come next. A deep breath filled my chest like gravel.

"Ahhh, that's sweet, you said we are friends. Kinda touches my heart," he chuckled. "Quid pro quo?"

Right, consideration. Things never change. "What about the fact that I saved your skinny ass—twice? Doesn't that count?"

"The events of my almost demise were greatly exaggerated. I think you were just searching for a medal. You should thank me––I'm the reason you received two. Payback, pure and simple."

I took in a deep breath and exhaled loudly as if getting suckered in. Bear had the connections, and I only had him. "Okay, whatever. What do you want?"

"That's my boy. I have an AWOL that I need a line on, Patrick Ackerman."

My eyes widened. "The senator?"

"Yep. He went missing between July 13th and the 16th. I need you to find out where he was."

"You know his whereabouts now?" I glanced up to watch the light change and eased my foot off the brake.

"Of course we do. He was only off radar for four days, but we need to know why."

"Done, but for the senator I may need a touch more . . . uhhh . . . solicitation for this case."

I knew in the silence the gears were grinding. A full two minutes passed. My mind could picture him signaling some sweaty browed assistant as he pecked on a computer. He let out a stream of expletives and a long grunt. "Pick up the DVDs from a detective Brower at the county."

Silence. I peeked at my phone to see if I had lost service. In bold print, in the right-hand corner, "*call ended*" flashed.

Such a friendly goodbye.

10

Carson

I waited in a hallway, watching the shuffle of worn shoes and somber faces. Here, ignoring anyone who might ask a question was commonplace. Detective Brower wasn't much different, except he was taller and less friendly.

"Carson?" His voice was stern and a touch effeminate, like an old-school nun.

I stood. Even with my height, I stared into his angular chin. He jutted it to the left for me to follow. His stride was hard to keep up with. I'd always thought big bodies like that moved slowly. I followed him down another hall, through an open door, into an interrogation room with a giant eyehook bolted to the table. The smell of blood, urine, and antiseptic made me want to cringe, but I wouldn't give Brower the pleasure. Mop swirls created a pattern on the cement floor.

A cardboard box, the type that held reams of paper, sat on one corner. He pointed to the prisoner chair. I glanced back. I'm pretty sure he was grinning, but it was hard to tell from his scowl. He sat. His large fists lowered to the table like double sledgehammers. Detective Brower was one of those first-one-to-speak-loses kind of guys.

I lost. "Well," I glanced around at the cinderblock walls, "I love what you've done with the place. The grey works well with the cement floor. Could use a recliner, though."

He wasn't amused. "I looked you up. You're a citizen. You've got a shitload of money and live in a crap cabin on a bunch of acres of rattlesnake paradise. An ex-Marine with a handful of medals, master's degree in organic psychology, and no traffic tickets, ever." His head tilted back and he glared at me down his nose. "Still, just a citizen."

I tried a smile. His face didn't change. "A concerned citizen."

"Bullshit. I'm not even going to ask how you got someone higher than God to make our chief *order me* to pass a little missing person's file over to you."

"I'm just doing a friend a favor—not real sure about any of the other stuff. Just trying to make a friend feel okay about things."

"You working for the sister? She's a pain in the . . ." He ground his teeth. "I had to break away from an important interview, just so I could play secretary and make sure all this crap was copied." He nodded toward the box. His face scrunched down hard as if he would grind his teeth into dust, then me.

I almost laughed at the mean look but knew better. I held out my hands and played dumb.

His brow furrowed. "You think you're smarter than me and Detective Landon?"

I didn't say anything. I wasn't about to get into a pissing contest with Brower. I watched his knuckles tighten. My jaw hurt with the thought of one of those connecting. He kept still for a full minute, then slid the box over to me. "I'm keeping tabs on you, so you know."

"I'd appreciate that." By the downturn of his lips, I knew that was the wrong thing to say. "If anything turns up, I'll call you. I don't want anything to do with an arrest or anything like that. You guys are the professionals." I watched his mouth flatten out as he thought about that.

Detective Brower reached in his pocket, fumbling for a time with thick fingers and pulled out a card. He tossed it to me. His eyes seemed to withdraw as his scowl increased. With a shake of his head, he turned and walked out leaving the door open. I assumed I was dismissed and chuckled to myself.

Outside the air was better. I inhaled deeply, then coughed, as exhaust fumes rushed through my lungs. I walked a half block south, to where my second vehicle, an old Ford 1500 truck, sat waiting. All the dents appeared to be the same as when I parked it. I noticed the ticket under my wiper and glanced at my cell clock. I still had fourteen minutes. Yanking the ticket out, I noticed the writing in sharpie—"*Just a warning.*" I'm certainly making friends today. One of Brower's partners, no doubt.

11

Carson

At Annie's suggestion, we met at her condo. She insisted on watching the DVDs with me. She answered the door so excited, I expected her to start clapping her hands and jump up and down, like those wind-up monkeys you find at state fairs. Her eyes twinkled above a contagious smile. This lady was a conundrum. On one hand, she was a touch of a high-maintenance elitist; on the other, an impetuous cheerleader. She was like two people, but they both seemed to fit her. I don't think I was partial to one or the other.

I glanced beyond an energetic Annie. Deep in my chest, I chuckled to myself. Annie's place was modern contemporary, all whites and greys as I gazed around. White walls, white carpet, black and white blown up photos of empty buildings, framed and hung at eye level, a silver-legged dining table with thick glass, light grey drapes, and a speckled black countertop in the kitchen with black cabinets on two walls. I was afraid to glance in her fridge in case it was color coordinated. Her flat screen sat on a glass table with a thin DVD player directly in front. On the shelf below lay a stack of local newspapers and three *Better Homes and Garden* magazines. *Never would have guessed—a gardener?*

"A drink?" she asked. I was still glancing around, not sure whether to sit down or pay admission. "Carson, you care for a drink?" She pointed to a sparse wine rack with one hand and her stainless-steel fridge with the other.

"Oh, sure, sounds great." I turned toward the front room. My jeans just didn't seem appropriate for sitting on her stylish, uncomfortable furniture.

She noticed my hesitation. "Try the couch. I know it

doesn't fold up like those chairs around your outdoor office, but it should do in a pinch." Her fingers flicked her forehead. "Sorry, I'm not trying to be condescending. Not at all. Once I got through your . . . Yellowstone-adventure attitude and your gallant, grab-your-own-camp-chair hospitality, I found your furniture comfortable."

I peered over at the couch. "Yeah, I know, it's uncomfortable, but doesn't it look great?" She held up a wine bottle.

"Just water from the tap—if you have it. And ice." I eased myself down and tried to find a soft spot between the tight tuck and roll leather. It was like sitting in a dry creek bed.

"I've got bottled wa—"

"Tap is great."

I pulled out one of the DVD's from my back pack, then pushed the button with an open icon on the front. Tiny lights came on and the door slid open with little fanfare. Annie sat down after putting my drink on a square, silver coaster.

It took three hours to go through one with stopping and reviewing. My cell told me what my stomach had been saying for the last hour. It was 5 p.m. and I hadn't really eaten for six and a half hours. Annie ordered pizza while I drank more water and finished off the candy-coated pretzels and second refill of shelled pistachios. *Where does someone get pistachios already shelled? What's the fun of that?*

"You ever see the Marine before?" I asked, glancing back over my shoulder from the floor. My time on the couch had lasted about thirty minutes. I'd rather swallow gravel. She had giggled when I slid her coffee table over and dropped down on the carpet. My butt gave a sigh of relief.

Annie was throwing together a green salad at the counter. "The guy with the short hair and zipper smile?"

"Yep."

"No, I would have noticed him. He wasn't Tia's type, but she seemed to listen to his every word. Once he disappeared she sat at a table with those three legal types—the two boys with collared shirts and the girl in the grey pants suit."

"He came back," I said. "He also talked to Allie, who was actually at the bar. The little liar. She told me she had heard Tia met a cool guy at the bar."

"Really, you didn't say anything." Annie set out a couple of black paisley placemats and three store-bought dressings on her counter. She cocked her head as if considering this. "When?"

"He was off to the side, while she was back at her table with her friends Amber and Pauline. He'd put on a blue beret and was leaning against a corner. His eyes were on your sister's table. He kept sipping his drink, but the level of the liquid never lowered."

Annie's eyes widened and she leaned her forearms into the counter. "He was like—stalking her?" She seemed to stop breathing as she stared at me.

The doorbell rang. Annie didn't move.

I got up and answered her door. A chubby music-teacher-looking gentleman handed me a pizza. His white shirt had tomato sauce in a line above his worn-out belt. I pulled out a few bills and handed them to him. He was indifferent to the fifty percent tip in his hand. I shut the door with my heel and peeked over at Annie. She hadn't moved, even her eyes appeared to have lost all their life. She gazed blankly into nothing.

"Pizza?" I set the carton down on the far end of the counter.

She looked straight ahead. "That guy had such an innocent face. He seemed like one of those gym fanatics." She paused; her eyes met mine. "That boyish-grin. Son-of-a . . . I actually thought he was . . . someone who might be good for Tia." She slapped her forehead. "I'm a complete idiot. What's wrong with me?"

"Annie," I stood close to her and put my hand on her shoulder, "I'm going to watch this many, many times. It may be a lead; it may not. Let's just see what we find."

She burst into tears. I waited. My stomach growled.

Five minutes later she wiped her cheeks with a paper towel. I handed her another. She accepted. Without notice, she turned on her heels and opened the cupboards. Plates were plopped down and forks clattered across the counter. I stopped one from going over the edge but remained silent. Green salad was sort of smashed into the plates along with generous slices of pizza which overlapped the salad. I felt it best to remain silent as she drained a glass of wine, then stood watch over the counter. I waited, uncomfortable.

"Okay, let's eat." She slid a plate toward me.

"Thank you." In these situations, I wasn't positive what to

say or do. I sat on a bar stool and grabbed a slice of pizza. She scowled at me, but I bit in anyway. She poured herself more wine.

Her plate sat idle as she grabbed the remote off her table. "I want to see this guy again. Will you take me to the place where Tia first met him, then to the one you mentioned earlier?" She dabbed a spot under her nose with a tissue.

I wasn't sure about this, but I got up after shoveling cheese and crust into my mouth like a chipmunk. My fingers fumbled with the remote. I envisioned sauce and oil smearing across the keys. She handed me a folded paper towel. I tried to say thanks, but it came out *"ouuuuks."* She waited, watching me with little interest. Her shiny cheeks had gone from red to a soft pink.

I chewed hurriedly on a wad of dough, forcing it down. I needed to be around people besides Hub more often. She seemed to not even notice. Finishing a glass of water, my speech came back. "Sorry, let's see where that was." The screen sped through split-second images until I found the spot. Annie moved closer to the TV. I heard her whisper, "Bastard."

12

Carson

I hardly realized I was driving until I heard the rumble of the cattle guard under my wheels. That bounced me back to reality. On the whole ride home, my mind was focused on the Devil Dog.

I knew right off he was a Marine. I'd spent so much time around Semper Fi, I could spot one from a mile in a crowd of a hundred. Their shoulders and chin had an arrogance to them, even the ones who topped the scales twenty years after boot camp. I once awakened a homeless drunk in San Francisco, knew what he'd been through immediately. Later I bought him lunch. Smelling like a restaurant dumpster, he had mumbled "Sir, yes, sir," as he slept under a tree in Golden Gate Park. They stand out, at least to other Marines.

The second tape from a security camera across the street from Brother Zac's had a grainy picture. A couple had exited the bar. The man seemed to be holding up the girl as she moved drunkenly down the sidewalk. The camera lost sight as they turned a corner. Annie was positive it was them. The picture was bad, but I thought there was about a 50/50 chance of it being Tia and the Marine.

My plan was to let Hub and Maria give me their thoughts after viewing the tapes tonight. A couple of cottontails scattered into the straw-grass as I turned into my ranch. The truck bottomed out. I should think about new shocks.

I knew Hub would have some insight if I could keep his neurons from migrating. He called it traveling on planes—which he meant as a geometric concept, not United Airlines. All I knew was that it was out of my realm of science. Once Hub was steered, he was a hound dog. Maria would have her own viewpoint, usually different from Hub's, but just as important.

The lack of dream time hit me as I slid the key into the lock. I'd only had a couple hours of sleep last night. I needed at least a couple more, but breakfast first. After four eggs, a mound of grits, a ham steak, and two glasses of Tang, I fell onto the bed sideways.

I woke up to Maria's soft Mexican voice and the sweet smell of fresh coffee. Our exclusive dating had been going on for almost three years. This thing we had seemed like one that would stay—though I'd never had much luck before. *Past does not mean future, but it sure helps keep the log rolling downhill*, Hub would say. Her long dark hair dangled down as she leaned toward me. There was a calming that overwhelmed me whenever I heard her gentle voice and sensed her touch. I was half asleep with a grin on my face.

Her nose crinkled and her lips tucked in. "Ahhh, Diablo," she said. "No candy for those lips until you brush." Her whole body angled back. "Brush them twice. You eat a muskrat?"

I balanced myself up on one arm. "I thought love meant more to you than worrying about little inconveniences."

"Amor doesn't mean caca." She punched me in my arm, and it wasn't any love tap. "Mouthwash, too."

"I'd listen to her." It was Hub's voice from the kitchen. "Remember your first Christmas?"

I wouldn't get up early one Christmas. Maria wanted me to see the present Santa had left. She had spent all night decorating the tree and talking about each and every December 24th from two-years-old on. She had that holiday energy usually reserved for five-year-old's. I feigned interest throughout the evening. We had several toasts to the holiday, and she finally went to bed with me about two a.m. Four hours later, she was bouncing on the bed for me to wake up. I mean bouncing, like it was a trampoline. Through the ruckus, I feigned sleep. By 7:30, I thought she had given up, until a pitcher of apple cider was poured on my face, and she stormed out of the bedroom. Spanish expletives echoed through my cabin. Adrenaline shot through me as I listened to my front door slam hard enough to send it through the back wall. I apologized for two days after. I knew I'd never miss Christmas morning again.

I nodded at Hub and found my way to the bathroom.

I finished my glass of orange juice and leaned back, giving room for a well-fed tummy to expand. Hub smiled. He knew his famous eggs Benedict and onion potatoes were my favorite.

Locking my hands behind the back of my neck, I tipped the chair on two legs. "You haven't made that since last February when I came back from that thing with the Columbian." I let out a long happy breath. "You're not going to wave some bundled weed and horse hair at me again?"

"That was Indian Paintbrush and Thistle. You needed their releasing wind."

"Yeah, that helped." My eyes rolled to the back of my head.

Maria came around from behind me, planting a soft kiss on my forehead. "Mi novio, you wouldn't know if it helped or not." She spoke perfect English, but she used Spanish when mad or loving. It was a subtle distinction. Sometimes I ducked, and there was only a hug coming my way. Playfulness filled her voice this morning.

With a half-smile, I decided silence was the best bet.

She turned my head upward toward her. Large brown eyes bored into mine. "So, where's the movie?"

"Movie? Oh, the surveillance tapes." I leaned the chair back down. "You want to see them, now?"

Hub slapped the table. "Of course we want to see them now. Maria and I have been like two giddy sleuths since you asked." Maria nodded her head and grasped my hand.

"Let me grab one more cup of coffee before we find our theatre seats." I poured the end of the pot into my cup; then Maria and I sat on the only couch, which was actually a futon.

I didn't own a television or have two hundred channels sucking my wallet. Hub set my laptop on a bar stool and searched for a plug. He found it. I handed him the first DVD. We watched his graceful fingers play with the keys until a faded picture came on the 14-inch screen. Hub sat down next to me, and we all leaned in. The three of us stared for about ten minutes.

"So, what are we looking for?" asked Maria. "The lighting sucks."

"Annabelle's sister Tia shows up in a minute or two. I want

you to watch her, and everyone she talks to. Anything that hits you as strange." I reached forward to touch the screen. "That's her—skinny, cute, rust blouse, innocent eyes."

"Move your finger. I can't see," demanded Maria. Her eyes narrowed as I backed up. "She's not skinny; she's got a nice figure. Tia's a size three, maybe four, depending on where you buy a dress."

We watched as Tia moved from her friends to the bar. On the way back, the Marine leaned out, asking her a question. She laughed and they exchanged a few words. He slid out a chair; and she stood still for a time, then waved to her friends, Pauline and Amber, and sat down. She had a full glass of wine; he finished off his mug of dark beer and signaled to an over-extended waitress with more weight on her tray than most people lift at a gym.

I'd have to see if Hub could enhance this enough for me to try my hand at reading lips. I had never been good at it before, but it was worth a try. I would bet Hub reads lips.

Next, we checked the outside tape—streetlights giving little definition. "He's not your guy," said Hub. "He's got hormonal rings; they're vibrating in his neck muscles. Watch when he talks." He backed the DVD up then hit forward.

I glanced at Maria. She shook her head then raised her eyebrows. "I don't see a thing. No rings. No vibration."

"It's lavender, man. Let your spirit ride the wave." Hub pointed one long finger at the screen. A smirk crossed his face as if he knew something no one else could. He was probably right.

"That guy's looking to get laid. I'm not picking up any threatening aura." Hub scratched his hair in concentric circles as if that might help us solve the case.

"No," protested Maria, "and quit twisting your hair. You know that drives me crazy." Her mouth tightened. "This Marine is a creep. He's a predator. In the bar, he was way too sure of himself."

Hub lay back on the carpet, his hands behind his head, his knees bent. "I don't doubt he's a predator, but not in the kidnapping sense. Mr. Marine is all about himself and taking home a pretty girl. I even think he senses there was a recent breakup. He reads people—well, female people. I'm not sure how he does with the gents, but people like him are usually good with either sex.

Though the motives are different. With a guy, he's probably . . ."

"You have a gift, but you're not always right," Maria's voice raised. She's an alpha female, and when she gets around the two of us—both card-carrying members of the "leader of the pack" category, she struggles for dominance. She usually wins, too. "He took Tia, period. A woman can tell." She flipped a cashew at Hub. He opened his mouth as if to catch it and got a nut in the nose. I breathed in thick air. Silence. The propane fridge kicked on.

"What about the other guy?" asked Hub.

"What other guy?" Maria and I both asked, barely a beat apart.

"The one by the pole. You know, with his hands in his pockets and his eyes watching Tia," said Hub.

"What? Who?" I pinched the top of my nose as I thought hard, rolling the tape through my mind. Nothing was registering. I glanced at Maria. She mirrored my puzzled face, then raised her eyes.

Hub slid across the floor and exchanged the DVD in the player. He sped to the part where Tia walked over to the bar. As she began to walk back to her table, he paused it. "See the guy by the pole to the right?"

"Yeah, but with the lighting he looks like an out-of-focus, fat ninja," I interjected.

"You can barely tell it's a man, if it is," Maria nudged Hub in the ribs with her foot. "He stands like a guy, but you can never tell anymore," she giggled. "If he adjusts his crotch, it's a guy."

"But check out the eyes," Hub said.

"Hub, it's too grainy to even know if those are eyes. He's in the shadows." I leaned closer, almost spilling the coffee cup in front of me.

"Okay, now watch him while I slow-mo to where she's at the Marine's table."

I still barely saw an outline, let alone the face. Then, for a split second, the shadow moved forward to put down his drink. There was a quick image of a face, though still fuzzy. His eyes could have been staring at Tia—or not.

"Did you notice that?" asked Hub.

Maria snickered. "You still doing that peyote you picked up on your last trip?"

He ignored her. "The eyes followed her every move. And he has those red marks on his forehead." Hub turned toward us as if we understood. I know he has skills that transcend normal barriers. But, science rules for me, so even though Hub's right about so many things, I'm still a skeptic. He could read it in my face.

"Like the cattleman in New Mexico? That rich racist?"

I remembered. He had told me something about red spots on Flack Newton when we first met the man. The "good-ol'-boy" wanted me to find an employee of his that had disappeared. It took me a week to find the guy and only a few minutes to realize the cattleman wanted to hide him in a shallow grave on his 2,400 acres. The whole thing was all about heavy revenge, for a slight embarrassment.

Maria turned her head to glance back at me. Puzzlement filled her eyes. I explained. After a few minutes, she shook her head, raising her outstretched fingers in the air. She was a true non-believer in Hub's Shaman acuity. I was merely a skeptic. But I knew for certain that Hub was an anomaly. He sees things when no one else does. Sometimes, in a conversation, he closes his eyes and is gone. A trance is the best explanation. For a minute or ten you can't get his attention. He becomes still and peaceful—then, he comes to and has answers to questions I never even thought to ask.

"Can you enhance the picture of the Marine and shadow boy?" I asked.

A grin crossed his face. "I've got all afternoon off, until the party. Shouldn't take more than two or three hours. I'll check DMV pictures after and see if we can get a name—they are without a doubt the easiest source to tap into."

Hub had a basement in his 100-year-old home, and except for the Persian rugs and the smell of incense burning it reminded me of Cape Canaveral during the space shuttle era. Of course, his stuff was much higher tech.

"Can you check military records?"

"I only go there as a last resort. Those pentagon types follow their paperwork like an obsessed mother."

"You know I won't visit either of you in prison," Maria crossed her arms with a stern slant to her lips. "I need to run home and pick up supplies for the party. Try not to be wearing cuffs when I get back."

I glanced at my wrist, then wondered why—I hadn't worn a watch in a decade. I pulled my cell off the counter, it read 10:42. We had eight hours before the festivities. With a quick peck on the cheek, Maria turned, hurrying out the door.

"She mad?" asked Hub.

"Nahhh," I said, without much conviction. "She loves us both . . . just hates it when I listen to you."

13

Carson

"I invited Annie." I shuffled my feet, wondering if this might upset Maria. I didn't need that tonight. She wasn't the jealous type, but the other day on the phone she had asked, "How are the sleeping arrangements in Idaho?" There was teasing but also a touch of insecurity in her voice, and she rattled a couple of Spanish words at the end that I wasn't too sure about. I had paused a little too long and answered, "Didn't get a lot of sleep." I could envision her eyes scrunched, mouth tightened. "There . . . were . . . two . . . rooms," I had lightly inserted.

Maria cocked her head slightly as if surprised. "I would love to meet her. I feel so sorry about her sister and all. It'll probably do her good."

"Annie asked me what she should wear."

The three of us laughed. Maria excused herself to run home for a few things.

Later, Hub and I went over the pictures he fixed up. There were seven of them, from different poses. "The Marine came out just like his revoked license. The guy at the pole became a big blur." He showed me the blowup. What I thought was a figure was the pole and an attached beer sign.

"And the Marine?"

Hub acted as if he had won the lottery, doing some kind of celebration dance. "I was right about him. There's nothing nefarious in his face at all. No red spots. No followers of any kind."

He had explained "followers" to me several times over the years. He believed he could see either diaphanous demons, or spirits of decency, that moved in and out of a person's soul. The demons were gooey and viscous and made a smacking sound when pulled from a bad soul. And they were multi-colored. The good spirits passed freely and were a light blue.

I wasn't sure if this was true shamanism or the after-effects of peyote teachings. Hub's voice lowered, "The Marine has nothing. Neither side wants him. He's not capable of hideous crimes. He's purely limbic."

I let out a stream of air through flat fingers tented at my mouth. He kept prattling, until I finally said in exasperation, "Do you have a name?"

Hub's lips parted and he held still for several seconds. "Of course I have a name—Mansell William Handley." He unfolded a piece of paper from his back pocket and handed it to me. "See?"

It was a copy of a driver's license. Five feet eight, one hundred and eighty-five pounds, brown hair, and green eyes were listed on the bottom. *Suspended* was stamped across the license. "You think this might be the right address?"

Hub grabbed my shoulder and leaned in, his dark eyes meeting mine. "I'm not an amateur. The current address is on the back." He paused, lowering his forehead. "Phone number underneath. I didn't call—figured you'd want to do that."

"You figured right." I felt like a hummingbird lost in an acre of sunflowers. My heart was beating about the same. It was always a rush to get a solid lead.

"I pulled his tax records, too," Hub snickered. "He doesn't make enough to eat more than rice and beans."

"I love you, man," I said. "He may have other income, off the books."

Annie's car pulled in. A stream of dust followed it and then flowed past where Hub and I stood by the fire pit.

I whispered to Hub and tucked the folded paper into my shirt pocket. I didn't want Annie to know I had found Handley until I determined if it were a real lead, or false hope. It sure sounded solid. She stepped out of her car in tight pants tucked into riding boots and a man's collared white shirt. She glanced around, probably searching for the polo field.

Hub leaned toward me, "White blouse?"

I reached out my hand to welcome her. One of her heels caught on some gravel, and she almost went down. I helped her over to more sure earth and introduced her to Hub. "This is Hubbard Tinning, my neighbor and friend."

A puzzled stare caught her face. "Neighbor?"

Hub held her hand between his two palms. The dust was settling again. "I've got an antique house about five miles south of here. Perhaps if you're around long enough, I could show it to you."

"It's filled with antiques?" Her voice was excited.

"Well, I've got a couple of metal lawn chairs from the fifties. Inside it's decorated in usable-disposable from Ikea. They're like antiques after two years, if that counts."

Her face appeared slightly constipated. After a moment, she nodded, then turned to me. "Any new information?"

"Still searching, but I bet I'll turn up something real soon."

"What was that look you gave Hubbard?" Her head cocked as if realizing something. "Is he the one who's the Shaman?"

I wasn't sure what look she was talking about, and I really didn't want him to go into Shaman-babble. I turned as I saw a red Jeep pull across the cattle guard. "Oh, here's Maria. I want you to meet her."

Annie turned as gravel churned and dust rolled off the Jeep's tires. She coughed, grabbed her middle button with finger and thumb and shook her blouse. There was silence as we all watched Maria hike over from her parking place under the Chinese elm. By her short quick steps, I could tell she had downed a load of coffee. She miss-stepped a couple of times on the gravel road. I watched her mouth spit a couple of Spanish expletives toward the ground. Glancing up, mascara and lip gloss highlighting her desert sun face, she radiated a smile as if she weren't cussing a moment before. I admired the woman's quick change of moods.

I waited until she was about two meters from the three of us. "Maria, I want you to meet Annabelle Linford."

Maria pushed me to the side and grabbed Annie's hands in hers. "Ohhhh, you poor, poor thing; Carson told me about your sister." They embraced each other, patting backs and making girl sounds. "Don't worry, my Carson will find this Marine and pop his head from his shoulders. He will bring back your sister. He is worthless at some things but not this."

Annie shot a look at me, "What Marine?"

Maria grabbed her by the arm and headed into the cabin.

As they walked away, I concluded, "This is Maria Sorento Canteña."

Hub chuckled.

14

Carson

Maria and Annie acted like old sorority sisters as they waited for the divorce party to begin. They giggled and chatted. I sat out on my camp chair watching the small fire I'd made and feigning attention to whatever it was Hub was rambling on about. Something to do with ghosts being released and a carnivore pudding he'd invented. I wanted to say something about the absurdity of his pudding, but instead I stayed in my own trance, considering Tia and her plight.

People arrived to help touch up the horse stalls, if you can call them that. They hadn't held horses for three decades. The stalls were no more than dry, grey wood panels nailed to a foundation of old cedar posts, with a roof showing almost as much light as shadow. Several friends ran crepe streamers in black and white around the rim of the ceiling. Two days ago, Art, the electrician, had put white Christmas lights throughout the rafters and in nearby trees. My job was to roll my generator out to the far corner and let electricity light up the place. I worried about my insurance, in case the whole stall came down. But, oh well.

I got up, reluctantly, and signaled at Hub to follow. I listened to his story about the cosmos and how it was smaller than first thought. I glanced back to the cabin. Maria and Annie were still in there. Faint laughter drifted out of the window.

Dust clouded the road as a platoon of ATVs and trucks made their way to my ranch. In small farm towns, people either come by truck, ATVs or occasionally, horses. Cars were for Sunday. The celebrated couple would arrive about 8 p.m.

"You have horses?" Annie said, startling me. She and Maria were to the side of us peering into the corral.

"They're just here for the night," I answered.

"He's afraid of horses," Hub said.

"Scared to death," added Maria with a grin that swelled her cheeks on both sides.

"He doesn't have the patience or soft energy to calm them." Hub rolled his hands in the air. "He drives them to anxiety attacks; you can feel it in the air—man against horse."

I felt my face redden quickly, the rush of blood raising from my neck up. "Let's go help with the party."

Tables had been set up along the tree line and were filling up with bowls of whatnot. The wonderful smells sifted through the dust of horses and 4-wheelers arriving. My stomach growled at the cooking fragrances as if hunger followed food scent. Danter, our area's self-proclaimed chef, had hauled out his fabricated trailer that contained two welded fifty-five-gallon drums set horizontally and fitted with a propane grill. Smoke and the pleasant odor of long-cooked pork radiated out. Ice chests with soda and beer were strategically placed around the corral. The hustle and bustle of organization flowed around us. I donated the place; everyone else did the work.

"You have a lot of friends," Annie said.

Maria burst into giggles. "Carson is the valley's hermit." She spread out her hands rolling them slightly. "These people love Carson. They think of him as one of their best friends. He, on the other hand, regards them as barely acquaintances."

"Sure, I enjoy some alone time. Who doesn't?" Irritation tightened my jaw and hands. "I'm not a damn hermit."

"Yes, you are, and it's one of the reasons I love you." Maria winked at me. "You live out here, miles from anyone else. You seldom go to town and rarely speak to anyone; but if anyone in the area is in trouble, you are the first to help."

I cocked my head. "You make me sound as if I'm working on sainthood."

"Not sainthood, maybe redemption."

Annie gazed at me with something between pity and admiration. The whole conversation made me uncomfortable. I walked away to greet a few people—my "acquaintances." I heard Maria whisper to Annie. "Now he's going to pretend to be Mr. Gregarious. Men . . . are they like that in the big city?"

"They're like that everywhere," answered Annie. "They hate being told what they like and don't like. Even when it's obvious to the rest of us."

The crowd swelled. It seemed as if everyone in the valley showed up, except for the inmates at the prison. Cheers began. I turned to my left. The couple could be seen a way's off, arriving dressed in togas and cowboy hats—like the day after a frat party. I swallowed my irritated pride and took my hermit body back to where Maria and Annie stood. I gave Hub a thumbs-up and watched him prepare the area for the ceremony. He was to officiate, since he was the closest thing to a preacher the couple knew.

I deliberately ignored Maria and pulled Annie to the side. I pointed down the secondary road. "That's Carl and Amblin, the couple this whole carnival is for. He is a long-haul driver who wanted four children. Amblin works at the water commission. She's bedded down a good part of the male population in this county and is totally infertile. They married twelve years ago to this date, and for irony, received their divorce decree this morning."

Annie craned her neck to see better. It wouldn't help. "I think they're both smiling, but it's hard to tell."

"They are," Maria said.

We watched while twin streams of clay dust flowed behind the hoofs of the palomino she rode, and the appaloosa he was saddled upon. Everyone grew quiet. The swallows' songs, a slight rustle of leaves, and nearing hoof beats announced their way. They were such incredible people and their couple-ness had always felt comfortable to me, but by this time I knew they were better people apart than together. Their marriage had unraveled one thread at a time, until little cloth remained.

Annie leaned closer to me and Maria. "Who's that riding behind?"

I laughed a bit too loud and received unwanted stares as if I'd disturbed a sacred ritual. I whispered, "I think they both brought dates."

Annie's face tightened. "They were the cutest couple. I adored them," Maria said. "Still do, it's just hard thinking of them as apart." Her eyes saddened as she shook her head. Carl and

Amblin dismounted with a short cheer from the solemn, happy crowd. Amblin held up their divorce decree like a banner—with a smile as big as the sky.

Hub shook hands with their dates who were waiting on their horses, both glancing around impatiently. Hub bounced over and put his arms around Carl and Amblin, then leaned in and gave Amblin a long kiss on the mouth. He turned toward Carl, who peeled Hub's arm off and backed away in mock fright. Laughter filled the stalls. The generator hummed in the background.

The ex-couple disappeared into the crowd, and Hub moved over to the mike. "I would like to thank everyone who's come to this auspicious occasion." Heads turned toward Hub. He rattled on about the divorcees finding other galaxies to discover and other worlds to conquer.

Maria gave a hearty laugh, "So, divorce means a voyage on the Starship Enterprise?"

"Pretty much," I answered.

Maria locked arms with Annie and me. She began moving us toward the food. Hub prattled on, while most of the group turned toward each other in conversation. The tables made a long track of white tablecloth and heaping bowls parallel to the cedar fence line. Maria pulled us toward the middle and smiled over at Annie. "You have to try my pozole."

"Pork or chicken?" I asked.

"Puerco, por supuesto," she licked her lips and rolled her eyes. "And my homemade Chile Verde with a hint of the lime."

"Sounds terrific," said Annie.

I glanced back to where Hub's voice still bellowed. He had his group of followers gathered around him in awe—four people in their early twenties and Harold, the drunk. Thin clouds barely shielded the sun, which appeared to be about three-quarters of the way to sundown. Gazing to my right, I watched cattle feed at the edge of the lake, two miles away, they looked like a small herd of ants.

A bowl of pozole and a paper plate of salad pressed into my ribs. Maria had prepared me a generous helping of each and stood with an odd grin on her face—forced, with a slight show of white teeth.

"I made you a plate."

Annie watched on. It took me a moment to realize Maria had become domestic. She had always been a "serve-yourself" kind of gal. She was showing a touch of jealousy mixed with definite ownership I had never seen before. I leaned down and gave her a kiss on the cheek for confirmation. At the same time, my lips moved to her ear, "Does this mean you're going to bring me my newspaper, while I relax in the recliner?" She peeked over at Annie, then turned back with eyes that burned a hole in my forehead. I smiled back with affection.

Hub could speak for hours. His voice carried on a light, warm wind. He kept signaling for the ex-couple to come to the microphone; they waved him off. He was fine with that.

Hub trolled on. "In some species, marriage is little more than a quick romp and then the female devours her mate. I'm sure Carl is grateful for the way the Supreme Being put him down here as a Homo sapien. Other species are truly monogamous, like penguins and wolves. We humans take the buffet approach with about half of us paired for life. Now, my aunt Verda . . ."

My cell rang, and I excused myself, trying to balance a flimsy plate in one hand and the phone and bowl in the other. I gazed at the digits on the readout. My mind took a moment to center. Setting the bowl of pozole on the top of the fence post, I said, "Now what's up?"

"No wonder you have no friends, if you always answer like that. I'm simply checking on your health."

The voice on the line made my stomach twist. I glanced back at Maria and Annie. They were in full bore girl talk, all animation and giggles. It was Bear again. His voice was a grind of gristle. He's called Bear because of his deep growl whenever he fought someone. He was nicknamed during our basic training. He's thin, bald, and wears Buddy Holly glasses. He has the bearing of a high-school algebra teacher but the precision and quickness to lay any opponent flat in two moves or less. I knew he would call, just not this quickly. *Health* was the word we used for assignment on open lines.

"I still need to find a doctor. I'm terribly busy as you know."

"Okay, we're secure now." There was clicking on the line. "I need this done immediately."

"I'm still searching for the girl."

"The girl can wait. This can't. Your short-term memory is fading. Remember, I gave you the tapes. Besides, this is a one-day thing."

I stayed silent, while I restrained my irritation. Maria gave me a puzzled stare. I held up one finger. "I'll get to it, but I'm going to do them parallel."

"You're my man."

"No, I'm not anyone's man." I could still hear Hub in the background, droning on about a voyage through the fluctuations of space and time. His voice seemed to calm me. I never understood why.

Bear cleared his throat. "Are you listening to a TV documentary?"

"I don't have a television—you know that."

"You solve my problem fast enough, maybe I'll buy you a flat screen."

I kept silent and bit into my lip. Two seconds later, the line went dead. He really needed to work on his phone etiquette. I slipped my cell back into my pocket and headed toward the girls.

They were circulating—Maria introducing Annie to everyone. Most of them I vaguely knew. As I crossed the pasture, I peered back at my plate and bowl balanced on the fence post. Flies swirled around it and Harold the drunk's mangy lab began sniffing it with his stretched neck up the post.

There was a sizable line backed up at the food table. My stomach debated getting in line or going back to share my cold pozole with the insects. Maria signaled me over.

"Important call?" she asked.

"Just an old acquaintance."

"You looked irritated. Was it bad news?"

Sometimes Maria was too observant. I knew she wouldn't let it go, so I puzzled over a stretch of the truth.

"Too long. You're going to lie to me, aren't you?" Her arms folded in front of her.

Annie perked up. "You lie to her?"

Taking a fleeting glance at both their expressions, I walked off toward Hub.

"El cobarde." She flipped me off. "Coward."

Annie nodded in agreement.

15

Carson

Pulling up to the Monson Apartments, my eyes scanned the buildings, cars parked in stalls, and the empty street. According to Hub's research, Mansell Handley, the Marine lived in Building Two. He drove a blue Toyota truck and had a three-bedroom. I wasn't sure if there were roommates or kids, so I had decided to be cautious. No need to wake a baby.

The buildings were labeled Joy Ann, Ruth Marie, and Jamie Lynn—the Monson's kids' names, I supposed. There weren't any one, two, or three designations. Common sense told me the middle one, Ruth Marie, was two. Twelve apartments—three floors per building. Mansell Handley's was in 208. I wedged on an old ball cap that said *Rugby* in thick woven letters and headed for the side facing the street.

I spotted the Marine's Toyota in a covered stall directly behind the middle building. I decided to take a peek, reached his car, and fumbled to find my keys in case anyone was watching. On the back seat rested a gym bag and a wadded-up, ratty sweater. The truck bed held smashed beer cans and fast food debris—the outside displayed enough grime to have been unwashed for several weeks.

A white Mini pulled up with a pizza sign stuck to its roof. An eighteen-year-old bobbed his neck to earphones and jumped out of the car. As he was grabbing two pizza warmers from the back seat, I waved my hand at his side. He glanced back and pulled out one ear bud.

"Those must be mine." I pointed to the containers.

He scanned the receipt. "You Busterbaum?"

"Yeah, Marty Busterbaum."

The kid appeared puzzled; I wondered if he'd delivered

here before.

"I thought it was Sonya?"

"That's my sister." I reached in my pocket and pulled out a wad of cash. Nothing says legitimate like a stack of bills and a customer waiting to pay. A wave of guilt passed through me as I thought about the trouble he'd get in when Sonya re-called. The thought passed.

"$27.38." His eyes gazed up from the paper in expectation.

"Here's thirty-five; keep the change."

He grabbed my money, slipped the warmers off the boxes, and handed Busterbaum's pizzas to me. I waited until he drove away, then walked up the stairs to 208. As the door opened, I walked in all smiles and puffed cheeks, backing up Mansell with a sharp edge of the pizza box. He appeared dumbfounded. Despite my size, I was way too friendly to be a threat.

He had arms like twisted rope, defined broadness in the shoulders, and stood erect at about five-foot-nine. His T-shirt was ripped down low under the armpits like some gym jockey. A Marine tattoo was inked with the standard eagle, world, and anchor on his bicep in blue and black. With a quizzical glance from the pizza to the tall, smiling, duffer face in front of him, he asked, "Pizza?"

"Angelo's for apartment 208," I set the boxes on the table. I opened the top one and checked inside. "A Hawaiian." Lifting a corner of the other one, I announced proudly, "and a . . . pepperoni and sausage. Good choices." Someone spit into a sink in the bathroom down the hall. The smell of peppermint mixed with pizza was pleasing in an odd way. However, I knew this wasn't going to go down easy. Politely asking where the lost sister was clearly wouldn't work. He had that look.

He cranked his neck to the side and called down the hall, "Luden?"

I took in a peripheral view of the apartment. Semi-clean— garbage can full of foil dinners with a sack that proclaimed, "Protein Boost" on the side; a sound-bar above the gas fireplace played old Shania Twain (wouldn't have guessed), leather couch and avocado green recliner that faced a 60-inch flat screen set on cinderblocks; and the scent of old bacon lingered from dishes that rose above the sink's lip. *Good, no kids here.*

A pudgy baby-faced man came out of the bathroom. He stared, his face contorting as he tried to figure out if he knew me. His pants and shirt were so wrinkled I wondered if he'd slept in them for days. Luden edged his glasses up on his nose.

Mansell Handley pointed to the pizza, "Yours?"

Luden said, "I didn't order them. What kinds are they?" He walked in closer and peered in the boxes. "Are they paid for?"

I gazed at the receipt, holding it out with a stretch of my arm. "You owe $27.38." I centered myself between the two roommates. Figuring the Marine would give me the most trouble, I watched his stance. His knees locked as he stood up straighter. His muscles relaxed. Knowing the military, the way I do, I figured he would be great at guard duty but way too removed from basic training to be quick. I decided I had to do this fast, then question him after.

Hooking my right foot behind Mansell's ankle, I swept his legs forward. His elbow smashed the counter edge. The back of his head hit cheap, thin carpet. With my eyes darting back and forth, I forced my body weight and a left jab into Luden's belly. Air and a hollow grunt came out. "I just want to ask you some questions," I said firmly, pausing for a moment.

Mansell shook his head. He edged up on one arm, his elbow seeping blood. The heel of my boot loosened his jaw. The sound of a solid crunch rang through the room. Spit flew. I hoped I hadn't overdone it. He curled up like a snake, extended in a burst, and struck my legs. I lost my footing. I tried to stop my fall but only grabbed the pizza boxes, making them drop with me. The Marine reached around and gripped my calves. Blood gushed from his open mouth—a few teeth flowing rivulets of crimson between them. His eyes were satanic and wild; his breathing, winded. I thrust my knee in his jaw, and he winced in pain, which was enough for me to roll loose. The smell of male sweat filled the room.

I turned. Luden stood above me with a fire poker. A straight-up punch to his jewels. He dropped the poker, fortunately to the side. His hands flew to his crotch, eyes wide, and his mouth gasping open. He folded and rolled over the couch, colliding with something that crashed into pieces.

I turned. Mansell wasn't anywhere near done. He elevated

himself on one knee, cramped over, rubbing his jaw. Cheek swelling and bleeding, eyes wild, he was searching for a weapon. Both of us saw the knives in their wood block on the counter. I kicked the trash can in front of him and he stumbled. It gave me enough time to grab the poker from under the table, where it had rolled. I heard the door open and slam, spotted a glimpse of Luden darting out. The Marine dove across the counter and grasped two steak knives—sharp but short.

Damn, I shouldn't have let my attention shift.

I backed up, feigning fear—eyes combing the room. A shattered glass tabletop spread across the carpet in front of the couch. Mansell was moving around the corner with knives tucked under his wrists. He might know how to use sharp instruments, but I knew how to avoid them. And I had the poker—ten times the length.

I slid by the couch. Taking a step back, I reached behind me and locked the deadbolt. I certainly didn't want Luden bringing friends to the party. I started swinging the poker in a figure eight. It was more of a scare tactic than anything. I didn't want him dead, just hurt enough to talk. He feigned a move toward me. I jabbed him between his knuckles. He held tight to the knives. "I want to talk to you, Mansell," I insisted.

His brow pinched and his eyes narrowed at me knowing his name. He came charging with the knives held high. Big mistake. With fluid motion, my boot connected to ribs and thin muscle with enough force to jar his heart a few beats. Ribs cracked and he gasped for air. He had enough momentum to double over; with stupid luck, he stabbed my leg. I jumped to the side as he fell. The steak knife stuck out at an angle. My pants reddened around the wooden handle of the cheap knife.

The Marine writhed on the floor as I searched my options. He cranked his neck and eyeballed me in terror, then plopped down flat. "Wuddy-hell-waan?" He had decided I was crazier than he. Blood soaked the collar of his shirt and down his front. His chest heaved. He cringed as the breaths came in.

I nudged under his nose with the poker. He winced. "Stay still or this thing goes through your skull."

He was breathing in short gasps. When I was sure he wouldn't move, I limped down the short hall to a closet, watching him the whole time. Inside, I found towels and cleaning products. I selected a beach towel and hobbled back into the front room. My leg throbbed. A biting pain ran down to my foot. Blood seeped in rhythm to my heart. I dabbed around the blade. It wasn't as deep as I feared—maybe an inch or so.

"First aid kit?" I demanded.

Mansell seemed to be trying to gain strength, but with each move his teeth clamped as pain bolted from his ribs and a loose jaw. "Stove," was all he said. It came out "stof." Maybe my foot had loosened his jaw more than I thought. He eyeballed me with hatred.

With teeth gritted, I eased over to the stove and checked the drawer next to it. His eyes followed me. I held the poker to his neck. No luck. I glanced in the cupboard above, pulled out a Red Cross embossed box, and opened his fridge. With two beers in hand, I walked back to a chair and ripped my pants open around the knife. The handle moved with every flex of muscle, causing more bleeding. The blade was wedged deep into my thigh.

Tying the towel around my upper thigh, I tightened the knot as best I could. Mansell raised his head. I pulled the poker off the table and twirled it in front of his face a couple times. He laid back down.

Taking a deep breath, I yanked the knife out and flung it across the room. It stuck in the wall next to an NFL poster. Blood oozed out at a good pace but didn't squirt. Thank God. I opened one of the beers and poured it over the wound—only antiseptic I could find. Cold, red foam drizzled down my leg. I held my breath with teeth clamped for a few seconds, while searing pain shot through me.

I found ample gauze in the first aid kit, a couple of cotton balls, scissors, Band-Aids, Neosporin, and a tongue depressor. No tape. I shoved the cotton balls inside the cut, wrapped the 2-inch gauze around my leg, and tied it off. I glanced down at Mansell while holding hard pressure on the wound with the ball of my palm. I was a touch light-headed, so I took slow deliberate breaths.

Opening the other beer, I took a generous swig. The swirling in my head appeared to dwindle. I kept wondering whether Luden was going to come back. Where the hell had he gone?

I slid my chair closer to Mansell. "Tell me about Tia Linford."

"Who?"

"Girl from Brother Zak's a few weeks ago."

"Tia?" Blood drizzled down his neck. The odor of meat and tomato sauce lingered in the room. "Zak's?"

I jabbed him with the poker in the side, hard enough to watch his face lighten. "You need to use more than one-word sentences."

He grabbed his ribs. His eyes shut tight. I could tell he was thinking as best he could. Mansell's eyelids parted, he bellowed a snort, and four expletives came out strung together. Then, "Tia from the bar? Shit, that was like forever ago, man. What the hell? You her boyfriend or something?"

"I'm something. Now tell me about that night."

The Marine glared at me, then the fireplace poker. He was defeated, but he didn't know it. He slid his leg around to give him leverage. I tapped his head with my hard heel. He rolled his legs back—knees flat on the tile. I waited.

"Hey, man, I didn't know she was yours. We hit it off. She's pretty. I swear she didn't act attached."

My mind shifted. "Where'd your friend go?" I winced as I shuffled over to the front door and propped a kitchen chair under the door knob. The pain was agonizing.

"Luden? He takes off like that sometimes. S-4 bastard. He did the same shit in Qatar. He won't be back . . ."

He started to say "tonight," then thought better of it. His roommate was a Marine? I remembered some of the S-4's—geeky, worked in payroll, necessary, but not real Marines. I kept the door in view anyway. "What'd you talk about?"

"You know, regular stuff—music, movies, friends. She was cool, came on to me as much as I came on to her." He moved wrong and there was a catch in his breathing. His face scrunched until the pain went away. "Man, I think you busted stuff." He looked down at the floor. "You the guy she broke up with?"

She told him about Tyrell. Tia may have been out searching for a one-night stand. I guess that's probably more normal than I would think. He didn't seem like the type to kidnap. A low IQ, born slow, or banged up overseas; things felt off. He had strength and a little of the animal in him, but he didn't strike me as psycho. I'd knocked him down a few notches. If he were good for Tia's disappearance, I didn't care. If not, I'd probably mull over hurting him later, way too much.

He tried to roll on his side, muscles tensing in pain. I wacked the poker on the floor, inches from his face. "Stay where you're at." The Marine lay back down in surrender.

I got up from the chair, wincing as searing pain raced down my leg. Picking up the knife from the floor, I went around the counter and began searching through the drawers. Stuff was jammed in each, but nothing I could use. Wooden spoons, measuring cups, pens, and folded towels dropped to the floor. At the sink, I noticed a cell phone charger plugged in, the light red. I yanked it out. I hobbled back to where Mansell lay and ordered, "Put your arms up behind you." He shook his head.

I pressed my boot into the side of his ribs; he squealed like a frightened puppy though his eyes were feral. His arms carefully pulled back in slow, agonizing movements. Grabbing his wrists, I wrapped the thin cord around twice and tied a double half-hitch. The plug dangled to the side of reddened arms. His muscles bulged and twisted, testing the strength. It would hold well, and he knew it.

"I'm going to search your apartment. You are going to lie still." I picked up the knives and tucked them into my back pocket, my blood covered the handle and blade of one. With an echoing thump, I dented the pine wooden table with the poker. "Understand?" He nodded.

I walked down the hall, asking questions. "What time did you leave the bar? And speak up, I want to know where you are."

I tore through every drawer and closet in the place. We talked and talked. The only thing I found was a plane ticket to Miami under Luden Anton; a half a bag of weed in a vase; $7,000 and change in cash, taped in envelopes behind a picture of coastal Italy; and pictures of the two roommates in the Middle East. I wondered about the money. Mansell said he didn't know about it. I believed him. He was pissed and swearing about Luden shorting him on rent money.

I kept the Marine under enough threat of terror that I think he told me everything he could remember. He could have lied, but

I'm a pretty good judge of human nature. I cut his binds and asked him if he needed me to drop him at an ER. He declined with a glare.

"Enjoy the pizza; it's on me," I tried to joke, already feeling guilty. I gazed down at crust and sauce stuck to the carpet.

The parking lot was quiet. My '68 Corvair started up without much ceremony. Anderton had done a good job tuning the old girl up. I grabbed a coat from my back seat, one I really liked, and sat it under me. I didn't want blood on these seats. The early evening air was cooling down a touch. My adrenaline had worn down about the time I opened the car door. My muscles turned flaccid when I moved; the hole in my leg throbbed as if it might erupt at any moment.

I pulled over. With my mind slightly hazy, I robotically pulled out my cell—glad I hadn't left it back at the cabin.

"The ID says Carson?" answered Teresa. "I'm not sure I remember anyone by that name."

"Yeah. You busy?" I worked on the words. It had been a long time.

"You sound a little breathy. Hope you're not calling for phone sex after four years–actually four and a half. I'm just having dinner drinks with a couple of the girls."

I heard giggling and glasses clinking. I hoped she wasn't wasted. "You still live at the same place?" There was a long interval of silence. "It's important; can you meet me?"

Teresa is a gynecologist and an ex-girlfriend. She wanted me to live with her. She wasn't about to live in my cabin, which she referred to as a nicely decorated outhouse. We split up. Mutual indifference. The two of us hardly ever saw each other anyway. I thought we might still be friends. We sent birthday cards—well, at least a time or two.

"Did you not hear? I'm out with friends? Candy's had an offer in Boston and she's leaving tomorrow."

I sucked in air. I remembered Dr. Candy–Isabelle Candy–incredibly smart, but hard to take her serious with that name. "I need some medical attention."

"Try the ER." Her voice had lost its bounce.

"That would cause a lot of unneeded paperwork–please?" My voice came out more pathetic than I meant it to. "I haven't been able to completely stop the bleeding."

"Ohhh, you," she let out a loud exhale. "You, man."

My mind's eye watched her shake her head.

"Bullet?"

"Knife."

After a string of expletives, she laughed. "Girls, a man needs me."

I could hear three giggling voices in the background, "Don't they always?"

"Same address, I'll stop by the clinic for some suture. It'll be about 20 minutes. You close?"

"Meet ya there in twenty—and Teresa, thank you." I breathed out a sigh of relief. I wasn't sure how clean that steak knife was.

"You're going to owe me, big time." She sounded mad, and I swear I heard her teeth grind.

Teresa pulled into her driveway as I shut my car door. She didn't glance back, just stormed into her place leaving the door open. I knocked, just in case. Her head angled around the corner. She drew a finger across her throat and motioned with an acidic nod. I followed with reluctance. She placed plastic trash liners on the floor by one of the kitchen chairs. I hobbled in and sat down. She gazed at my torn pants and red bandage. Exasperated, she said, "Drop your drawers."

"You sure that's safe?"

She scowled, then blew out a long stream of air between tented fingers. "You still find yourself witty, don't you?"

She was in no mood for humor. Maybe we didn't part as good of friends as I thought. "My pants are pretty well totaled. How about I cut this side up like shorts?"

Teresa fumbled in a drawer, then handed me the scissors. "Suit yourself." She slid another chair in front of me and covered the cushion with a white plastic bag. She tapped the top of my wound as if soothing a baby. My eyes scrunched shut while I waited for the pain to abate. I handed her my pant leg. She handled it with her fingertips like a contagious disease and tossed it into the trash.

I tried a manly calm, but breath-holding anticipation turned into sweat spilling from every pore. Without warning, she ripped

Jef Huntsman

the bloody bandage from my leg. Another fling and that hit the can. She opened a Macy's bag from the table and pulled out suture, tape, gauze, a tube of something, and forceps.

We made love on this table. Not real sure why that thought crossed my mind.

She pulled a bottled water from the fridge and poured it over my cut. I whispered through gritted teeth. "You're sure cold water is the best thing to use?" Goose bumps formed as the water ran off, and cool air rolled across it.

She used the forceps to carefully open the wound, pulled out the globs of cotton balls, and peered inside. She dabbed it with gauze as blood began filling. "It's about 3 centimeters deep, but they didn't cut anything important." She glanced up, "lateral leg muscle; you may have trouble pivoting to the right for a bit."

She grabbed the suture with the forceps. "How's Maria?"

I pulled my leg away, to the side a bit. "Shouldn't you use gloves, or antiseptic, or wash your hands, or something?"

"I washed my hands this morning." She glanced up at me with a smirk.

I clutched my shirt and tried to smile. Nerve fibers shot like lightning down my leg. I gulped air as I realized I hadn't taken a breath in quite some time. My lips were dry.

She got up from her chair, reached in the bag again and pulled out a pair of surgical gloves. As she was putting them on she said, "See, I can be witty, too. It's fun, isn't it?"

I held in my annoyance and slid my leg back over.

Thirty minutes later, I was hobbling back to my Corvair in the dark. Tomorrow I would send her a gigantic bunch of flowers–daisies—she was fond of daisies.

16

Carson

I sat in the car for a minute, scribbling in a notepad all the information I had so far on Tia and the night she disappeared. I knew a little more but not enough. Dim city lights tried their best to break through pollution.

A text from Bear. It read, *FLY VALLARTA–NOW–FLT. 244* Ugh. I'd hoped he'd give me more time.

I called Hub. He had found the information I needed. Agony spiraled my leg as I drove. I was beyond tired and my pants had one normal leg and short-shorts on the other. I needed a bath and a handful of aspirin. As I glanced in the rear-view mirror, the face of a prize fighter who took home the low end of the gate stared back at me. I'd stop at a Walmart for some clothes and use their bathroom for a shower. The bandage Teresa put on me was the cleanest thing I had on. With an almost wimpy sigh, I called the airport.

Damn, damn, damn. The red-eye flight took off in fifty-eight minutes. How'd he know I hadn't left Salt Lake? No time for a stop. Did the airport sell pants?

Weaving between cars and the shoulder of the road, I made it to the airport in record time. I left the car in a cab-only area and raced to the door. Horns honked. Someone yelled, "Hey, asshole." The car would be towed, but I'd pick it up at impound later.

Security eye-balled me as I passed through the metal detector.

I pointed behind me, "A dog attacked me in the lobby." They half-smiled, not sure how to react. Without luggage, I zipped through the evening airport security. I jogged to terminal B. People seemed to jump out of my way. Disgusted glares from all.

Jef Huntsman

After using the plane's cramped bathroom to clean up and finger brush my hair, I walked back to my seat. The passengers weren't sure whether to quickly cast their eyes elsewhere or laugh at the man with one pant leg, whose only carry-on was a cup of coffee. As soon as I sat down, the stewardess gave me a grey blanket. I could tell by her hesitation she had been told to give me the covering. I watched her rump wobble as she darted away.

I awoke as the flight touched down at the Licenciado Gustavo Diaz Ordaz International Airport. The landing was rough but not unsettling. Luckily, I always carry my passport with me. Things like this seem to pop up in my life.

Outside, the airport was already filled with tourist panthers—"two for one, the condo is almost free, girls"—they took one look at my bruised face and bandaged leg and left me alone.

I found a cabbie and gave him the name of the hotel Hub had booked me in, the Melia.

Still dressed in my absurd one-legged pants, I picked up my room card from a reluctant young lady. The hotel was spacious and festive, filled with the sound of tourists heading to the breakfast buffet. I was too exhausted to even think about food—a first for me.

Fifteen-foot palm trees embraced the brass-doored elevators. My room overlooked the beach, three pools connected by what appeared to be cement-lined rivers, and an impressive view of *Bahia De Banderas*—the Bay of Bandits.

The smells of salt, fish, and humidity, though pleasant, made me wish for home. I had spent too many years working in tropical lands to be giddy about a vacation paradise. Thinking back, there were also too many years on dry, scalding sand where breathing dust was the norm. My cabin and sitting in front of the fire pit were my idea of a holiday. No agenda but my own.

I crawled onto the bed, grateful to finally stretch out.

I awoke hours later, just before one, Vallarta time.

I took a long hot shower, shaved and changed my bandage. Each chore sent spikes radiating from my wound. The single-cup coffee pot perfumed comfort through the room. After two sips, I looked at the pathetic clothes I had to put back on. That would have to be addressed.

I focused on the man in the mirror. The purple bruise around my jaw had turned to a sickly amber shade and a demon shadow circled my left eye. I looked even worse than I felt. I turned away and picked up my phone to make a call.

Hub is a touch eccentric, but he's also amazing. He had found out that the senator used his middle name and his first name to register at this hotel. Senator Patrick Ackerman had become Wayne Patrick. He had used a celebrity's jet to fly here and a fake passport under the same name. He had obviously done this before. Often the government gets so tangled in their own nest, they don't look for the simpler solutions. Hub always started with the basics.

I approached the front desk and, with a terrible Texas accent, asked if my good friend, Wayne Patrick from North Carolina was staying here. I chewed gum about as hard as anyone could. The check-in clerk inspected me with complete disdain. My smile didn't seem to change his disposition.

I grabbed his hand, leaned forward inches from his displeased face, and tried a different tact. Firmly gripping his manicured fingers, I kneaded each digit enough to induce pain as I instructed, "Press your fingers to the keyboard and look up W-a-y-n-e P-a-t-r-i-c-k." His genetically tanned face whitened, nut-brown eyes darted for help, then sank into vulnerability. I released his hand and patted it softly. Angelo, as his name tag stated, released a held-in breath. He began clicking away at the computer. Soon I heard the churning of a printer hidden under the desk. He rubbed his fingers and bent down to retrieve the printout. He handed it to me and stepped back, hands to his sides.

"This is between two amigos," I said forcefully. I had lost the accent. He nodded.

I went up to my room and made a phone call. "Portner?"

"Who's this?" came a raspy reply.

"Carson." I waited a beat. "Remember Yelapa and those two ladies from Boston?"

"Major Carson, of course. It's been . . ." he chuckled. "We tossed those two lovely crazies over the side."

"We?"

"Well, you," he snorted. "I was right there as backup."

"You were lying on the deck, screaming like a banshee." I

took a sip of a can of lemonade from the mini-fridge and propped my feet up on the chair next to me.

"Well," he paused and took in a deep breath with a short cough, "she stabbed me in my privates. I thought I was going to die. Totally ruined my favorite swim trunks."

I smiled. He hadn't changed one iota; every thought was grander than reality. "You realize, you were cut across the butt, and it was superficial."

"Let's just say we have different memories." His tongue clicked a couple of times. "So, you must need something if you're calling me after all this time."

Portner Latternee was a terrible fishing guide but a proficient salesman. He knew less about fishing than his out-of-town clients. However, he dressed like a shrimp-fisherman, had an amazing teakwood boat with double screws with enough horsepower to raise a thunderous wake, and a load of bullshit several fathoms deep. He kept his customers drunk, well fed, and had Señor Gonzalas to bait the hooks. I wondered if he was still a guide.

I jotted down his address, and we decided to meet that evening at seven. In the meantime, the clouds were forming sinister anvil shapes across the sky. The wind picked up, spinning trash across the road as I jumped into a cab.

I asked the cabbie to take me to "*la roperia*"—a clothing store. He asked, "Ropa marca o ropa chafa?"

"Tourista." My fingers danced circles across my chest to illustrate flowers. He laughed, pointing to a man on the sidewalk in an orange shirt plastered with lavender fish. I nodded. He took me south of city center and introduced me to Chada's shop. There were quiet words between the two of them, and I knew a finder's fee would be exchanged.

I bought a T-shirt with a frog drinking tequila on it, with "Puerto Vallarta" in red letters below, and a pair of white linen pants that fit surprisingly well.

Hours later, dressed like a tourist who just got back from the inner-city flea market, I caught another cab. A few sprinkles dotted the windshield—the smell was refreshing. Out of the corner of my eye, I caught quick hand movements within an older-model

Mercedes S65AMG sedan. In the rain it appeared black, but it could have been blue or dark green. Keeping track of my surroundings was deep-set within me from field work in countries where people wouldn't consider vacationing. Beams kicked on and the Mercedes U-turned behind a loaded watermelon truck. I watched its headlights in the rear-view mirror as the driver tried to decide whether to pass. Our distance lengthened. They finally sped around the slow vehicle but stayed five car lengths back, the downpour distorting the car's lights in rivulets. I assumed my tail had something to do with the senator.

It took twenty minutes to reach the edge of the town under a downpour known only in the tropics. Except for a few hazily lit signs, Vallarta hid behind rain so thick most people would assume we were underwater.

We turned up a street between two bars that were blazing music. The carnival inside seemed incongruent with the weather. The Mercedes followed. A river flowed toward us as we rode the narrow steep path. Huddled vendors and tourists watched like abandoned pets from covered doorways and shop windows. My driver held the wheel as if navigating through massive ocean waves in a 19-foot Boston Whaler.

It took some time to get the driver's riveted attention. I made sure he got a good look at Ben Franklin then tucked the bill into his shirt pocket. "Lose the car behind us," I said. He cocked his head, puzzled. I pointed behind us. With a glance in the mirror, he smiled and patted his pocket. We sailed around a corner. The cab floated on top of the water for a few seconds then tread caught and grabbed. I braced myself as we seemed to dive in and out of the asphalt. I thought we were riding a road; I just couldn't see it under the rush of the new river. A quick left, up a torrent jammed with silt and streaming refuse, the cab sailed with loose contempt. I felt the springs hit bottom.

The Mercedes drifted behind, though relentlessly pursuing. They knew we were trying to lose them but struggled to maneuver up the flooded streets. Five minutes passed. The cab planed atop water and dipped around corners until the rain shut off like a hose. Canopies dripped. The water level lowered. Streaks of sunshine broke through. My driver, Eduardo, told me about a restaurant and a plan. Our pursuers had fallen behind.

Jef Huntsman

Several minutes later we pulled up to the Vista Grill, high above the city. Eduardo talked briefly to a heavy-set Mexican who could have been a greeter. I cracked the door open. My adrenaline peaked, and I sucked in gulps of humid tropical air. I waited until my stalkers were within sight then jumped out, my sneakers landing in a puddle just deeper than the rim. Emotions charged, I laughed and shook my head, walking soggily toward the door. Water squeezed out from my socks with every step. Glancing back, I noticed four faces in the car—dark complexions, thick mattes of black hair, watching my every move. The mouth of one in the back seemed to be screaming at the others. The Mercedes was a deep green.

Eduardo pulled out, just as I walked inside. The pudgy man, dressed all in black, motioned for me to follow him and uttered two, quick, indiscernible sentences in Spanish. The restaurant radiated with happy chatter. It viewed over the city center and Banderas Bay. The man in black darted around a corner and down a short set of stairs. We strolled through a busy kitchen with pots steaming and the sizzle of grease on the grill. A wonderful mix of cayenne, cilantro, and lemon perfumed the hot air; the cooks ignored us. We went out through a swinging door, down a hall, to a back entrance. He scooted me out the door, pointing toward a wet cobbled road no wider than an alley. I turned to thank him, but he was gone.

My feet suctioned to the ground with each step, then released with a gushy noise. I came to a small intersection in the road. Eduardo was parked to one side, motor running. Without our tail, we made it to Portner's place with little fanfare. I deposited another hundred in Eduardo's palm. He asked if he should wait. His eyes and smile said he'd surely stick around for another Ben Franklin. I shook my head and made my way through the courtyard. Rain dripped slowly from the red stucco roof. The vegetation bent low as if exhausted by the heavy downpour.

Portner hadn't changed, rhino-shaped with thin strands of red hair protruding in curling wisps from his thick neck. I sat near his brick fireplace, shoes and socks off; my legs stretched close to the flames. It reminded me of my fire pit back home. The melancholy moment faded quickly as my thoughts turned toward the Mercedes.

My old friend and I talked about times past and caught up on new. He had leased his boat but would, now and then, take *special* fishing clients out. His live-in girlfriend, Melinda, made us strong coffee and hummed sweet songs from the other room. Fishing was still his passion and with arms spread wide, he talked about various catches. Finally, with a quizzical cast, he asked, "So, what's up, Carson?"

I downed the last slug of my coffee. "Yeah, there's a reason I'm in Vallarta." I let that linger.

"And?" his thick eyebrows raised.

"I'm checking up on Senator Ackerman. He was here some months back."

Portner chuckled and rubbed his palms together. "You want some tequila? I just picked up a half-a-case from Jalisco's newest distiller, La Flor."

"What do you know?"

"Tequila first."

"You and your rituals; okay, I'd love two fingers, with lime."

He yelled out to Melinda. I turned. She had a sturdy structure and a petite mouth. She was beautiful in a backwoods kind of way. He gave her our order. Dimples popped out as she grinned, turned and hummed back into the kitchen. Portner remained silent as we waited. I knew better than to push him. Melinda came back with a tray of cut limes, iced glasses, and a bottle centered perfectly. He thanked her and swatted her butt. *If I did that to Maria, I'd get a frying pan to the side of the head.* He poured. We drank after a light clink of glasses.

"You know, women quit being servants after 1950." I shook my head.

Portner shook it off with an upturned lip and a flip of his hand.

I eyed him with anticipation; he pretended not to notice. Quiet time passed.

"You know about the beauty the senator visits?" he finally broke the silence.

"Tell me."

"Dark long hair, legs you want to climb, mid-eastern indifference—you know, the type everyone second glances, and she knows it." He pulled a swig from his glass, then bunched his face. "Not sure what she sees in the senator. He's got that flat wide face and a second trimester belly."

"He's been here a lot?"

Well-garlicked steak sizzled on a hot grill, and some clanging of dishes came from the kitchen. I pointed to the kitchen and whispered, "Is this okay?" My fingers motioned from him to me.

"Melinda's fine."

He tapped the side of his glass. "No. He's not been here a lot that I know of. I only heard of one time. They spent some time at the hotel—you know—dinner, drinks by the pool. Then they slipped up to her place in the hills. I've heard rumors she has a husband, but no one has ever seen him. Also, I've heard there are many men who visit. Perhaps she is insatiable."

"You know anything about a green Mercedes with a bashed-up right fender?" I asked.

"Nothing comes to mind. I'll check on it if you'd like."

"I'd like." I'd only sipped the top eighth of my glass of tequila. I wanted to have my wits with me tonight, after being pursued. Something added up, though I wasn't sure what, yet.

Portner poured himself another glass and tilted the tequila bottle toward me. I shook my head. He shrugged his shoulders. "I could probably get you a picture of her. That might be worth," his reddish eyebrows jumped up and down, "something?"

He was asking for money. "Depends on the picture."

"I'll have something delivered to the Melia hotel in the morning. Perhaps you could take the pictures and send back the envelope?"

"Filled with a touch for your time?"

"Only if you wish," he answered. He held up his glass in salute. "I knew it would be good to see you."

My room at the Melia cast a scent of sanitizing. The toilet paper was folded in the shape of a butterfly. The towels arranged perfectly, and the bedspread folded back. I dialed from my cell and left a three-digit number when an answering machine clicked on. Searching for bugs, I left the room bearing signs of a rock group having stayed there. I strolled by the pool, waiting for my cell to ring. I really wanted to call Maria, but that would have to wait.

The phone finally rang as I walked the beach. Bear asked, "What's the good word?"

"I found Senator Ackerman's wanderings, but I need $5,000, no wait, $10,000 delivered tonight to the Melia hotel in Puerta Vallarta."

"So, you want a beach vacation in a five-star hotel, and you want some heavy spending money to enjoy yourself?" A fake chuckle boomed through my cell, and I pulled it back a couple of inches.

"He was here. Just send it and give me a clear email address. I'll have pics and names by morning."

"You're my boy. You'll have an envelope shortly. What room?"

I watched the waves roll, crawl forward, and recede. The sun had disappeared into the ocean, but its last light still glimmered across the water. "Room 614. What does the courier look like?" I heard clicking and Bear blowing his nose.

"Mmmmmm. Ahhhh, it will be Brent. He's six-three and has the face of a guy that gives lectures on actuarials. Says here he's mastered most of the Japanese arts. Great cover over those bones."

I waited to see if there was more. There wasn't. He hung up with the usual no goodbye.

After a warming talk with Maria and a late dinner, I hit the elevator back to my room. No sign of the Mercedes' crew, though I'm not sure I knew enough to spot them. But I could speculate.

Two hours later, with my eyelids more shut than open, I startled to a loud knock on the door. The peephole revealed the guy Bear described. When I opened the door, he had a stiff smile as if trying to learn enchanting. His face came off more like a tax accountant about to tell the head of the mafia they need to pay taxes. Brent handed me a lime-green box with a white bow—the kind flowers come in. He held out his hand as if waiting for a tip. I gave him a puzzled look.

He chuckled with a real smile. "Wanted to see what you'd do. Plus, I could use some Starbucks money." He handed me a card—Boston Savings and Loan and a phone number. "Call me when the package is ready."

I couldn't see him in a black belt of anything, unless they gave one for geometry. I closed the door, poured some wine, and fell asleep before I had one sip.

I woke to three bells, ringing over and over. I rubbed my eyes. It was the tiny speaker on my cell phone sounding off its obnoxious alarm. I didn't remember setting it and fumbled forever trying to turn it off.

Shaved, showered, and dressed in another set of tourist wear, I made my way to the hotel buffet. I was famished and needed vats of coffee. I engulfed a perfect omelet, potatoes and onions, a heaping mound of cut-up fruit, toast, several glasses of juice, and enough coffee to keep the Marines marching.

A bug-eyed, thin-nosed gentleman slid in next to me. He laid a small manila envelope on the table and waited. I finished one last sip of coffee, then opened it up. A lovely tan face stared up at me. To her left at the table sat Senator Patrick Ackerman, or Wayne Patrick as he apparently calls himself on trips without his blonde, pale wife. He smiled as he had every right to. She was gorgeous with mysterious eyes. Most of the other pictures were similar, until I gazed at the last one. She was stepping into the back of a green Mercedes–no dents. Ackerman was nowhere around. *Ah ha,* a little voice inside my head pronounced. Thin-nose sat impatiently, one set of fingers typing on top of the other.

I paid Portner's runner and called Brent. He stopped by 20 minutes later and picked up the pictures.

I caught a plane late that afternoon with $2,500 left in government money to cover the plane fare, hotel, a present for Maria, and any unexpected bribes.

17

Carson

Maria was waiting when I re-dusted the trail to my cabin. A quarter moon did little to light the way up the stairs, and I rammed my shin on the first one. I'd had eighteen calls from Annabelle, who I decided could wait a bit longer. There were two urgent messages from Hub, who could also wait. Maria offered me a beer and two aspirin. My lips kissed her cheek as I headed for the bed.

I woke to a bright morning, with my favorite woman cuddling naked in my bed and that pleasant air of home. She moved, canting her hip high and then stilled with soft breathing. My arm was wrapped across her breasts and for a short time, I thought about never rising. With wistful exasperation, I slipped out soundlessly and tossed comfort clothes onto my rough frame. My thigh grabbed as muscles tensed, and I grimaced. Coffee perked, while I buttered toast and sliced up a peach. I hauled my breakfast out to the fire pit on a thin coffee-table book I often used for a tray. Settling into my camp chair, I inhaled home; the scent of strong grounds and sagebrush relaxed me.

The roar of a motor and incessant honking displaced the peace. Turning and spotting my lap with hot coffee, I watched Annie's car barrel around the last turn. She shot through the trees, gained air and came down with a thud over the culvert, then headed sideways toward my gate. The car caught at the last second, spinning gravel as she missed the post by inches. I unclamped my teeth as she came to a halt behind the cabin.

The door slammed; I could hear her voice well before I saw her. "Where the hell have you been? I'm paying you to find my sister, not chase around to God knows where. You don't answer my calls or my texts." Her arms waved like an off-balance skier as she approached, shouting. It was seven a.m.

"I was just about to . . ."

"Right." She peered at my phone with disgust. "Maria told me you were getting in last night. LAST NIGHT!"

I wasn't sure whether she was going to cry or smack my face. I set the coffee and my tray on the ground. The coffee was empty anyway. I glanced down at the coffee spot on my crotch and flicked a peach slice off my leg.

"I suppose your phone shut down." She crossed her arms so tight I thought her breasts would pop through the back side. "Well?" She stood over me in a pose I remembered from my fourth-grade teacher—Mrs. Battenhower. "Well?" she repeated.

"Hi, Annie, I didn't hear you arrive." *I thought I'd try humor.* The angle of her eyebrows scolded me. I sighted Maria leaning on the porch rail with the grandest smile. Annie loosened her grip on herself.

"You want some coffee?" Maria asked, "while we find out what Carson's been up to?" Her eyes locked on mine in a saved-your-ass kind of way.

Muscles relaxed as Annie answered, "I'd love some coffee," she glared at me. "It'd be nice if we had real chairs to sit on." I got up, winced as leg muscles tightened, and unfolded a couple more camp chairs. I tried a melting grin on her; it didn't work.

She noticed my bandaged leg just below my shorts. The cords in her neck loosened. Her mouth opened as if to say something. She stared at my leg for a while, then pointed toward my two-day-old wound with concerned contemplation.

"What's that?"

"That, my dear, is my get-out-of-jail-free card." Maria brought out two cups. "It seems Private Handley doesn't like pizza."

They both regarded me with confusion. I picked my cup off the ground and stood up.

"Where you going?" asked Annie with an annoyance that didn't quite fit her but still passed a strong message.

"Coffee." My voice felt weaker. It seemed as if gravity pulled a touch harder as I began to take each stair toward the porch.

With a full cup, I returned to two expectant scowls. The three of us sat in a triangle with the fire pit in the middle. The grey-dead ashes swirled momentarily as a gust traveled through. I knew Maria was being supportive of Annie and keeping her just below postal. To myself, I thanked her for being there. The two of them waited for me to begin, but not too happily. "I had to do a favor to get the information on Tia and perhaps receive more help in the future. I'm sorry it took a couple of days, but . . ."

"Three days." Annie stated in an obtuse tone.

"I'm sorry it consumed three days, but I'm back now and can spend 100 percent of my time on finding Tia. I also spent some time on the flight, figuring out who to check on next." I explained the information I received from Handley but left out the trip to Puerta Vallarta.

"That's it?" Annie spat.

"Pretty much. I'm headed back to Salt Lake after breakfast. Hopefully I'll have more answers later tonight."

Annie dropped in the chair as if all her bones had suddenly evaporated. Tears began streaming. Maria got up to comfort her. Her breaths caught between tiny moans. I felt inadequate, so I sipped my coffee and watched the ashes lying inanimate in the circle of rocks. The compassion and painful sobbing seemed to go on forever. Fear of disturbing anything held me still.

In a whisper, Maria asked, "Tissue?" I thrilled at something to do. Running quickly, I returned with a box of Kleenex. *Good dog.* I stood by their side to dash off for anything else they needed. After agonizing throbbing, my leg went to sleep waiting.

I kept glancing at the clock on my cell until Maria invited Annie in for breakfast and to hang out with her for the day. Around ten o'clock they released me, and I headed to the big city with a short stop at Hub's.

My stomach reminded me of lunchtime as I parked in front of Brother Zak's. I rummaged through a sack Maria had given me and found a Snickers and a bottle of lukewarm water. Hub had re-watched the surveillance discs while I was out of town and noticed a Chase Bank down the street a bit. There was a camera by the drive-through, gazing at the parking lot. Banks keep their surveillance tapes for months. I thought about asking nicely, or pretending to be FBI, but both might put me in jail if the manager became jumpy.

I had an improbable idea and drove toward another part of town. The police station was the same glass and cement structure I had visited weeks ago. At the desk, I asked for Detective Brower. I wasn't too surprised he was in—most police work is done from cubicles, on the phone, or staring down at a computer screen. Halfway through a third magazine on hunting and guns, he came out, stood over me, and reviewed me with disdain. I began to stand, then noticed his body close enough to mine I had to lean back and brace myself on the back of my chair. I could tell we'd hit it off better today.

"You solving another one of my cases?" Brower accused.

I glanced at his big fat fingers. "Still checking on the same one."

He stepped back a step; I stood upright. He leered at his wrist as if checking a watch. "Wow, haven't solved it yet. Ahhhhmazing. You out there, and yet the streets still aren't safe."

"Okay, so you like me and I'm out shopping for your birthday present. Nothing's changed, except a young girl is still missing, and it wouldn't hurt for you to close the book on it."

"What have you got?" he asked as if he didn't care and checked his nonexistent watch again.

"You have time to take a ride with me? I'll tell you everything I know to this point. Maybe I'll even stop and buy you an ice cream," I said jokingly.

He showed no sign of reaction, poised like a gigantic mannequin. The inflection in his voice was another thing. "You buy lunch; you can talk all you want."

I drove—I could tell he was impressed with the Corvair. Detective Brower picked the place, Italian, with a picture in the window of spaghetti with meatballs the size of cantaloupes.

We talked—actually, I talked; he listened. Brower had a heaping plate of spaghetti—not quite as big as the one in the window but impressive nevertheless. I had the chicken Marsala and a dinner salad. I wasn't sure he was listening, so I raised my voice to be heard above his slurping. His brow crinkled as if annoyed. He didn't say one word until his plate was emptied and mopped up with garlic bread. He leaned back, patted his barreled stomach and considered things with a glower.

I waited, sipping the life out of the remaining ice cubes in my glass.

"Let's go check it out," he finally said and stood up. With his index finger, he slid the check toward me.

After a quiet ride, we pulled into the lot at Chase Bank. Inspecting Brower's detective ID thoughtfully, the assistant manager had us follow him down some stairs and into a room marked "Employees Only." He had called someone named Dan to meet us. After a short explanation, Dan sorted through files and dates on the computer. The assistant manager went back to do whatever it was he did. Dan banged on the keys for about 15 minutes while we stood by lazily, with full bellies—at least mine was full; Brower could have probably packed in a side of lasagna and dessert.

"Here's that night," Dan motioned us over.

"Skim through to later, perhaps ten or eleven o'clock?" I asked. At about ten forty-five, I spotted Tia's car to the far right of the screen. "Okay, now go to the morning."

Dan glanced back at me. "About what time?"

"Nine."

Her car was still there at ten. At eleven-fourteen, a truck pulled up and stopped behind the car. Tia got out of the far side. I couldn't quite make out the driver, but he seemed familiar. Tia grabbed something from her car—a notepad or folder and then returned to the truck. They drove away. I had Dan go through it frame by frame several times.

I leaned in close to the screen. "I thought that was a truck with a shell."

Brower pulled his glasses out of his jacket and bent forward. He moved the glasses up and down on the bridge of his nose. "Ummmm."

"Is that a Humvee?" I asked.

He nodded, then wiggled his hand in a maybe gesture.

"I'm fairly sure. You mind checking DMV?"

He ignored me and set his finger on the man on the screen. "Recognize him?" asked Brower.

"It's a touch hazy, but I know that hunched profile from somewhere."

"Make a couple of copies," demanded Brower.

Dan didn't hesitate. I'm pretty sure Detective Brower was used to people following his directions.

On the way back to the station, an out-of-shape jogger crossed the sidewalk in front of us at a stop light. It came to me. My chest filled with air, and I felt better about the day.

18

Tia

A putrid-vile smell woke me from a stupor. Twisting, I felt my pants stick to the dirty floor. I had been lying in my own urine. The truck jostled. Empty bottles of orange soda and water rolled in the short span between my body and the sides of my coffin. Whimpering echoed against the pine box; I didn't realize for some time that it was my voice. My arm moved and a spike of pain shot through to the bone. Rubbing it, I sensed the smooth texture of tape and something that felt like a thick thorn under it. I followed it to an attached tube. A stab jarred me alert. A dangling IV. I didn't remember that from before.

The truck hit the soft shoulder and threw me against the wall. I knew by now I was black and blue from the ride, even though the darkness hid anything but basic shapes. *How many hours had passed? How many days?* I rubbed the scrape on my knee—wet.

I ran my fingers through dusty matted hair and wished for the phone to ring. Annie called every day. Her stupid, prying questions, so obnoxious and so thoughtful, drummed through my mind. *What did you have for lunch? Why don't you dump that loser? You need to have that car checked.* I missed her so much! What was she doing? Was she looking for me? Of course she was. I bet she had asked the governor to send out Marines. I smiled for the first time in I didn't know how long. How many days had I been here? I rubbed my tongue along my teeth. They felt as if germs scuttled across them in troops. My gums seemed swollen and rough. Tears flowed. "Annie, Annie," I whispered over and over again, my brain swelling and on fire. My throat burned. "Annie."

Jef Huntsman

The rustle of gravel under the tires pulled my attention back to the present. It was endless and grated on my mind. I searched for a can of pop, or water, but found only empties. Whenever I had awakened before, there had been fresh bottles of water, cans of orange soda, and a few energy bars. They tasted incredible, even in the stench of urine and female sweat. Now there were only empty wrappers and open cans. I squeezed the life out of an uncapped plastic bottle and threw it at the wall. The sound of it hitting the pine box was pathetic, weak and trivial. Everything was puny and pitiful in this box—especially me. My headache told me the drugs had worn down, and I would have to face reality. Bold, ugly reality.

After an eternity of grinding rock, the truck downshifted, and the brakes squealed. I was hopeful and scared to death at the same time. My teeth chattered with the wait—eyes wide in the thick blackness. Several winks of light broke the darkness. I listened to a slight scurry of the others in their boxes as they squirmed with anxiety—at least the ones not comatose and dreaming. Metal creaked with rusted fittings, the truck door lifted, and sunlight pierced through the holes in my crate. My breathing stopped.

Minutes passed as tense hours; then I heard a gruff man's voice. The tone was different from before, with more authority.

"Okay, back up to the barn."

A push into gear and the idle raised. The sun slowly fell into shade.

"Whoa, asshole." The truck jerked to a stop. The vehicle's door opened and slammed.

"Turn off the motor; you trying to kill us in here?" Quick shuffling and the door opened again.

I could make out shapes moving in the thin bright light and voices, deep and hollow. There was movement at the end of the truck. A girl's voice, broken and crying in weak sobs. It sounded as if they were lifting their captives out of each box and forcing them into some large enclosed area. It was a tone change, maybe a slight echo. I could only make out a hint of silhouettes. I sat up straight and stiff, breathing as quietly as I could. Tears dropped to my chest. Maybe they would pass me by.

The top of my crate popped open, and a wide, short man

with a ZZ-Top beard reached in. I saw the glimmer of a knife. My heart stopped. He cut my binds. His eyes were wild and black; his teeth, yellow and broken.

He lifted me as if I were no more than a rolled newspaper. I wanted to fight with all my might, but I couldn't move. He sat me down on the wood plank floor. Both legs tingled in sharp bolts of pain. My IV bag was thrust into my belly. By instinct, I cradled it like a baby. A hard shove on my back and a slap to my head brought me to my feet. I stumbled and turned to glare at the bearded man, then thought better of it as I read his eyes, black and lifeless. I stumbled forward, slid and bounced off a crate. He kicked me hard in the back, and I tumbled off the edge of the truck onto the ground. I was yanked to my feet and lined up behind the others. My muscles were sore, my neck ached, and my legs barely held me up. Tingles of pain shot up my bare legs.

Off the end of the truck bed was hay and hard clay. An Asian girl twisted her ankle, fell, then they forced her up and pushed her thin body into the line. A terrible squeal left her lips.

It was warm and humid. I wondered if we were in one of the southern states. All I could see was the corrugated tin walls of a rustic barn, an empty hayloft, and three men ushering us to a wall. A fourth guy came in the barn, dragging a blonde girl with a black stripe in her hair behind him. He threw her against the wall with us. All the men had beards, camouflage pants, and black T-shirts. I was fairly sure two of them were Cedee and Tony, the truck drivers. *Fake beards?*

Most of the girls stared straight ahead, their faces weighted with fear and worry. Two leaned against the wall, still stoned from whatever drug they had given us. A short blonde and a busty black girl showed defiance. They glowered at the kidnappers with their hands on hips, legs straight and feet flat. They seemed to know each other.

The one that lifted me from the crate walked up to the two. "You bitches want to say something?" He put his face within an inch of the black girl's nose. The short blonde blurted. "Wha . . .?" His fist doubled her over before the second word. A gasping sound, like a blown tire, hissed from her mouth. The man punched the other girl in the face, knocking her head back into the metal wall with a clang. He turned back toward the rest of the group.

"Silence is golden. Do we understand each other?" All of our heads dropped, and we studied the hay-strewn ground. Dust billowed with each footstep as he paced in front of us.

"Get the bags," shouted the short, husky leader who had punched the two girls.

The two bearded drivers started at one end of the line, turning off and disconnecting the IV bags. They left a short port line dangling across each elbow. Cedee gave an evil smirk and eyed each girl up and down as if picking out a hooker. As he ogled at me, a knot the size of a gopher burrowed deep into my chest. Sweat drenched me. I held my breath until he passed on. Tony put the bags on a narrow, wood table by the door.

The man-in-charge nodded toward the door. Cedee and Tony left. Shortly after, I heard the truck start up and diesel fumes spilled into the air. The truck lurched forward and pulled to the left as the barn doors closed.

Silence.

We all glanced at each other like feral dogs—scared and confused. Murmuring began as we watched the man-in-charge motion to the other guy. Bile rose through a new-found silence. A moaning whistle of wind came through the gaps of light in the barn. The other guy pulled a hose with a nozzle out from behind a lone bale of hay. He uncoiled the roll of clay-colored hose and handed it to the man-in-charge.

The bear-sized leader stroked his beard. I watched his skin pull—the hair was real. He stood like he had a 2 x 4 embedded from his butt to his skull. That smirk never left his face. "You girls stink," he said with a shallow laugh. The other guy, a farm-fed boy of about sixteen, with a face hidden behind a coal-black beard, nodded. The kid leered at us like a bully dressed up for Halloween.

The man-in-charge pulled the silver trigger and began spraying us. His cheeks rose with fiery pleasure as he pointed the stream from head to toe. One girl turned her back to the water, and he screamed, "You don't turn until I tell you to." She faced forward, her lips quivering. He aimed the gush of water directly at her face. She held her breath and clenched her eyes tight for a full minute. He turned the spray to the next girl. I stood two girls down, forcing myself not to pass out.

The water came at me with the force of arrows, pinging

every inch of my skin. It felt good and horrid at the same time. I couldn't wait until he went on to the next girl. An eternity passed.

When he reached the end, he laughed, saying. "Okay, now you can turn. I want your pretty little backsides to me." We all obeyed. As I faced around, I noticed the girl he had punched. Her cheek was swollen; there was a cut above her eye. The place already stunk of damp hay. He sprayed us again.

My thin underclothes stuck to my rear. This was beyond humiliation. I could hear the other one, Sidearm, with his low, repeating laugh behind me. I wanted to kick him in the groin.

Time slowed. I thought of my mom playing piano while Annie and I twirled, hands raised high in the air on the front room hardwood floor. Mom's voice circled my thoughts. Her hands were so thin and perfectly manicured, dancing over the keys. The music echoed happy and invigorating times. Annie's and my cries of joy twisted together in that hollow room with only a sitting chair and an ancient piano for furniture.

Someone nudged me, and I glanced up. It was the thin girl next to me—brunette with blue highlights. She signaled me with a head nod toward the men. I saw the rest of the line moving and followed quickly. Sidearm handed out crumpled long t-shirts and baggy shorts. I scrambled to put mine on, momentarily, incredibly grateful to Sidearm. We formed a circle around the man-in-charge. He waited with bulging arms folded in front of him. When we were all in place, he said, "This will be your home for a couple of days . . ."

Sidearm broke in, "While we wait for the boat."

The man-in-charge turned sharply toward him with a glare that could have started a bonfire. Sidearm shrunk and backed up a few steps, then lowered his head.

"Like I was saying, this will be home for a bit. You will have food and water. Sleep wherever you want; the mice don't mind. Not sure about the rats," he chuckled at himself. "Don't try to leave the barn. It will be guarded from outside." He spat on the ground, then inspected us as if we were mangy rodents. "Anyone gives me any trouble, and you'll be locked up in the chicken coop. And trust me, you don't want that to happen. Any questions you have—don't ask. I'll let you know what you need to know."

All eyes glanced around, darting, and wondering, and

scared shitless.

"Okay," he yelled over his shoulder. The barn doors opened and the two crazy drivers, Cedee and Tony, with their cheap fake beards, brought in two giant coolers. On top of Cedee's cooler was a 5-gallon, plastic bucket with a full bag lopping over the side. They set them down in the corner by the hose and hay bale. Cedee walked over and handed the bucket to the big guy with the permanent scowl.

He kicked the bucket toward us. It rolled haphazardly between two girls and came to a thud against the wall. He tossed the bag in the same direction as the overturned bucket. A roll of toilet paper bounced out and unrolled along the dusty floor. "All the amenities of a fine hotel." His face lit up as he belly-laughed. The others followed suit. Their cackling twisted every cell in my body, but I kept still.

The man-in-charge motioned with his stubby fingers and all four men walked out. The thick wooden doors were shut. We all stood still listening as a padlock clicked outside.

Eyes rippled with tears and glazed with drugs stared into nowhere, like lost sheep. A yearning for normal, for home, for friends, pasted heavy on each of our faces. Three girls edged timidly over to the ice chests. I leaned closer to get a glimpse. With a hungered glance, one of the three opened the grungy chests. I inched a few steps forward. One was filled with orange sodas and plastic water bottles, the same as the ones clanking around in my crate. *Couldn't they buy another flavor or two?* The second had cans of Vienna sausages, potato chips, beef sticks, spam, graham crackers, and what appeared to be chocolate pudding cups.

One by one, each girl grabbed an armload and carried it back to a place she designated, without words, as her space–her stuff. The atmosphere carried anxiety and suspicion; mouths nibbling, drinking; eyes darting. Feminine faces with no makeup and hair striking out like sagebrush crouched in their spaces and watched.

I held tight to my waters, chips, and a *Snickers* bar I had tucked in with my elbow. I couldn't imagine what would happen next. I think we all knew we had to work together if we were to get out of this. Whatever *this* was? I pulled my knees to my chest and closed my eyes. Birds were chirping outside. A slight breeze that smelled of fish seeped through cracks in the barn. I glanced up. Light streamed in sharp bars with floating dust twirling inside. The dirt on the floor was fine like desert sand. I could smell the dung of animals who had passed through. I heard water running. Glancing over, a redhead with one loop earring was crouched a few feet from me peeing. *Oh crap, we have no bathroom. We have a bucket?* For some reason, it wasn't as big of a deal as it would have been last week.

Empty time passed.

The girl who had been hit in the face stood up, dropping her cache to the floor. "I'm Adriana," she blurted. It seemed to shock some and amuse others. Her voice dropped to a whisper. "We need to find a way to get outta here." She stated what all of us were thinking. She eyeballed each of us with her hands high on her hips. "Anyone in?"

We all watched as Adriana yanked off the tape and eased the needle out. Her arm was red with black streaks and blotchy specs of adhesive in two lines. Everyone gazed in horror. After a few seconds, others began ripping the IV ports from their arms as well.

I stared at mine, then pulled quickly. It was like a freedom––terrifying, biting freedom.

The group began to laugh, almost maniacal.

Adriana asked again, "Anyone in?"

"How?" said the girl next to me who had just emptied her bladder.

"I don't have all the answers; that's why I need you girls. I know we need weapons and maybe a tool to pry our way out. Perhaps a shovel?" Adriana gave a disgusted growl. "You wanna stay here, fine with me. You wanna help me get us out—let's talk."

The group of girls began searching. The barn was heavily built of thick lumber and corrugated steel. A few breaks allowed light to leak in, except around the door. Nails for hanging things were pounded in solid. A noise came from outside the door, like someone kicking it with heavy boots. Something hit the wall to the right of the door—something metal.

"What the hell you doing?" came a voice from a ways off.

"Never you mind! I heard voices, and I'm letting 'em know who's the boss." It was Cedee. I'd know his voice anywhere.

"Peety ain't gonna like it."

"Peety ain't here, so I'm in charge."

"He said that?"

He kicked at the door again. "Didn't need to." Another kick to the door. "Got any cig's left?"

We could hear mumbling and big boots on hard earth walking away. Everyone sucked in a big gulp of air and let it out quietly and slowly. At least we weren't in pine boxes. My legs shuddered. A line of coagulated blood marked my calf where it ran from my knee.

Hours passed, and anxious exhaustion enveloped me. I fought with gravity on thick eyelids. It had been dark, black really, for some time. While listening to mutterings across the room, sleep overtook me.

The sound of an owl hooting from the barn roof woke me. The horror of the kidnap threw water on my face, and I bolted upright, my hand covering a shriek that wanted to spill forward. The night was cold. Tucking my knees to my chest, I wrapped my arms around bare legs. I rubbed my goose bumps with enough force to start a bonfire. Everyone was asleep—motionless.

A flicker of light from behind a bale of straw caught my attention. I listened and watched. The owl fluttered from the roof. Leaning as far as I could on my extended right arm. I could see the light poking out to the side—fingers paraded across it. The rectangle of a cell phone. Who had a cell? I inhaled long silent breaths. The cell clicked off, and I heard movement. I lay down quietly but swiftly. My eyes had fully adjusted to the dark, and I saw the blond hair of the girl who called herself Wren. When we first arrived, one of the men had thrown her in with us, in the barn. I could tell by the wide swath of black hair that separated her bottle-blond mane. She slid the phone inside the hay bale and surveyed the barn with skittish haste.

I wondered if she could see my heart beating through my chest as I feigned sleep and peeked through semi-closed eyes. What was she doing? Who was she calling? I watched her find a place on the floor and lie down.

Twenty minutes later the lock rattled. The man-in-charge, Peety, and Sidearm came busting into the dark, yelling. Flashlight beams raced around the barn. More yelling. The tone was telling—

the words garbled. The group curled into various corners, huddled, shaking. I stayed put and kept my head down. Two lights focused on the cinnamon-skinned girl, Adriana. Peety grabbed her by the hair, dragging her out screaming. Her legs flew like a rag doll. Sidearm shut the barn door and the lock clicked into place.

My heart raced as I listened to Adriana yelling "NO!" repeatedly. Her screams faded slightly into the distant wherever. Banging vibrated through my ears. My heart pounded. There was a scuffle and a door slammed. Adriana's voice had become hoarse, but she kept wailing at a shrill pitch that hurt my marrow. A door opened again. The sound of fist against flesh carried through the night. Then a soft whimper like a scared dog began. I listened, leaning forward. Something heavy thumped onto wood planks and a door shut.

19

Carson

The Monson apartments came across much nicer in the dark and at a distance. Closer, even under sparse lighting, the outside bricks needed a good scrubbing. Struggling grass peered through the Creeping Charlie and Dandelions. The corrugated metal over the parking stalls appeared well kept.

I inched the Corvair up, so we could view Apartment 208. A full trash bag lay just outside the door. The neighbors had an old battery to the left of their door, their idea of a potted plant or door stop. I didn't spot Mansell's truck or the one from the video. I eased the car down the entry to the parking lot hoping to find Mansell's white Ford 1500. *No luck.*

I glanced over at Detective Brower. He sat relaxed but coiled. "You mind waiting here while I check out the place?" I asked.

"Sure as hell do." He opened the door, then tried to crane his size fourteen foot out.

"Or you could come up with me," I hurriedly finished.

The air had a lingering taste of rotted food and exhaust. Detective Brower let out a grunt, lowered his massive head and eased out. I felt a sinking and release motion as the shocks rearranged themselves on the passenger side.

As we suspected, no one answered.

Strolling over to the next apartment, I knocked on 207. We both glanced down at the battery; Detective Brower tilted his head in bemusement. A yipping dog sounded the alarm of visitors. An older feminine voice yelled "Teater, hush!" from behind the door. It took a while to undo internal locks. The door swung open, revealing an elderly woman, sunken and hunched from a severe life. A beehive hairdo and pink furry slippers greeted us, along with a smile that brought out the deep furrows of her face. At her heels was a tiny rat of a dog—bug eyes and a bow between its ears. I could hear the TV blasting, and cocked my head when gunshots startled me.

"CSI," she said and nodded her head inside the doorway. "Can't get enough. They solve everything with licked envelopes and chewed gum. The police should watch this—solve a case or two. I was robbed three months ago and . . ."

"Ma'am," I stated abruptly.

"Oh, sorry, what can I help you with?" Her head swayed as she checked both of us out. "You two don't look like vacuum salesmen." Detective Brower's bush eyebrows jumped up and down a couple of times, clearly annoyed.

"We're wondering if you know your neighbor, Mansell Handley?" I asked.

She spent some time thinking about that. We stayed silent.

"He owe y'all money?" She held her hand out. "I'm Mrs. Orlane, Vera Orlane. You two look big enough to get it from him. I know for a fact his rent is two months past due. Doreen, the manager, and I talk about it most every day over coffee and pastries."

The mouse dog licked my shoe. I noticed Mrs. Orlane's well-worn slippers were matted, probably by Teater. The dog scooted over and rested its tiny face on the comfort of her feet.

"Now, Teater, you behave."

"Does he owe a lot of people money?" asked Brower.

"I see unsavory people stop by all the time." She held up a finger, "Not that I am like a stalker or something. I mind my—"

"Any of them dressed like a Marine?" Bower tried a smile; it didn't fit.

"Oh, honey, they're mostly girls. You know—bar trash. Though, I'm not making any judgment. They come for Mansell. What he's got that they want, I can't imagine."

"How old?" I asked.

"Now Luden, on the other hand, he's a nice boy. Takes out my garbage. Brings me the Sunday paper after he's done with it." She leaned closer, "I can't afford it anymore since Harvey died. We were married four years. He was my second. The first one wasn't good for much; even had a low sperm count." She threw up her hands.

"How old were the girls, Ms. Orlane?" I asked, again.

"The girls?"

"The ones that visit Mansell or come home with him?"

"Honey, they ain't old enough to know nothing. Twenties, maybe a little younger. And necklines that leave nothing to the imagination. If they were—"

"You ever hear any names?"

"The girls, no, probably Bambi or Trixie. Something like that." She held up a finger, "Well, Luden has that fellow Cantoni or something Italian. Sounds like a pasta dish." Vera paused and bit at the edge of her lip. Her finger went back up. "Renaldo, he calls him—Renaldo Cantoni."

"Tall, short, dark hair, muscles, you notice anything about him?" Brower asked.

"He's stocky and wears suits with big lapels. Aren't they out of style?" Her head tilted as if picturing it, "He has really white teeth. I think they're capped—probably the son of a dentist."

We questioned the old lady for 30 minutes longer than we should have. She was a fund of information on all the tenants, but not much more about Mansell or Luden. As we were saying goodbye for the fourth time, she asked, "Now, who are you boys?"

"They just know me. Friend-of-a-friend thing."

We darted to the car and could hear her rambling as we crossed the lawn, oblivious to the fact we'd gone. Brower eased his big body into the car. "With all that information, I could throw half the complex in jail, except Mansell and Luden. Sure glad I did this instead of going home to rest off a 12-hour shift." He let out a funnel of air through his teeth. I nodded.

"Dear little Vera's as helpful as a box of rocks." Brower waited for my response.

I started the car.

"I'm hungry again. And I know there's nothing in my fridge but an empty six pack and cheese that keeps changing colors." He waited for my reaction.

"Do you want me to grab you something at a drive-thru?"

"My figure can't handle all that grease and fat." His fingers wrapped around beer fat and jiggled it a little. "I was thinking the buffet over on Main."

"Sure, that's the least I can do; it'd be my pleasure," I said sarcastically.

He put his massive arms behind his head and leaned back, smiling. His elbows lifted my ragtop.

"Renaldo," I mused.

20

Carson

"The neurons are firing in every direction. My heart's going to split ribs at any second. Momentum, man, momentum."

I hated it when he became cryptic. It was so irritating. I sucked in a long, deep breath and asked, "What's up, Hub?" A high-pitched whistle whined in my earpiece. I yanked the cell back and heard cursing. "Hub, Hub, you there?"

Something crashed, and I heard more cussing. Silence, then a tapping sound. "I just ruined a perfect high—a psychic understanding—an out-pocket voyage. Down the old shoot-er-oo."

Out-pocket voyage was his term for his spirit leaving his body. I didn't understand any of it—never would. Hub could be coherent at times and asylum crazy at others. I waited while he babbled for a bit. I knew he would get to the point sometime. He always did. He told me about breaking his ceramic teapot, a gift from a descendant of Mayan lineage, Pateao Monez. I'd met him on a journey with Hub to central Mexico. All smiles and broken teeth.

"I'm in love," he said, then paused forever.

I waited impatiently as I jotted a note on a pad.

"She has so much unfiltered joy, but it's stifled under the refuse of teen and college years. It was like traveling through the city dump. And I'm not talking about walking on top, we burrowed."

"So, you're in love again. Makes me tingle all over." I rubbed my brow. "Who is it this time? Don't tell me it's Lucy from the theater?" A horn honked and I glanced over. Just a dog crossing the road. The *Heinz-57* walked in front of my parked car and headed down the sidewalk.

"She came out of it like springtime after a hard winter," he said.

"Who?"

"Annie. Who'd ya think I was talking about? She kicked off those high heels and her board-of-director's suit. There was a woman in there. A comfortable person with all that girly sentiment and charm."

"Hub, you didn't?" My fists tightened around the steering wheel.

"It was intervention. She's wound tight with all this Tia stuff. I didn't give her too much. We took things slow and worked out those demons. I won't be able to loosen her up completely until you find her sister. You need to hurry. If she drops again, I'm not sure I can pull her up."

I was grinding my teeth. "You gave her peyote?"

"It was the least I could do. She was a mess after you left the other day. Lucky I happened to stop by. Maria didn't know what to do."

I wanted to strangle my best friend. Every fiber of my body tightened. My heart rate soared. I knew my next question and wasn't sure I wanted an answer. "Hub, did you bed down Annabelle?" As the words came out, I knew it was none of my business–but.

"Not like you think. The potion had completely worn off. We ate breakfast—drank coffee. Consenting adults and all."

"Consenting? She was drugged!"

"Hey, amigo, don't be a prude. Hours had passed since the counseling session. She kissed me. What was I supposed to do? The love gears cranked in."

I felt the Hub headache coming on. "You called to irritate me?"

"Hahaha. Love the humor, buddy. Oh, yeah, why'd I call?"

I envisioned him stroking his forehead and staring skyward. It was a mannerism Hub used frequently. A truck with a plume of diesel smoke whizzed past me. I'd parked across from Mansell's apartment after feeding Detective Brower enough to power twelve normal humans for a week and dropping him off.

"Ohhhh, when I was scanning the universe, just sailing with no real destination, I must have skipped into a time warp—a reversal. I watched the whole scene take place."

"You were hallucinating," I boomed, my voice caustic.

"No . . . No, hallucinations are false visions. All my senses were performing. I was there. Well, not there in the physical sense, but there in the spiritual. I hovered above."

I'd heard all this crap before. My thumb softly rubbed my temple, and I tapped my foot on the hard floor. After endless prattling about spiritual awakenings and four-dimensional alertness, Hub finally told me who he, supposedly, saw take Tia. The irritating part was that it happened to be the same person I'd centered on. I often wondered if he came to conclusions based on the same facts I relied on, or, as he proclaimed, his ideas came from "his shaman tendencies." I wasn't sure which, but I half-listened to his ramblings, even when he talked about spiritual travels. There were always kernels of wisdom in the craziest of Hub's thoughts.

At 10 p.m. my mind rested as alert as a hibernating bear. My eyes barely caught the blink of car lights that pulled into a stall at the Monson apartments. I had wadded my jacket up as a pillow and stayed in that position while I grabbed my monocular. Luden exited the car, clicked the locks with his key, and headed up the sidewalk. I thought about waiting until he entered the apartment, then decided against it. I wanted him out in the open. My eyes darted around. No one appeared to be in sight.

I pressed the button so the interior lights stayed off and exited my Corvair without making a sound. Following the hedge of overgrown barberry, I curled around behind Luden. He whistled one of those numbing radio hits. I knew the tune from years of top-forty feeding but couldn't place the title. Glancing around, there was still no one in sight. I readjusted my plans to address the six-pack of beer in his left hand—didn't want to get clobbered by that. I knew I had to scare the crap out of him or he might run screaming. I couldn't allow the whole building to spring to life and watch me talk to him.

I kicked his elbow with just enough torque. Budweiser glass shattered on the walkway, still in its paper holder. Luden reached for his elbow and started to turn. I palmed his right ear with ample force to pivot his head back. Dazed, his hand went from his elbow to his ear. He raised up on his toes to take off running. I shoved him through a patch of trumpet vine and into the side of the building. His head hit dusty, yellow bricks. His legs rubbered. He dropped. It had been years since boot camp for this flabby Marine. Stepping over spilled beer and brown glass shards, I picked him up by his armpits. My left foot slid on wet glass and took us both down. His doughy body cushioned my fall. Short seconds passed, I twisted around him and pulled us both up. His eyes rolled as I stood him against the wall. Blinking, he centered his grey-green eyes on me, recognition coming slowly.

I leaned in close, "We need to talk."

He cupped his ear and remained silent, trying to gain some of his faculties. I noticed blood ooze out of a three-inch scrape across his cheek. Brick is unforgiving. There were sounds in the near distance. We both glanced up as voices came closer.

I put my left arm through his and grabbed his wrist with my other hand. "We're taking a walk to that red car," My voice low and stern. I jutted my chin in the direction. A conversation between two girls became closer. We would see them in two seconds. "I'll snap this fat arm like a toothpick if you do anything. Nod if you understand."

His head jiggled, then tucked into his chest.

"Hi, ladies." A genuine smile filled my face.

Their facial skin tightened as they eyeballed Luden. Their pace slowed. I put pressure against the bone in Luden's arm. "Gotta get my pal here to the doc. Damn dog tripped him on the stairs."

They gazed at the broken beer and looked around for a dog.

"Do you know who has that black wolfhound?" I asked.

The girl to the left bunched up her face, setting deep crevices between her brows. "A wolfhound?"

"Yeah. Seemed kind of lost and hungry."

They shook their heads and scooted past us and down into a basement apartment. They didn't look back.

From the edge of my sight, I saw Luden bend down lower on his knees. He was ready to bolt. I twisted the skin and added some compression to his doughy forearm. He straightened up. I guided him into the passenger seat.

"Don't try anything stupid. I'd truly hate to have anything

squirting all over my clean seats." I tapped the pistol tucked into my belt on my back. He nodded with a brief startle. *He wasn't scared, but the gun gave him a pause. Good for him. Even as a desk jockey, he'd been through stuff.*

I slid into the driver's side, dropping the gun onto the dash.

I decided on the direct approach. "So, Luden, where'd you take Tia that morning?"

His eyes dropped just faintly, but enough to tell me his thoughts. Hub and I were right. He was wondering how I knew. He searched for an escape. He looked over to the butt of the gun. A stream of blood ran down his face, dripping crimson onto his cargo pants.

"You can tell me here and now or talk to the detectives in one of those smelly rooms. However, they'll throw you into a cell with someone calling you 'girlfriend.' Your choice."

He sucked in a breath of air, trying to appear dispassionate and uninterested.

I threw a tissue at him. "Don't bleed on my seats."

We were both caught up in the waiting game. I decided threats of police didn't faze him. I'd need a different tactic.

With his hands tied up in front of him, we headed up Parley's Canyon and turned off at Little Dell Reservoir. The slob lost bravado. Sweat beaded below a receded hairline as we drove around sharp curves heading into thick trees. At one point, he covertly reached for the doorknob as he readjusted to the side. I elbowed him in the nose and told him to stay put. Blood gushed from his nostrils, so I threw him a clump of napkins.

He yanked on the rope holding his hands to his stretched belt. He tried to bend forward to retrieve them. Exasperated, I grabbed the wad of paper from his lap and shoved it at his face. He grabbed it and held it to his nose. His eyes tightened at the pain.

"None of that on my seats."

Toward the top of the mountain, I pulled down a dirt road that was shorter than a hundred yards and shut the car off. A stream gurgled in the distance. His hands cupped his nose and his back curled forward. I jumped out. He glanced up.

Opening his door, I said, "Get out, we're taking a walk."

Luden's eyes became defiant. He pressed himself deeper into the seat. I grabbed him by the arm. He immediately grasped the left side of his seat. Uncut fingernails dug hard into the seat.

"You're making a mess of my seats, dammit. Now, let go. Or I'm going to make you feel like you just gave childbirth."

Luden held tighter. His hands dug firmer into the vinyl. I shook my head, grabbed him with both hands by the hair and dragged him slowly out. He had planted himself down pretty well, but yanked roots are a motivator. I dragged him through the trees. He grabbed at branches along the way. I jerked him harder.

We came to the edge of a stream. I shoved his face into the water, bouncing it off the pebble bottom. He braced himself on elbows and knees, jerking and twisting like a fish on land. I shifted to his side. With each lift of his head, he gulped for air. Water and blood burst from his nostrils. His weight was the only thing going for him. I shoved my knee into the small of his back, pressing him further into the shallow water. He shook, trying to escape. The sound of him gasping water into his lungs made me back off. He bucked, and I thrust him hard into the wet gravel stream.

"You ease up, I'll let you live."

His body writhed and butted. Another couple gulps of muddy water and resistance faded. He collapsed.

I dragged him to the mossy side and pumped his chest. Seconds passed, then he vomited a stream of water and foam to the side. He sucked in a gurgled sound of air, then threw up again. I jerked him on his side, annoyed at the mess. Water globed out of his mouth and nose—yellow-red and odious. His eyes opened as deep breaths filled his lungs. His eyes hungered for life.

Before he gained any more fight in him, I snatched off his belt, rolled him close to the trunk of an aspen tree, and jerked his hands back. I tied him sitting up. Luden's wide eyes rolled around as he tried to center himself. His cheeks were red and pocked from pebbles, and mud blotched his face and arms.

We stared at each other for several minutes.

21

Carson

"You crazy bastard! You could have killed me," Luden blurted. Spit dribbled from his mouth. His eyes scowled like a rabid coyote. His back was hunched; his fat neck pulled tight to the collar.

I leaned back against an aspen and crossed my arms. "I see it as, I asked a question and you wouldn't answer. Just a difference of opinion."

"I don't know a damn thing." He bared his teeth in frustration and hate. Red rivulets of blood rippled across puffed cheeks. "You should talk to Mansell; he's the one that screwed her. That morning she couldn't wait to get out of there. Her face had regret written all over it. She's not the first one to be taken by Mansell. They all fall for that face and charm. Maybe the muscles too." Luden glanced toward the stream, his face turned sour with restless searching.

"You can't outrun me," I laughed.

"She must have called eight friends trying to get a ride, at six in the morning. No one wanted to answer. She asked me for a ride to her car. I just helped her out. That's all, really. I don't know a damn thing."

"Sure, you took her to the car, but then what happened?" He had smooth lies and kept reverting to his honest face—as if astonished that I would think otherwise.

"I drove to work." He coughed, eyeing me with contempt.

He knew I knew it was a lie. Pushing myself from the tree, I closed the distance and jammed my face near his. "The day she came up missing, you didn't show up for work. And you missed the next two days." I leaned in a quarter of an inch, eye to eye.

There was more gray in his iris than green.

His face squirmed. "I don't know a damn thing." He bit down on his lower lip. I was getting tired of his lame mantra and didn't think he could handle another drowning. I circled around in a slow rhythm of shoe crunching dry twigs. His head swiveled. I made a full pass, then stopped behind him.

"Well, if you don't know anything, I really don't need you. Do I?"

He turned frantically to face me around the tree then rubbed his tied hands. His eyes were wide with worry.

My voice lowered, and I pronounced each word with pedantic clarity. "I wonder if these woods have bears." I rubbed my chin and nodded. "Sure they do. Mostly brown, but some black. The black ones are the meanest. You know, they can eviscerate a man with one swoop of those powerful hairy arms." I pantomimed the motion, then rubbed my chin and glanced upwards. "Course, it's their claws that really do the job." I curled my hand and stared at my fingernails. "You ever get a close look at those claws?"

Luden gazed into the far distance. "You're not going to freak me out. I really don't know nothing." He emphasized the "really."

"You realize that's a double negative. You're saying you know a lot. Now's the time to tell me." I popped his forehead with my palm. His head made a thud on the tree trunk.

Luden tucked his chin into his fat neck. Pink rubbery tubes circled below.

I strolled in a circle again, then stopped. I pointed toward the thick trees. "You know what bothers me about the out-of-doors?" I paused and circled around him. "The bugs–mosquitoes, come out around dusk–West Nile–Zika. I read in a medical journal the other day there's evidence they carry GBM–glioblastoma. It's the worst form of brain cancer. No survivors, and it grows so fast, pushing everything to the limits of the skull. Your limbs become useless. Migraines so bad, you pray to die." His head lifted as he tried for defiant. I noticed his body shudder slightly. I undid the belt that strapped him to the tree. He seemed relieved. I knew he could squirm out of that belt in no time.

"Follow me." He made whining noises as I ran him through

the trees back to my car. His eyes bulged as I grabbed a length of rope and a rag from my trunk and hauled him back to the stream. He gulped in breaths as though he had stage three emphysema. I shoved him roughly up against a thick lone pine. He squirmed, kicked, and screamed while I tied him upright to the tree. Expletives blurted out as if I'd arrested a hooker. I crammed the oil-stained rag deep into his mouth. His cheeks reddened and puffed out.

"Nocturnal, that's what they call those creatures that hunt at night. Raccoons, owls, mountain lions, foxes—pointy little teeth and jowls of steel. Luckily, they only come out after the bugs leave." I kicked dirt at him. He startled and began a long, muffled scream.

"Wolves—they're the bad boys. They hunt in packs and surround the prey. Come at you from all directions and try to get to the jugular. Messy." I shook my head. He began bounding against the aspen as if in a seizure. The tie on his arms stretched but didn't loosen. His nose ran blood and snot that flicked as he jounced.

"Yeah, I can imagine being tied up."

He worked a tiny bit of rag from the left side of his mouth. "Ain't no such thing here." His muzzled voice quivered slightly.

I glanced at my cell phone. "We're getting close to sunset." Reaching down to his binds, I jerked him around closer to the tree. The nylon rope pressed hard into his soft neck and legs as he bucked and squirmed. Holding his head tightly to the trunk, I pressed the rag deeper into his throat. His face was as red as a ripe apple.

I tossed my keys in my hands. "Well, if you don't know anything about Tia, you can't help me." I turned on my heels and walked back to the Corvair without glancing back. I could hear his muffled squeal behind me.

I drove down the canyon, turned on I-80 and headed toward Park City.

22

Tia

My eyes were shut. Fear kept them closed; curiosity wanted them open. My heart pounded enough to explode my skull. I turned to try and sit up. Mice skittered to a far-off corner. A weak southern voice drawled, "Shhh." Soft footsteps, then the breath of someone kneeling at my side. I forced one eye open just slightly. A voice said, "You awake?" It was the thin girl with the blue highlights in her brunette hair. She had on a ripped oversized T-shirt with Duke University printed across the front.

My vision swept past her to where I saw Wren last night. I couldn't see her. Anxiety tightened my chest. "Never slept," I whispered and turned to brace myself on one elbow.

She held her fingers flat to her mouth. The knuckles were bruised and cut. Her purple-painted fingernails were coated with the dust of the barn floor. "We need help. We're going to dig our way out. Oh, I'm Corrina." Her lips quivered as she attempted a smile.

I put my finger to my lips and scrutinized the surrounding, both eyes wide open and searching, my neck scrunched. I found Wren asleep atop spread hay near the door. My finger pointed in her direction. Corrina's neck curled and she spotted my focus. An inquisitive raise of eyebrows turned in my direction.

I mouthed, "She's with them."

"She's a hen?" she blurted.

I shook my head, with my palm down padding the air, urging her to hush. Her brows lifted as she waited for more. With mouth to ear, I whispered, "She's one of them—a snitch. There's a cell phone hidden in the bale. Wren told on Adriana."

Deep lines appeared on her forehead. She cocked her head

back and forth like a puppet.

With her puzzlement, I leaned in again, my bruised knees scraping on the dry dirt. My breath caught for a few seconds. "I watched her use a phone and minutes later Peety and his buddies hauled Adrianna out and into the chicken coop."

"Phone? Cell? From where?"

"That bale of hay." I nodded to my right.

Corrina quietly spat out a rattling band of swear words. Most, I'd never heard together. She scowled back at the blond lump on the hay and said, "I've gotta go tell the others. You watch her. Make a ruckus if she wakes."

She didn't wait for my soft, "Okay."

Soon, she brought three others. They crouched by me like conspirators. A few of the other girls gave us looks. Corrina motioned with her slender hands, "Lisa, Perri, and Mati. They're all from Arizona, different cities, but nearby. I'm from Evanston, Wyoming, by way of North Carolina. Where're you from?"

"Salt Lake—Nevada originally."

"All Rocky Mountain States," said the one introduced as Perri. She had deep black hair that flowed over her wide shoulders and down the middle of her athletic back. Strong legs and firm arms seemed ready for a marathon. She rolled her R's, giving her a hint of Spanish in her voice. Lisa had hips made for mothering and a kind face with sparkly eyes; Mati had a bruised cheek that barely showed through her Mediterranean tan, but you could tell it hurt.

Corrina glared over at Wren, curled alone in the corner as Lisa said, "Let's take her out!" Her words were so incongruent with her gentle appearance, I would have found it funny under different circumstances. Her elbows were bent, and she held a boxer's stance, with feminine clenched fists.

Perri rolled her eyes. "You definitely need to quit watching TV."

With a nod, Perri signaled for me to follow her. We all kept watch of the sleeping Wren as we tiptoed in a mother duck line behind Perri. She showed me where a rodent had burrowed under the concrete base of the barn.

"Stick your hand in there; it goes through to the outside," she said softly. She gazed around in quick motions. None of the other girls paid us much attention. I think most were in shock. The others were scared to death. Most of these girls had never left the safety of mom and dad's place.

I started to kneel, then shook my head and hurried to stand upright. There was a rodent nose and whiskers just below the surface. It backed up, burying its path. "I'll take your word for it."

Corrina grabbed my arm. "I was raised on a ranch. Whether it's a rat or a weasel, they're more afraid of y'all than you are of them."

"I don't think that's the case. My sister's first apartment had a mouse. Scared me senseless. I jumped on the couch and pushed her TV on top of the thing. Missed it. Annie barely missed me with a slap. The mouse took off quick after that. Wow, Annie was mad. It took everything I had to haul that TV out to the dumpster."

"Okay," said Perri. "You want out. You'll get on your hands and knees and dig."

I peeked a little closer at the hole and said nothing.

They showed me a dusty board that was as wide as the length of my foot and about three-feet long. It lay half buried under floor dirt and hay. Corrina whispered that it would work to cover the hole. We set up with one of us to block the sleeping Wren, another with their foot ready to kick the board in place, another to dig, and Perri to watch the barn door. We rotated every fifteen minutes or so.

My turn to dig came up, and I pushed back my queasiness of rodents, dropped to all fours, and dug like a dog over a hidden bone. Perri was right, I wanted out! A rush of fear-linked adrenaline surged through me. The two girls to my side pushed the dirt further away. Before long, my nails were broken and filled black with filth. The plan was to dig mostly the inside and break through to the outside the next night. I grazed something hard that cut my finger. Blood oozed through the dirt on my hands and ran between my fingers. I winced in pain. Corrina shoved me to the side and leaned down to carefully feel the soft dirt. I pinched the wound between my forefinger and thumb to stop the blood, after wiping off the cut on the shorts Sidearm had given me.

"It's a metal rod, the kind they put in cement," whispered Corrina. "We gotta move the hole to the left."

Jef Huntsman

The sound of metal clicked behind us. My heart rose to my throat.

23

Carson

Blood drizzled from cuts on my knuckles. I tried to brush the dirt off them. Throbbing penetrated the bones just below my eye socket. Luden had reared back several times with his thick skull bouncing off my upper cheek. I rubbed it with a cold bottle of water from my ice chest in the back seat. Each movement caught my breath. Scrapes on my knees and elbows sent shooting pain through my legs and arms. He might have broken one of my ribs, but I think the ache was just tenderness. I peeked at myself in the rearview mirror. It was me but torn and battered by that chubby ex-Marine. For an out-of-shape man he had more strength and stamina than I would have given him credit for. *We'll see how the dark wilderness treats him. See if that loosens his lips.*

I pulled over to a gas station just off the interstate and grabbed a large sack I kept for emergencies. Slipping bandages into my pocket from an overused first aid kit, I ducked into the bathroom. The spider-cracked mirror wasn't in much better shape than I. Coagulated dark red etched a crooked line from my forehead to where it met with another oozing stream from my cheek, before the stream rippled halfway down my neck. Eight wet paper towels later, I began to recognize myself. Exiting down the aisle of chips and pork rinds, I dabbed the corner of my lip with another paper towel. Blood sponged in. The cashier gave me a worried look.

A few minutes later, dressed in my grey sports jacket, a black golf shirt, and blue dress pants, I hopped in the driver's seat, somewhat presentable, though battered. I used my sweaty, torn shirt to wipe dried specs of Luden's blood off the passenger seat. It wouldn't pass a forensic test, but you couldn't spot anything from a short distance. Tossing the shirt and bag into a waiting dumpster, I headed through Kimball Junction toward Park City.

I parked and walked to the first café I found, sat at the counter and ordered a turkey sandwich and coffee. The food brought me back to life. I drank two more cups of coffee with deliberate slowness. The unknown and anxiety fester when you're trying to waste time. Only one hour and thirteen minutes had passed since I'd left Luden tied to the tree.

I walked up and down Main Street, gandering at paintings, sculptures, stuffed bears, nuevo-western wear, pottery, T-shirts, and smiling tourists. Sitting on a bench, I thought about Maria. She was a wonder, filled with hot blood, cute expressions, a sexy look that could stop traffic, and the wonderment of a child. Her patience with my delinquent behavior had always astounded me. I pulled out my cell to call her, thought better of it, and shoved it back in my pocket.

Following the crowd, I entered a bar, nursed a beer for so long the bartender scowled, probably thinking about the tip based on one beer. Several tables hooted and clacked glasses together and laughed way too loud. I shook my cell to make sure it hadn't broken as my eyes gazed at the clock for the fortieth time. With my beer finished the bartender perked up, and I strolled out to the street. Just as I began to cross through late night traffic, my phone rang. Maria's picture came up. I hesitated, then decided to take it.

"Maria?"

"Good evening or no? You, perhaps, home tomorrow night? I was having a few people over for lasagna, you know, Harmon Dobbs, Emily, the Webster sisters, and Sonny. I'll probably call Hub, too."

I leaned on the brick window sill of a restaurant/bar. The amplified voice of an old Billy Joel tune vibrated the window. "I'm working, not real sure what will shake out after tonight. You mind if I call and let you know by tomorrow morning?"

"Not at all." I heard disappointment in her voice. "Any luck with the Tia thing?"

"I'm waiting to discuss that with an acquaintance shortly." I leaned away from the thumping glass.

"I know I shouldn't ask, but you aren't doing anything illegal or dangerous?"

"Nah, just checking on leads, pulling a string at one end and seeing what comes up on the other."

"Okay, I get it—don't ask."

"Lasagna sounds wonderful. I hope I can make it." I knew I wouldn't be sitting down to dinner with her tomorrow or for some time. This Tia thing had me too absorbed. I caught myself breathing loudly. Luden had to give me more information.

"Love you," she whispered.

"Yeah, back at ya. I'll call in the morning."

"Back at ya? You make my legs all rubbery when you talk like that," she paused, "asshole."

My fingers covered a growing grin. "Love ya too."

She clicked off. I hopped down from the sill and began walking up the steep sidewalk. Stopping at a jazz bar, I nursed another cup of coffee. My heart shook from all the caffeine; my fingers drummed the counter.

At two-twenty in the morning, my car pulled out of its parking stall behind Main Street. Thirty-five minutes later, I pulled over to the shoulder of the road up the canyon. My lights were off for the last ten minutes as I crept along in the dark, trying to find the pull off. After I turned off the key and my eyes adjusted to the light, I headed toward Luden. By the time I could see his drooping silhouette, I'd skinned my knee, took a branch to the neck, and buried one shoe in some dark muck. One leg of good pants was ripped at the calf. Good thing I'd left the jacket in the car.

Luden's eyes were open, his body perfectly still as I approached. He could hear me, though I doubt he saw more than a shadow closing in. A crescent moon peered over the south mountains lighting him more than me. I stood about 16 feet away and began cracking dry branches.

"Hello," he said in a quick quivering voice.

I wanted him scared, motivated to tell me whatever he knew, so deep in my throat I growled.

He began kicking his feet and yelling like a madman. The rag he'd held in his mouth spat to the dirt. His body writhed in fast jerks against the tree. I wondered if the binds would hold.

I watched for a few minutes then started forward.

Screams of agony bellowed from the fat Marine. He kicked dirt high into the air. Spit flew in all directions.

"Calm down crazy man." I slapped his face.

His body slumped against the slight looseness of the rope. His breathing echoed in hard, gasping sounds. I waited until his chest rose and fell closer to normal.

"Thought I'd stop by, see if you wanted to chat." I pointed my flashlight down on his face. His eyes glared up at mine. Using my foot, I pressed him back against the tree. His mouth started to open, then clammed shut. I could almost hear his teeth grinding.

I pressed my shoe deeper into his upper chest. No response. So, I shimmied the toe of my sneaker into the flexible tissue of his neck. A child's high-pitched moan came from his throat.

"I can't keep coming back here every few hours," I said. "I'll untie you, when I know what you know." I shook my head in disgust. "You really want to tell me now. I have commitments, places to be, I won't be back this way for . . ." With two fingers, I tapped my head. "Today's what? Tuesday? Yeah, I think so. I'll be back on Friday, maybe Saturday, if nothing else comes up." I pressed closer, my foot cutting deep into his Adam's apple. "You'll be okay for four days, right?" Tucking the flashlight under my arm pit, I reached in my pocket, fumbled around deep, and came up with car keys. "Crap, I don't even have a stick of gum for you."

He said nothing.

Pulling him in against the tree, I tightened the ropes. His face tried for defiant, but it came out exhausted and worried. I yanked my belt off and strapped it around his neck and the tree. It cinched up nicely. I started to walk away, then turned and walked back. I picked up the rag, re-wadded it up and shoved it with my thumb into his mouth. He tried to bite down, but I smacked the side of his head. His ears were probably ringing.

With the flashlight as a guide, it would be easier going back than coming in. After I stepped about 10 feet away, I heard a hurried squeal. I stopped and smiled, breathing in a sigh of relief.

With a sober face, I turned around. His head jounced to the side trying to let me know to come back.

"You sure?" I asked.

He nodded.

With the rag out, a raspy voice said, "Water."

"You're sure you're ready to have our talk?"

He nodded again.

With the beam of light, I found the stream and dipped my hands in the cold water. Cupped as tight as I could, I hauled three handfuls over to Luden. He seemed relieved.

"Just a minute," I wandered back to my car to grab a notepad and pen. Luden started screaming after a few seconds and kept it up until I returned. The sound was unearthly.

I got back. He calmed after several minutes.

"Okay, shoot." I held out my pen and sat down by his side. He asked me several times to loosen the rope. I repeated, "Shortly, shortly."

Luden leaked everything out. Two and a half hours passed. The light of the impending sunrise began to silhouette the mountains. I had to haul a couple more handfuls of water to him.

He had given me names, dates, places, and how seven girls had been abducted by four men. I squeezed out tiny details that might help along the way. He didn't know everything, but he knew plenty. Probably more than his bosses wanted him to or had any idea he knew. I recorded the most important things on my cell phone. Things that would indict him for kidnapping and even murder.

When I was sure I had it all, I untied him and strapped my belt back on. He begged me to give him a ride down the canyon. My fist tightened, I wanted to pummel this piece-of-shit. Tia's sweet, full-of-life smile from the picture Annie gave me was imbedded in my mind. My eyes bored into his. I turned before I took out all the fury buried inside me on him. He was on his own. Maybe the long walk down would add some conscience to his warped mind; I doubted it.

Part way down, before the lake, I had to pull over and heave. Even with as many times as I had seen all the horrid inhumanity people could produce, I never got used to it. At least when I had the task of being a soldier, and later in the CIA, it seemed like there was a greater good. In this case there was none.

I called Annie and woke her up, asked to meet her at her condo. She was all questions, but I hung up without answering any.

Next, I pressed speed dial for Maria and explained to voice mail that I wouldn't make it to her dinner. Probably wouldn't be back home for a while, perhaps weeks. I'm not sure why, but I knew she'd understand. She and the people I help are the reason I feel good about myself. Maria got that.

But Annie wasn't going to like what I had to tell her.

24

Carson

I pulled up to the condos and shut the motor off. Annabelle Linford was at her door, waiting impatiently, arms crossed and face as rigid as granite. When I didn't immediately jump out of the car, she eased over stiff-legged toward my vehicle. The top was down. She noticed the cell phone to my ear as I mouthed, "One minute." She had a tight squeeze on her elbows, arms under breasts. Her teeth chomped into her bottom lip. I turned away.

Detective Brower's voice gave no indication of emotion, after I spelled out most of what I knew about Tia's disappearance. I kept my voice almost conspiratorial, lowered, and I covered the cell in my long bony hands. Some things I wouldn't want Annie to know about, though I'd give her an armload of bleak information. Brower would have Luden's place watched and agreed to hold off on any arrest. He'd check things from his side; I'd stick my nose a little deeper in the badger hole. He seemed to like that.

Clicking off, I turned to Annie. She had a sick, lost-sheep glaze to her face. I opened the door, walked around to where she stood, put an arm around her sagging shoulders, and walked her back to her condo. She knew the news would be bad, even though I hadn't said a thing. I felt the spasms of her tears as we entered her home. I sat her down on that hard couch, went to the kitchen and poured her a glass of water. Her hands quivered as I held it out to her. She automatically grabbed it, like saying "Fine," to a stranger's question about health.

I sat on the couch with her and waited. Five minutes passed before she glanced up. "Is she dead?"

"Not that I know of."

Annie's butt slid forward and her back dropped into the

couch in one fluid motion. Both hands covered her mouth. She let out a moan between her fingers. I wasn't sure if it signaled relief or something completely dark.

"She's alive?"

"I'm working on that assumption. Look, Annie, I'm going to search around in your fridge for some eggs and brew up some coffee. I've been up all night and I want to gather things together in my mind before we talk."

"But . . ."

I held up my palm. "At this point, her kidnappers need her alive. So, that's the good news. Let me eat and think. We'll go over everything I know so far." I rubbed her shoulder absently and stood up.

"Your face?" she asked.

I said nothing.

Opening her fridge, I pulled out a half carton of eggs, Havarti cheese, a container of salsa, one iffy zucchini, and some processed ham slices. "You want an omelet?"

She cleared her throat with a little girl cough, "No."

I wondered where all that girl strength had disappeared to. She had seemed to be holding up so well, until now. I placed a glass of orange juice in front of her. It was ignored.

After listening to the echo of kitchen noises for ten minutes, I split a giant omelet into two halves and slid them on a couple of plates. Setting one down in front of Annie, I shoved big bites into my hungry mouth. I'd toasted a bagel and that went in as well.

She stirred her eggs around like chasing chickens with a fork. Her eyes were centered on the plate, but her mind clearly wasn't.

I swallowed the rest of my juice. "You ready?"

25

Carson

Annie had fallen asleep—exhausted from worry, tidbits of insight, and overloaded by a touch of knowledge and truths. Her purring in the next room relaxed me to the point that I had fallen asleep, too, despite her unforgiving couch.

When I awoke, full daylight streamed through Annie's condo window and the beating patter of a running shower intruded. I sat up. My spine felt as if put together with gravel and rusty tin. I rubbed the back of my neck and glanced around for my cell. Finding it stuck to the back of the couch, I hit power and read five-forty-two p.m. I'd slept nearly nine hours. I rotated my head to clear the kinks and snaps of neck bone and muscle. Standing up and twisting my shoulders sent horrid stiff pain down into my lower back. I could smell coffee, pungent and on the verge of burnt. Robotically, my feet padded across kitchen tile, and I poured myself a cup. My knuckles and arms, skinned and bruised, gazed back at me.

The shower stopped. Within minutes, I heard scuffled feet and dresser drawers opened and slammed. A half hour later, Annie stepped out. Her hair was wet, piled in a spiral on top of her head and clipped. She wore slim denim pants with a yellow collared blouse tucked in.

"You sleep okay," she asked?

"Like a princess."

She giggled, "I'm sorry. My couch isn't made for overnighters."

"I must've been really tired." I rubbed the granite countertop with my palm. "Perhaps this would've had more give." I peeked over at her. "How're you doing?"

"Somewhat better. I got up after an hour or so, logged in to work for a bit, then took a shower. Had some time to think about things. You really think Tia's okay?"

"Relatively speaking, yes." I sipped a little more bitter coffee. "How about if I buy you an early dinner?"

"I could . . ."

"I looked. We used up all the eggs and orange juice. There was some Chinese takeout, a foil wrapped slice of pizza, and a couple of condiments left in your fridge." I raised my eyes. "We wouldn't want to get stuck here during a hurricane or flood. Besides, I could really use some steak and eggs. And coffee." I pushed my cup away.

Annie had a lost glaze to her eyes. She inhaled deeply. "Okay."

I wiped my plate clean with the last roll. Annie had nibbled on a slice of apple pie. You could barely tell any was missing. We hadn't talked. I ate forcefully and listened to her sigh ever so often. After paying the bill, I stood up to leave. She didn't move.

"Annie?"

Her head lifted. She had chewed through the lipstick on her bottom lip. Without a word, she raised out of the booth. I held her elbow, guided her out to my car, opened the passenger door, and helped her in. We drove back to her condo in silence. I wasn't sure what to say.

With her keys, I unlocked her door and guided her to a chair. I stayed standing. "I've got to leave. I need to find your sister and I need to do it now."

She stared at me. "She'll be okay, right?"

I thought about my promise to her. *I'd bring her home.* I just wasn't sure how far gone she might be. She could be fine. Not likely, though. Being abducted and forced to do things that never entered your mind does terrible things to people. But I had survived living like a mole in Afghanistan rock—beaten and starved in total darkness for months until my escape. And I'm back to normal. (If normal is night tremors and solidifying fear of crumbling dust.) When that cave exploded, I thought all was lost. But it turned out to be my escape. Tia could make it. She could be okay. But would she?

144

"I'll find her. I'm good at what I do. You have to trust me."

Annie's shoulders slumped and her hands relaxed. "Thank you."

I knelt in front of her. "Annie, you need to be with friends. Call some up. Go to the movies. Get absorbed in work. Don't stay by yourself for long periods of time."

She gazed up at me with confused, watery eyes. "I don't have friends. Tia was my only friend. We talked every day." This was a far different side of her than the demanding woman I'd first met.

"You have friends. Call somebody." My eyes met hers until she nodded.

I stood up, grabbed her purse from the counter, searched, and pulled out her cell. I put the phone into her lap. She nodded, again. "I'll call you with anything I come up with. I'll try to call daily, but don't fret if two or three days pass. Remember, I'll find her." I hoped my voice held the conviction she needed.

26

Carson

My brain spun with details. I jotted down names and a stitching of lines to denote associations on a yellow pad. What I knew involved sketchy facts and too many gaps. I knew I could fill in most of those gaps with supposition, but not fact.

Two of the names Luden had given me, Private First Class Sandoz and Sergeant Bandy, probably wouldn't know much more than the chubby Marine. They were both in different cities: Omaha and Spokane. But the third guy interested me, a retired star, General Stanchy, who lived just outside Camp Pendleton in Oceanside. He would have the most clout.

I wondered about this military affiliation as I called Hub.

"Hey, my friend," he sounded hurried. "I'm just about to leave the house. Borrowed Raymond's little truck—mine's in his garage waiting for parts. The oil pump went out. I'm sure it was karma; just can't remember what I may have done. The mind's a touch squeaky; really need to cut back on burgers. I've had two this month, course I know better than to add fries to it, but I couldn't help myself."

"Hub," I said curtly. My ears were ringing from all his prattle.

"Oh, yeah, man, what's up?"

"I need you to check on a couple of names: Private First Class Sandoz, Sergeant Bandy, and Brigadier General Robert Stanchy." I had taken a turn too wide and slid on the gravel shoulder. My heart raced, but I cranked the wheel just enough to hear the Corvair's tires make asphalt sounds. My mind's a touch squeaky, too–whatever that means.

"No can do. I'm leaving on a Salt Lake run to help a

distressed maiden. Gotta go."

"You're headed to Annie's?"

"Yes, and I'm breaking hell and high water to get there tonight. I've left fifty plus emails from clients and friends floating out there."

He talked faster than normal, which in Hub's case was hard to do. Our lives were so different. Everything he did was emotional; I saved my passion for a limited few. He was affected by the cry of a cat, the bleating of a young lamb, and a burp from a toddler. My ears spent as much time paying attention to such things as to a wall of tongue-and-groove pine.

"Hub, slow down a minute. These people I need information about are involved with Tia's disappearance. You help me, you help Tia, and you help Annie. They need you on this and it must be now. Time matters." I could hear him clucking his tongue. That was a good sign. I hated using him like this, but I needed his expertise. "You know if I called Annie she would want you to help find her sister."

"Okay, you've got me on meltdown. Let me phone Annabelle and let her know what's up. Give me those names again."

I could hear a door slam as he re-entered his house and fumbling noises as he searched for pen and paper. I gave him the names. Twenty minutes passed before my cell rang. I pulled off at a park.

"Carson, that general was on the news last night with Senator Patrick Ackerman. Big square-faced dude with a gut that makes him look about 8 months along. There was a ceremony. Ackerman gave some medal to Stanchy." He began humming, and I could hear the soft tap of keys. He must have set the phone down next to the computer. "Here it is. There was a big ceremony at Pendleton. He received a commendation medal for meritorious achievement. It says the senator was a major general in the Marines and worked with Stanchy in the Gulf, years ago."

I waited, listening to Hub as he hummed the United States Marine song. "Anything else?"

"Not really. The article's mostly about stats on the Marines and Camp Pendleton. Oh, Stanchy's the father of three girls. I can't imagine that face reproducing on a female. Pure voodoo. He's been a general for fourteen years."

So Stanchy was big time, but the lowest level of generals. I wondered why he had not advanced further in so many years. But then I didn't. He probably messed up along the way.

I realized I'd been grinding my teeth. I watched as a group of kids played soccer in the park.

"Anything else?" asked Hub.

"Check the affiliations of each and see if any other names pop up in the group. This is organized and it appears to be military related. Let me think it over for a bit and maybe I'll have more to research, but this should tighten some of the strings up." I started my car. "Anything on the other two?"

"Not yet. Give me a while. I need to call Annabelle. I may have her come down."

Alarms went off in my head. Two parallel lines creased between my eyes, and I tried to rub them out. "No experiences, all right?" I was talking about his drug therapy, and he knew it.

"Okay, but she's in a bad way. We'll only do dry runs. I can do that if we have a good night sky."

"She's a strong woman, but she's fragile right now. She just needs someone to talk to."

"You're the psychologist."

I clicked the phone off.

A couple hours later, I stood up and rubbed my neck. The clock on the library wall told me I'd been here nearly two hours. I tried to do research on my own after talking to Hub about what he'd come up with so far. The librarian kept eyeing me as if I didn't belong. I'd never seen anyone who could scrunch their lips so hard without sucking on a lemon. She could. I smiled for the thirteenth time. She gazed quickly down at her desk as if something important had arrived. I paced around the stacks of books, slapping my yellow notepad at my thigh. The librarian made a call—security probably. She kept peeking over her shoulder.

A meek little man with hunched shoulders came up the stairs. He glanced up long enough to see me, hesitated, watched the librarian nod and then with great effort walked my way. He had thin hair, wire rimmed glasses, and moved as if pushing water.

"Are you finding everything okay?" His voice tried to sound masculine but came out froggy.

I realized I still had cuts on my face and arms from dancing with Luden. I thought I'd try humor. "I'm trying to figure out the differences in pickles. Dill is sweet with a touch of tartness. Bread and butter are cut in a waffle pattern, and Gherkins, even the name sounds small. Do you realize there's no fat in pickles?" The meek little man stepped back a step and sucked his lips into his mouth, then held his hands at his chin as if praying.

"What's your take on it?"

He froze for the longest time. Finally, he said, "What? . . . Pickles?"

I waited a few beats. Then I smiled, "I'm kidding you."

He unclamped his hands and a touch of color flushed through his face. His relieved eyes met mine and a lopsided smile gleamed. He nodded happily.

"No, I'm just researching some old Marine friends and had to get up and walk a bit." I held out my hand, "I'm Carson." We shook.

"Miss Thornton wondered if you are okay. You know, with the bruises and all," he lied.

I felt along my cheek and forehead. "I'm fine but let me give you some advice. Don't ever take in a stray cat." I snarled my face and scratched the air with my cupped hands.

"My Buttercup loves to play, but there are times she opens up my forearms. I know she doesn't mean to," he whispered.

My cell vibrated in my pocket. He pointed to an empty study room about twelve feet to my right. I nodded and walked away. It was Hub. He jabbered for five minutes about re-incarnation, then mentioned something about General Stanchy. He lost me on the significance. This happens every time he gets excited about something or other. I finally had to stop his tirade.

"That's interesting," I broke in, "but tell me about any specifics you found on the three."

Hub let out a long exhale as if deflating a beach ball. "Sometimes you vacuum all the fun out of life. This is interesting stuff."

"Hub, I have limited time. The longer it takes, the further away Tia could be, the worse off she could be."

149

"Annabelle's almost here." The phone dropped, and I could hear him fumbling around on the floor. "Crap, I'm nervous. This is such an enveloping sensation. I'm like a teen ringing the doorbell for his prom date. This isn't me."

I laughed. "You love women with problems." I watched the librarian poke her head around a shelf to check on me. The meek little man had disappeared, but it was practically closing time.

"No, it's not that. Yes, she has the drained look of loss, but Annabelle's still solid—holds her neck high. She's amazing."

"Sandoz, Bandy, and Stanchy. Please."

"Fine," he said. "Sandoz lives in Omaha, Nebraska. He's on vacation from a recruiting office. W-2s show he makes barely enough to pay the rent on his year-old house in the subs. Wife, two kids, one from a previous marriage. But get this, he drives a yellow Hummer. There's a 28-foot Eliminator racing boat registered to him and a 2012 Porsche 911 GTS registered to his wife, Sandy. His work thinks he's on his boat somewhere. I called his house; the wife and kids are there; all she said was that he's out."

I sat down on the conference table in the study room. "You think he was there?"

"Not at all. I don't think he's been home for a while. Also, I don't think she cares."

I digested that for a moment with the information I had found on the three of them. They were all at Camp Lejeune at the same time, along with Luden. Sandoz and Bandy were arrested with three others for drunk and disorderly at Myrtle Beach. I'd jotted down the other three names.

Hub continued, "Bandy has a wife, no kids, and he opened a bar by the river five months ago. It's called Bandy's."

"Clever."

"He's been in and out of rehab eleven times in seven years. Heavy alcoholic. A few arrests–marital disputes and bar fights."

"Alcoholic with a bar; life couldn't be better."

"Yeah, my thoughts, too," Hub paused.

I could hear his fingers punching down on the keyboard. No wonder he always wears those keys out, banging them like he's pounding in nails. Ms. Thornton, the librarian, did another walk by. I waved with my fingers fluttering. She sucked more lemons.

"He also hasn't been home for a week or so. At a tavern

convention, his wife said. Do they even have conventions for beer bars? His wife sounded relieved that he was gone, too. He picked up two bullets in Iraq. One in the shoulder and one took off a major part of his left ear. Probably why he wears his hair longer than military. He also works at a recruiting office. I found a letter of recommendation from, guess who?"

"Brigadier General Robert Stanchy."

"The very one. Looks like the three stayed in each other's lives for a long time after meeting in North Carolina."

"You see Luden or Mansell in any of your searches?"

"No, but I didn't check. You want me to? Never mind I'll do it," Hub said.

"E-mail me everything you have." The librarian tapped on the door. I held up two fingers and mouthed two minutes. She purposefully glanced at her watch.

"One other thing. When I was checking on the general, a vibe arose. Someone wanted to know who was looking over his files. I got a ping."

"What? You actually had someone back searching to your computer or another intuition?"

"Both. Psychic confirmation and physical fact."

Ms. Thornton tapped on the door glass. I felt like throwing my phone at her. I smiled and turned away. "How close did they get."

"Right on the door steps. But I turned them in another direction and shut down. I'll have to completely re-route to get back in."

"This sounds as if someone more than the Marines is monitoring the general. Perhaps one of the acronyms. Be careful. In fact, stop your search on him for a while."

I told him I'd call first thing in the morning and walked out of the room. I pointed a hand pistol at the librarian. Her eyes widened and she began shuffling papers.

27

Carson

A hushed cell rang inside the bag I'd just finished packing. *"Highway to Hell,"* muffled under boxers, shirts, and neatly folded pants. I dumped everything out on the motel bed and scrambled through the pocket of last night's unwashed khaki shorts. The music stopped as I pulled it out. Hub had called. So had Annie, thirty minutes earlier. Maria had phoned late last night, I must have absorbed her call into a dream. I gazed back at my jumbled heap of clothes. I really needed to wash them. I had scrubbed the T-shirt I had on in the sink with the tiny bar of hotel soap, rinsed it in the shower, and hung it out to dry last night over the balcony. It stuck to my chest where the cloth was still damp.

I pushed 3, the speed dial to Hub. He answered in his morning voice, with the tone of someone talking through a paper tube on way too much caffeine. He explained that Sergeant Bandy and Private Sandoz had both purchased tickets to San Diego International. They had arrived last night, two hours apart. Sergeant Bandy had made a reservation in Carlsbad, California, for a mid-sized car and a three-night stay at a Fairfield Inn with two double beds.

I decided Southern Cal' would be a nice place to visit and booked an overpriced flight for that afternoon. I doubted Bandy and Sandoz were there to see a whale jump through a hoop.

I listened to Maria's cell ring as I drummed my foot on the pavement.

"It's about time you called me back," she answered.

"That's a charming hello."

She let out a long "Holaaaaaa," as if falling off a cliff.

"How about a vacation?" I asked.

"Wow, I don't have anything going for the next seven or eight days. Hub would see that as a sign of paranormal mind communication or something." She paused for a full ten seconds. "I assume this is a working trip and has a lot to do with finding Tia? But Carson, a nice hotel, not one of those *you* stay in to be inconspicuous. I don't like mice, or winos, in the stairway. Got it?"

"Uh huh." I leaned against a pillar.

"Okay, but it better be somewhere with rolling surf, white sand, and Gringos baking like lobsters on hotel towels."

I chuckled. A man and a woman walked by in a hushed argument. The man struggled to keep up with her quick step. "So, eight nights in Newark, New Jersey at the finest budget motel wouldn't suit my Mexican princess?"

"I'm hanging up."

"How about San Diego and the finest hotel?"

"Only if they have seared tuna and rows of insincere waiters." I could hear her neighbor's yapping dog in the background. She must have been out weeding in her amazing garden.

"We leave today at four-fifteen."

"Surely you jest? I am a woman and a Chicana. There is packing and a million little things."

"What time?"

"A lady of my reputation couldn't possibly fly out before eleven-ish tomorrow."

"I'll text you the info and we'll meet in San Diego."

We talked for several more minutes about Carmella, her house plant that died, and the dinner I missed. I told Maria about the connection of the three Marines and gave a vague reason for the vacation.

Sand molds of my feet followed me as I walked the beach that night. I had called my old friend from college, Luis Brown. He became one of the A-listers after leaving the prosecutor's office for politics. He sounded good, even happy, with his third wife. He had the clout to get me invited to a fund-raising party the Governor's wife was putting on for some children's hospital. Luis found out that General Robert Stanchy and Mrs. Stanchy had RSVP'd for the event with six guests.

Jef Huntsman

Luis had been one of my roommates in Autumn Hall. He had called me a few years back to find his 15-year-old daughter when she fell in love and ran off with a 22-year-old druggy of a boyfriend. I had found them two days later, just after midnight, at a truck stop in Nevada. The love had faded. She was terrified and speeding on amphetamines. She wadded up eight napkins and laid them out between us as I talked to her. She told me she wanted away from the freak. He was in the bathroom shooting up heroin.

Luis arrived for his daughter five minutes later from the motel we were staying at. He almost killed the boy. I had to break my friend's rib with my foot to loosen his grip on the loser's trachea. Later, wrapped in bandages, Luis thanked me. He tried to slip me a check for a thousand dollars. I ripped it up and tossed it at him. That cemented our friendship even deeper.

The beach was empty and the moonlight cast a silvery glow. Maria would arrive about one-thirty the next day. We would attend the party at eight o'clock. Luis had set me up with formal attire. Maria explained in some detail that she would pick out a new dress for the party. She was as excited as a prom date.

The ocean breeze cleared my mind. I made mental notes, then transferred them to a recording on my cell. I couldn't help thinking that something was churning for all three to gather in one place. And how many more soldiers were in on whatever this was? Something clanged in the back of my mind. I couldn't seem to bring it forward enough to grasp it. The more I tried, the softer it became. Then there was nothing, but the feeling that it had almost surfaced.

My mind whirled and I knew I couldn't sleep yet, so I ran barefoot along the wet sand for about three miles, turned and sped at a quick pace back to the hotel. I'd thought of something to do. As futile as it might be, the thought energized me.

Huffing and puffing, I put my hands on my knees and bent over as I waited a few moments for my breathing and heartbeat to slow. Sweat dripped off my face onto the carpet of my room. After a couple of minutes, I stripped, jumped in a cool shower, threw on tan slacks and a green golf shirt, and raced out into the night air.

I found the Fairfield Inn. The only description Hub could get of their car was a blue mid-size, either a Toyota Corolla or a Chevrolet Cruze. I had no idea what a Cruze looked like, but I

154

assumed it would have the raised letters on the back. Searching the parking lot, I found two Corollas, one red and the other an atrocious green. Hub could have the color wrong.

I pulled over in an empty parking space and dialed Hub. My watch said two-twenty-three a. m. in bold numbers. The call went to voice mail. I left a quick message. As I began to back out of the space, Hub called.

"Sorry, I didn't mean to wake you." I did mean to wake him. It was important.

"Not a problem, man. Annabelle and I are just sampling some new tea I just got in from Havana. Castro didn't play well with others, but he knew how to grow tea leaves. Not himself, of course, probably poor farmers under the watchful eye of Cuban military, or worse, their police. I understand this was one of his favorite herbal remedies after age dwindled him to a wheelchair and left him gazing out from his balcony."

"How's Annie?" I bit hard into my lip, not sure I really wanted to know.

"She's mellowed. All that inner turmoil vanquished. She shines this perfect grin that never leaves her face. It's fantastic. You should talk to her."

A beep told me I was blocking somebody's late arrival. I pulled the rental back into the parking space. "Not now. I'm wondering if you had a unit number on Bandy's hotel."

"Oh, yeah," a pause, "let me go check. My mind's a bit muddled for numbers right now." I heard giggling in the background and an unoiled door opened and shut. A couple of minutes later, he came back on the phone.

"101. Ones and zeros man; it's a sign. This whole thing has something to do with computers and abstract thinking. Government issued, I would assume. Let me meditate on this; do a little mind travel. I'm positive I can come up with something on my voyage. Wow, ones and zeros. I should have noticed that before."

I knew better than to discount his sorcery practices. I always figured he had a fifty-fifty chance of coming up with something, though he was luckier than that. "Sail away my friend. I've got to check this out."

I got out of the car and walked around to where 101 should

be. Two vans with "Go Trojans" scrawled on the windows, a motorcycle, and several tiny rentals sat in the row in front of 101. I sauntered back to my car.

In a last attempt, I drove around the area to find a bar they might be in. After two parking lots of late night drinkers, I found a blue Toyota Corolla parked at a strip joint called the "Zip Up." I glanced at their pictures Hub had sent on my cell and walked in. I was greeted by a linebacker asking for a twenty-dollar cover. The two tens slipped into his pocket. He nodded me in.

I never understood the fantasy of men thinking they will go back to their hotel with one of those dancers, boasting to friends at work; then telling their wives what a hard time they had on the road. The girls—they're in it for the money. Unless it's one of those sleazy outfits that takes a sizeable cut of their tips and an even larger cut of the take on prostitution in the back room. Those girls I feel sorry for. The men, not at all.

Sergeant Bandy and Private Sandoz sat at a table in front of the main dance pole. The girls were changing shift. The music was loud, drinks watered down, and strobe lights were spiraling around the room. Both Marines were bar stool soft.

I ordered a beer from the bar, keeping myself to their backs. The barmaid, aged by a rough life, set a draft on a cardboard circle and waited for my money. I gave her a twenty. Twenty minutes later, she still hadn't brought my change. Stiff price.

Sandoz and Bandy were well lit. They spilled drinks and patted each other on the back. A new batch of three girls came out and Bandy gave a loud *oorah*. I thought about grabbing the table next to them but didn't want them to recognize me tomorrow night at the fundraiser. That is, if their beloved general had invited them, which I was fairly sure he had.

I kept an eye on them for twenty more minutes, then decided nothing would happen tonight. I downed the last of my twenty-dollar beer, nodded at the bartender and got up to leave, hoping she didn't expect a tip on top.

I was sound asleep by 3:45 a.m.

28

Carson

My heart thumped a couple of extra beats as I watched Maria's bouncy gait when I pulled into the pickup area. She led two large bags and a hefty leather purse across the asphalt. They floated behind her like sailing birds. Her thick black curls were tossed off her shoulders; I had missed her but hadn't realized how much until this moment.

We embraced, holding each other until the jerk in the car behind us honked. I told her she could freshen up at the hotel before we grabbed lunch. I was starved. Maria lifted a brow as she dispensed instructions to instead take her to a mall she had found online.

I dropped her off at the entrance to an open-air mall. I wasn't about to sit outside the changing room and watch ladies haul truckloads of try-ons, a ritual I had subjected myself to once and vowed to never do again. I had almost chewed my tongue off from boredom that time. I never understood how I could pick up three shirts, a pair of shoes, and two pairs of pants in the time it takes Maria to go up the escalator. Of course, she turns out stunning, and I turn out, well, me.

The Governor's house made the Sistine Chapel look insignificant. It was more of a hotel than a home, with carved entrance doors you could walk circus elephants through. The reception room spread out from the center with inlaid wood in a pattern of lights and darks, radiating like a geometric sun. Emerald green carpet framed the room below a high ceilinged upper balcony. I wondered if the Chargers had ever played there.

Maria and I followed a pack of smug bankers and their

wives. The flow of partygoers funneled out into a delta that opened onto what might be mistaken as a golf course. At least a hundred white-clothed tables were placed strategically around the park. Lanterns with numbers were surrounded by a wreath of fresh flowers and dotted each table. Later I realized the numbers corresponded to our invitation, a caste system of peasants and royals set in specific islands on the vast lawn. Our table sat in the shade of a weeping willow but still far enough away from the buffet tables to make getting a plate a journey.

I began humming Carly Simon's old hit about walking into a party. When I got to the part about his shirt being apricot, Maria delicately elbowed me in the sternum. I gasped. She had hit me in a tender spot that was still healing from my talk in the forest with Luden. She grinned. I glared. A rental stage lay a distance from us. Soft rock from a fourteen-piece band feathered through the chatter of meeting and greeting.

We walked toward the food, more with the intent of finding something to do than anything else. Long tables were filled with shrimp as big as a young girl's hand, crab claws, sliced tenderloin, fruit of every color, and elegant salads. A row of white clad servers stood behind each table, waiting with arms folded to begin serving the feast.

"I'm famished," said Maria. "Don't the rich ever eat? Or do they just parade the food? Their bodies appear to be eating. And well."

"Protocol, my dear. The banquet is laid out, then the Governor must give a lengthy welcome speech, then food."

"My new, beautiful dress will fall off my starved bones by that time."

"Should we slip over and run with the bowl of shrimp?"

"Now you're talking."

"Patience," I whispered in her ear. Her frown deepened even more.

I noticed Luis and his wife thirty feet away, talking to a group of black-hatted men. He saw me and nodded to his left.

On the far side, a gentle slope dropped to a flat plane of grass and waves of sun heat. As we walked closer, we found tables spaced like an overstuffed restaurant. That area had its own buffet laid out without the charm of the rest of the party. No orchids. At the edge of the drop, I saw a full table of loud-talking Marines in full uniform. Sandoz and Bandy sat on opposite ends of the circle.

"I see it in your eyes," said Maria. "Those are the naughty boys you're searching for."

"Yep." My lip curled in and I made a smacking sound. "The far north and the guy just opposite spilling good beer all over the tablecloth. I need the names of everyone at that table." I watched them and thought for a minute. "I'll wander down, try my Navy commander persona and get to know those boys."

"Noooo," Maria commanded. "You really want them to know you yet? Give me five minutes, and I'll have everything you need."

"Maria, these guys are dangerous, and I don't even know how dangerous. I'll figure it out."

Maria let go of my hand and shook her rump. She walked quickly down the slope right toward the table. I hated it, but I knew there was no way of stopping her without drawing attention.

The table of Marines all smiled as if they'd hit the jackpot. A corporal stood up and offered her his seat. She declined. Within seconds, they were all laughing at whatever she said. Bandy tried to grab her by the leg. She slapped him so hard that I could see the facial surprise and redness from where I stood. She shook a finger at him. They all laughed.

Ten minutes later she walked by me, signaling with her eyes for me to follow. I waited a few beats, then walked in a semi-circle toward her. As I came up behind her, she was texting. Maria turned to say something, but a big fellow in a grey hat and wide-striped coat barreled in and blurted, "I'm Sanderson, Amal Sanderson. My law office is right down by the beach in Newport. I can work on an affidavit, while my bare feet tingle in the surf. You two friends of the bride or groom?"

We forced out a laugh. It was probably the same line he'd used for hours. He wanted everyone to think he was a funny guy, but that line was all he had. He stood waiting for us to speak. We both shook his clammy hand, talked to him for a few minutes, and noticed someone we had to see. He took it well. Probably happened a lot to ol' Sanderson.

"I texted you all the names of those dangerous cowboys down there," Maria said sarcastically. "I didn't get all the ranks, sorry."

I leaned in and gave her a hug, my nose taking in her wonderful scent. "Have I told you how beautiful you are lately?"

"No, but while I have you in this mood, keep going. Earn a few points."

I backed away from her and held her by the shoulders. "I could go on for hours."

"Please do." She crossed her arms.

"Here comes Luis and his lovely wife."

"Por supuesto, you give her a compliment, but not your señorita princess?" Two defined lines scrunched between her eyes.

Over the shoulder of my friend, I spied General Stanchy and the governor talking with someone I recognized. My international playboy, Senator Patrick Ackerman, stretched his neck out in a heated argument with Stanchy. The governor motioned with his hands, trying to quiet their conversation down.

I excused myself—too abruptly, judging by the glare on Maria's face. Moving quickly, I headed for a small grove of birch rising from a thick display of yellow flowers with emerald leaves. As I leaned down to gently smell a bouquet, I stood eight feet from the three gentlemen. Years of surveillance taught me to dabble in reading lips and focus on intimate conversations. This wasn't one of them. The men spoke in hushed loud voices with arms and stance changing rapidly.

"You need to solve this . . . There's a seventy-percent pull on it, and I'm looking upward." The senator's eyes narrowed.

"Fine, fine. The last two shipments have been stalled due to rough weather. I can't control hurricanes. Maybe you can." Stanchy puffed his chest, but it deflated quickly.

The senator moved in closer and mumbled something. The governor backed up, held his hands up as if in warning, then walked away. General Stanchy had the curved back and red face of a man who was just kicked between the legs.

I strolled back to Maria.

The governor's wife, a petite redhead, hurried over from a pack of expensively dressed women and grabbed the Governor by the elbow. She escorted him to the podium. She had the taut face of several trips to a high-end nip-and-tuck-boutique. Both she and her husband wore shining smiles showing expensive dental work.

Several taps of the microphone and everyone turned toward the stage. A thin, white-suited man stood and grasped the microphone stand as if caressing a cat. "Ladies and gentlemen," he pronounced, "it is my pleasure to introduce Governor Stannack and his lovely wife, Barbara, the hosts of this wonderful event." He held up his arms and lifted his neck as if angels were approaching. The band played a few notes and all the hungry visitors with thick wallets applauded.

Maria giggled and shook her head. "You Caucasians are a silly bunch. These people need to get their stiff asses to a Mexican barbeque." I noticed a few of the people at our table sat straighter and clamped down on their lips.

The governor grabbed the mike, thanked everyone for coming and then gave a short speech that ended with his ad for the next term. His wife talked for thirty minutes, primarily dropping names. More applause and cliquish chatter. Then the governor leaned in and said, "Let's eat, but keep your pocketbooks at the ready." I'm not sure his wife was finished.

Maria mumbled Spanish profanity, then steered me toward a line forming at one of the buffet tables.

I texted Hub the names Maria acquired and some of my overheard conversation. We took our place in the buffet line. Even with four separate tables of food, we were back far enough I thought I was watching from a commercial plane. Maria rolled her eyes and pretended to pass out from starvation.

Hub called back just as I sat down to eat. I excused myself from the table. Maria listened intently to the boutique owner next to us and her girlfriend talk about a new band—Maria's fork moved in rapid scooping motions as she nodded in full agreement. I wasn't real sure she even noticed my cell rang, or that I had excused myself.

"Hey, man, jackpot. All the boys on the list did a stint at North Carolina at the same time, except your Ken Van Dorius. He's a civilian procuring military equipment and supplies. He's worked the circuit – Afghanistan, Honduras, El Salvador."

"He seemed pretty chummy with the others," I said.

"Get this – the name Van Dorius set off fireworks in my skull. The Fourth of July kind that goes on for thirty minutes or more. I focused, had some jasmine tea, a few yoga squats and voila, it came. Oh, crap!"

I waited, wondering if the signal dropped. Silence. "Hello .
. . Hub?" Minutes passed.

"Sorry, one of those big lion-face spiders was stringing a
web from the counter to the toaster. I had to flick her in a jar and
haul her out. I showed her several much better places for her web.
Nothing shortens a date more than a giant spider and her enormous
web strung over the food prep area."

I heard water running on the other end. "Hub?"

"I'm here, just cleaning up. Okay, where was I?"

"Van Dorius."

"Oh yeah, like I said, neurons were crackling and all of a
sudden I remembered that when I researched the general, the name
Van Dorius kept coming up. The general and Ken's Dad have an
overseas trade business together. It's listed as corn and grain
export and import; only they never buy any corn. They ship
military electronics–laser sights, weapon parts, high-end tracking
devices, and much, much more. There's a full website. I felt
creeped just viewing it."

I began writing notes on a napkin. Maria caught my eye.
She waved a crab claw at me then took a drawn-out bite. "You're
missing out," the crab claw said.

"Get this," Hub broke in as my stomach churned. "They
named it–Best Buy Livestock Feed. Now with his son as a buyer
for the good old USA, sales are listed at seven hundred and twenty
million a year. Not a bad haul. Especially when Uncle Sam's
checks never bounce. There are three other businesses listed
through information: A peat moss farm in Iowa, a turkey
processing plant in Kentucky, and a swimming pool supply
wholesaler in Modesto, California. All of them are listed as
corporations of daddy Van Dorius and son. I'm still digging."

"That's a lot of money." I moved further over into the
shade. The heat caused more hunger. As I glanced back to our
table, everyone seemed to be getting along just fine. "Anything
else on the others?" I listened to keys being slammed and Hub's
humming.

"Press Eagins, actually Preston, is a real estate broker. He
has a live-in girlfriend, doesn't pay much income tax, so he either
hides profits or he's one lousy salesman. Amyl Nanda left the

Marines five months ago. No notable means of income. His Facebook page said something about his attending college, but no verification yet." I heard keys clicking hard. "This Niles Sanderson lives in Detroit. I got a chuckle out of him owning a brand-new Toyota Corolla. Brave man–buying overseas. He's managing a Marine recruiting office with a staff of two. Takes care of his mother. She's at stage three lung cancer."

I waited for more. I guess Hub was waiting for a reply. "Okay." I glanced at my napkin notes. Nothing else came. "How's Annie?"

"She's home and back to work as we speak," he said. "I think she's going to make it. My therapy did wonders. A glow, man, a solid glow. She left here all Christmas lights and Easter baskets."

"Yeah, that's it. Must be the Hub therapy." I shook my head, wondering what happened this time, though I didn't want to know. "Call if anything else comes up. None of this relates to Tia, as far as I can tell, but I know there's a piece missing." I hung up and went back to cold shellfish and sun-warmed salad dressing.

Later I danced with Maria to the band's version of new pop hits. I tripped on the uneven grass as I watched Niles break off from the group and head toward the pool. With swift steps, I hauled Maria by the hand in pursuit. She pulled my hand from hers. Within seconds, her face lost the irritation of being yanked from a slow dance. She stopped abruptly. A relaxed grin crossed her face. "You're working," said Maria. "You chase them, and I'll check out that tray of star-shaped brownies for any clues."

I nodded. *Love the way she flows with my crazy lifestyle.* I began striding toward the plateau of lawn where the pool rested. Niles stood outside one of the dressing rooms that had a little boy peeing on daisies stenciled upon the door. I approached. Cute.

"Hey, Lieutenant, where're you stationed?" He looked over at me with puzzled eyes.

"I'm in Detroit as a recruiter. Boring stuff, but I did a tour searching Taliban in that wasteland they call Afghanistan. Miserable heat and earth you couldn't grow sage brush in. You musta been in?"

"Yeah," I answered, "I was a jarhead, spent some time in Iraq and Afghanistan. Mostly waited for orders while the sailors floated us around the Gulf."

He smiled, "Been there." The bathroom door opened, and he turned away. "Later."

I strolled slightly down the hill to where I could intercept Niles again. Maria started to walk in my direction. I scooted her off with a quick flick of my fingers. Her lips rounded and she veered the other way. I watched Niles come my way and started to intercept him. Glancing to the right though, I realized his Camp Lejeune group was watching me. Narrowed eyes spoke enough to alert me. They were wondering who I was, and why I kept following Niles. I rapidly decided to ignore them and sprinted past Niles. I came up quick on a man in a suit, stopped, and put my arm around him.

"Sonny, how you doing?"

He glowered over his sizeable dark glasses. There was a silence, then a lift of blond eyebrows. "I'm not Sonny. Who the hell are you?" He tried to shake off my arm.

I held him firm. "Look, my friend. I'm security, and I'm watching a couple of guys over there." I smiled and warned, "Don't look. I just need to make sure they aren't the hecklers from the governor's water rights meeting last week." I stood for a few more seconds. Perspiration dropped down his neck. "Now shake my hand, nod, and laugh."

He did. I nodded and walked away. The Marines had lost interest in me and were sipping on their imported beer. I heard Maria's laugh and turned in that direction. She was gabbing with two other women. Complete silence ensued as I stopped behind her. After a few seconds, the three giggled about something I would never know.

I thought I was better at this, but Sandoz, Press, and one other Marine, whose name escaped me, came up and stood next to me. They had that alpha-dog look in their eyes. The other two women scuttled away. I had screwed up somewhere.

Sandoz moved in close to my face. "What's your interest in us, homeboy?" His voice had a deep growl to it. Probably scared the willies out of fourth graders and architects. "You had your girlie here coming on to us like a whore in heat."

"Watch your tongue soldier." I stepped closer. "Truthfully, I don't give a shit about any of you. You trying to pick me up?" I

164

crossed my arms.

Maria's eyes opened as big as I'd ever seen them. She bit down on her bottom lip. At first, I thought she had some sudden fear, then I realized she was just plain mad. I made a quick movement with my head for her to stand down and walk away. She shook her head.

"You little boys go find another playground or my man here will turn me loose on you stupid rednecks."

Sandoz laughed, and the two others followed. He glared at me. Sandoz began to say, "You better keep your girl . . ."

Maria drove her spiked heel just above his black leather shoe, stepped forward, and kneed him in the groin. Her new dress never wrinkled.

His eyes went blurry as he bent over grabbing his thighs and took short, deep breaths. The other two glanced from Maria to me, trying to figure out what to do next. Fists tightened. Out of nowhere, General Stanchy stepped in saying, "This is neither the time nor the place for this bullshit, Marines. Get back to your table."

Sandoz hobbled off. The other two marched away without glancing back.

"I'm not quite sure what happened here, but I'm sorry." The general had a treble voice with a two-word rhythm to it as if reading a poem. "My boys don't usually act like that."

"Not a problem, Sir," I said.

He turned to Maria. "You okay, little lady?"

"I can handle my own."

General Stanchy laughed. "So it seems. Can I buy you two a drink?"

"We'd be happy to have a drink with you, but they're free," I smirked as I toasted with a fake glass.

"So they are." He looped his arm through mine and Maria's and led us away. "Let's go down some of the governor's best scotch. Or perhaps you'd prefer wine, young lady?"

"Scotch is good."

I knew she'd prefer wine.

He led us over to the affluent side of the yard, signaled a waiter by a lift of his close-shaved chin, and sat us down. He leaned in with the breath of garlic, seafood, and booze.

Jef Huntsman

There was a definite interrogation from the general. He had the air of knowing how to find things out. I'd been through this before but with much crueler techniques. Still, I was starting to feel like the Taliban before we left his presence.

29

Carson

I woke up about two a.m. There was a scratching at the door and voices in the hall. I slipped my long body out of the covers, trying not to awaken Maria. She purred. Glancing through the peephole, I saw an empty hallway. My pants hung over the desk chair. Without much trouble, I zipped them up and yanked a yellow T-shirt over my head. I headed out without my 9 mm Walther.

The front desk sat quietly while a flicker of light shone from the side office. Tan industrial carpet had good spring on my bare feet. Surveying the entry, it had an abandoned feel to it, though in a few hours suitcases would roll and feet would scamper. The double doors opened. I walked out into the early hours–no moon. A lime-green Mini drove down the street in a hurry. I walked past the drop-off and peered around the side of the building. My rental sat hidden by an outcropping of curb filled with a tall, thick hedge. In the darkness, I saw nothing. My teeth clamped as asphalt bit into my bare feet.

I felt for the gun at my waist, then realized it remained locked in the room safe. A rat scurried by, startling me. Laughing quietly, I chided myself, it was just a parking lot filled with cars, nothing else. I decided to take a glance at the rental to make sure it was locked.

As I wandered to the car, something seemed askew. Two more steps and I realized the driver's window had been smashed out. I hurried for a closer inspection. Maybe it was just reflective light. No. Glass had been spilled onto the seat. The glovebox gaped open. Maria's empty sack lay tossed out the window, and the trunk sat ajar. I started to open the door, careful not to step on any glass fragments.

I smelled beer and cologne just before my head bounced hard off the curved roof of my rental. My mind went musty and leaden, then things happened fast. Punches pounded my lower back. I reached behind me, half turning, and grabbed a shirt. Buttons popped just as a pipe clanged hard into my forearm. Another whack. I felt my brain bounce against my skull. Two kicks were fired to the back of my knees and my legs noodled. I fell forward and smashed into the car door. My head slammed again. I tried to reach for something but only grabbed empty space. My face hit the pavement. Two of them kicked my ribs. I tried to cover the blows, but tendons and muscles failed. I felt myself losing consciousness. A horrid blackness filled my head, though I could still feel boots slamming into my sides. I passed out.

Water splashed me awake. I lay still while wetness dripped from me to the ground. By the smell, it was a cola—sweet. They stood me up. My eyelids were like locked doors. I tried over and over to open them, but nothing. One of them leaned down and spat on my face. My eyes opened with enough of a slit to make out a figure. His breath reeked of beer. He held me up by my hair. It was Sandoz.

"You and your bitch stay out of our business," he said. "Next time you'll be wearing a flag, Marine," he let me fall. I didn't have enough in me to cover my face. "You understand?" he asked.

His boot jarred my teeth. That was the last thing I remembered.

30

Carson

Hospital smells brought me out of nightmares. Being awake wasn't much better. I rolled through blurry vision and pain meds. Maria told me I'd been there two days. It took me the first day to understand what she was saying. The second day the catheter was removed–thank God–and things started to come back to me. The first trip to the bathroom, I pretty well scared myself, this battered, stitched, puffy face stared back at me. My stance was hunched over–unsure of itself. I dropped my gaze to my arms and legs, blackened and cut in the stark light. I clung to my IV pole as though it was a cane. I hated the fact Maria had to help me back to my bed.

My recuperation marched forward at a slow pace. I despised the comfort, the irritation of the TV flickering, and all that incessant beeping. At least I knew my ears worked.

They had done a thorough job. The Marines thought I would turn tail and run. They didn't know me. The beating wasn't a deterrent; it put steam into my step. Maybe not today, but soon. Something really bad and profitable was going on. I needed to find out what. Of course, with two broken ribs, the face of a botched Frankenstein, and a swollen cracked jawbone, it might take a while. I couldn't find a part of my body that didn't hurt, but I told Maria I was fine.

The doc said I would be on solid food the next day. I knew there was something wrong when even that didn't interest me. I kept fading in and out of sleep. Maria was taking good care of me, with the sad eyes and voice of someone trying to heal a bird with a broken wing. "Pathetic"—I mumbled to myself. I had been in worse shape than this before–deep in foreign countries with self-serving leaders and religious crazies. My heart cared about nothing but finding Tia. And, smashing the faces of those four bastards. It had given me reason to heal quickly.

"You're going to have a headache for a while," said Doctor Andoz. This was his third visit that I knew of.

"I knew that, without spending years in medical school," I replied.

"You are feeling better. Sarcasm. I love it."

"Be nice to the doctor, Carson, or that headache might get worse." Maria held her flat hand up and gave me a threatening face.

Doctor Andoz laughed. "Ahhh, more sarcasm."

"No, she means it," I said, feigning fear.

He glanced at her stern face. "I think you're right." He lifted the chart. "You are very lucky. Only two broken ribs, like we talked about. The burr hole alleviated the head trauma and most of your cuts and bruises will heal nicely. The small fissure on your bone," He gently touched my jaw, "will fuse over the next month or so. Careful with the gash on your knee, I want you to ambulate but not overdo until the stitches heal a bit more." He patted me on the arm.

I held inside a long groan. My body ached as bad as it looked.

"You will probably be released tomorrow, if you can make yourself ease back into life. What did you say your line of work was?"

"I make charts."

Maria laughed. "Among other things."

"You got those bullet holes making charts?" The doctor's eyebrows raised.

31

Tia

My shoulders pressed into the cage wires. Four eyes of terror gazed back at me. The smell of fear rolled through my nostrils. I could barely move off my elbow, tingles of blood flow made me catch my breath. My eyes cringed as the pain subsided, and I tried to adjust my arm out.

Dried blood spotted down Corrina's muddy face. Her thin features hung gaunt and pale in the silver of moonlight. "None of us have room, girlie," she whispered in harsh tones. Her eyes slashed like claws through me.

"My legs and arms have gone to sleep. I can't help it," I replied. The honeycombed wire bit deeper into my back.

Perri groaned. Her dark hair clung to the sweat on her neck. "Assholes." She spat mud from her cracked lips. Bits of straw were embedded on her far cheek.

"Why the hell did you scream?" fired Corrina. "That wasn't nothing but pebbles on the roof. Those cretins were just trying to scare us." She tried pointing a finger, but her shirt sleeve caught on a nail.

"That was Mati," said Perri. Her teeth glowed between black lips.

"Then why the hell ain't Mati out here in this chicken crap?" Corrina whined.

"She's not the one that snitch Wren saw digging," I said. "Good thing Mati and Lisa didn't get put out in this coop with us. This isn't even as big as my coat closet."

"You're right there, girl," laughed Perri. "Lisa's hips alone would have pressed us through these wires like grated hash browns."

We all giggled, forgetting for a moment we were covered in white feces, cobwebs, and dusty feathers. The tapping of mice feet across the rafters was drowned out.

A squeaky door opened in the distance. It came from the direction of the house. Trees hid the view, but a flicker of porch light made it through the pine needles and leaves. "You three shut up, or I'll toss a badger in there with y'all." Our mouths clamped shut, but muffled laughter kept us from the reality of our situation. We closed our eyes, though I'm sure none of us slept a moment that night. A hard rain hit about sunup.

By late afternoon we were let out, kicked to the ground, and taunted by three of the men—Cedee, Tony, and Sidearm. We huddled together with our arms locked tightly around each other, knees set deep into wet earth. We had blood and wet filth caked to every part of our bodies. A doughy palm popped my jaw. Someone yanked my arm, and I was peeled away from the others. My legs were so cramped I couldn't even stand up. They dragged us to the barn and tossed me in. Corrina landed on my legs in a heap. Perri hit just inside the opening. The door closed and latched. The other girls stood around us, afraid to get too close at first. Then they all came to our rescue, brushing us off and inspecting our wounds.

We whispered a bit, I was confused by the fact not even one of the girls had been assaulted or raped. Why? It made no sense. We decided the captors had to be afraid of someone above them. Who else was there? Where were they taking us? What was going on? Why? Fear silenced me as I held tight to my knees.

Three days later, all of us except the snitch, Wren, were loaded into the back of a semi that arrived in the morning. Wren still had a sizeable black eye from where Corrina had popped her with the digging board. The sky was overcast with a thick black coat like one continuous cloud. There were no wooden crates to put us in. That was a relief. We huddled in blue moving blankets at the front of the trailer as it pulled out and drove down muddy roads. Small unnamed cliques had formed during our time in the barn. I kept close to Corrina, Perri, Lisa, and Mati. Other groups were as small as two and as large as five, like ours. A feeling of safety in comradeship held each of the groups together. It was never talked about, it was just there.

I slept off and on as we traveled for what felt like days—maybe a week. The water jugs were empty. The crates of bananas, oranges, and apples were gone. None of us had eaten for at least a day. My stomach churned. Dizziness seemed to keep us all still. When the truck's brakes screeched and finally the door lifted, thirteen frightened faces peeked out. I hoped, crazily, that we were pulling over for a Big Mac.

Tony and Cedee yanked us out into the cold, wet night. Palm fronds were scattered across the narrow road. I could smell the ocean, and rain, and decay of plants. We walked into the weedy parking lot of an abandoned crappy motel. The remnants of a fountain centered a shell-paved turn-around.

Three men we had never seen before stood with open beers, watching our every move. Peety, the man-in-charge, came from behind a building and nodded to the other five men. Wind swayed the tops of the trees. A cold chill of weather and fright ran through my blood stream. I wrapped my arms tightly across my chest.

Our abductors split us up into three rooms. There were no un-boarded doors or windows, except the entrance. A gecko raced across the littered floor and into a hole in the grimy sheetrock.

Cedee put a battery-powered lantern down in our room. Nineteen-seventies wallpaper curled, trying to escape from the walls. Remnants of orange carpet lay hidden under old handbills, newspapers, and beer cans. Green mold climbed around the door casings. Two of the men dropped a box of tomatoes and a banded bunch of carrots on the floor. One had a serpent tattoo crawling up his weight lifter's arm, disappearing into a tight T-shirt. The other had the face of a sloth. They disappeared then came back with a rusty metal tub of warm soft drinks and four loaves of bread. "Eat up girlies," the sloth said.

Mati scrunched her face. Her Mediterranean heritage lost its color. She glanced over at me.

"Carrot sandwich sounds wonderful to me," said Corrina. Her eyes were blackened with loss of sleep. She reached down, took a big bite from a tomato, and began unwrapping the twist tie on the bread.

"What the hell." I tossed tomatoes to Perri and Lisa and grabbed one for myself.

"Okay guys." Mati separated a carrot from the bunch and

began nibbling as if it were an ear of hot buttered corn.

Perri came forward and yanked out soft drinks, and I handed her a couple slices of bread.

"I'm hungry enough to roast that gecko," remarked Corrina. I think we all felt the same.

We all hunched down as thunder slashed through the night and the short fuse of lightning lit the room through the cracks in the boarded-up windows.

32

Carson

The sun glowed through misted clouds in orange and red hues. I winced as the car turned right, off the asphalt. Even perfect shocks couldn't lessen the impact as the car dropped and bounced onto semi-packed gravel.

Maria glanced at me, "Whoops."

We passed over the Sevier River. Cattails and tamarisk crowded the banks. Ducks rippled the ponds. The wind combed through the cornfields, changing the green shade just slightly.

It felt like home. Even the bumpy ride breathed a pleasant feeling into my lungs. As we turned through my gate, I couldn't wait to put my feet down on my few acres of earth.

Maria opened the door carrying a few groceries in. She almost punched me when I bent down to pick up the sacks. "Make you some dinner?" she said.

I didn't answer her right away.

"Carson?"

I strolled over to the fire pit. "How about I start a fire, and we cook those brats we bought, over the flames," her cheeks deflated. I knew she wanted to make something special for my first day back. By the raise of her eyes, I knew brats didn't do it.

After a long expel of air, she said, "Okay."

I hadn't seen this side of her for a long time. I must really look pathetic. I considered milking it but knew her well enough not to. "Can we throw a few ears of corn on the fire too?"

She brightened. "I'll make salsa, chips, and black beans. Can you get the fire going?"

With the sun rimming the western mountains, I finished three brats, two ears of corn, and a heaping bowl of beans. She ate an eighth of everything I downed. We barely talked—mostly sighs of contentment. It wasn't long before the stars gathered and our necks tilted upward. She held my hand for hours. I thought about Tia and where she might be. It was hard not knowing.

About the time we were ready to turn in, my phone sounded. I ignored it and watched the stars flutter. By the third ring, Maria grabbed my cell from my jacket pocket, glanced at the caller, and answered it. She spoke in hushed tones for a moment, then handed the phone to me.

"Hello," I said, as if inconvenienced. I startled for a second when I heard the voice. It was Annie.

"I'm so sorry about what happened. I've been afraid to call and bother you."

I watched the last embers glowing as the wind shifted. "First, it's not your fault. I let my guard down for a split second too long. Second, you call anytime you'd like." I leaned forward as a pain whipped through my side. "We're going to get Tia, and some people are going to pay."

A worried, but business-like voice replied, "You sure? The hospital—it sounded like you'd be down for a long time. I'll pay you for what you've done so far," she paused, "and your hospital bill."

"I'll be fine. Give me a couple more days. I feel like I've pulled hard enough, I'm almost to the end of the string. I'll find her."

"But, I really like you and Maria and . . ."

"I'll find her. If you want to hire someone else, that's fine. But I'm still working on this. I can't let it go now. Tia is not the only one that needs help." My toe kicked a rock. It rolled into the weeds. "I'll find her," I said again, determined.

"I'm embarrassed," Annie stated. "I was hoping you'd say that. I know you care. That means a lot." There was dead space on the phone for thirty seconds, then she came back on. "Can I come down tomorrow and help someway?"

"Maria and I would love to see you. Drop down anytime."

"I'll move things around and be down in the afternoon," came a schoolgirl's excited voice.

The next morning, I slipped out of bed silently, threw on some throw-away sweats and a pair of Nike's and went jogging past the corral and up the mountain road. Slow at first, then limberness settled in, and I pushed the needle up. My wounds grabbed and squirmed, but after a bit, the muscles stretched into a rhythm.

I had to get back in shape. And soon. God only knew what Tia was going through. Revenge wasn't the answer, but perhaps when I found Tia, the Marines and the general would tumble into an arroyo of legal thorns. One could only hope. It had been a full week since the beating. My face still had the coloration of a facelift victim, though the swelling had subsided a touch. My ribs would heal slowly, like many times before.

I gazed out over the valley below. The sound of my lungs filling with air broke the immense silence. Mist hid the river, green crops were being watered by sprinkler lines, and trees guarded my little cabin like a protective fence. Peaceful.

Maria must have seen me coming down the road. She sat smiling in shorts and a thick wool sweater; coffee steam rising from cupped hands. Another cup sat on a log by my camp chair with a blueberry muffin cut into fourths.

"How'd you know?"

She nodded toward the binoculars on the top step.

"Ahhh, a stalker."

"Stalker, my ass. You take off up the mountain, barely out of the hospital, with a face bearing so many colors I'm wondering if Hub slipped *me* something." She pointed a finger gun at me. "You probably scared the poor snakes out there."

I sipped my coffee and smiled.

After forty-five minutes of her talking and me listening, two more cups of coffee, and a light kick to my ankle, she rose. "I'm making breakfast. Give me five minutes." She meant, get up now and meet me in the kitchen.

After huevos rancheros and a plate of potatoes with Anaheim peppers, I laid down on the couch. Sputters of pain rolled up and down my body. I said nothing. Maria tossed the pain pills and a bottle of Ibuprofen onto my belly. I downed a couple of Ibuprofen and eased onto my back. I'd call Hub after a short nap, then maybe take another run up the road.

Leaning over, I clicked my phone on. It said 2:19 p.m. in

fuzzy green letters. I popped up on my side. A sharp jolt and a stretched-out burn ripped my ribs. I held my breath until it subsided into only an ache. Glancing around, Maria wasn't anywhere near. Good. I grabbed my phone from the floor and headed out to the wooden porch off the kitchen. Just as I clicked the on button, it rang.

"Hey, my friend. You're back. Last time I saw you, the morgue orderlies were waiting outside the door."

"Hi, Hub. You trying to brighten my day? I was about to call you. Now I'm not sure why."

"You scared your compadre here! Maria tells me you're feeling better, but you're not acting so smart. Did you really take one of your crucible runs up the mountain?"

"Halfway, I needed to limber up—make myself human again." I leaned into the rail and put pressure on my ribs. It helped, after I found the right amount. "So, anything new on the Marines' or the general's business?"

"How about if I come over there and give you an ancient Hopi Indian release. It'll yank those pain demons right out. I've used it on Emial's chickens. Remember that bad case of fowl pox his hens had three summers ago? It worked on most of them. They were back to laying eggs faster than an automatic weapon."

"Didn't the vet use antibiotics?" I heard a car pull up and park on the far side of my cabin. "Besides, I'm not sure I want to be laying any eggs."

Hub ignored me. "That afternoon, after I'd already healed them." A car door opened, "I'm here."

Hub came around the corner carrying a couple lengths of frayed rope and his damn ceramic medicine pot.

"What the hell is that smell?" I turned my head away.

"Herbs, couple of apricot pits, and a mix of fermented fruit. All natural, no beast flesh." He came up the steps and held it out to me. His other arm lifted from behind his back. "A bottle of wine might help too."

"Hub," I almost gagged at the smell, "get that off my porch and bury it somewhere far away. That's not fermented. It's rotted." I held my arm out and headed for the door. "Replenish the soil with nitrogen. Crap, the native plants might die first." I turned back, "Bring the wine in on my counter."

He followed me in. Maria came up from the basement, grabbed Hub by the shoulders, and pushed him back out. The door shut. She flipped the latch and scooted him with her fingers.

Hub's puzzled face dropped. He leaned forward, his nose pressed into one window pane of my cabin's French doors. "Don't you want to hear about the general?"

"Get rid of Satan's bowl first," said Maria. Her voice hung a notch below yelling.

"You guys are serious?" His forehead furrowed. "I'll put it in the car, but I'm bringing my rope and leather headband. You have matches?"

She gave him a look, and he turned to flee. He was back knocking on the door within a minute. The ropes hung loose around his neck. Maria peered through the window, then opened the door.

Hub tried to give me a hug. I've always been uncomfortable with men and old aunts hugging me. This time was no different, but I knew it would make him feel better.

Hub pretzeled his legs in one of his yoga relaxation postures on the tan carpet. His spine was so straight, I found myself sitting up a touch more erect. It hurt like hell. I irrationally resented him for making me uncomfortable.

"How's the pain meds?" he asked, a gleam in his eye.

Maria slapped him on top of the head.

"Haven't taken them since the second day in the hospital. Tylenol is about as loopy as I want to be."

His mouth opened. He peeked at Maria and clamped his teeth together.

"So, what's up with the general and the boys?"

33

Tia

On a private dock, worn and sagging to the left, an ancient shrimp boat lifted and dropped as the waves pounded in. One side of a double mast was sheared about a third of the way down. The boat clung to the dock like drunk friends in a storm. Waves dropped gallons of water across worn planks, then spurted forth out the drain holes and down into the bilge.

Perri and I were peeking through a slit between pieces of old plywood screwed over the one window. The moon blinked as dark clouds skittered above. Our hearts raced. The wind moaned across the roof and bubbled in the plywood. A wooden crate somersaulted into the door with a loud crack. Rain inched through everywhere.

Peety and a tall man were cinching up the ropes on the boat. The two were braced, their bodies angled against torrential gusts. They tried to hide from the storm behind the captain's cabin, to no avail. Jackets billowed. The hull rammed into the used tires that were nailed in a row on both sides of the dock. The girls screamed, unheard in the thunderous wind and rain. I watched a tree uproot and drop just feet in front of the semi. The storm raged through the night.

By morning, the sun had broken through a rising stack of black clouds. A light breeze whistled softly through the cracks. I had slept curled in against one wall. Stretching, with pops from my neck, I twisted my head and torso in every direction. My temple throbbed. The other girls in my room either stared into nothingness or huddled in shivers and goosebumps.

I gazed through the slats again. The tall man tossed debris from the boat. Shellfish littered the ground. Tony and Cedee were checking for damage to the truck and pointing at the fallen tree. I ate a carrot and a tomato; the bread was all gone.

My body sat cold and tired as I breathed into cupped hands for warmth. The other girls were worn out too, displaying black-ringed eyes and hair like buzzard's nests. Their skin had lost melanin and sported splotchy makeup of bruises and cuts. I was thankful there wasn't a mirror.

Corrina turned from spying outside, "That boat, they're taking us somewhere," her voice caught.

Perri glanced out. "It barely looks seaworthy." She pushed oily black hair from her eyes. "My uncle Willy has a waterskiing boat. Runs through waves like a hot knife through butter. I love lying on the open bow, slick with lotion, the warm sun and a lake breeze. Relaxed like you've never been before." She shook her head, "How the hell did we end up here?"

"Those bastards aren't taking us on that," said Corrina.

Mati moved over toward the boarded window and peeped out. "It's a big boat, but what're all those poles and wires for? Is that a fishing boat?"

"Shrimp boat," I said. They all looked at me like I was crazy. "I did a report in college on shrimp fishing after the gulf oil spill. Got an A." I let out a big exhale, "Like that matters now."

Lisa began crying. Her tears were contagious. The blubbering noise level increased and a group hug ensued.

That afternoon, we watched the men go into the other rooms and haul four girls at a time out to the boat. Screaming and crying could be heard loud enough to make me cringe. Blood seeped from my bleeding lip. Adriana squealed profanities so woven together they flowed as one word. One of the men elbowed her in the face. It didn't slow her down a bit. Acid burned deep in my gut.

We all became silent as four men came toward us from the boat. Room C was next. We began huddling together as stomachs tightened. They couldn't break us apart if we remained a group. Our faces betrayed the truth though; we knew we were helpless to stop them. Hands grabbed tight to each other. We heard the padlock snap open. I could hear thick cries from the boat. As the door opened, we moved like a centipede to the far corner. Deep male laughter reverberated like nails on a chalkboard. A tussle of strength over willpower ensued. Screaming, yelling, vile groping and then knuckles hit Perri's chin. She let go to fight back and disappeared out the door.

A weighty elbow caught me on the bridge of my nose. Blood spurted down my front. My legs wobbled. I felt a loose grab of fingers across my hand. Everything went black.

I woke up with my wrist tied to my leg, a horrid headache, and the smell of an Asian fish market filling my nose. I tried opening my eyes. They stuck together like glue for a moment, then light from a porthole startled me. My face throbbed. I reached up with my one free arm and touched the bridge of my nose. Pain flared to the point of nearly losing consciousness. I wearily glanced around. All the girls were sitting on the floor in the hull of the boat. Perri seemed disoriented. Mati and Corrina looked seasick as did most of the others. Everyone was dazed. Slimy filth gleamed all around. The smell of urine bit my nostrils. How long had I been out? An hour? A day? A week? I had no idea.

Wherever we were, it was close to land. I could hear seagulls squawking. Boards creaked as the men moved around above us. One hatch sat straight above me, another lay beneath a curved metal stairway at the back of the boat. The diesel engine idled.

A growl from my stomach turned painful. I began feeling lightheaded. I curled my legs into my chest and held tight. I dry heaved a couple of times. The bile burned my dry throat.

There was a commotion on deck. I could pick out Peety's low drawl, but the other voice I hadn't heard before. The other girls were gazing up now. The sounds became louder. I closed my eyes and concentrated on the words.

"What do you mean another storm's coming? We've been waiting out this weather for a month or more already," Peety yelled at someone.

"I'm the captain here. I'll tell you when it's safe." It sounded like a fist slammed down on something solid. "There's a Coast Guard weather warning, you stupid piece of shit."

"You're paid to get us to the island and that's what we're doing. It's sunny, no clouds, and the air is as still as an icicle. You dumb idiot, get those engines up to speed."

I heard a smack and something hitting the deck above with a hard thump. A tussle.

"You don't tell me shit. I run this here boat. I ain't taking it through a storm that's only a few hours away." Someone stomped their foot. There was another shuffle of feet above deck.

A shot rang out. Then another. A heavy thud. More feet scrambling. We all sat still as statues.

"Nobody hammers me and gets away with it." It sounded like Peety. A thud of something solid being kicked. "Nobody smacks me."

The air held still for the longest time. I listened as my heart pounded and I held my breath. The girls all stared up; frozen, unblinking.

"You killed the captain," someone above said.

"I'm the captain now. Who knows how to run this damn boat?"

Silence.

"Nesson, you came here with that piece of crap. You know how to run it?" asked Peety. "Don't look at me like you're stupid. Get in there and get this tub moving."

"I don't know how to find . . ."

"What?" There was a tapping of metal on metal. Then a hard suck of air.

"I'll figure it out."

"That's my boy," said Peety. "You two, pick up this lanky son-of-a-bitch and toss him over." Boards creaked from different directions. "I know he had a hose somewhere. Spray this crap off."

I heard more quick movement, then a grunt, and a splash. A moment later someone threw up over the edge.

"Don't get that on this boat," said Peety. "I don't need to be smelling that. Dammit, find that hose and clean this up before it dries. You can vomit after that."

The transmission dropped into gear and the boat lunged backward. Several of the girls fell from the ledge some of us had perched on as a bench, screaming. I held tight to the metal edge. There was a grinding sound and the boat jerked forward. I slipped to the side into Mati and a redhead. We tumbled to the hull floor. Peety called someone an idiot. We waited to see if the vessel kept going before sitting upright on our bench.

An hour or so passed. The fear of not knowing shook my hands and twisted my belly. The back hatch opened and two boots appeared. It was Cedee, He carried a crate down the spiral staircase, the metal creaking with each step. He set it down next to a white metal box I hadn't noticed before and opened each. The crate contained oranges and packages of beef jerky. *What's with these guys and their beef jerky? At the farm, they chewed on it all the time.* The metal box contained bottled water. Crap, why hadn't I noticed that before? Cedee glanced around, staring at us like prize cattle. He spat chew onto the top of the metal box. Brown ran down the side.

Cedee stood by for a moment then disappeared up the winding metal stairs. I heard a lock clamp shut.

With slight hesitation, I slid forward to get to the boxes. My one leg was still tied to my wrist, so I had to move hunched over. I'd tried earlier to untie it with my free hand, but the knot was slippery wet and tight. All the other girls followed. We each looked like the hunchback of Notre Dame. It was too pitiful to be funny. I grabbed two oranges, two waters, and a bag of jerky and slipped, then maneuvered clumsily back into my spot.

As we gulped down the meal, the boat continued its slow up and down motion. Shortly though, we were deep into a gulf storm. The boat rolled and swayed and slammed into wave after wave. Water leaked down through cracks in the deck. I wiped the drench from my forehead, but it didn't help. My hair felt like mud and smelled like shrimp. I listened to frantic feet above and constant shouting. The wind wailed outside and whistled through the boards. The shrimp boat rocked and bounced in turbulent water. The vessel creaked like it would burst apart. We held on to the boat's ribs for dear life.

Most of the girls were periodically bent over vomiting what little we had in our stomachs. I managed to hold it down. The storm pounded the boat. Each rise and drop compressed my spine, almost breaking it like chalk. I was scared to death we would capsize, so I bent down and began chewing at my binds. Things shook and rattled. I tried to yell to everyone to untie their ropes. There was so much noise and fear, I couldn't be sure if anyone heard.

The wooden crate of oranges banged into the knees of a black girl, Cedelle. The most ungodly sound spilled from her throat. I bent down and gnawed at my binds like a feral animal.

Strings of rope curled open. The boat leaned far to the left and I lost my grasp. I fell forward on ribbed metal. Dazed for a moment, I paused, then hurried back to the task. My mouth tasted of fiber strands, fish, and saltwater. My jaw hurt. A new cut on the back of my head throbbed. Every so often, I caught the nub of my swollen nose on my knuckle or knee. I held my pain deep as the need for survival took over. Someone rolled into me. I kept my grip on the rope, chomping and crunching each fiber. It began to loosen. My fingernails ached as I ripped at the strands.

Something heavy fell hard on the deck. I looked up. All I could see was darkness and waves spurting across the now open hatch. It hung from one hinge. When I realized I couldn't hear the men above, I panicked. With all the strength I could build, I yanked my leg from the knots. It burned. There was slight freedom and I sucked in air through gritted teeth. My hand was numb. Scrapes burned into my wrist and ankle. Waves poured the sea down into our chamber. A charley horse ran down my leg, and I screamed. At the same time, the rope snapped. I was free. A giant gulp of air filled my lungs. It stunk. I didn't care.

I tried to slide the metal water box over to the port. Water splashed up to my knees. The lid opened and I fell backwards. Girls pled for help. I eyed them, then the lid. I hadn't been thinking. My jaw was killing me. I rubbed the back of my head and scrunched as I located a wet bump.

I signaled to the other girls. Fear and confusion crossed the other thirteen faces in our bouncing, grey, rocking tub. The sounds were deafening. I motioned with my wrists across the exposed edge of the lid. A light seemed to come to most of their eyes. A few tilted their heads in confusion. The others moved forward and began, one by one, rubbing the rope across the sharp metal lip of the container. Then they began helping each other, while I dashed up the spiral stairs to the smaller hatch. It was locked. Then I noticed the motor had shut down. How long ago?

Corrina helped me as we searched for tools. A shovel up by the bilge pump, a few giant wrenches, and two crushed beer cans were all we found. All the girls rubbed their wrists and legs. As I unsteadily moved over toward them, they all beamed at me. Their chins were up and they were obviously waiting for my instructions. *Crap, I'm not a leader. I do insurance estimates. We are*

185

somewhere in the Gulf of Mexico, in the belly of a sinking shrimp boat with a kidnapping captain that knows nothing about boats, a storm rolling us around like tin cans, oh yeah, and a dead motor. Why the hell are they all looking at me?

I held on to the side. The boat took a harsh dip. I couldn't help thinking I never wanted to be near water again. Corrina patted my back. I shook my head.

Then I remembered what I was thinking about before. I gained strength and straightened my spine, just as the boat swung sideways. We all fell in a heap. Water splashed through the center hatch. Girl panic rose. Screaming and crying echoed through the hull.

"Get up!" I yelled and moved toward the metal box. "Come on, we're not going to die here. Corrina, grab the shovel," I pointed. "You two find those wrenches back there. We need weapons. The rest of you help me with this damn box." My hands went to work unloading the remaining water bottles. I nodded to the others as I gripped one corner. "We need to get it on its edge, the long side up."

The box was heavy. Grunts and loud cussing lifted it up. With the movement of the boat, it was precarious at best. Several held the sides, while, unbalanced, I climbed on top of it. Mati and Perri held my legs stable. I wobbled upright, grabbing the porthole cover. The door moved unexpectedly in a swivel. I danced to keep a smidgen of balance. The palm of my hand cut on the hinge. My teeth went from chattering to vise tight. More hands supported my legs. Slowly, I walked my fingers to the port opening.

"On the count of three, push me up as far as you can." With wind and rain pelting, I wasn't sure they heard me. But my feet lifted, and I rolled an elbow over the edge. With a hard kick, I struggled above the rail. The edge dug into my belly. Another swing of my legs created momentum, and I was up on deck.

I could see about fifteen feet ahead at times, my hair drenched in my eyes. Other times, the distance cut to a third. No one was there. Waves as high as my chest tossed the boat and me around. One mast straddled the length of the deck. Everything was a twist of rope, wire, steel, and shattered wood. Was there a life raft? Did those thugs take it?

I crawled, holding tight to anything I could grab, ducking

over and under twisted metal and snapped wood. Rain and waves drenched my freezing body. Suddenly, I couldn't breathe. I tried to scream, but nothing came out. My eyes locked on a young body–the one they called Sidearm. His chest had been smashed by a falling mast. His eyes glared into the storm above. I backed up. *Yes, my legs worked*. I moved to the front of the shrimp boat. I could hear faint cries from below deck—my name.

I spotted a metal rail that could work as a ladder. I inched my way closer. Icy water sprayed my face and neck. I almost tripped over something big. I peeked down at Cedee. A hole between his blank eyes. Crimson blood seeped out, then another big wave washed it away. I wanted to feel bad for him. I didn't. He just looked like a harmless backwoods boy, pudgy cheeks and a tummy rounder than his chest. Seeing him didn't bother me like the boy. Sidearm was about nineteen, not yet sure of himself. Now he never would be.

A double rail with rungs lay against what was left of the forward cabin. I stepped over Cedee as if hopping off a curb and grasped the loosened rail. The ship dropped. I fell onto battered knees. Pain surged up my body and tears flowed from my eyes. I turned, eased up, and hurried back with precarious balance and precious cargo. Walking between the ships rolls, I used the twisted rail as a cane and yanked on sturdy thick rope as I inched forward.

I grasped the edge of the porthole as water dumped me to my side. I scrambled back and peered over into the boat's belly. The girls were frantic. I slid the rail-ladder into the hole.

I yelled down the makeshift ladder. "Forget about the shovel and wrenches. There's no one up here." I climbed down the ladder to wait out the storm.

Night came and gradually the water calmed.

As the sun rose amid the storm clouds the next morning, one by one we exited the underbelly of the boat. Eyes wary, we scanned the boat debris. We gazed at the tail end of the rolling storm as it headed away. The water still churned but with less ferocity. The craft rolled and swayed in four to five-foot swells. The gulf gradually waddled, becoming relatively quiet; the squawk of birds returned, two flying just off the rear. This was the end of the squall. I hoped.

By midday, the sea lay motionless and the glorious sun

warmed our faces—our dirty, filthy, cut-up faces. The shrimp boat drifted, taking on salt water that seeped into the below deck. The bilge pump was silent. By afternoon, we were hungry and disoriented. The slowly sinking boat drifted.

Lisa, Perri, Kin, and Cedelle had taken the task of unburying the young boy and Cedee from the rubble. All of us bowed our heads, more from queasiness than sorrow, as the four girls tossed them over. An echoing splash was heard. They were gone. Several of the girls burst into tears. I wasn't certain if they cried for our abductors or themselves. I peeked over the edge. Two bodies floated, their lifeless eyes staring into mine. I regretted peeping over. The image burned into my brain.

"What should we do now?" asked Corrina. It took a while for me to notice that she and the others were waiting for me to answer. I gazed at all their tattered faces, hair askew in every direction, mouths agape like listless statues.

I wiped my mouth with the back of my arm. The smell of diesel fuel cringed my nose. I peered at the deck. Shambles. I sat on the wet wood and leaned on a broken pole. My eyes filled with water. I sobbed into hands that were cracked and filthy. Nobody made a sound. It was just me, shaking and blubbering like a girl.

I am a girl. I may not look like one now, but I am. I sat upright. I wiped the tears from my eyes with my knuckles. A wave jostled me to the side, shattering a plank of displaced wood. Pain shot from my hip bone. I squealed—more of an overwhelmed sound than one of agony. Shortly, I focused and calmed myself as waves lapped over the side. A few ideas came to me. I stood.

"Okay, Corrina and Mati, grab a couple of others, and search for food. Those bastards couldn't have taken it all." With fingers outstretched, I waved my arms parallel to the deck. "The rest of you throw as much as you can of this crap overboard. Make sure it isn't something we might use. We need to lighten the boat, find food and water, and pray for the Coast Guard." Everyone began busying themselves. "Oh yeah, any of you girls know anything about motors or pumps?"

Lisa spoke up, "My dad used to rebuild old cars in the garage. I'd hand him sockets and he'd tell me everything he was doing. He even let me help him put together a carburetor one time," she nodded. "I kinda know how things work."

One of the Arizona girls said, "Great, we really need to get that bilge pump working. I'm not sure how long we can float with the seepage down there." That didn't help spirits much, but she was right.

The cabin lay smashed in, but we found a case of oranges, a partial box of beef stew, some crackers, three cases of cheap beer, and an unbroken bottle of scotch. Mati found a tool box and a first aid kit. There was a small fridge that had tipped over, but with one of the masts sitting on top, we couldn't open it. We'd have to get everyone to help with that. Corrina found a hatch by the captain's chair that contained white bread and Twinkies, floating on top of three inches of water. She pulled them out. Most of the loaves were dry in their plastic bags.

We passed around Twinkies and beer to everyone as a celebration. Soprano voices cheered. It was the first I'd seen smiles in a month. Mati ate hers down as if having an orgasm. We all giggled.

By the end of the day, the ship looked more like a boat than a freeway crash. We could move around. We had lifted the mast from the fridge enough to pull it to the side and open. It contained diabetic supplies, cheese, a few spoiled fish, and unbelievably, eight dozen un-cracked eggs. The small freezer contained only empty ice cube trays.

Lisa got the stove working, and we had scrambled eggs and a slice of bread each. It was the best meal I'd ever tasted. By the sounds on deck, the others felt the same. After dinner, we all fell asleep on the hard deck with a three-quarter moon as a night light.

Laughter and splashing rose over the edge of the boat and woke me. I scanned the boat, two of the girls were missing. My heart surged. I looked toward the noise. Within five minutes, most of us jumped into the calmed waters. It felt good to just be girls.

34

Tia

The next five days we drifted. Adriana, the black girl who was put in the chicken coop first, found a way to siphon water from the clean water tank below deck. The boat rode lower and lower in the endless gulf. Lisa still couldn't get the bilge pump to work, so we formed a fire brigade and bailed the water out as best we could. We had to repeat the process most days. Spirits were low. We were drifting in what seemed to be the same endless patch of ocean. Nothing but water and sky everywhere.

On the ninth day, Lisa traded the battery at the front of the boat for the one that ran the bilge. I have never been so happy as when the first squirt of water came out of the side of that vessel. The pump worked! It gave us all hours of satisfaction and our arms a much-needed break. Now, if she could only get the motor to work.

My stomach growled a little more each day as we had to keep tightening the rations of oranges and bread. We were down to a dozen eggs, a partial bag of potatoes, six more clumps of those damn carrots, one loaf of bread, and four fish that two of the girls had caught in some netting that had survived the storm. The Twinkies and beer were long gone. We were all lethargic and sunburned. Mostly, we laid on the deck and complained to ourselves. Little mutterings, waiting for someone to tell us it would be okay. I counted on each one of these thirteen girls for comfort; at the same time, I felt I could barely stand being with them for a moment longer.

On the evening of the twenty-second day, Mati began yelling. Screeching really. The sun had dropped and formed a crescent of light behind us. She was pointing. I turned. Off the bow, I spotted her excitement. Trees. At least the outline of trees in the distance. Maybe a mile away, glowing as a sliver moon rose behind them. The shrimp boat turned into an uproar.

We screamed and clapped and waved. The bottle of scotch began being passed around.

Two hours passed. We fell into total silence despite being wide awake as the night darkened and our torn-up vessel floated slowly past a tiny patch of land.

35

Carson

Hub opened the door. Rope and strips of thin leather were tucked through his belt and ran down the side of his knee-torn jeans. It wasn't until then that I noticed the wire-rimmed glasses with rose lenses. *He has perfect vision.*

"Oh, man you won't believe it," Hub swept a strand of hair from his cheek.

"Probably not." I glanced at Maria, who raised her brow.

"After too many hours on the computer with little luck, I tried the dark neural pathways. A place to tread slowly. Juan, the top dog of all Mayan Shaman, taught me. The general was a hard nut to crack." He held his skull and squinted as if his cranium would explode. "Way too many hate knots. It took hours. Finally, I picked up a short synapse–trucking company."

"Trucking company?" Maria asked. Both of us knew it always took Hub a long time to get to the meat of the story. Her face was tight as mine, waiting.

Hub's eyes widened. His hands gestured with every word. "Yeah, that's when I started the journey back. My mind hit a plane and jutted to the right for no reason. There I was, lavender room, all curtains, and a white piano to one side." He clapped his hands. "Wahoom, curtain parted, and in walked John Lennon." Hub's hands rolled in the air like a crashing helicopter. "I could have messed my transcendental pants."

"You do know John Lennon's dead?" I asked. I began to wonder about whatever information he thought he had found. "You talked?"

"Of course he's dead. Breaks my heart to think about it." He sat on a barstool, sweat dripped from his forehead, the rope still draped from his shoulders. "We talked. Not the way you and I converse. It was more vascular. I felt the words flow through my veins. It was like white cells carried each letter on a platter. I was in awe. Never, never had I had such a rush of energy."

"I'm sure it was odd for you," I scoffed. I became impatient and grabbed his arms from whirling around so much. Getting close and breaking his personal space, I asked, "Does any of this have anything to do with Tia?"

"John kept repeating 'island.' Then he said once, 'Follow the truck—search the island." A full tooth grin smiled back at me. "Shamanism, don't you love it." He patted his heart.

"Follow the truck and search the island? What a clue." My tone grew overboard sarcastic.

Hub's face folded, reminding me of a kicked dog.

"Sorry buddy, I'm full-bore left brain and you tend to dwell in the right side. No offense, we just see things differently." I tried to apologize through my tone.

Maria nodded, then began laughing. "You two couldn't be more opposite. That must be the key to your friendship."

Hub softened. "There's more."

Now's the time he tells me there was a cow, a donkey, and Socrates that led him to a revelation.

"The great Brigadier General Stanchy owns a trucking company with Ken Van Dorius. I found it on Google. Three trucks, losses every year for five years. I passed through some of the company's barriers and found all the bills of lading. They said: Government Supplies. The name listed was Humble Pie Trucking. There are six drivers working in pairs. I texted you their names before I swung by."

I grabbed my cell from the counter. Hit power. Blank screen. I hit power again, still blank. I peeked up at Maria. "Where's my charger?"

She scowled, a hard thing with those pretty eyes. "You start keeping track of my shoes, and I'll watch your charger."

Point taken. I strolled into the bedroom, went out to the car and truck, and came back and searched every plug in the cabin.

"My shamanistic senses won't work on cell phones. You want to check my 'sent'?"

"Yeah, Mister left-brain," Maria laughed.

Jef Huntsman

I held Hub's phone and grabbed a yellow pad on the counter. The names weren't familiar as I jotted them down. "Anything else?"

"Coincidently," a grin formed on Hub's face, "all six were jarheads at Camp Lejeune about the same time as Sandoz and Sergeant Bandy. All grunts."

I slapped my hand on the table. Frustration rode up my chest. With a twisted smile, I asked, "You couldn't have told me that to begin with."

"Carson, it's like the pebble tumbling slowly in a river; one has to follow an assigned path."

"Whatever." I shook my head, exasperated, "Can you drop me off a hard copy of the list with addresses and any other facts?" I asked.

"Let's work on your health first. Where are your matches?" Hub pulled the rope from his side and dangled the loose strands in my face.

I have found it is better to go along with Hub's eccentricities than to try and argue with the man.

My cabin smelled like burnt hemp and my ribs still hurt. Hub had left an hour ago, pleased with my progress. I was going over all the information he had printed out and dropped off. I spotted the charger, snaked-up behind my Mr. Coffee.

Maria handed me a beer, just as I heard a gentle knock on the door. I glanced through the panes of my French doors. Annie peeked through. She jumped back when she noticed us watching her. Maria opened the door.

Annie gasped when she saw my face. She held her hand out as if to rub my yellow and black blotches. Her mouth tightened. She slowly curled her fingers into a fist and dropped her arm to her side.

"You think that's bad," said Maria, "you ought to be the one that has to kiss it."

"Has to? It?" I interjected. My chin sunk into my chest in fake rejection.

"Sympathy, really . . . sympathy?" Maria turned to Annie. "He runs miles up the mountain with two broken ribs and whatnot, and the poor child wants to be pampered." Her head shook, "Men, barely out of the caves."

194

The three of us talked about inconsequential things for an hour or so. We laughed, drank a bottle of Merlot, and tried hard not to mention Tia. At dinner, I began telling Annie about where the case was at. She listened intently. Her voice was professional as she asked questions and made comments. The whole meal felt like an acceptance of grief—matter-of-fact. She might cry all that night, but first she needed to know.

At eight-ten, Annie rose to leave. We protested. I grabbed extra blankets and a pillow from the closet and set them on the couch. Annie refused, saying she had to be back to work in the morning. After extensive hugs, she walked out and drove away. Maria thought we made her feel better. I wasn't so sure.

The next three mornings I ran up the trail, waking pheasants and rabbits. Evenings I did the same. The stiff edges began to soften. The trail flowed under my feet. The ace bandage around my ribs, wet with sweat, cooled me as I would slow to turn through the gate.

Maria was always there with a steaming cup in hand. She chastised me at the end of every run. We'd laugh, then sit affectionately in the cool mountain breeze. Annie called every night around seven.

Five mornings after Annie left, I rose early, had a quiet breakfast with Maria, and tossed my bags in the Corvair. My color had returned and the discolored wounds had shrunk.

The line through airport security was tedious. I watched as a mother scolded her kids for swinging on the chrome bars as adult travelers inched through the maze. The little boy and girl had yet to understand all the lines they would be herded through in the future.

At two-twenty, the plane set down in Jackson, Mississippi, a sprawling city on flat earth. In a white Ford Escape, I googled the address of *Humble Pie Trucking*. An hour through mostly parking-lot traffic, I found the building. It was a shanty of a strip mall—dry cleaners, a Korean market, a shoe repair shop, and two businesses with no signs. I drove around back. No trucks, just weeds and an industrial complex in the distance. I slammed the side of my fist into the console.

I pulled back around and got out. Given the neighborhood, I clicked the locks and glanced around for a weapon. Nothing, unless street litter might frighten someone. There were three cars parked outside. The shoe repair sign said, 'be back in an hour.' Glancing through the window, I thought the sign could have been put up weeks ago. People were stocking shelves in the market. Few customers walked the aisles. The next store had lights on. There were six or seven people in cubicles with head-sets on. I walked in.

"Afternoon," I looked around, "Ladies. Do you know where *Humble Pie Trucking* might be?" A bosomy black lady gazed over her reading glasses at me. Her name tag said Manda.

"Who's askin'?" she said.

"I heard they's lookin' for drivers," I said, rolling my R's a bit and letting each word roll off my tongue like a light breeze.

"You ain't foolin' nobody with that there accent." Manda shook her head and emptied the ash off her cigarette. "Your clothes give you away. You either from Denver or Arizona. One of them cowboy states."

She was one smart lady. "Sorry, ma'am. Just trying to find the company," I smiled.

"One of the drivers use your face for a walking mat?" She set her headphones on the table. All the other girls were listening, their heads cocked just so.

"Something like that." I sat half my rump on an unused desk. "You know the truckers?"

She rubbed her chin and looked around at the others. "We know any truckers?" They all giggled.

"I don't get the joke."

She leaned her chin in the palm of her hand. "Man, we just answer phones. We don't know nuttin."

"Any idea of how to get in touch with them?"

Manda shrugged her shoulders. The others giggled.

I stood up, reached in my pocket and slipped off a twenty from my money clip. I sat it down on her desk.

It could have been day-old sushi, the way she grimaced. She turned away.

I dug deeper and set a hundred down on top of the Jackson.

She leaned over and sort of sniffed it. Her nose crinkled. "That ain't even enough to get us girls some decent Chinese."

I pulled off another hundred. Her finger wagged. I grabbed one more. "Three hundred and twenty is my limit."

She snatched it up and tucked it deep into her bra. "I

probably would have done it for fifty, but the girls, I'm just not sure." She tapped on her computer. A few minutes later, I heard a printer sound in the far corner. She pointed to the sound.

I strolled over and picked up four sheets of paper. One told me about the owners, information I already knew. Another was about the drivers and held their cell numbers and addresses. The other two listed routes and destinations for the last two months. As I opened the door to leave, I turned to Manda. "If I'd known what you had, I'd probably have paid $500."

She padded her soft chest. "You're welcome here any time."

I stopped at a diner on the way back to the airport. The burger was good, not great, the fries coagulated in a lump to the side of the plate, and the coffee was burnt. My mood was somewhat the same. I texted the drivers' names and addresses to Hub. A minute later, he replied, *I'll let you know.*

I slid the plate to the side—soggy fries untouched. Finishing the water, I declined the waitress's offer of a warmup. The big hand had moved halfway around the cola clock behind the bar. A three-tone whistle sounded, and I checked my email. Hub had sent me a newspaper article about Dupree Chella, a truck driver who was found dead from gunshot wounds. A maid found him in a motel in Atlanta. No leads. Police thought it was drug related.

I gazed down at the pictures and addresses Manda had photocopied at the answering service. Dupree's chin jutted straight out as he stood stiff in his military uniform. A scar on his temple. I searched through the names and pulled out the three that lived near Jackson, Mississippi: Charles (Cedee) Kacey, J.B. Sanders, and Raul Martinez.

After loading addresses into Google Maps, I took off for a visit to Martinez. He was the closest.

An hour later, the landlord told me Martinez had skipped out two weeks ago, his rent thirty days past due. Raul drove a 2001 light-blue Ford 1500 with a front grill smashed in. He drank a lot, judging from the beer littered bushes off his tiny porch. The manager offered me twenty-five bucks to collect the $600 rent. I smiled, uncommitted.

Charles Kacey's house took a while to locate. He lived

back in the woods off a gravel road. He had a wife and three kids. They greeted me as I pulled up to their two-level white house. They were both hesitant and excited to see anyone coming to visit. The last mailbox I had seen resided at least a mile away. I gave a folksy smile and a wave.

As I exited the rental, a black terrier came barking at a gallop. I crouched down close to the ground and put my palms out. My breath caught as ribs shot flames through my abdomen. The dog stopped and growled, without much behind it, about two feet from me. Neck stretched. It crept closer a couple of steps and licked my palm. I scratched behind her ears and we were best friends.

With the dog at my mercy, the kids strolled off the porch and came up to me. The oldest, a puffy cheeked girl almost entering her teens said, "Wha-cha-wan?" The other two snickered, until the oldest gave them a look that could melt steel.

"I'm looking for Charles," I said.

They peeked at each other with worried faces and backed up a step or two.

I realized I may have screwed up. "Doesn't Cedee live here?"

Their stance slackened. Mom brushed her apron off.

"You know Cedee?" the mom asked. She peered down and cocked her head slightly.

"Not well, at least since the service. We spent some time on the ship and in Iraq."

"That must'a been the USS Austin."

"Yep." I rubbed the dog some more. "He told me to look him up if I was ever in Mississippi. My ex took most everything, so I thought I'd do some traveling, see old friends, and check out the sights."

"I'm Sarah," said the mom, "He's here less than when he was in the Marines. You want some coffee?"

I nodded and walked toward the porch. The kids kept a distance, except the pre-teen girl. She wrapped her arm around mine and headed me forward. I found out later her name was Dulah and the two young boys were Eddie and Charlie Jr.

The clock on the wall said 1:00 a.m. The kids had been put

to bed three hours ago. I'd found out Cedee worked for a secret government operation that he couldn't talk about, and they had bought this five-bedroom on fifteen acres for cash, three years prior. Cedee had a big shop out back with all the toys—boat, hobby tractor, ATVs, enough tools to fill a Sears, and a $2,400 fishing pole. He was home, maybe, two months a year and I think Sarah preferred it that way.

After two pots of coffee and a plate of chocolate chip cookies, I was shaky and wired. My brain pounded the back of my eyeballs. Sarah had talked to Cedee, and knew where he was, three weeks ago. She also mentioned a dozen times that he wouldn't be home tonight. Between wanting to escape her not-so-subtle romantic hints, and my banging coffee head, I finally told her I'd better get on the road.

36

Carson

J.B. Sander's house was a three-story monolith of ugly. An upright cinder-block rectangle, few windows, a cracked and chipped cement porch, and a front door from a warehouse—the kind that slides sideways on a track. A long-haul truck with the initials J.B. centered on the chrome front grill blocked any view of the south woods.

I knocked hard on the metal door. From my periphery, I noticed the heavy curtains move to my right on a barred window. A few minutes later, J.B. slid the door open about eight inches, leaving three-quarters of his sizeable body hidden behind the door. The way his shoulder was tilted and his eyes narrowed, he was holding a shotgun, readily concealed and positively loaded.

I thrust out my hand to shake his. He peered down at it like I held a turkey liver.

"Germs, I know, they bother me, too." I lowered my arm. "I'm here with Chemical Petroleum out of Detroit. You've probably heard of us."

His mouth opened, and I wasn't sure if he was going to drool or spit on my clipboard.

"Anyway, love your place here. What do you have?" I looked around as if in awe, "About twelve acres?" I already knew he had fourteen, a mortgage of over four thousand a month, and enough in savings to make the payments for five years.

"Who're you?" He spat a glob of Copenhagen into the dirt just off the porch.

"Sorry, my manners. I'm Clement South." I started to raise my arm for another attempt at a handshake. His glare said to put it down. I did. "I noticed that tat of yours; you were in the corps, huh?"

His chest inflated a couple inches. "Yep."

"I used to feed you boys. I was a naval cook on the USS Austin. Wanted to be a Navy Seal, but with asthma and all." I rolled my eyes.

"Well . . . Navy, what the hell do you want?" His hand tightened on the edge of the door.

"Get down to it. I like that." I lifted my clipboard, "My company, CPI, wants to dig a trench on the far side of your property and lay down some piping. We'll pay you nicely for the privilege."

"What's nicely?" His lips puckered. "I already do just fine."

"Mr. Sanders, if I could walk around a bit and take some soil samples, I would have a better idea of our costs and what we could offer you. It would be substantial, I assure you."

With his half-smile and narrowing of one eye, I knew the money angle had worked. "Mr. Sanders was my gran-pappy." J.B. slid the door open, leaning to his left to set something down. He nodded me in. A 30-30 deer rifle sat next to the door. He offered me a whiskey. It was still morning hours, but I wanted him as a friend for now.

The largest flat screen I'd ever seen rested on a thick coffee table. The other walls contained three well-worn couches—the kind that lie back and have drink holders. The room had bookshelves filled with empty beer cans, stacked in neat pyramids. The place was relatively clean, with the warmth of a shipping dock.

"So, is it just my property or do they want Sheffield's across the way?" He opened a built-in cupboard and grabbed out two glasses and a tall bottle of dark liquid. "You ain't one of those on-the-rocks assholes?"

I took the glass as if three inches of straight whiskey was nothing. I pretended to drink. The cheap liquid stung my tongue. "All this yours? Looks like you could have some great parties here."

"Yep." He admired the dreadful place, his hands firmly planted on puffy hips. "Got some boys that stop over now and then. And gals from the casino on the reservation. They ain't just waitresses, you know." He sat. "Now, what about the doe-re-me?"

I had watched while he fixed drinks. He didn't pack a weapon unless it was a small knife in his pocket. No sign on either leg. He had me by at least 80 pounds, and I wasn't about to let those chubby knuckles break more ribs. I had to use finesse and stroke his ego.

"We'll have to check the area to see how hard the earth is, and how stabile. That's the first step. We need to know how much it'll cost to dig." I glanced at my clipboard holding an empty notepad and some bogus law papers I'd copied at the library. Time to stall. "I forgot my soil containers from the office. Mr. Sanders, do you have any of those small plastic bags I could borrow?"

"Name's J.B." He gave me a sour stare. "I was born with a last name, but I don't have any use for it now. I've got some shopping bags under the sink. I'll grab a few of those."

He was dumber than I figured. "Yeah, that'll do."

J.B. handed me the bags. His phone rang. He walked back into the kitchen for privacy. I overheard something about a problem, and that he'd be right there. I busied myself studying the bags as he came back in.

"Gotta go. You get your samples and let me know how much dough." He gazed down his nose at me. "And it better be enough." He pantomimed counting money with his fingers.

"It'll take me a while. Maybe I'll know by the time you get back," I smiled.

"Won't be back for a few days." He grabbed a pen from my pocket and wrote a phone number on the notepad. "Text me the figure and make it a final offer. I don't like dancing, Navy." He nearly shoved me out the door.

I took the bags over into the trees and scooped some dirt into one. I heard his semi start. After a few minutes, he swung the truck around his house, glanced at me and took off down the road. I texted the plate number to Hub, dumped the dirt back out, and tossed the bags in my rental.

I walked around the redneck's house. While I was inside, I hadn't noticed any alarm system. I checked the two windows on the main level. They had rusted bars bolted into their cement frames. Dogs barked somewhere in the distance. A light breeze cringed my nose as the smell of an unemptied septic tank sailed by. A vent pipe curled out from the grass. The steel back door was bolted solid. I strolled to the other side—no windows. A ladder lay in the dirt next to a garage big enough to hold a herd of elephants. The windows on the upper floor had no bars, so that was the best entrance.

A thought came to me. I turned and headed to the front of the house. The padlock on the front door sat covered with age and rust. I found a four-foot length of pipe and began beating at the hasp and lock. The short screws pulled out of the hasp, and the whole thing dangled to one side. I slid the metal door open. A mangy cat ran by me. My heart took a minute to restart. I entered quietly, with breath slow and soundless, stepping carefully.

After thirty minutes of searching the main floor, I headed up the stairs. While the main floor lay relatively neat and clean, the upstairs was a tumble of clothes, empty potato chip bags, and beer cans in every room. A rubbing noise came from one room. With caution, I eased the door open. A reptile-like smell escaped. Two rows of aquariums lined the walls on two-by-four framing. I pulled my shirt up around my nose and ventured in. Snakes, coiled, some sleeping, others darting sharp tongues in and out, their eyes watching. A feral taste filled the air. Rattlers, a large boa, and several colorful snakes began waking to my entrance. I heard something slide by my leg. A six-foot, tan snake with dark markings curled quickly past me, then slid under a workbench to my left. My lungs ceased to function. I backed out of the room and shut the door. I checked to make sure it wouldn't re-open. My chest filled with a rush of needed oxygen.

J.B.'s bedroom smelled of sweat and bath fungus. I checked through everything with a coat hanger. Touching anything in there might have meant signing my own death certificate. Finally, under his night table I found a spiral-ringed notepad. I scooted it out with the hanger like it contained plutonium. A used cough drop was melted onto the cover. The other stains I was unsure of. With a covering of tissue on my fingers, I opened it. A grin formed as I scrolled through one page after another. Jackpot.

37

Carson

The wind combed back my hair as I raced from the Dothan Alabama Airport. It seemed indulgent, but a Subaru BRZ convertible was the only car left that wasn't a mini-van. I thought it helped with the tourist persona. Traveling Interstate 231, I found the right exit just north of the Florida border.

A gas station with one of those mini fast-food franchises inside sat on one corner. I picked up a few supplies and headed out. Following directions from the scribbled-on pad I'd found in J.B.'s room, I turned and headed the Subaru four miles north until the road forked down a dirt road. A recent rain had left puddles in the low spots. After forty minutes more of teeth-chattering rock-bed, I reached a tired mailbox with a partial name, stenciled years ago. I could barely make out a "DEW" something "R." Had to be the old Dewnar place.

I pulled past the mailbox a hundred yards or so and got out to open the trunk. Minutes later, I had the car jacked up and had rolled the rear wheel into the bushes.

I picked up my only weapons—three Roman candles, a string of fire crackers, a bottle of vodka, matches and a Swiss army knife. My gun wasn't fond of airport security. I headed through the trees. The growth thickened as I traversed, hidden, fifteen feet from the entry road. The quiet grew, interrupted only by the flutter of birds. My cell phone sang. My heart lifted to my throat and back. Panicked, I slid the phone out, silenced it, and then shut it off. I leaned on a tree trunk until my breathing calmed. I'd assumed I had a mile to walk, but one never knew. A white truck stormed down the road. I ducked. It didn't slow.

I waited a minute, then moved on, my feet silent. A patch

of mosquitoes attacked while I peered into a clearing. My eyes were alert as I studied the barn, house, a couple of small outbuildings, and an empty chicken coop. Two white trucks, a Dodge and a Ford, with oversized tires were parked at the edge of the trees, near the far side of the house. I jotted down their license numbers

There was no sign of life, except the vehicles. The place sat unnaturally peaceful. Smoke curled upwards from a recently used fire pit. I edged around the clearing to check all angles.

At the back of the house, near the door, I smelled fried meat and heard low laughter. A gun shot. I dropped hard to my belly. Two more shots. I lay still, my ribs radiating pain. Screams tore through the air, coming from the house. I cocked my head, then chuckled to myself, realizing what the noise was. *The damn TV.* I moved back into the trees. My heart slowly dropped back into place.

Hours passed. My legs were going to sleep, and my mind was edgy by the time a T-shirted man came out the back door. Tattoos covered both beefy upper arms. His gut needed more exercise on a stair-stepper than time would allow. He chugged a beer, flipped a cigarette into the yard, turned, and went back in.

There were too many windows for me to venture unseen to the house until dark. I crab-crawled backwards, then lifted up behind three woven pines. Making my way over closer to the barn, I spotted another man sitting on the front porch. A rifle leaned against the house on his right side. His head lay back, resting on the window sill. A knife the length of a table leg was strapped to his denim pants. A capped bottle of whiskey lay on the table next to him. His chest raised and lowered in rhythmic movements.

I moved back into a grove of trees and high green grass, rolled my jacket up as a pillow, and laid down to rest until dark, only a few hours away. I quickly fell asleep.

A rodent in the bushes woke me at dusk. I made my way back to the car and replaced the tire. If I had to leave, it would have to be quick. The sporty car looked out of place. I started it and drove the way I had come until I found a grassy turn-around about a mile and a half back. With some maneuvering, I backed the convertible into a narrow strip between two trees. Bushes scraped at the bottom and sides. I stepped back. It lay hidden from the road.

Jef Huntsman

The car had brush marks on both sides. I hoped it was just the dust and not paint scratches. I grabbed a pen light from my travel bag and headed out.

There were three of them sitting on the porch drinking and finishing off plates of food. The only light came from a window off the porch. I'd noted two spotlights earlier, one above the barn and one on a pole by the small chicken coop. I headed toward the back of the house. Inching my chin up to the window, I saw a messy kitchen, empty, with an opening into a larger room and the porch beyond. A staircase rode up the side of one wall. There was no one inside, that I could see. The way these guys were settled in with feet up and two twelve packs, I figured I had about twenty or thirty minutes. I tried the back door. Unlocked.

A slight squeak of unoiled hinges set me on edge. I spit on the hinges to provide some lubrication. It was a trick a French burglar had taught me years back.

Patience. I slowly opened the door enough to squeeze in. I held my breath as the door closed, then made my way to the pantry. Costco-sized cans of everything lined shelves caked with spills. As I closed the door, a glint of metal caught my eye. Behind a broom sat a shotgun. I eased it out and opened the chamber. It was loaded. Five rounds. Glancing back in, I found no boxes of shells. Five would have to do.

Feeling a bit surer of the situation, I snuck upstairs. There were five small bedrooms and a disgusting bath that drooled shampoo off the top of the toilet tank. Nothing of any use except a knife that I slid into my back pocket. Just as I was coming down the stairs, high beams bounced down the roadway, lighting up the main room. All the boys stood, and I slipped down and out the back door. My heart pounded; teeth cinched tight.

I crouched low and tore through the bushes. I wanted to see who and how many were in the truck. I knew it was a semi by the distance its headlights rose from the ground. I found a spot behind a large acacia tree. Headlights whizzed over my head as I held myself low in the bushes, still as a deer. Their tires squealed and slid to one side, coming to a stop about twenty feet from the porch. The house lit up like day. I grasped the shotgun tighter and peered around the tree.

The pudgy face of J.B. Sanders poked his head out of the

Peterbilt window. *Where's the trailer? He must have dropped it off somewhere.* The men formed a semicircle around the open window. J.B. muttered quickly and pointed in various directions. I could tell he instilled fear into them.

I cupped my cell. It was 1:34 a.m. They followed him like giant baby ducks into the house. The ambiance of drinking, swearing, and laughter went on for an hour. The lights went out. I snuck over to the locked barn but couldn't hear a sound. My knuckles tapped on the tin. A squeak muttered from somewhere inside. *Probably a cat.* I checked the vehicles then headed back to my hideout. With my body weary, I passed into a light sleep, my mind still combat alert on the inside.

I woke to hustling sounds and light peeking over the trees. The backwoods boys were on the move.

They scuttled about after J.B.'s brief orders from the porch. One went to the barn and unlocked it. I crawled to my left to gaze inside from the distance. Three young women with fright in their eyes were backed deep into a corner. I hoped that Tia might be there hidden in the dark shadows. The man grabbed a handful of empty milk jugs scattered on the barn floor. He exited and slid the door shut. I heard high-pitched whimpering. He filled the jugs from a hose, walked into the barn, and set them just inside the door, spilling one over.

The others had headed for the house and were now coming out front with duffle bags. Two were tossed into the Ford truck, the other went into the bed of the white Ram. J.B. backed the semi into a hollowed spot, north of the entry road, then headed over to the Dodge. Two of the men jumped into the Ford pickup and started it up. The other man came out of the house carrying full plastic bags, locked the door, and ran to the barn. J.B. waited in the Dodge Ram, swearing at him to hurry and pounding the side of his door.

The man had a limp but hurried back to the barn. He tossed the bags in, then locked the door and ran to the passenger side of J.B.'s truck. Churning up dust, they hustled down the entry road, their lights turning left onto the main road.

I bolted to the barn and found a shovel against the side wall. With five or six solid hits, the padlock broke and fell to the ground. The light was still on, and I could see three pathetic faces huddled with their knees against their chests. One made a squealing sound, and all three began whimpering. My eyes darted around the barn, looking for Tia. There was nothing but shadows and water jugs.

I turned back. "It's okay," I assured the girls in a soft voice.

With their feet, they dug in the loose dirt pushing their backs against the corrugated steel wall. Eyes were wide, panic written on their faces.

"They're gone. I'm here to get you out." I motioned for them to follow me to the door. I didn't want to get any closer for fear of scaring them further. "We have to hurry. I'm not sure where they went or for how long." I back-stepped to the open door and peeked out. My eyes returned to the girls.

A weak voice asked. "You're not . . . not one of them?" Their eyes became hopeful, but shiny with tears ready to burst. The three began whispering between sobs. "You a cop?" she asked.

"I'm looking for a girl, Tia, curly long blonde hair, about twenty-two, light complexion, five-foot-five. Have you seen her?" I asked.

A lanky girl of about eighteen stood up slowly. "Those creeps dropped us off here yesterday." She glanced at the others. "Two of them drove us all over hell in wood crates, in the back of a delivery truck. I don't even know where the hell we are." The others stood.

"We have to hurry. I need to catch up to those guys."

"Not with me you're not," a thin-nosed girl said. She crossed her arms. The other two stepped forward.

"No, no, no, I'll drop you off, so you can call the sheriff." I motioned with my arms for them to follow me. "Now!"

The three caved into each other.

"Sorry, but I need to go. You can stay here if you'd like." I knew I wouldn't leave them, but I had to do something to get them to move.

Fifteen minutes later, we were all in the Subaru heading down the road. The young girl in the passenger's seat kept twisting her hair, her mouth gaped open. The strong smell of urine reeked from her clothes. The car's speedometer marked sixty-four, and I held tightly to the steering wheel to keep it on the gravel road. My fingers vibrated, and the skin on my knuckles stretched taut. The other two girls huddled in the small back seat; they appeared more in shock than relieved. Their clothes soiled. Their arms and faces bruised. Not a word had been spoken since we left.

The car slid sideways as I braked for the intersection and eased onto a paved road. I raced forward not knowing which way to go. One of the girls let out a scream, then another. I glanced in the rear-view mirror. Both were pointing to the gas station we had passed. I screeched over onto the shoulder. Before the vehicle came to a full stop, I turned and yelled, "What?"

They both melded together. I peered in the direction where their fingers had pointed. One of the trucks was pulling out from the pump. It stopped to the side of the mini-mart. The girls ducked down. The one in the front passenger seat had her hair ratted tight to her fingers and was covering her eyes with it. A second later, one of the original men came bounding out with a case of beer. He tossed it in the truck bed and jumped in. They sped away in the opposite direction. I waited for a couple of cars then flipped a U-turn and plunged down the road in pursuit.

All three girls started howling and pounding my back and side. High-pitched shrieking rang in my ears. I caught one or two words, but most of it came out as gibberish. With one hand on the wheel and the other out for protection, the Subaru veered all over the road.

"Stop!" I yelled. Silence and the scent of sweat filled the interior. Laborious breathing started after a few seconds. My heart roared. "I am going to drop you off someplace safe." My voice softened, "Trust me. I won't let them have you again." They stared with wild, frantic eyes. "I promise." I tapped the shotgun at my side.

Air filled my lungs in one full inhale, and I let it out slowly. "I need to follow those damn . . ." My anger wouldn't come up with a name for the sick bastards. "I'm looking for that girl, Tia, that I asked about. They took her, too. We need to find out where they're going, but I promise, I won't let any harm come to any of you." Their shoulders sloped slightly. We dropped off the asphalt for a split second and bounced back into the lane. Everyone stiffened, and I held tighter to the steering. My attention fastened on the road. "I can't drop you off at that gas station. It's too close to their farm. We need to get further away."

The girls remained stiff. "Okay," one muttered from the

rear seat. The other two gave hesitant nods. Wet tears lathered their cheeks.

"Keep your eyes on that Dodge Ram and keep a look out for the white Ford." The slender-nosed girl in the front seat stared at me with puzzlement. "Watch the trucks?"

A car and a delivery van were between the Ram and me. I wanted to keep it that way, though I struggled with the urge to overtake them and shoot them on the spot. I knew I would have to plan on the fly. I needed to know where Tia was.

Fifty miles later, we had entered Florida and headed down the 231 toward Panama City. They stopped at a Waffle House in Cottondale. I flipped around and pulled into a grocery store about four streets back.

I handed the thin-nosed girl three twenties. "Go into the store and ask the manager to use the phone. Talk slow. You girls look like poster children for a television charity. Call the police first, then your parents." They tore out of the car, headed to the front door. Filthy torn clothes clung to their sweaty backs.

"Easy . . . you're going to scare people!" They turned and waved after they opened the door. It was the first time they'd smiled since I let them out of the barn.

I waited and watched through the glass. They talked to a woman at the checkout. She left her two customers and guided them to the back. I lost sight of them and pulled out of the parking lot. I nodded to myself and opened the window. It was the first time I had felt calm in forever. A calm that only combat soldiers know.

The truck still sat at the breakfast joint. I drove just past, where I could watch. I found parking at a convenience store and backed in. Desperately needing energy, I hurried into the store and picked up a large coffee, three questionable muffins, a case of water, and five assorted candy bars.

The white Ram was still there. I chugged down a gut full of water and chomped on sugary muffins. In my old line of work, I had learned to relax my body and rest enough to relieve the sagging eyes I wore. In a complete state of calm, I watched through eyelashes a spot on the truck's mirror that reflected the morning sun. It was a yoga-type sleep. Hub would have been proud. The coffee and candy bars waited, while I took long relaxed breaths.

The bright spot moved and startled me awake. The digital dash readout told me I'd slept fourteen minutes. With renewed energy and a couple of head shakes, I followed, three cars behind them. The Ram jumped on Interstate 10 through Tallahassee, then cut down the peninsula on Interstate 19.

Hours passed. I'd downed enough candy bars to strangle my gut into knots and give me the permanent shakes. The coffee cup sat in the cup holder, empty.

"Finally," I yelled into the windshield. They pulled into a truck stop just past the city of Perry. My legs had been crossed for the last hour. Pulling the car to the opposite end of the parking lot, I turned off the key. I rummaged through my bag, found some dark glasses and a black Raider's cap, and sprinted to the men's room. The two of them came in and strode up to the urinals on my left. I pulled the cap tighter and gazed slightly to the right at grey tile. I waited until they finished and were out the door, then washed my hands and zipped to my car without drying. They were gassing up, and I did the same.

The Ram pulled over to the restaurant in the back. They all went in. I followed cautiously with my ridiculous covert costume—hat and glasses.

My plate sat with the remnants of steak bone, egg yolk, and syrup. The place had high back booths that helped hide me. The lowlifes I was following sat by the window twenty feet away. I had grabbed a free magazine and sat as if immersed in buying real estate.

I figured out why they were taking their time when the two other men from the house came in, craning their necks to find J.B. Sanders and the young guy I had heard them call Sidearm. All of them wore tight T-shirts and tighter belts. One had a mermaid tattoo swimming up his bushy arm. The other walked with a slight limp. Prosthetic, I'd guess by his canted large body movements. The two sat down and lifted coffee cups to the waitress. She smiled as if holding in a gas bubble or thinking about the extra tips.

I dropped money on the table and headed for the gas station store to pick up supplies for the road and a different hat. Ten minutes later, the men jumped in their trucks and headed back down the road.

My cell rang. It was Annie.

I answered with, "Making progress." My gaze locked on the trucks. A Jeep on the incoming lane almost sideswiped me as our tires spun and my back end inched past the front fender of the Cherokee. They curled sideways on the graveled edge. Dust billowed. The car stopped and a single digit waved at me. My phone had fallen from the seat to the floor. I could hear Annie. My hand reached down and nabbed the cell.

"Really?" There was excitement in her tone. "Really, Carson?"

My breath came in short gasps. My heart banged on bruised ribs. I switched the phone to speaker and set it on the passenger seat. "I'm not sure how long I can talk." I paused and rubbed my unshaven chin, calming my breathing. "I think I found the place they had Tia. I'm following two trucks. Four men. My hunch is they're headed to another location. Hopefully where Tia is."

"Was there any sign that Tia had been held at . . ."

"I found three girls from Houston who had been kidnapped like Tia." The Ford pulled off to the side of the road. The Ram kept going. I looked in the rear-view mirror and saw the man with the limp slip into the trees on the side. I slipped on the hat I had bought. It was something between a forest ranger and a gardener hat. I glanced in the mirror and stuck out my tongue. I looked absurd.

"Carson? You there?"

"Yeah. Anyway, I should know more tonight. It looks good."

Annie began firing questions. Her voice trembled and skipped words.

"Annie, my concentration needs to be on the road and these trucks for the time being. Okay if we talk later?"

"Sure, sure, I don't know if I'm happy or scared to death. I'm sorry."

"You are the first one I'll call. Can you do me a favor?" One of the cars between me and the Ram turned off the interstate. I slowed. "Will you call Hub and tell him I need information on the pictures of the plates I sent him?"

"Carson, Hub's at a Rub-4-Life massage thing for some

youth home in Arizona. He won't be back until late tonight. He was sweet and asked me to go, but I'm frazzled."

Crap. I chuckled at the odd things Hub gets into. "Not a problem, just as soon as he can." I tilted my hat back, "Will you also call Maria? Tell her everything's okay, I'm in Florida, and I'll call tonight if things work out."

"I talked to her just before calling you. She's worried about you. How are your ribs?"

"They're fine," I lied.

At a sign saying, "Crystal River three miles," they turned down a thin highway with little traffic. Orange groves lined the road. I kept my distance at about a mile behind the white Ram, barely making out its image. A few abandoned fruit-stands and ranch roads broke the monotony. The terrain changed to unkempt jungle fifty miles in and the road veered close to the coast. The smell of iodine and decaying vegetation let me know we were closer to the ocean than I figured. A glint of sun on windshield told me the Ram was turning. I slowed.

I pulled up to a toppled sign, twisted and leaning, moss hiding the lettering. The un-maintained entry turned about thirty feet in. Pressed grass told me the path was newly driven. I pulled a half a mile further and found a stack of trees shredded by a hurricane to hide the car behind. I buried my rental with dead palm fronds and grabbed the shotgun I'd acquired from J.B.'s house.

I high stepped it back toward the entry road, my eyes scanning for snakes. Florida is famous for poisonous snakes and constrictors. Not a good way to die. Not sure there is one. Roots banged my shins. I'd duck one limb and slam into another. The going was slow and cautious. Thirty grueling minutes later the growth ended in tall brush and buildings off to one side.

I crouched in the brush watching. I couldn't see the white trucks, but I could hear someone was barking orders from the far side of the building—J.B.'s voice. A rickety dock moored a twenty-seven-foot Avalon pontoon boat. The craft appeared to be showroom new, resting on still, dark water. The Avalon looked way out of place on the old dock. A big backside with grizzly hair fussed around on the boat by the console.

Ducking down, I watched and listened. My cell vibrated in my pocket. I crawled behind a group of small palms and read an email from Hub.

I'll call when I can. J.B. Sanders has enough of a portfolio to put a dent in the national debt. So does General Stanchy and Ken Van Dorius. The others just make a decent living. The Ranch where the girls were is owned by an overseas business out of Singapore, which is owned by another ghost corporation in the Bahamas. Nothing on the three girls yet. Except all are Aquarians. February. Eerily significant. I'll work on the spiritual ties to that. I'll check the plates in a few. Sorry man, they're calling me to do another massage.

I texted back, *Later. SHTF.* He would understand—"Shit's Hitting the Fan." I pocketed my cell and turned. J.B. Sanders carried a shotgun loose in each hand. The other two followed behind with a cooler and a cardboard box. Both big men hunched with the weight. The deck boards bowed as each man entered the pontoon boat. The motor started.

I waited. As the Avalon ducked out of view around the sawgrass and a patch of gumbo limbo trees, I stood. I checked the old motel first. Keeping low and entering with caution, I surveyed each room. Nothing except candy wrappers, empty water bottles, and rotten fruit in abandoned rooms. In one, I found a high-end girl's tennis shoe without the match. Another had a strip of yellow soft cloth. There were old apple cores and orange peels on every floor.

I checked the trucks. Keys were hidden on top of the tires. Crooks are usually as stupid as one imagines. The Dodge Ram had a 45 Smith and Wesson in the glove box. The magazine held seven rounds, three were missing. It fit in the palm of my hand. There was a fishing pole behind one of the seats and an ammo box filled with sparse tools–three plyers, a wrench, and five screwdrivers. Both vehicles were registered to Pickles Construction out of Atlanta, Georgia. I texted the information to Hub.

A quick run along the dock and the shoreline yielded no clues. I checked for another boat with no luck. I jumped back in the Dodge and started it up. With the sun in my eyes, my hand flipped down the visor. A pad of paper dropped. Glancing closely, under the Red Roof Inn stationary, embedded scratches caught my eye. I pulled over. With a tire crayon I found in the glove box, I highlighted the scratches. It was two three-digit numbers. They made absolute no sense to me. I texted them to Hub and took off toward the highway.

Four miles down the road, I found a sign that said "Hummel's Fishing and Boat Dock." With my credit card racked up a sizeable amount, I took off in a V-hull with twin screws.

Six hours later, with my eyes dizzy from staring at rolling water and little else, I pulled back into Hummel's. I'd found the old motel and took off north in the direction the Avalon took. I passed several boats, but none like the one that left the ancient dock. "Discouraged" didn't even come close to the funk I was in. I opened the door to the Dodge Ram and slid in.

The engine kicked over at the same time my cell rang. I was on about half power and the charger was back in the rental. A familiar voice said, "What's up, slick?"

"Isn't that a nickname for one of your apprehended thieves?" I asked.

"Depends on what you're up to," answered Detective Brower.

My eyes went to the front seat, then the dash of the stolen truck. "Me? I'm vacationing in Florida. Maybe I'll catch one of those Tarpon."

He snickered in that deep-chested way I'd heard before. "Had my eye on trucking abductions; seems three girls were just found in northern Florida. The man that saved them had a description similar to you. Mmmm, and you're in Florida?" I heard him puff out a stream of air. "Cept one said, 'handsome in a rough way with kind eyes.' I knew right then it wasn't you."

I wiped sweat from my brow. "What's up, Brower?" He must have been in his cubicle. I could hear other voices in hushed tones in the background.

"Off the record, what're you finding, Mr. Concerned Citizen?" He let out something close to a laugh, but deep enough I wondered if he gagged. His voice lowered to serious, "Another girl went missing across the border in Idaho. Same as Tia, in a bar with friends."

I explained about the girls, the farm, and following the two trucks. I described the Avalon boat and my futile search, then I pulled the truck off the road. I realized I wasn't sure where I was going.

I jumped out of the truck, the heat and humidity hit me. My short walk put me right into a swarm of mosquitoes, and I began slapping my arms and face, still on the phone with the detective. I raced back to the truck.

"You okay? What's happening?" shouted Brower.

"I'm fine . . . stopped to clear my head."

"Sounded like you were in a fist fight. I heard slapping, and it sounded like you fell on the ground," he had concern in his voice.

"Just visiting with some native critters. Anyway, I'll text you those plate numbers. You might check on a Pickles Construction out of Atlanta. That's who registered the trucks."

"You realize you're swimming with alligators?" He paused, probably typing in the information I gave him. "If there isn't already, there'll be an APB out for the two trucks. You might find a different type of transportation."

"Am I detecting concern?" I asked.

"Carson, I don't give a rat's ass about your lanky butt, but I do care about those girls. Don't screw anything up," he clicked off.

I started the Ram. The tires spun in the roadside muck, then grabbed. The sun threw long shadows off the palmettos and gave an orange tone to the asphalt. My phone sounded its irritating music–Highway to Hell. I was finding Maria's sense of humor for my ring tone less and less funny.

"I'm coming out. Where's the nearest airport?" Annie's voice boomed, determined and curt.

My fingers tightened around the steering wheel. "No! You stay put. I'm on this; to be honest, you'd just be in the way."

"Carson. I'm coming. This is my sister." A noise like a hissing teapot came through the cell.

"Look, Annie, this is admirable. I appreciate the gesture, but I need to do this alone. I promised you I'd find your sister. I will."

I listened to that hissing sound again that warbled toward the end. "It's been months. I'm not eating. I've missed so much work they've probably fired me, and I haven't been in enough to find out."

"That's not the . . ."

"What airport?"

She was mad. I could feel the frustration in her voice. I glanced ahead and almost missed the turnoff into the abandoned motel. The truck slid as I cranked the wheel into the overgrown path. Tools slid out from under the seat. Something punched my ankle. I overcorrected. The bumper snapped a tree. I jammed down on the brakes and slid to a stop, adrenalin surging through my veins.

After rubbing the back of my foot, I shoved the jack back under the seat and glanced around. My cell lay on the floor with assorted papers and tools. I picked up the phone again. Annie had hung up. Easing down my heartbeat, I backed the truck a couple of feet, then proceeded down what used to be a road.

The discarded motel lay quiet. I pulled the truck to where it had been before, straightened the jumbled mess on the floor, wiped off any fingerprints, jumped out, and high tailed it back to my rental. I took the path this time. No sense banging my legs on all the roots or having a snake kiss my ankle. Halfway back, my cell buzzed again. I was feeling more popular than I'd ever been.

It was Hub. "Carson . . . Carson?"

"I'm here. What'd you find out?"

"Annabelle is racing close to a psychiatric chair." There was urgency in his voice. "She wants to fly to Florida or wherever the hell you are now and search for Tia. Her voice rattled my aura. She sucked energy like a coal-powered generator. I could feel the black soot as she rambled on. I tried to get her to come down for a health visit. I know I could help her." I heard him slam his fist on a table. His voice softened. "She hung up on me. Can you believe that?"

"Yes, I talked to her twenty minutes ago," I thought about that determination. "Call her back. If anyone can, you can talk her out of it. It's moronic and dangerous here."

"I've tried. She doesn't answer." His voice pulled away, "Not now. I've lost my center." Another voice said something. "Tell her I may not do any rubs for the rest of the day."

"Hub."

"Sorry, I'm back."

I tossed the branches off the Subaru and cleared the path a bit. Fumbling for my keys, I told Hub, "Keep trying." I unlocked the door and slid behind the wheel. "What else do you have for me? I talked to Detective Brower. The three girls are safe, but J.B. Sanders and three others have taken to the water, and I lost them."

"Hold on. Let me check my laptop." Keys pounded, "I'm looking at their picture now—Megan, Tilly, and Sara. They all look like high school kids. Says here, Megan's seventeen, the others are nineteen. The parents are flying into Tallahassee in the morning."

The sun was just a thin orange glow on the horizon, my stomach growled, and frustration pulled my face into a scowl. "Can I call you back?" I said. "I'm getting loopy. I need coffee and a thick steak. I've got to figure out my next move and this restaurant's calling my name." I hadn't eaten in hours.

I pocketed the phone.

With food in my belly, my mind sharpened its pencil. Things became clear.

38

Tia

The hull lazily slipped between the knee-like roots of the eighth tiny island. Our clean water tank had squirted green foamy liquid for the last day or so. We slurped it up like lime Jell-O, half-conscious and spent from days of overhead sun and the never-ending rolling drift to nowhere.

The ocean had been endless. We castaway through seven days of heat, exhaustion, and a delirious craziness.

The boat floated close to a tangle of mangroves. The four of us on deck tried to focus despite the sweat dripping into our eye slits. The port side spun around and slammed into a solid tree.

My tongue swollen and glued to the top of my mouth, my throat thick, I tried for words. My mind weaved along slow pathways. The heaviness of my small frame reluctantly rose as if held back by rubber cement. I watched Adriana wave her arms around as she leaned over the far side. The trees knocked the metal of the boat as waves tossed us further toward shore. Adriana's eyes met mine. Our open mouths turned into lopsided grins. My lips moved to say something. A subdued elation rose in my chest.

A shriek of joy flew from my mouth; my throat felt as if gravel had shot out. Adriana laughed crazily. Corinna and Lisa came out of their haze and gazed up at us as if we were lunatics. Our sunburnt bodies were peeling, like old paint. We both pointed as the shade of the mangroves enveloped us, then a wave tossed us hard to the deck. I reached up and touched another cut to my head. A dab of blood reddened my fingers. It didn't matter. The four of us began laughing, until we could barely catch our breaths.

"What's going on up there?" Mati's soft voice barely spilled out from below deck. Most of the girls were hiding from the sun. It was our turn to take watch. I'd stared at so many days of water and sky, I wasn't sure where the horizon split the two.

Heads popped up when we took too long to answer. "Trees! Shady flippin' trees," shouted someone from the opening. The hatch exploded with arms and legs as they fought each other to get a glimpse. All at once, an energy began that lifted our spirits and shone off the smiling and crying faces that erupted out. The deck was filled with as much spirit as a touchdown at my High School football games. Our bow dipped with the weight of everyone gathering in sweaty embraces.

Adriana grabbed one of the branches, trying to steady the boat. I zipped across the deck into what was left of the pilot house and grabbed the rope that lay curled on a hook. With speed and babbling shrieks, we tied both sides from the boat's cleats to the trees. We stood elated and loud in the shade of knurled trees. We bounced and clasped each other's hands as if saved.

Corinna stood back, "I watched this island from some ways out, it's about the size of a mall. I thought we'd pass it by like every other place. After a few minutes, I lay back down." She held her palms out, "Stupid island pulled us right in with me half asleep."

I turned back to the trees–thick, moss-covered branches lifted toward Heaven as if arms of the dead. Colorful birds fluttered in the upper branches. Besides the constant roll of the gulf and a few birds swimming through the tight nest of branches, a watery silence enveloped everything.

The fear of another unknown, perhaps a perilous doom, began to seep into my heart. By the despair in their faces, the others felt it too. The noise of celebration ceased and stillness caught our breaths, undisturbed by the rise and drop of the craft from each new wave. A darkness of twisted trees stared back, a creepy black place. We deflated.

Adriana broke the spell with parched lips and wide eyes. "Who's going to get out there and see what's here to see?" All of us stared at her. She slapped her bosomy chest with salt caked fingers. "Not me."

Everyone's head turned downward toward the brackish water. I found myself staring at the thick trees, dripping spider webs from hanging moss. The ocean curled and the birds shook the leaves.

Someone, somewhere said, "I will." It took a moment for me to realize those two silly words had come out of my chapped lips. I thought about taking them back, but all the girls began patting me on the back and clapping. I stood stunned. All their faces had lost any semblances of female. They were raw and weary, but there were hesitant smiles of dim hope. I tried to tell them I'd spoken too soon, but no words would come. They needed a hero, but I wasn't the one.

Adriana came up to me and put her arm around me. "If this puny, frail cracker can handle it, I'm going with her." We embraced, gaining strength from each other.

Dusk came soon after. It was the first time I'd noticed the sunset in days. Hazy reds with clouds lined in orange. The mosquitos hit. They were so thick it felt like we sucked in a hundred with each breath.

As the moon rose and the sun dropped into the endless horizon, everyone helped gather supplies for the trip inland. Kitchen knives were pulled from the drawer. A chef's knife, a boning knife, and a small cleaver were wrapped in sail cloth. We had two bottles of green "fresh" water and slices of fish that Perri had caught in a net the night before.

Adriana grabbed a long wrench and tucked it into her rope belt. "Just in case I need to pop a snake in the head."

That didn't make me feel too secure. I borrowed long pants and a thin cotton sweater from quiet Sarah, and Adriana donned greasy overalls the Captain had stuffed by the pump in the hull. One of the girls made a backpack out of canvas, wire and rope. The sun sizzled into the ocean. The island hung mysterious and daunting as black branches swayed.

The moon lit the tattered vessel in grey-blue hues. I lay down on the mid-deck. I tried to focus on the stars, but anxiety kept my brain focused on all the jungle perils I'd ever watched in movies. Adriana snored at my feet. Other girls kept checking on me–telling me how all right things would be. *Yeah, so why weren't they going?*

Somewhere between thoughts about teeth-gnashing gorillas and sun burning through my red, peeling eyelids, I must have fallen asleep. As I woke, I raised up on one elbow. My eyes squinted at the morning brightness, for a moment, until a figure stood between me and the sun. Perri came into view.

She knelt and whispered, "You sure about this?" Her words were husky and concerned. Wide eyes peeked at me above her burned cheeks.

All my thoughts from last night came streaming through. My breathing shortened. I sat up further, my arms extended behind me. "Somebody's got to." *That sounded as if I meant it.* I stood. Blood drained from my head to my feet. My toes throbbed. Dizziness surged over me for a few seconds.

Kin, my Asian friend from the barn, came up to me. She held out some well-used, high-top, red Converse and pressed them to my belly. "These will be better than those sandals." I accepted them gladly and slipped off the brown sandals I'd found at the barn.

"Thank you." I slipped them on and stood, walked two steps and realized they were several sizes too big. My feet slipped back and forth.

Kin reached in her pocket and pulled out strips of white canvas. "I had to wad these up and shove them in the toe. Maybe slip a few under your foot." I sat back down, and she helped me. The shoes were workable, but it took a while for me to get used to the floating fit.

We had a breakfast of coconuts that had floated to us a few days prior and we'd caught in a fishing net. Everyone seemed to be watching Adriana and me. I felt self-conscious with every bite. Adriana glanced up and eyeballed each one. "What'ch'all staring at?" All heads bowed and chewed on their pieces of coconut.

Adriana stood and signaled me with a lift of her head. Unsure, I got up and followed. My throat tight, my pulse raced. The walk to the bow stretched for miles. I peeked over the edge at the foam and debris that swirled in the space between the hull and the mangroves. The black, wet roots curled out like serpents. Waves pounded and splashed across the dark trunks. Deep in the jungle, little light shone through. Mosquitos swirled around my face. I swatted, slapping my own skin more than hitting the bugs.

Adriana gripped my hand and placed her one leg over the edge. I couldn't breathe. My foot eased into the water. My back slid down the edge of the boat and into waist-high moss-green water. My fingernails dug into my palms as my shoes sucked down a few inches.

Adriana laughed. "Open your eyes. My brothers and I used to swim in water darker than this." She reached out, "Grab my hand."

We moved slowly. My jaw was clamped tight, until a buzzing mosquito flew up my nose. I began slapping the bridge of my nose, blowing frantically and clinging onto Adriana. Her eyes spoke a million words as she shook her head.

The water became shallow. Waves rocked us toward what I considered full-out doom. My ankles and knees took a beating from the solid roots. Each time, I felt sure it was a python or an eel. Adriana kept pulling me forward. The mud squished around my ankles. We hopped over the roots in a few inches of lighter ocean. The two of us walked on crushed shells into a beach of the same. Beyond, the forest was so thick I could only see about five feet ahead.

Adriana was no longer holding my hand and panic filled my chest. There was something about that dark, murky water–the unknown. My breathing became uneven. We turned, stood silent and took in the dense jungle in front of us. I grabbed a stick and beat a massive cobweb to death. The imagined glimpse of a giant, fleeing spider shocked me into dancing frantically for a few seconds.

"Keep your eyes out for alligators."

She didn't really say that. My body froze.

Adriana glanced back a few steps ahead, stopped, turned, and stared at me. My sight kept darting back and forth in frantic search. My legs were leaden. My mind bounced between spiders and alligators. The girls in the boat cowered behind the hull.

"I'm scared to death, too," Adriana whispered as if something horrible might hear. "But, would you rather float around and die starving and thirsty on the ocean?"

I shook my head but wondered which would be worse.

"Tia, we have a chance at food here. We haven't hardly pulled in eight fish in the last week. And those coconuts were a fluke. We have what, thirteen girls?" She wiped the sweat from her brow with her T-shirt. "It's shallow here. Should be easier fishing."

I closed my eyes tight and muttered, "Okay." There wasn't much behind it.

Adriana smiled, flicked her hair back, and began moving away from me. No way was I going to stay here alone. I followed.

After twenty minutes of hacking our way through ominous vegetation, we came to a clearing. The ground changed and the vegetation struck me as different from the mangroves. Thick trees and bushes surrounded a shell beach the size of a small bedroom that humped up in the middle. A keyhole shaped pond lay encircled by eight feet of beach. The water shimmered clear except floating foam that lined the edge. It brimmed with conch shells and lazy brown fish; small crabs speckled the bottom. The crease of an inlet on the ocean side showed signs of filling during high tide.

Adriana put her finger to her lips and backed up slowly. She signaled for me to follow as she eased into the haphazard path that we made getting there. I kept pace with her. It seemed just as hard to exit as it did to enter. With a few yelps and rubbed shins and arms, we made it back to the boat. The girls were lined up, staring over the bow as we approached. They cheered. Our dirty faces smiled back, even though all the mosquito bites from the night before seemed to rage upon our skin.

I headed for the boat. Adriana suddenly grabbed me by my waistband and yanked me back. A snake with its head raised high wriggled past on top of the water. We both froze. My jaw stayed open and loose as the tail passed on by. The girls in the boat were in hysterics. It took all of us fifteen minutes to calm down. My eyes never left the water.

Adriana decided to have the girls toss the supplies to us. We only wanted to cross back to the boat once.

After the net and other items we needed were gathered, Lisa said she'd bring them to us. The others gazed at her as if she were homicidal. I scanned the calm roll of waves for any odd ripples from long tails. With everything strapped to Lisa's back, her wide hips rolled over the side of the boat. She swam through the shallow water until her knees banged on tree roots, then she slowly trudged toward us. She grinned. I was panicked. She took her time as if happily wading in a chlorinated pool. She dipped her face in the dark waters and came up with her hair back, combing it with her fingers. Silly girl.

Adriana and I glanced at each other and sucked in a breath of fresh air. Strength in numbers, we thought. The three of us took off, being careful where we stepped. Lisa jabbered about her mom's garden and complained about the mosquito bites.

With a raised finger, I hushed Lisa as we neared the pond. She'd been talking non-stop since we left. I think it was fear. A light breeze carried the scent of decay and salt water through my chapped nose. A rustle in the bushes made us jump. An eerie chill climbed up my spine. I slapped my cheeks softly and wished it away. The noise moved further into the brush. Leaves blinked.

As we ducked under a fallen tree, the pond came into view. Lisa pulled the hammer out. We inched closer. The crabs and fish appeared unconcerned. Adriana motioned for the two of us to move to the far end of the pool. Lisa quietly handed me the net and gave the hammer to Adriana. She pulled out a sharp rod of metal and laid her pack on the ground.

The pond sat peaceful and undisturbed in the jungle surround. Brown fish huddled as if in formation.

Halfway around, we all gasped. A fish longer than my arm came out from under a root-knotted embankment. It had a long pointy tail and a small mouth with sharp teeth. Adriana whispered, "I think it's just a small thresher shark. I'm sure I've seen some just like those in our city aquarium back home."

The words *shark* bounced around in my skull. I backed up into the trees. My throat became dry, my jaw clenched, and my lips parted. I made tiny whining noises through miasmic teeth. All our eyes were wide as the large fish cruised by with speed and swallowed a reddish fish. As it swooped past her, Adriana clobbered the water with the hammer, barely missing the now circling fish. Its tail in a nervous flick, the fish shot for the shallow entry to the ocean.

In a wild frenzy, Lisa slashed the narrow stream with her metal pole. The fish writhed across what was mostly broken shell, Lisa slammed the rod behind its dark eyes. It wiggled on the pole as she held it tight to the ground. An open mouth and rows of thin teeth bit at the air. I wasn't sure if I was happy or ready to heave. The poor, sharp-toothed fish splashed and sputtered for an eternity. Lisa beamed.

The crabs had scattered below me. I shook out the net as if

doing laundry and dropped it over four crabs and two thin yellow fish. They tangled themselves in the net and dug into the shell base. Adriana and I stepped into the water and dragged our cache from the bottom. Dripping water on the shore our haul of mostly crushed shells began to move–a claw here and there.

On our way back, Lisa spotted limes in a tree. She poked the ground with her spear, hoping to scare any snakes and rustled through the growth toward the tree. When she approached, the bark moved. A thick tube slithered higher into the tree. Lisa stiffened. Adriana darted ten feet down the path. Lisa used her rod to swing dangerously at the tree. Puny, brown-spotted limes tumbled to the ground. She filled her T-shirt with limes. A black fish tail wiggled from the backpack.

We had crab and fish soaked in the cooking juices of limes, like ceviche. It had to be the best meal I'd ever eaten in my life. The large fish we saved for the next day. The three of us were heroes and pampered by the other girls.

Sleep came easy that night. Even the mosquitos were light. We slept on the hard deck next to each other like we were having a grade-school sleepover—up late giggling and sleeping in.

The sun was high overhead when we awoke. After a breakfast of the last of the coconut and a lime, I was ready to search the island again. My fears had disappeared. With a healthy stretch, I watched as the group began to get things together.

"Look!" shouted Perri, arm outstretched and pointing. "Is that a boat?"

In the distance, a boat motored its way toward us. It was just a dot on the horizon, but it seemed to be coming directly at us. We waved our arms and cheered. Two of the girls danced across the deck. Several embraced with tears running down their cheeks. My fingers high in the air played an imaginary piano. The boat grew closer, maybe only a couple of miles out now. Its black silhouette bounded over the waves. Everyone began waving.

I glanced over at Adriana. She leaned over the back of the boat, staring at the ocean. "What's up?" I asked.

Adriana turned, her mouth tight. Two furrows divided her forehead. She wet her lips. "Is that help?" Her eyes narrowed. "Or is it Peety and his men?"

A feeling of dark premonition spread over me as we watched the approaching boat.

39

Carson

After hiding the Subaru convertible in the trees, I hiked back to the vacant motel. I had the pistol tucked in the back of my jeans and the shotgun loose in one hand. Little sounds of life fluttered in the trees. A six-foot python slithered past the dry fountain and into the trees by the gulf. The trucks lay quiet. I slinked around the perimeter and located a point where I could watch the dock and the trucks. The moonlight cast a grey-green tone over everything.

I'd previously stolen a green blanket from the one motel room that had two mangy beds and a camp stove–the abductors' quarters, I presumed. With branches and brown palm fronds, I made a camouflage dome that would hide me if someone wandered off to pee. At one a.m. I shoved the convenience store food, chips, jerky, four foil wrapped hot dogs, two tins of spam, and five quarts of water to one side and lay down. Sleep found me quickly.

The flicker of the sun through dense trees and a cold ocean breeze woke me. I wished for hot coffee as I gulped water and feasted on cold hot dogs on dry buns. Within minutes, my stomach rebelled and began burping a noxious meat gas. More water didn't help.

In the distance, the humming of powerful outboard motors caught my attention. I set the water down and waited. My pocket vibrated. Crap. I pulled the cell out and Hub's picture stared back. "Let me call you back," I whispered without need. The noise became louder as the tip of the Avalon passed through a break in the trees.

Swinging into the feeble dock, a single figure stood at the

wheel. There was a thudding sound of props hitting mud, then a crack as the boat clipped off the corner of the dock. The idiot didn't know anything about boats. *Raise the props,* I shouted in my mind. Tannish-brown water bubbled behind the boat as the blades cut through the mud.

It was the man with the limp, one of J.B.'s men. He leaned back, craning his neck as the boat bucked from the bow and stuck deep into the shore line. Finally, he found the key and turned the motor off. Silt flowed out into the bay. The pontoons were stuck two yards from the dock.

Limpy gazed at the dock as if wishing it would come to him. After checking the other side, he jumped from the bow into knee deep mud and grass, fell forward and then crawled onto the dry ground. With mud from waist down and dry dirt chalking the rest of him, he walked to the motel.

I changed my strategy. With the pistol in hand, I eased out of my cover. The windows were boarded up, so the only egress and ingress was through the door. Actually, the door frame. The bedded unit had no door. I could hear him whistling and smelled propane. I eased around the building. Waited and listened. A pot of coffee was beginning to boil.

After subduing him, I'd have a fresh cup of coffee. Wonder if he has sugar?

My face pressed hard to the frame, I peered into the opening. His back faced toward me. He whistled on. The tune hit me− 'Girls Just Wanna Have Fun,' by Cindy Lauper. I almost felt sorry for him. He began turning, and I ducked back. I'd left the shotgun in the bushes, but the pistol was under my belt.

His head stuck through the opening, his neck extended. I braced my body against the siding, grabbed his head, and rolled him down and forward. My weight landed with a crack of broken shells beneath me. His heavy body hit the ground hard. I heard the air escape his lungs as he grasped his chest. I rolled on top of him, pinning his arms with my legs. The shells cut my knees as I landed.

My hands squeezed his thick throat, tightening. Limpy pressed his palms into the shell and bucked and bounced. I held tightly to his neck and rode him like a cowboy at a rodeo. He tried to throw me off, making wheezing noises. He'd used too much energy. My hands clasped deeper, trying to subdue him. He twisted, then slackened. His puffy face turned white. Then his pupils rolled back and his muscles loosened.

I checked his pulse. It was weak and inconsistent. *Crap, he can't die on me.* I jumped off him and began slapping his face. Limpy lay motionless. I leaned down and pressed my ear to his mouth. He wasn't breathing. I pressed on his lungs with the palms of interlocked hands. I pounded his heart a few times. Nothing. The wind had gradually come up and whooshed in a high-pitched roar, I couldn't tell if he was breathing.

Reluctantly, I gulped in air and pressed my lips to his, hoping to blow life into him. A burst of rain began pelting my back and putting a shine to the shell path. I kept forcing air into his lungs. I pounded on his heart. More air. More pounding. I gained a rhythm, to no avail. Sitting up with the rain running down my body, I slapped his face. "I need you alive," I yelled.

He coughed. His chest raised and lowered. I couldn't hear his breathing through the pounding rain, but I could sense it.

I grabbed under his arms and pulled on his 200-plus-pound body. A sharp pain trudged across my ribs. My knees strained to stand upright. In squishy, slow steps, I dragged him into the motel room and dropped him by the bed. His eyes opened, and his mouth loosened. He tried to talk. A mumble. I edged closer.

"Who the hell are you?" Limpy said in a breathy whisper. He tried to sit up against the bed.

"I'm the one who just saved your ass," I answered.

He glanced around. His eyes stopped at the doorway. The rain formed rivulets flowing out toward the shore. His head jerked back toward me. "You's the one tried to tear my head off." His eyes darted around the room for a weapon. His knuckles were white, in fists.

"Hold off, hero." I raised the pistol from my pocket. "I'm just trying to find J.B. He told me to meet him here." I nodded my head toward Limpy, "I thought you was a thief or something. J.B.'s truck's out there, but he's nowhere to be found."

"You're a friend of J.B.'s?" he asked.

"Yeah, I was up at his place in Alabama. Had a couple of things to finish up, then I was to meet him here." My forehead crinkled, "Who are you?"

He sat up and rubbed his temples. His eyes tried to refocus. "I'm Ken Fishe, an old friend of J.B.'s. We were in school together. I lived at the end of his street." He paused, "You wanna put the pistol down?"

"Were you a Marine?"

"No." He slapped his right calf. "Cause of my leg. It never healed right after the bicycle accident."

I glanced at the stove and pointed. "You want some coffee?" I smiled, trying to make a new friend each day.

"Sure. There's some cups in that closet. Key's on the ledge above. I think there's a package of them raspberry donuts in there too."

I grabbed two cups and tossed him the box of donuts. Shutting the door, I noticed six pairs of handcuffs behind a box of cereal. After a few minutes of silence, I handed him a cup, pulled a five-gallon bucket over and sat down next to him. "So, where's J.B.?"

His mouth puckered in. I could tell he wasn't sure how much to trust me. I smiled. "He's out finishing up some work," Fishe said. "He'll be here later."

"Does it have to do with those girls?" I asked.

Fishe jerked his head. His eyes met mine. "You know about the girls?"

"Why do you think he asked me here to help him?" I shook my head like he must be stupid.

He rubbed his head, keeping his eyes on mine. It was quiet. The rain had stopped and water dripped off the roof in slowing intervals.

"Well, he needed a different boat. J.B. had a friend that lent him a bigger boat. He had me bring this one back." He peeked through the door at the mud-wet Avalon, tilted slightly and rocking with the tide. "He knows I can't drive no boat. He gave me a five second lesson on following the shore." Fishe pointed out to the boat and gave a puff of air from his mouth.

"Yeah, that's Sanders," I said. I thought for a minute, sipping coffee. "He ever find those girls?"

"He will. Peety put a transmitter on the shrimp boat. You know Peety?"

I gazed into my empty cup. "Not well. Is he that big guy?"

Jef Huntsman

"That's him and meaner than a raccoon. I keep my distance from him."

I poured us both another cup of coffee and thought about those handcuffs. "How you feeling?"

"Better," Fishe said. "But my head feels like something's knocking around my skull to get out."

I glanced in the cupboard, looked back at him with his head bowed into palms, and grabbed two sets of cuffs and a bottle of acetaminophen. The cuffs I slipped into my back pocket. I handed him a couple of gel caps. He swallowed them down with black coffee. "You well enough to help me dislodge that boat out there? J.B.'s going to be plenty mad if he finds it burrowed in the mud."

Fishe raised his eyes, peeking below fingers, he rubbed his forehead. "You think the rain loosened it a bit?"

He set his cup down on the floor and began to get up. I grabbed him by the arm and steadied him. "Head's spinning, but it'll be okay in a minute," Fishe said.

His face had been grey, but a touch of color seeped through it. I wasn't sure he would be much help; I just wanted to keep an eye on him. I tied the boat with ten feet give to the nearest tree, then started the motor. The stern had some good buoyancy, but the bow had wedged in solid. After some heavy vibration and mud spattering, I got the props raised enough to grab water. Fishe watched from the dock as he leaned on the algae-covered rail. The Avalon bucked and jerked. I alternated between forward and reverse, the props squealing when the RPMs were raised. The double pontoons struggled in the thick ooze. Suddenly, the boat leaped back, I let off the gas. It yanked on the rope I'd tied, the tree bent to the ground, then the rope snapped. The boat barreled backwards, tossing me into the console, and rolling with the waves. I eased it into gear and pulled forward gently to the dock.

After tying down the pontoon boat, I walked past Fishe, who hadn't moved, back to the motel room. I grabbed some supplies, tossed them into a crate, and headed to the dock. Fishe was on the shore, his jaw loose and eyes pinched together.

"What's that for? We got the boat out of the muck," his face scrunched.

"Change of plans, buddy." I handed him the box. He took it. His mouth lay open. "Come on, put it in the boat while I unhook

232

these lines."

His back straightened. "We're not going anywhere. J.B. told me to stay here."

I grabbed the box from his hands and put it on the starboard seat. I clutched him by the elbow and muscled his two hundred pounds into the boat. His head still hurt, face ashen. He plopped next to the crate of supplies—dazed.

"J.B.'s gonna be mad as hell." He began to stand.

I hopped over the rail, used his momentum to slam him flat on the fiberglass deck and centered my knee in his back. I grabbed his beefy arms and handcuffed him. He made a groaning sound as I tried to lift him off the deck. He fought. His back and legs writhed on the floor. I decided to forget it and let the stupid beast lay face down. I finished untying the boat and started it up. As I sat in the captain's chair, a biting bolt ran across my healing rib. I let out a slow breath until it subsided.

Fishe rolled to the side, on one elbow and sent me a prison stare. His puffy cheeks made it look clownish, and I began to chuckle. I backed the boat up. Fishe slid forward, slamming into one of the seat posts. He braced himself with his legs, twisted his neck, and scowled.

"You're going to tell me where they headed."

"I ain't saying nuttin. Who the hell are you, anyway?" He tried to show his mean face; but lying contorted, lifted on one elbow with his arm behind his back, he looked more like he was trying to pose for an amateur sex magazine. His long hair lifted in the breeze.

"You'll tell me." I stared at him until he turned away. I swung back around. The waves squirted around the bow with each lift and drop. The boat plowed through each crest at 33 knots. My ears focused on any movement Fishe might make.

A half hour went by in silence. I cut the motor back and dropped to idle. We bobbed in the gulf and I pivoted. Limpy was lying on his side again, hands behind his back, pinched in handcuffs. "Which way?" I asked.

He grunted and cranked around. I smacked his ankle with a strip of stainless steel I found under the console. My body jumped back as his foot swung out to kick me. It slammed into the table pole. He yelped and tried to grab the top of his foot. The boat dipped. I balanced myself with legs apart and one hand on a starboard cleat. I pulled the gun from my waist band and pointed it at the crest of his nose. He curled and leered at the gun.

"Go sit on the bench to the left of the bow," I said.

He lifted himself, setting his sore foot down gently on the deck. His eyes darted. Probably checking for something to bash my head in. He got to his knees, then hobbled over to the seat. I pulled out the other pair of handcuffs, looped them around his, and clamped them down on the front rail.

"You're going to lead me to J.B., or I'll pull out some of that rope and you can body surf behind at full throttle."

Sternness filled his face, though I could tell it was mostly a façade. He glanced over at the shore. A restaurant and dock could be seen in the distance. I cocked the gun.

He spoke into his chest. "It's about forty-five minutes to an hour along the coast. Past a couple of mangrove islands and a bunch of small docks."

I pulled out a fifty-foot length of nylon rope from under one of the seats and sat it on the deck by the steering wheel. He followed it with his eyes. His face washed out. I tied his feet together with the rope, while he cussed and squirmed. An elbow hard into his calf took some of the fight out of him. I undid the handcuffs and tied his wrists to his legs. He fell on the deck in a ball, turning his head so I wouldn't see his tears. It's always good to have someone think you're crazy. I sat him back up in the chair, the pistol pointed hard into his ear. He got the point.

I put the Avalon back up on plane. Rivulets of water ran down Fishe's shoulders and chest as the boat bounced between the swells. "You lead me to the wrong place, I toss you over."

Fear marched through his dark, inset eyes. His chin dropped to his chest.

40

Carson

An hour on fast, rough water is a harsh hour. Fishe's face had lost all color. His mouth contorted. I wondered if he might heave at any moment. I eased the boat down and gave him a little water. Apparently, he was already too sick. Within a minute, he lost everything over the edge of the boat and across the rounded seat. I kicked on the pump, grabbed the coiled hose from a cubby hole, and sprayed him and the edge of the boat. With his face dripping wet, he emerged from his seasick stupor.

"Look around. Do you notice anything familiar?" I asked. There was an old shack with a bait sign attached and an old man fishing off the dock.

He eyeballed the shore, then turned back to me, "Nah."

He was lying. I'd watched too many people in too many countries lie, while their body language shouted the truth. I reached over and tied the end of the rope to the mooring hook. I slid him over to where the rail ended and lifted his legs toward the water.

"Wha'cha doin'?" His jaw dropped. There was a catch in his voice.

I reached back, grabbed the shotgun and poked his nose a couple times. "I've been doing this awhile. I know when people try to deceive. It's in their eyes. It's in their hands and neck muscles. You, my friend, seem to need some encouragement." I tapped the shotgun against his forehead. A small chunk of skin peeled away. A trickle of blood oozed out. He rolled to his side, and I pulled him back upright with the sight pointed into his ear.

"Okay, man, I'll tell ya." He swayed, nodding up and down. His chest raised up and down in short gasps of air. "That dock over there . . ." He pointed with his head. "That I remember.

The next dock is real nice. Painted white. A big cabin sits off in the trees. That's where J.B. got the speed boat."

"You know, this time I believe you." I set the gun back on the console.

I kept the boat further away from the shore as I crept around a bend Fishe pointed out. As the white dock came into view, I noticed that the only boat there was a green canoe up on the grass knoll. In the distance, a gigantic cabin with massive windows rose behind a frame of two catalpa trees. The woods were thick. A shell road curled south of the cabin.

I shifted away and pulled the boat into a mangle of trees about a hundred yards from the dock. With Fishe gagged and handcuffed to the steering wheel, I slipped into the dark water and swam over to the edge of the property. I eased into the shore and made my way through dense vegetation, careful not to step on any of the varieties of poisonous snakes slithering in Florida. The place appeared empty–no cars, no outdoor furniture. I crouched and ran for the glass door. At the first enormous window, I peered in. Empty. A few more feet and I wiggled the door. Locked up solid.

I finally found a sliding glass door on the backside. With a large knife, I jimmied the frame enough to slip the door out. I laid it against the side and walked in. There were pictures of a Hemingway looking man with two grandchildren on his lap, and one on the wall of him in dress uniform with a row of lesser stripes. J.B. was standing third from the left in the picture. Ken Van Dorius stood to the side in a suit. An older gentleman with the same cheekbones and thick eyebrows stood next to him. I assumed it was Daddy Van Dorius.

The house was empty, although a stocked fridge and cupboards awaited. I made myself a ham and cheese sandwich, grabbed a half dozen water bottles, and snuck back out to the boat. Fishe was squirming around, struggling to get loose without results. I uncuffed him from the steering wheel and headed in the direction he had told me. I tossed him a sandwich.

Several mangrove islands dotted the passage.

As I came around the first island, Fishe began getting jumpy. I gazed out to the open sea. A thirty-foot, single-hull boat angled to its port side. I cut my speed and turned into the mangroves. A narrow passageway was cut through them, and I followed it until it opened just enough to turn around. It took five passes back and forth to point the two hulls outward. With the motor barely above idle, the boat inched its way to the entrance. On the last twist of the passageway, I stopped and waited for the boat to pass by. Limbs and leaves blocked my view, but I found a place where I could see a sliver of the bay.

As they cruised by, I could only see three men in the boat. No women. One could be J.B., but I wasn't sure at this distance. They were heading toward the dock at the cabin. The information I needed was known by these men. I made a quick plan. Quick plans are usually clumsy and hard to predict all outcomes, but I figured *what the hell*. I'd done this type of thing before and was still alive.

The first part took seconds. I cut Fishe's leg binds which released his hands from his ankles. The cuffs held his thick wrists tightly. I shoved the key to the handcuffs into his pocket and tossed him over. He wasn't expecting that. He thought I needed his help. His wide-opened mouth and eyes as he hit the brackish water said everything. He went under and came back up kicking and struggling with the handcuffs around his wrists. He knew how to cuss.

With a raise of the brow, I waved goodbye and headed out into the open sea. I noticed his Clemson hat had fallen off, swooped it from the floor and topped my head, pulling it down low.

They slowed when they saw the Avalon day boat coming their way. I waved and peered behind dark lenses. The cap shadowed most of my face. One man on the stern behind the cabin waved back. J.B. stood topside next to the driver. His arms were crossed. I assumed he was wondering what the hell Fishe was doing there.

I kept the speed at 35 mph and swerved in an arc, facing the starboard side of their boat. My velocity increased. As I headed straight at them, the man at the back ran to the side and began waving his hands. J.B. undid his arms and leaned out, shaking his fist in the air. I watched his jaws spread wide as he mouthed expletives. The pilot looked straight ahead at the dock. At about thirty feet away, I pushed the throttle forward until it stopped and flung myself off the back of the boat.

I dove deep, then watched a flash of fire from above as

water and fiberglass exploded. Pieces of litter dropped and floated on the surface. I kicked up to get air. A quick breath, I dropped down again and swam toward the shore in haste. I came up by one of the dock pilings. Air filled my burning chest. I slipped behind the piling and peered out. Just as I figured, the pontoon boat was a mass of floating fiberglass and splintered wood. The small thirty-foot yacht tilted to one side as water rushed through a hole in the hull, sinking. The driver lay curled over a metal rail on the front. I couldn't see J.B. Sanders or the third man. I waited and listened.

I was ninety-percent sure the crash hadn't killed them all, but the silence pressed heavy on my chest. Five minutes passed. I clung to the post. The boat had settled to one side in perhaps twelve feet of water.

A deep cough came from the other side of the yacht. J.B. staggered around the gunwale on the high-tipped edge of the boat. A three-foot length of stainless-steel rail stuck from out of his right side, just above his pecs. A spattering of crimson soaked his shirt and wetted it down to his waist. His mouth was open, his neck turned as he eyed his surroundings.

I ducked down into the water and paddled toward the shore, under the dock. I eased my body, careful not to disturb the surface. I pulled the pistol out from my belt and set it in the grass on the hidden side of the dock. Opening the chamber, I slid the bullets out and placed them on the sunny grass. I shook the gun to rid it of excess water and set it by the bullets. Reentering the water, I pushed off with enough shove to send me back to my piling.

J.B. stumbled, staggered off the lower window on the captain's cabin, and sat where the cushions used to be. He slumped down, keeping a watch on the waves for anything that didn't seem right. His gaze held agony and hatred. J.B.'s hair sprouted out like a burning bush. His chest rose with each careful breath. He glanced over at the pilot of the boat, hunched over partially in the water. He gave no reaction. I thought he might be in shock but wasn't certain enough to venture out.

After more waiting, I decided to get a closer look. J.B. seemed preoccupied with trying to breathe and keep from bleeding. His hand pressed to his chest, wrapping around the metal pipe. I slid down behind the piling and swam underwater in slow rhythmic strokes. I came up on the far side of the yacht and took in quiet, full breaths. The wind was starting to kick up a few whitecaps about fifty feet out. I floated closer to where the Avalon had hit the yacht. Part of one pontoon nestled several feet into an open hole, its tip shattered. I glanced in the hole. A sandal floated inches away. I backed out. The third man was attached.

I needed J.B. to live, though I figured he would be the hardest to crack. Any information he had was likely to go to his grave.

I swam around to the back of the boat. A ladder at the stern had unfolded during impact. I climbed up and slid onto a flat area for loading. The upper cabin raised five feet in front of me. A window in the door had shattered. I glanced in. Things had scattered across the floor and table. A cantaloupe nestled on a shoe. Books had shifted to the floor along with charts and a basket of emptied apples.

I struggled with the laces of my canvas shoes, wet and tight. A minute later I slipped them off and crept around the foot-wide gunwale where J.B. had come from. Hand over hand around the cabin, I pressed forward. My sight held firm on the edge, knowing any time I would see J.B. I took my time. As the window curved inward, I peeked around the lip.

J.B. had moved. Blood on the seat showed where he had been. My breath went still as a rock. I held my precarious position, leaning hard into the boat's cabin. My mind buzzed with anxiety. Sweat dripped off my chin and onto the boat. I listened to the only sounds–sloshing water and a light breeze. In slow motion, I peered around the corner.

J.B. held a gun pointed right at my forehead. "Come out," he said. I hesitated. He cocked the silver pistol. "Nothing funny now."

I began to slide into the open. "I just came to see if everyone was okay," I said in my most sincere voice, my hands stretched out and palms up.

He shook his head, trying not to let on he was in dreadful pain, but I saw him grimace as he moved. His chest was streaming blood around a one-inch diameter pole through his upper chest. He was tough. I gave him that.

He stared and rubbed his chin. It took him a few minutes to figure who I was. He smiled. "Hell, boy, you got that check for leasing my land?" He spat a glob of blood and chew onto the deck. "Who the hell are you?" He began waving the gun at me.

"I'm Carson." I took a step forward. The gun pointed back at my face. I stepped back. I could tell he wasn't thinking clearly, but he did want to know why I was there. He had lost a lot of blood. He also knew he needed a doctor. "Let me help you over to the cabin," I said. "We need to call an ambulance."

He spat out another reddish-brown glob. He extended his arm, holding the gun. His other hand clamped hard against his wound. "You're going to help me?" He laughed and began coughing. "You're the son-of-a-bitch that broadsided Hank's prize possession with that day cruiser. I'm gonna trust you? You're crazier than me, and that's saying something." He let out a long exhale. "Where's Ken?" He resituated the gun, pointing it at my chest.

"He's out in the mangroves."

He chuckled. "With that bum leg, he can't swim more than ten feet. What's your angle in this, anyway?"

"I'm looking for a girl. Tia Linford. I figure you know where she's at."

"One girl?" J.B. stared up at me for some time. "This is a bitch. I need you to get me to the cabin where there's a phone and you need me to help you find . . ."

"Tia."

"Tia. How'd you know the boat's radio's not working?"

I pointed at the cabin. "The antenna's sheared off up there, and I saw the radio guts strewn across the floor."

He glanced down at his wound. The bleeding had slowed but not stopped.

"You tell me who and where they took the girls, and I'll help you get medical assistance."

His face was pale and we both knew he had little time. He bit his bottom lip and shook his head. "The girls are headed to Jamaica on a sixty-two-foot yacht. A nice vacation," he laughed and wiggled the gun loosely in his hand. "Now you get me to land and I don't blow your head off."

I nodded, "Is there a life raft in here somewhere?"

"I wouldn't know," he answered.

"I've got a good idea. Move your feet."

He slipped them back, the gun never lost sight of my head. I reached down, slipped my finger into a hole on the deck and raised the lid. We peered down at a neatly rolled rubber raft. A red pull cord was attached.

Moving J.B. onto the raft with a gun poked into my ear was disconcerting. If he slipped, the trigger might pull and all the information I had gained would be spread across the small bay. My heart throbbed at double pace. The barrel lifted my inner ear.

I helped J.B. to the shore and supported him carefully toward the cabin. Partway across the grass, his arm dropped to his side. The gun hit the grass. His weight pulled him away from me as his limp body dropped onto his back. The rod stood straight like a flag pole into the salty air. He stared at the sky with the hollow eyes of death.

41

Carson

The beach house sat soundless. Searching with socks over my hands, I found an I-pad in one of the drawers and a charger underneath. The name Lilly was stenciled on several drawings taped to the wall. Sure enough, Lilly happened to be the password.

I downloaded a phone app and texted Annie. She immediately responded. She had been sitting in a crappy restaurant drinking coffee and trying to figure out where the hell I was. She skimmed over a map as I talked about the places I'd been. I fluffed up a pillow against the pink headboard and tried to recall details. I finally texted her to wait and I'd go check the entrance.

I ran downstairs, my shoes sloshing against the carpet. The well-beaten path outside circled about a half mile until I hit the paved road. A nicely painted sign stated, "Retired and gone fishing." There was no mailbox, but an address ran across the bottom of the sign. I hightailed it back to the cabin and texted Annie again. Apparently, she was only about forty minutes away.

I gazed out the window at the mangrove island about a mile away. "Crap!" I said to the vacant house. After relaunching the yellow raft and tossing the plastic oars in, I headed out to get Ken Fishe. I swam the raft past the first waves, then jumped in and began rowing. A hundred feet out, I found Fishe attached to twelve feet of driftwood. He was clinging onto one of the two topside branches. With his face pressed deep into wet knurl, he kicked with little strength. I headed toward him. Fishe lay exhausted after I pulled him into the small raft. His eyes were barely open–hair matted like a drowned dog. I didn't have the gun, but I wasn't too worried about him overpowering anything for some time.

I helped him across the grass toward the house. He stopped,

eyes bulging and neck tight, when he saw J.B. lying still and lifeless on the ground. Fishe turned and threw up, then dropped to the ground. I left him there, went back, stroked the grass by the dock and found my gun and bullets—dry.

Fishe and I ate two cans of ravioli and crackers. We drank coffee. I waited for Annie.

I took a quick shower and searched the house for dry clean clothes. With a belt, I made some denim pants fit, though they bulged around the hips. A shirt and jacket fit nicely. The boat shoes were a size ten, slipped right on.

Minutes later, I heard a car pull down through the gravel. I heard it back up a few feet and honk. I'd texted her not to pull all the way in. I didn't want Fishe writing down any license numbers.

I wiped off the I-phone after texting the police for help, then took a rag to everything I thought I'd touched. I had been careful before not to leave too many fingerprints. I told Ken Fishe to stay put, that I'd be back. He started to say something. I tapped the pistol in my pocket. He sat back down.

I opened the driver door. "Hi Annie. Slip over and let me drive," I motioned with the back of my hand.

She gave me the same motion back. "I'll drive. My name's on the rental, not yours. I'm staying with you until we find my sister." She patted the passenger seat with her hand, "Understand?"

I got in. Wheels spun as we backed out. "We need an airport and a flight to Jamaica," I stated.

She punched a few things into the car's GPS. "Tampa's our best bet." I pulled a lever and reclined the seat. Within a few road miles, I passed out. It had been an exhausting morning.

She woke me up at the airport. I lifted up the clear plastic bag that held my wallet. Water sloshed in the bottom. I knew I should have let that dry out. The man at the home security station wasn't impressed either. After a two-hour wait, we boarded the plane. Lots of people from the north were headed out in flowered battle gear, in search of rum and red snapper.

I called Hub before the plane taxied off. He seemed giddy that I was flying to Montego Bay.

"Last night this out-of-focus dream swirled in my head for an hour. You, Jamaica, and a fenced-in beach." Hub clicked his tongue. "I kept trying to finish *Magical Passes* by Castaneda. That dude," he chuckled, "had his perception arrow focused right on in so many ways, but his aim was always just to the left of the bullseye. He needed Don Juan to edge him back. I'm not saying he didn't know his stuff, mind you. His energy tilted . . ."

"Hub!" Several people in the seats close by eyed me with contempt, annoyed. I lowered my voice. "You mentioned before that you knew people in Jamaica. Anyone near Montego Bay?"

"Of course, Kemosabe, I spent a year there living in the mountains with fellow lovers-of-life. We've emailed for years." The phone went silent. "What happened to big bad J.B.?"

"I left him at the cabin with a friend of his." I didn't want to get into that with Hub right then. "Do you have someone who might help?"

"Sure, Akiel and his son Martin. They're farmers just outside Montego Bay. What kind of help?"

I glanced around, then covered the phone, "Guns, night-vision goggles would be nice, a place for Annie to stay, perhaps a phone."

"Annabelle's there?" His voice was accusatory.

"She refused to stay. I'm not about to argue with her." She smiled and nodded her head. "Tell me about your friend."

"Akiel owns fourteen acres of the best ganja in all Jamaica," Hub proudly said. "He might have a gun, but I've never seen one. I hope you're joking about night goggles. He'd love to have Annabelle stay. He has a lovely place in the mountains. I'll call him and have him or his son Martin pick you up from the airport. I'll text you the info."

The stewardess came by and tapped my wrist holding Annie's phone, reprovingly. "Looking forward to it." I handed the cell back to Annie and was soon catching back up on sleep.

Just as Hub said, a lime green, 1968 Ford truck waited across the street from the airport. Grey wood with green moss fenced in the back of the truck bed. A tall black man with long, dry dreadlocks waved at us. Hub must have sent a picture. After I shook hands with the roughest palms I'd ever felt, we exchanged a lengthy greeting, then Martin opened the dented door for Annie.

The ranch house was well built with stone and a wood shingled roof. We entered Akiel's sizeable room with a fifty-inch flat screen blaring a commercial about cleaning soccer uniforms. His wife, Isla, came out from the kitchen. She had shiny, puffy cheeks and eyes filled with immense warmth. Annie and Isla sat and talked while Akiel motioned me outside to the barn. He talked about Hub with strong affection as we walked.

In the barn, he pulled out two well-oiled rifles and a shoe-box-sized crate of old dynamite sticks—no fuses. I glanced at the crate, then squinted my eyes in his direction. He put a finger to his lips, turned and walked out.

During a late lunch, Akiel showed me a map of the area I'd asked about. It was down on the water about four miles away. On the narrow, meandering roads, the trip would take about thirty-five minutes.

Around five, I was ready to take off. Annie gave me a kiss on the cheek, her dark eyes wet with hope. I jumped in the back of the old pickup with Martin driving. I was a bit afraid of taking the ancient dynamite, but the sticks appeared dry and were not leaking anything.

42

Carson

After a rough ride, Martin slowed and pointed to his right. I jumped out and headed into the jungle. Two miles in, a clearing stretched behind a barbwire fence with loops of Cortina wire across the top. I climbed a tall tree. The beach curved around a small bay. Several navy ships were anchored in the distance. Three bunkers were built to one side of the clearing.

On the other end, up on a rocky hill, stood an elegant plantation house. It was more of a mansion than a house. Army guards were stationed along the front, below a ribbon of bushes and a stone stairway. A group of well-dressed men, some military, some not, were being waited on by comely women with trays of food and beverages. The hustle and bustle stretched across the veranda and onto the manicured lawn below. Soldiers walked the fence perimeter.

I repositioned myself in the tree overlooking the complex. I watched as the guards walked past me every twenty-five minutes. Cars came and went from a road behind the barracks. I assumed there was a guard post down the palm-lined asphalt, out of my view.

I jumped down after a couple hours. My arms and legs were numb. After stretching, I trotted silently and found the gated entrance. I walked the perimeter of the fence, through thick vegetation, until I stood just behind the mansion. The fence spread only thirty feet from the back of the building. There was a grassy yard, a few trees, and a wandering cobblestone path at the back. No back door was visible, just four large open-curtained windows.

My sneaker snapped an old tree branch across my path. I ducked to my left and slid into a ravine. A gate opened and two

Marines in full garb fanned their rifles in an arc, moving closer.

With care, I pulled a leafy limb over the ravine and peered out. One soldier stood two feet from me. My lungs froze, holding in nitrogen-rich air for minutes.

When the soldier took a step away, I let the stale air out and took in a careful breath. Monkeys jabbered in the background. The trees rustled with their play. The other soldier mumbled something and they both marched back through the gate. I heard it click shut. I raised up and spied the area for an hour or so, then returned to walking the fence.

The sky turned blood red as the sun lowered on the far side of the island. I found a place where the chain link had been wired together. Between patrols, I undid the bindings with the rusty pliers Akiel had lent me. It wasn't electrified but probably would be tonight. I left two wires in the shape of a "C," holding the fence together. They could be easily slipped off later.

I moved back into the jungle, settled in to wait, and ate two guavas and some jerky I'd packed.

Later, the only lights came from the grand villa, the barracks, a few drums with wood fires around the camp, and the guard's sweeping flashlights. My breath caught as I tapped the base of the metal fence with my knife. Sparks jumped. I surveyed the area to make sure no one noticed. It caused no apparent excitement.

After the twenty-five-minute guard pass, I wrapped leaves around the pliers for insulation and slipped off the two remaining clips holding the fence. I opened the hole with my boot and slipped my long body through. I re-did the process of closing the gap and putting the two clips in place. A sizzle of sparks lit the area around me as they closed. My heart pumped like a geyser.

I scuttled behind a metal tool shed, then marched with a guard's cadence through the open field to some bushes lining a path to the house. No one seemed to notice. Crouching in the shadow of the bushes, I ran across a pebbled walkway and up a trimmed embankment. My back hit the corner of the house.

Three guards huddled to my left. They were telling stories and laughing. Several were smoking, which didn't fit with formal guard duty. Rifles were strung over their shoulders and they wore combat belts. It was either lax here, or they were off duty. But, I hadn't seen anyone else walking on guard, so I assumed the first.

As one soldier flung his cigarette, I snuck around to the back. No guards, but they could come this way any minute.

I peered through a back window. It looked like the same crowd I'd witnessed on the veranda, only they were drunker and louder. There was a bar in the center with a corkscrew staircase going up next to it. I didn't see Tia. Inside, the villa had the jovial look of a family reunion BBQ at first glance, then the seductive atmosphere of glassy-eyed girls with obnoxious soldiers cast its black shadow.

As I started to think my efforts were pointless, I noticed a face I recognized. Senator Ackerman leaned into a table of four-star generals. The group laughed. With his hand touching shoulders and his permanent white teeth, he worked the crowd. I got a sick feeling in my gut. *Bastard!* I retrieved my cell from my pocket and snapped several pictures.

Three privates came around to the back of the house. My anxiety rose. My heart pounded against my ribs. One flicked his light on against the fence. He clicked it off and walked toward the once-lit spot. I heard a stream of urine. His two friends were telling stories and slapping each other on the back. The one buttoned his pants up, and the three took off to the far end of the house, disappearing around the corner.

I peered back in and noticed the girls inside the house appeared distant, almost robotic. They sat on laps of Marines in full uniform, lieutenants and above. They poured drinks and brought out food. I watched a short, bald, full-bird colonel as he took the hand of one. In a daze, she followed him up the winding stairs. The girls didn't stumble as if drugged, they just seemed unknowingly submissive. I wondered if Tia was like that now, if I was too late.

I headed back around the house. With stealth, hidden behind trimmed bushes, I slipped by the three. I kept low at the walkway near the bushes. Several fifty-five-gallon-drum fires were lit around the complex. I could see the black smoke but not much fire.

The moon was cresting, barely out of the dark ocean. I knew I had little time before it threw light on the whole place. Was it a full moon, a quarter? I should have checked. I beat myself up while marching across the open area to the shed. In the blackness of the shed, I heard a commotion going on down by the barracks.

I poked my head around the corner. Two guards were walking from the beach. A small vessel waited on a dock. The guards had three girls they were forcing up to the end barracks. If Tia was here, she was probably in those barracks.

The fence patrol team paced to my right. I pressed myself into the shadows. They walked on by, ten feet from me. I took in a relieved breath and picked up my pace, speeding toward the wired hole in the fence, then I heard someone yell, "Hey!"

I dropped to the ground and flattened out into the uncut grass. Slowly, I turned my head. A soldier walked toward the two who had just passed me at the shed. He had called to them. I blew out a sigh of relief and shimmied toward the cut fence.

The leaves were still laying on the ground nearby. I wrapped the pliers and was soon on the other side. Finding my back pack and the box of dynamite, I made my plan.

Night deepened, a quarter moon lit the facility in a grey shine. Barrel fires dotted the barracks, the beach, and the path up to the plantation house. I found a stream and layered my face and hands with fertile mud, then laid back and waited.

At about three in the morning, the moon slipped into the jungle to my west. I crept out of my hideaway with a rifle I wasn't sure about, six sticks of aged dynamite that might explode just from me walking with them, no fuses, a sharp knife strapped to my belt, and my best weapon of all, my brain. Well, maybe it was my hands. I've screwed up more than my share. I downed the last chug of my water, waited for the guards to pass, and opened the fence hole again.

Running in shadows and darkness, I headed for the barracks. Several men with a full load of weapons stood by the barrel fires. One turned and gazed my way. I was one with the grass—still and waiting. He faced back around.

In a crouch, I snuck toward the far barracks. I peeked in the window at the back door. I checked the handle. Locked. I eased up and peered through the window. It was dark, but I could make out sleeping soldiers. I counted only six. The other beds were wrapped tight.

I held the rifle angled against my shoulder. As a silhouette,

Jef Huntsman

I hoped like hell I looked like a guard. I marched past the barrel by the corner of the end barracks and headed for the one twenty yards away on the beach. I knew the girls that were unloaded earlier were in the barracks closer to my fence entry. I hoped Tia was as well.

I glanced around as I neared the barrel, no one was paying attention. I picked a dry stick from the pile by the side. With duct tape, I attached dynamite to the stick. The fire was low and perfect. I angled the wood to burn from the bottom, hoping the dynamite wouldn't blow before I got back to the girls' barracks. I turned and noticed an army guard as he hiked toward me. I nodded and started to walk away. He said, "Halt, soldier." I stopped, turned and moved toward him but into the shadows, away from the fire. He came closer. His hand lowered the rifle from his shoulder.

"Name, soldier?" he asked.

My mind sputtered. A synapse. "I'm a retired devil dog, just taking a walk from the house."

His rifle pointed toward my gut, "You're not supposed to do that." He took a step closer, "Where's your ID?" I started to pull the rifle from my shoulder. He poked his into my belly. "Why you got a gun?" His look was stern.

I blurted out a maniacal laugh, low and guttural, and slipped my fingers around the butt of my rifle. He looked at me as if I was crazy. His neck stretched out. I slammed the butt of the rifle into his lower jaw with lightning speed. His eyes went loopy. His clutch on his rifle dwindled and the gun dropped. I crowned him with my palm into his left temple. His eyes rolled back, and he thumped to the ground.

I checked all around. A patrol of two were moving about fifty feet out. I grabbed the private's gun and holster and kicked his rifle into the bushes, then pulled out a handcuff strap from his side pocket and tied his arms. With quickness and a prayer against the dynamite blasting, I dragged him into the darkness by a bush. I undid his shoes, stuffed his sock into his mouth, and lowered my shoulders and high-tailed it back to the barrel by the corner of the end barracks.

I tossed a stick into the barrel and rushed around the far corner. Flames shot up and a boom rocked the area. Within seconds, the other barrel blew—shooting into the air, tossing flaming wood across the beach. I passed by soldiers, running. Enough havoc spread to hide me in the turmoil. I pointed toward the end of the beach, yelling, "Someone's out there." They were storming every which way.

At the second barracks, I dropped two more sticks of dynamite into the barreled flames. It blew and drove a large splinter of wood into my shoulder.

I hurried to the third barracks, kicked open the back door and shoved my way past screaming girls and frightened faces, trying to locate Tia. Everything was in a panic. Women tried to get out the front door, while a single, skinny guard shoved them back. I shoved one of the girls into the private. He tumbled backwards. Several girls ran over the top of him toward the beach. The guard stumbled backwards, his weapon held in two hands above his head.

The screaming sounds raked through my mind. All lights were out. I grabbed my tiny flashlight and shined it into so many frightened faces. They clawed and kicked me in their scramble to escape. They thought I was the enemy. I began yelling "Tia . . . Tia Linford?"

A black girl grabbed me by the shoulder. She pulled at my clothes. "You're not a soldier. Who the hell are you?"

Someone pounded on my back. I shoved them back. "I'm looking for Tia Linford. Her sister sent me."

Her head cocked to the side.

"Do you know her?" Distrustful eyes stared back at me. Seconds passed. I grabbed her shoulders lightly and repeated, "Do you know Tia Linford?"

She pointed over to the side where a thin brunette stood, helping another up off the ground. The two worked to help up the other girls huddled in their corner. The girl turned. A dirty, tanned-red face with determined eyes gazed up at me. A frown tightened her lips. I wondered if she might attack.

"Tia," I said. "Annie sent me to find you."

A lopsided mouth opened. Soft features, like the ones I'd seen in her photo with her sister, appeared. Her legs gave out and she dropped to the floor on her knees. Tears began to run. Her friends patted her back.

I stepped forward, grabbed her hands, and lifted her up. "We have to go *now!*" I pulled her from under her armpits and dragged her toward the back door. She gained her legs, turned, and motioned for the other girls to follow.

Soldiers were searching the woods to the far side of the complex. The barrels lay split, on their sides, fires still burning within. A line of girls followed Tia and me to the fence hole. I kicked the fence wide open with my boot. Sparks flew. I crammed Tia through and began helping the rest.

Four soldiers ran toward us from the beach, guns out. Shouting instructions, I hurriedly wrapped duct tape to a stick of dynamite. I lit it, waited a few seconds, and tossed it. The girls were still shoving their way through the fence. The dynamite landed and the tape lost its fire. Three more girls. A warning shot hit the dirt to our side. They were getting closer. I watched the stick on the ground, hoping for life. Finally, it flickered, then glowed. A spark hit and the blast pushed the soldiers into the dirt. The last girl slipped through. I counted thirteen. More troops were headed our way.

I pushed through the fence, then led the girls up a steep incline into the jungle. Their feet slipped on decayed matter. Spotlights flickered through the thick brush, dead trunks, hanging moss, and interlaced trees. Voices shouted orders.

We crossed over a knoll that dipped into a shallow stream. Bullets fired into the knoll's soft dirt and clumped vegetation, which barely protected us from certain death. I took a few seconds to wrap more tape around two dynamite sticks, lit them, and tossed them back over the hill we had just climbed. One blast caught a dead tree on fire. I heard a scream. The bullets began frantically cutting through the jungle, but the distance between us and them had increased.

I led the girls down the stream about thirty yards, then headed back up the hill again. The soldiers were still battling away at the place we had been. One of the girls stopped, grabbed her knees and began sucking in air. I grabbed her by the arm, my face inches from her ear and said, "Rest later; you stay, you die." She glared into my eyes but stood and followed. We crossed a dirt road and ran into the bush on the other side, just seconds before a military truck barreled past us. Monkeys screeched in the trees and a few tossed fruits at us. We stormed forward.

I wasn't sure if we were going the right way. And what the

hell was I supposed to do with thirteen girls when we got there? Just Tia would be easy, but thirteen?

We came to a clearing and stopped. The girls were spent. Sweat dripped into the moist, green-covered soil. Voices yelled in the distance—getting closer. I shut my eyes and tried to picture the map. It came into focus. This was the larger of two grassy meadows. The one I needed hid to the southwest. That's where Akiel's son, Martin, would have the truck. I nodded to my right and we crept inside the tree line. We scrambled around the clearing. Two of the girls fell behind. I hustled back, put an arm around each waist and hurried them forward. There was a lost gaze to their eyes.

Daylight was just peeking through the trees in a thin belt of white and orange. Martin had said he could only wait until six a.m. He had a load of bananas to pick up and deliver to the market. I held up my hands and stopped the girls about halfway around the clearing. I listened and heard soft voices to my right and breaking twigs in the distance. It would be quieter to run through the meadow. I signaled with my finger, and we took off through the tall grass—backs arched low. Grass whipped at our legs.

Helicopter blades suddenly chopped the air, moving toward us. We darted back toward the jungle thickness and safety. We raced around the perimeter to the far side. Some of the girls were sobbing in fear but running hard. I helped the two who had briefly given up before.

Finally, I saw the truck. Martin stood talking to five Marines. We dropped onto our bellies. He had the hood open and was talking with a great deal of animation. It was like a dance with swear words. You could probably hear him across the mountaintops. Minutes later, the soldiers had had enough. They spread out and entered the trees opposite us. The girl's eyes were as round as globes.

I waited five minutes, then tossed a rock at the truck. It hit the old boards on the back. Martin turned and I stood and waved. A smile crossed his face. He strolled around and shut the hood, jingling his keys in the air. We all ran across the open area.

Martin glanced back at us. His eyebrows raised. His palms flicked open, jaw dropped. I loaded the girls into the truck bed and had them lie like a package of hot dogs. Tia helped them spread out in layers on top of each other. Martin and I grabbed fallen palm fronds from the forest's edge. I tossed the brown and green leaves over the girls, telling them to lie still. Soon they were semi-covered in leaves. I pulled out bundles of tall, wet grass and set them on top of the palm fronds. Soon, it looked like a load of loose hay in the truck bed.

We piled in. Martin drove, Tia sat in the middle between us. Martin pulled a cigarette from his pack, lit it, and we were off. I tossed the last stick of dynamite to the side of the road. That felt safer.

We drove about a mile, then came to a roadblock of Jamaican police—one jeep and three men. They glanced at me and Tia from the driver's side. "Get out," one said. Two pulled Martin to one side. The other kept guard on Tia and me. Their guns were held in both hands. Two whites with a Jamaican in the jungle usually meant a drug exchange. Their faces held stern and poised.

I leaned across Tia and said, "He's taking us to town. Our rental broke down, and I guess we walked the wrong way, trying to get back to town." Martin smiled and agreed with several nods that that was how it was. "You can call our hotel; we're staying at Sandals." That was the only resort I knew was in Montego Bay. I hoped it might lend some credibility to the story. They looked skeptical. "Perhaps you gentlemen could take us back to our hotel, if there's a problem with this nice farmer?" I asked.

The one with the most medals gave the other a full frown and spoke in quick Jamaican. They walked to their jeep and waved us on. I knew they wouldn't want to drive us into town. They had easy duty out here.

Our dust hid the road behind us. My heartbeat finally slowed.

43

Carson

Pulling into Akiel's farm, I felt a sense of exhaustion and fear. The leathernecks wouldn't be too far behind. They wouldn't chase us helter-skelter. They would make plans and search in military precision. Having so many upper ranks at the villa would slow it down a bit—too many roosters and too few chickens. They'd be at the airport, any major boat docks, and main roads out of Montego Bay. They probably had money shifting to the Jamaican police right now. We walked to the front porch.

Annie barged through the door, all red-eyed with worry. Her jaw opened wide, then her cheeks raised into a giant grin. She and Tia ran to each other, almost knocking themselves to the ground. They embraced, tears flowing freely in the midst of sunshine smiles. It was worth everything. My beat-up body rose just above the surface of the ground as I watched the two beautiful sisters reunite.

Akiel and Martin unburied the twelve other girls from the truck bed. Nervous chatter burst through the palm fronds. Unsure eyes gazed between the boards affixed around the bed. The wide-eyed face of the girl who helped me find Tia in all the turmoil of the building poked around the edge and smiled. She bounced out, ran toward me with arms open and jumped up, wrapping her legs around my waist. With a grin and her cheeks rippled with tears, she yelled a litany of happiness into my ears. I patted her back awkwardly and tried to set her down.

I was embraced by another crazy, happy girl for the longest time, then Tia yanked her arm, giggled, and they both dropped to the ground. The two girls laughed and rolled on the soft earth together, hugging, while the others beamed with bright smiles amid a flow of tears.

I noticed Akiel watching the road as he shifted his feet. His worried face seemed to be bunched up with old wrinkles. "We've got to get into the house," I said. "The soldiers may be coming by any minute." Faces blanched as the girls ran through the door. Akeil let out a troubled exhale.

Akeil and I talked on the porch, while his wife, Isla, made a pot of coffee and settled the girls into the couple's small main room. All the girls huddled together on the floor, while Tia whispered to them, trying to relieve as much anxiety as possible. Annie couldn't stop gently patting her sister's arm. The small front room looked like a sorority house after a party.

"Can I use your phone?" I asked.

Akiel's head motioned back and forth. "It been out all day. May come soon."

May come soon is a Jamaican expression, which means, roughly, that things may happen in a minute or twenty years from now. I'd heard it a lot on former visits to this relaxed paradise.

"It happens a lot up here," he said. His shoulders shrugged.

I held my exasperation in.

Akeil pointed to the barn on the far side of the marijuana field. "There's an old, cold, storage area under the barn. A hatch to the left of the door leads down a crappy staircase." He folded his arms as if in prayer, "If they come, go out the back door through the high plants and into the barn."

I nodded.

"The dust will probably settle back over the storage entry. I'll have Martin toss something light on top."

"Do you have water and food I could take down there?" I asked. "I'll pay you for all this."

"I know," Akiel said. "Hub told me you are a generous man," he paused and looked straight at me, "though your face doesn't show it. Hub told me that, too. I think he misses your aura. You have the colors of giving."

Great, another Hub with a different name.

"I'm sorry, what did you say?"

"Nothing. Just thinking about the girls."

He reads thoughts? I turned and bolted inside.

44

Carson

I'd just taken the last bite of a grilled plantain. The motors and rough road sounds hit my ears just seconds before my adrenaline skyrocketed. My brain whirled through scenarios, even with the bubbling sounds of girl anxiety that surrounded me. Annie started to pull back the drapes. I swatted her hand and placed one finger to my lips. I signaled the other girls, grabbed Tia and Annie by the arms, and bolted through the back door. Akiel and Isla motioned us out. Fear swallowed the old man's gritted teeth.

Heartbeats pounded. Birds fluttered and flew over the canopy of jungle. The backyard was circled in twisted trees and flowered bushes. A worn path headed into the trees. It curled around as Annie, Tia and the other twelve girls followed me in a bunched-up, single-file line.

The path Y'd. I veered to the right toward the noise of Humvees cutting across the open field toward the house. Annie let go of my hand. I stopped. She shook her head. The rest of the girls looked like scared wet puppies as they trembled and backed away from the sound of the military vehicles.

My forearm stroked the air in a hurried fashion. I whispered. "I'll keep you safe." Hesitant, they finally read my eyes and several nodded. I turned and eased forward. The soldiers were so close we could hear deep voices barking orders. A crunch of twigs to our rear stopped all our hearts. Someone was coming at a quick clip. I signaled for the girls to dive into the bushes. They made enough noise to send a family of monkeys into frantic disorder. I pulled my gun, moved into the bushes, and listened to the sounds from behind. I swiftly hid between some tall roots of a tree and waited. Some of the girls crammed together by me, others dropped behind the bushes. I heard only two feet running. As a shadow came into view, I slipped my foot out and watched a dark figure fall. I pounced, putting my gun to his head.

"Martin!" I helped him up. Leaves and fertile soil clung to his dark face. His white teeth shone through, and he tried to catch his breath. He leaned into my side. "I'll meet you at the barn," he said in a low voice. He returned to the trail and continued running.

We moved. Soon, we came to a long clearing with a six-foot width; it separated the forest from the crop. I couldn't see the soldiers but could hear them. I mouthed, "Follow me," and ran across the narrow clearing with Tia and Annie in tow. Tia grabbed Adriana's hand. The others followed.

The marijuana crop was thick with budding crowns and delicate leaves. We batted our way through the maze of plants in a path to the barn. Someone from the porch of the house yelled, "Fan out."

He must be a new WestPoint grad, forgetting hand signals and screaming his intentions to the enemy.

At the edge of the crop, I spotted Martin. He waved for us to get into the barn. The girls bore stressed long faces. Some limped as we hurried. Their chins hung close into their necks. I whispered, "Life or death," and grabbed Tia by one hand and Annie by the other. Tia had a hold on Adriana and we raced forward. A girl named Lisa was the last one through the barn door. Martin closed it slowly. It creaked and sent chills down my back. The only light came from a square opening at the highest point. With so little sunlight and Martin's dark complexion, I lost his whereabouts. I heard the creak of latches and followed the sound. Martin descended the creaking staircase, lit a lantern, and began helping the girls down into who knows what. Annie and I were the last ones in.

I glanced around. The place had the crossed comfort somewhere between an abandoned mine and a bear's cave. I hoped we wouldn't disturb anything from hibernation. A few logs braced the earth, but the area was mostly tied together by a map of roots. I shined my penlight down the row of girls and couldn't find the end.

"There's a covered opening at the end. Comes out in the trees," said Martin, then he shook his head. I knew by the tightness of his mouth that the exit wasn't a great choice.

Martin set a lighter down on a crate and blew out the lantern. "Don't light it until the soldiers are gone. I'm not sure how solid the boards above are." He slipped up the stairs and shut the hatch down.

We could hear him kicking dirt and debris over the wood door. Streams of dust funneled through the wood slats, then stopped. He slid a bale on top and kicked more dust. We watched as the tiny streams of light were snuffed out, turning our burrow into coal blackness. Silence passed over all of us. Finally, breathing started. It was a welcome friend in the damp earthen hole.

Seemingly abandoned, we listened for any above-ground noise. Our pulses were stoked with adrenaline so thick you could taste it. I whispered something about keeping their mouths sealed and sat down. With my pen light spotting the cave, soon all the girl's butts were settled on the dark layer of forest decay. I knew they were all holding hands and staring upward, even though I couldn't see them. There was an air of comradery one could feel, despite the fear.

Twenty or thirty minutes passed. The sound of someone approaching shot a current down my spine. I heard a few gasps. Then voices. I closed my eyes tight to hear better, though in the solid darkness it seemed impossible. Four footsteps, perhaps, crossed above us. Cut plants were shuffled. We listened to feet on ladder rungs as someone climbed to the loft above. His feet were weighty on the thin ladder that led to the loft. I heard a muffled voice with the sing-song vernacular of the Jamaicans. I concentrated to hear.

"Me nun waan truble," said Akiel. I smirked. He spoke better English than college scholars. "No oo'man, neva. Dem run?" They seemed to be ignoring him as he rattled on. After he tried to give them some free ganja, they exited the barn. I heard the last soldier shut the door. I leaned back against the soft earthen wall. Adrenaline still surged through my body, but I felt a quivering relief.

One girl about ten feet from me asked, "They gone?"

I gave her a short "Shhh." We waited.

Time passes slowly in perfect darkness, especially when the ground squishes and your mind wonders about all the earthen

creatures below the surface. Small noises twisted my neck—
endless and anxiety producing. I tried to check the time on my
phone as I shielded it from the unknown. With a quick bleep, the
batteries died.

Finally, we listened to feet charge through the door and
assemble just above us. I swallowed, though nothing but dryness
spasmed down. They stopped just above us and kicked the earth.
Dust fell into my eyes. All breathing stopped.

"Carson, it's me," said Akiel. He'd lost the Jamaican patois
accent. The hatch swung open, and Martin and his father gazed
down at us. The girls all crowded around the bottom of the rickety
stairs, peeking up with hesitant smiles. One began to laugh and the
others followed. My shoulders relaxed as I helped each one up.

We gathered above ground. Akiel held his hands up saying,
"Wait here, I'll bring food and water. They're still looking on the
other side of the mountain."

I handed him my cell. "Can you put that on a charger?"
Annie handed him a charger from her purse and tossed me her cell.
It had one bar. I scrunched my face. *Nice luck.*

We all relaxed in the barn. The warmth and brightness of
the morning sun raised our spirits. We ate bananas and yams and
washed it down with strong coffee. The barn had the rich odor of
ganja plants and swayback horses.

Hours later, Martin brought me my phone I'd given him to
charge. I told the girls to wait in the barn and if they heard
anything to head down below. I gave Martin a look. The loose jaws
and defeated stances of the girls told me they wanted me to stay. I
explained that I needed to make a phone call to get them out, but
that service was down at the farm.

Tia grabbed my hand and mouthed "Thank you." I don't
think she had it in her to say the actual words without breaking
down again. Tears flowed from several girls. The one I knew as
Adriana tried to joke, "Suck it up girls, this tall devil dog won't let
anything bad happen to us." She scooted me out with the back of
her hand. I took one last glance at Annie, turned, and ran into the
trees.

The trees were thick enough to hide most of the sunlight.
Forty minutes passed as I hiked up to the mountain peak Akiel had
told me about. I tried my cell. No bars.

Moving while limbs and roots grabbed my legs, I found an overturned tree, braced into two crossed palms and climbed to the edge. The branches bent and creaked as I moved forward, flat like a lizard but without its agility. A swift, short break of the bracing trees, and I found myself sideways. I hugged the tree for dear life. I hung thirty feet over the hill's edge and could see for miles across the mountain tops. The uprooted tree dropped about an inch. I waited. Everything stabilized. I hoisted myself up and checked my cell. I had bars. I shimmied up a foot more to brace myself on a larger limb.

It rang. I smiled as I clung to the tree, then glanced down and lost the happiness.

A recording sounded. An older, overly sweet voice came on. "This is Eva, I've stepped out to run to the hairdresser's. Please leave a message." I shook my head at Bear's answering machine.

"You know who this is. Call me back right away. I'm in a damn tree." In frustration, I pressed my chest into the dead tree. "I'm stranded in a tree, looking out over the mountains. Get your damn hair done some other time!" I clicked off and waited.

Ten minutes passed. Then twenty. I was sweating from every pore. The sun baked my back. My eyes pierced the cell phone, to no avail. *He couldn't be on a mission. He didn't do missions anymore.* A breeze chilled my sweat, but not my temper.

I was about to give up when that stupid, wonderful tune Maria had installed carried across the tree tops. I fumbled and almost lost the phone to the jungle below, before my grip slammed it to my ear.

"Hello! Hello!" I yelled.

A faint echo replied, "Hello." I heard a low chuckle. "That true? You in a tree, or is that code for locked out of your car?" A belly laugh.

"I've got Senator Wayne Patrick Ackerman nailed to the wall here."

"I'm listening," his gravelly voice turned serious.

"I'm in Jamaica." I swatted a big red ant off my wrist. "I need transportation back to the states for me and thirteen girls."

"Thirteen girls! I have no idea how you do it. Does Maria know?" His low burst of amusement almost sounded as if he were choking. "I have a hard time getting a date with the widow down the street."

"I am up in a dead tree on the side of a mountain so that I can get reception. I'm so happy you find this hilarious!" Two more sizeable ants had meandered down the trunk toward me. "Do you want to trade?"

"You already know the answer or you wouldn't have called," Bear said. "Keep your cell phone charged. We can get a signal, even though you can't. We'll find you."

I punched end and called Hub. I gave him the condensed version of what had happened and asked him to send all the information he'd collected to Detective Brower in Salt Lake.

Then my mind clicked, *uh oh.* "Please call Maria and explain the situation. I'll call her as soon as I can." I ended the call abruptly as I realized the ants had relayed information to one another and a battalion of them were creeping down from above— ants the size of cockroaches. I slipped the phone into my pant pocket and began shimmying down the trunk in haste.

I was greeted by kisses and hugs as I entered the barn. My face turned five shades of red as I pried myself away. Annie stood to one side, grinning as she quietly clapped her hands. The girls had a different mood in them, celebratory and jubilant. Their lost, frightened, hollow faces had gained dimples, and there was a tallness to their stance. I assured them we were going home soon. Giddiness erupted as they hugged and spun each other around on the dirt floor.

Before, I had been afraid to go to the house. I wasn't sure if the soldiers would be back or not, and if they were watching from the trees. Now, I decided to take the chance. I snuck back through the rows of plants. At the edge, I cut over to the jungle and found the path that led to Akiel's back door.

He greeted me with a glass of banana rum. I declined and checked my phone. No bars. A sliver of doubt swallowed down my throat. He watched the entry road through the curtains while I checked Annie's recharged phone. She had one bar. Maybe it was enough for the call. It wasn't.

I stared at Akiel and Isla's home phone. Maybe the line worked now. I raised my eyes to his. Akiel raised his palms in front of him. I picked it up. Dial tone. Nice.

I hadn't noticed the humidity until I relaxed into a chair. On the third ring, a grumpy familiar voice answered. "Is this that freelancer?" Detective Brower asked.

"I've got thirteen abducted girls and maybe twenty or thirty more back at a villa on the beach." I waited for that to sink in. He said nothing. "I need your help."

"Of course you do," he said sarcastically. "Where you at?"

"Montego Bay, Jamaica."

"I can't come there. My wife's been harping on me to take her to a tropical island for years. No way she would understand me going," he coughed. "I don't think the department would flip for the bill either."

"No," I said. "I need you to meet me somewhere on the coast."

"Well, that narrows it down."

"I'll have to give you instructions later." I stood and peered through the window with Akiel. Martin bounced across the clearing in his truck, coming back from somewhere. "Will you line it up?"

"Sure, maybe they'll give me the keys to the city before I go," he laughed.

"I can't live with the notoriety. I need you to take point on this and receive all the thank-you-for-your-thorough-police-work crap. Can you do that?"

"You make me sound so needy," he paused. "But, of course I'll take the kudos. I could use a stripe or two and perhaps the raise in pay grade." My ears picked up traffic in the background–a horn honk, diesel truck rumbling nearby. "Maybe later I can take the wife to Jamaica."

"And keep my name out of it?" I asked.

"Who needs to share the glory, when I did all the work?" His deep laugh sounded like an automatic rifle in a wind tunnel.

I hung up. Akiel and his son were talking on the front porch. I tapped on the window. They turned and strolled through the door. I handed Akiel my phone and explained that I needed to leave it on charge.

The girls were relaxed on bales of crop when I entered the barn. All eyes stared anxiously at me for news about how soon we would leave. I cocked my head to the side and held up my hands.

Chins dropped to their chests as they went back to waiting.

Martin scurried through the big door. The look on his face scared the girls. Heads darted back and forth from each other. "Mr. Carson, the phone." He grabbed me by the wrist and began pulling. "A very mad lady is on the phone, threatening my dad. He is pacing. She is shouting. I only understood your name."

I raced between the trees and the tall plants this time. Martin couldn't keep up. The back door had been left open. In two long strides, I burst into Akiel's main room. Akiel fumbled with a glass of rum in one hand and his ancient black phone in the other. Relief washed over his face when he spotted me. The earpiece was jammed into my hand.

I could hear Maria's irritated voice, even as I lifted the phone inches away from my ear. "Maria," I said.

"You have that crazy Shaman call me." It wasn't a question. "You're too busy to phone me." That wasn't a question either, so I waited. Her river of exasperation streamed on. She kept bouncing between Spanish and English. Martin and Akiel hid on the porch. *Cowards*. I waited until her voice became hoarse and the words had pauses.

"Maria, I am *so* sorry." I waited through another litany of profanity. Then her silence bled irritation through the speaker. "I have no excuse." I felt it best not to go on about my cell phone reception problems. "With everything happening, I screwed up."

"What's everything?" Her voice came through as a smoldering burn, ready to ignite with the first hint of a breeze.

"I found Tia and freed her and twelve other girls. They're all bundles of shock and tears. Marines are searching for us as we wait on a small pot farm in the highlands."

"Marines?" she asked.

I sucked in air. "A small group of the corps that followed orders from some self-entitled upper rank. It looks like Senator Ackerman put this baby together."

"Are there more girls than the thirteen?" Her speech had softened—in fact there was a slight, endearing quiver to her voice. Maria is fiercely strong and independent, but she melts at the thought of anyone being hurt or in harm's way.

"A lot. I have no idea how many, but according to one of

the girls, some have even been shipped out to various behind-the-lines' bases around the world. It's craziness."

I knew now that I could tell Maria that I couldn't talk much more. I let her know I probably wouldn't be able to call her until after I was in the states. She seemed okay with that. She told me to thank my Jamaican friend and apologize for some of the things she might have said. I told her I missed her, then hung up to the sound of a helicopter whipping the air from above.

45

Carson

Bear picked us up in a naval helicopter, then flew all of us out on a Caribbean Airline's plane. We landed on an abandoned air strip near Dallas, Texas. How he snuck us through customs with most of the girls not having passports baffled me. There were no other passengers on the ATR-72 besides my group, Bear, and three x-linebackers with flowered shirts who claimed to be U.S. Marshals.

We were whisked off in a brand new, military bus and taken to a Hilton in Dallas. The girls doubled up in seven rooms. Clothes had been bought and laid out on each bed. I heard sighs as they ran to their rooms to rid themselves of the light-blue onesies Bear's men had given them at the barn in Jamaica.

Three hours later, showered, legs shaved, and in denim jeans and button blouses, the girls came out smelling like a *Juicy Couture* factory. They joined us in the conference room with white-papered, banquet tables. We ravaged through salads, chicken parmesan, and mixed vegetables. Repetitions of the questions asked in the plane barraged each of us. I was used to it. The girls squirmed and threw shy, scared glances around as difficult memories were uncovered. Well, except Adriana, who couldn't stop talking. She was a fund of information—more than they could ever ask for.

At Annie's urging, I pulled Bear off to one side and told him, "Enough. These girls need to call their parents and loved ones." Most of the families of each girl were headed toward Dallas on the government's dime. I couldn't imagine how frantic and relieved they would be. The girls kept asking if their parents were there yet.

The other abductees at Senator Ackerman's complex were also picked up by naval helicopters. They were flown to a stateside hospital for detoxing.

The Marines in Jamaica were cross-examined by military judges. It was found that some were in on the scheme, but many were just following orders, no matter how absurd they seemed.

Warrants were issued in twelve states. The military was in an uproar as twenty-six of its own were taken into custody. The Commandant of the Marine Corps distanced his beloved Marines from the scandal stating, "Most of the suspects were retired, or had left the Marines years ago. The poison of civilian life and corrupt politicians apparently broke down whatever honor they once had as Marines." Reporters had a field day dramatizing the medals and stripes earned by those involved, generals on down.

The great Senator Wayne Patrick Ackerman, heir to the Ackerman fortune and son of one of the greatest naval commanders in the history of the United States, was hauled from his private jet to an undisclosed location. General Robert Stanchy and a civilian, Ken Van Dorius, were found at the same time, in Ackerman's jet, and taken away in different vehicles. Someone sold a picture of the three exiting the plane with "What, me?" looks on their faces.

Two weeks later, Ackerman and a gaggle of military brass were formally arrested for misappropriation of funds, conspiracy, and kidnapping. The evening news stated, "It seems he bought a large villa on acres of land in an unknown foreign country."

Apparently, the government had developed a refined date-rape-like drug that Ackerman used to control at least forty-three women and eight men, at last count. The drug's effects lasted for weeks and affected the limbic system in the brain. The victims subjected to it had no memory of anything except being kidnapped and hauled to an island. The drug made them do what they were asked, against their will, but without physical impairment during the *high.*

Several bases around the world were invaded and their officers interrogated as places where unwitting captives had been sold.

Ackerman's only statement to the news was, "My innocence will be proven."

Later, it was discovered that Ackerman had bought the forty-acre property and villa in Jamaica from a well-known author who hadn't used it in years. The purchase and upgrades were paid for by the taxpayers without anyone's knowledge.

The funds were siphoned from one agency to another until they landed as pay for supplies at General Stanchy's and Ken Van Dorius's company, Best Buy Livestock Feed. From there, the funds were diverted to a non-existent enterprise in Jamaica, referred to only as BananaCorp, then to an undisclosed bank in the Caymans. The ownership of BananaCorp was still being investigated.

Detective Brower was all over CNN and Fox News as the man who tracked down J.B. Sanders, which led to the abducted girls being found. By all accounts, the scheme was discovered as a result of the concerted efforts of Detective Brower, the Salt Lake Police Department, and the FBI. Everyone happily shared in the glory.

Serenity, as it was coined by a lab in Cincinnati, was apparently a derivative drug of GHB or Liquid Ecstasy. The lab, working in conjunction with the Pentagon, had developed Serenity to be sprayed over enemy troops and make them docile and unaware of their mission.

Senator Ackerman had requisitioned the lab to develop a pill form. The military had bought large quantities of the drug based on military procurement forms signed by General Stanchy and sent to an address owned by Ken Van Dorius and his father. Thousands of bottles were found in an underground bunker at the Jamaican compound.

One month after the arrests, Senator Ackerman disappeared en route to one of many court appearances. His remains were found three months later in a jungle outside Rio de Janeiro. The cause of death was determined to be strangulation. His wife had already divorced him, and his three girls did not show up to his humble funeral.

After the dust settled, Maria, Hub, and I invited Annie and Tia to a tin-foil dinner at my ranch. With careful fingertips, the two girls followed our lead as we opened the foil. Steam, and the aroma of vegetables and steak burst forth. As the sun closed out the day, my campfire danced happily in the evening breeze. Tia gingerly examined the lightly-charred carrots and potatoes. As she poked at them with her fork, I noticed the same disgusted look on her face that Annie's had held when she first surveyed my ranch, *definitely sisters*. Tia caught me watching her and quickly smiled back as she took a cautious bite. "Yum," she said.

Excerpt from

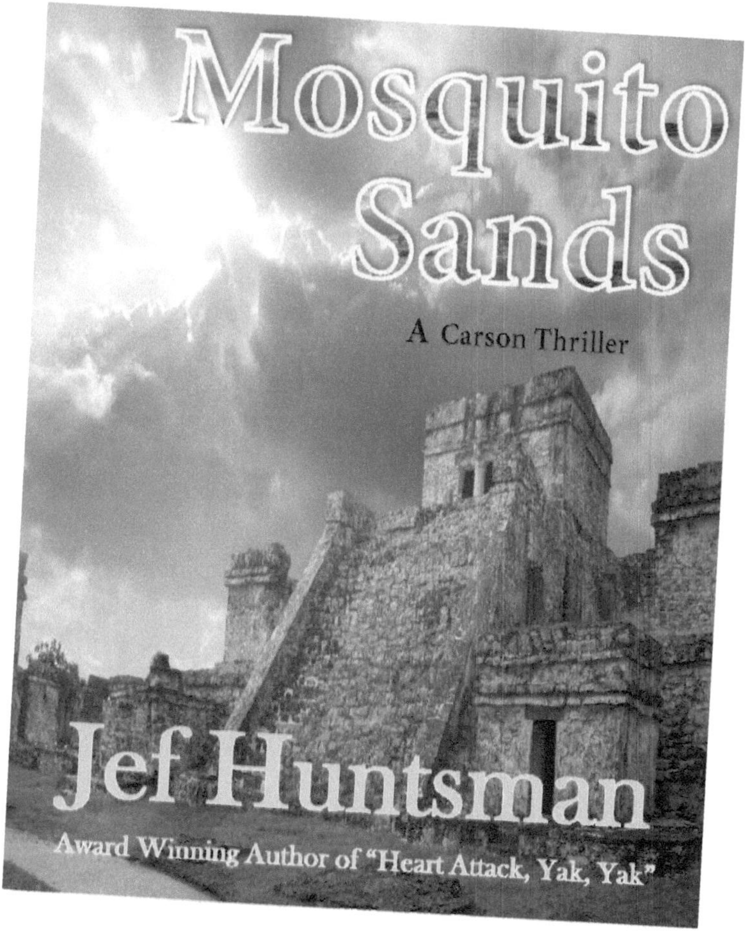

A Carson Thriller

Belray Books, LLC

Jef Huntsman

Mosquito Sands

1

Mosquitoes hung in speckled clouds as we searched the dry swamp for Harold Sims' body. April rain and crazy warm temperatures had brought out the bloodsuckers early. I couldn't even imagine how thick they'd be by summer. I walked the banks of the Sevier River, slipping on mud and grasping for tamarack bushes. Other searchers spread out across the dry areas. One yelled when she found a Cuervo bottle; a short swallow remained.

This wasn't the type of search I usually did, but there were enough stories swirling around about my recent exploits that the local police had grabbed me to help find Harold. Most forces would discount a civilian recruit, but this town had so few officers any aid was welcome. They even brought me a fresh cup of coffee from the Maverick store in town. Fair enough pay for battling mosquitos and dung intermixed with mud while looking for a dead guy.

After twelve years of living in my remote cabin, I was still considered an outsider. Oh, the town people were friendly enough, all two-thousand and eight of them. I got nods at the store but was rarely invited off the mountain for home-cooked dinners. It suited me just fine.

We fanned out along Fayette Road on both sides of the Sevier River. The brush was thick and the mud made movement slow. Rabbits and ducks fled in our wake. I watched as a garter snake writhed across still water, escaping from our disruption. We came upon several islands of dry sand beat by hooves and littered with cow pies and the occasional faded beer can. Dense tamarack surrounded the pockets of sand with tiny inlets like a maze. I had kept glancing at the sky searching for circling buzzards – a sure sign of carrion.

I edged around an abandoned salt lick and spotted a partial sleeve of a checkered shirt. Calling over Heath, the town's only detective, I held up the ripped piece of cloth with a gloved hand. Gloves courtesy of the city.

"Yeah, that's Harold's," Heath said. "He only has but two shirts, and I've seen him in both."

I noticed an overturned rock and a scuffle of foot prints dug deep into the cracked clay ground. We both squatted down to see if they meant anything. My eyes followed a path through the bushes. It appeared there had been four large boots, the kind that could be used to make waffles. Matted bushes and broken branches prompted me and Heath to follow the trail through a thicket of brush. I could barely see ten feet ahead as I parted the twigs that rose a foot above my six-foot frame.

I entered a sandy dry tributary from the river, then spotted the rest of the shirt. I rushed toward it, getting slapped in the face by the tamaracks. In a small ravine lay the body of old Harold. Dust caked his open lips. Blood had coagulated after running from a gash on his head, around his ear, and down his neck.

We had searched for about two hours; six hours had passed since Little Jim had confessed to killing him. The police told me he cried like a baby, blurting out nonsensical words about a fight down by some river. He was so drunk they had to wake him up four or more times to gather any semblance of what had happened. Little Jim and Harold were best of friends and spent most afternoons, into the evening hours, on bar stools in the *Horseshoe Bar and Grill* at the end of Gunnison, Utah.

My cell rang. I grunted with irritation and slapped my pocket. *Why the hell did I bring my phone? I never do that.* I answered mostly to stop the ridiculous tune my girlfriend, Maria, had installed. Heath raised his brow.

My eyes panned over to the body. "Yes," I answered curtly.

"Wow Carson, cut back on the caffeine, man." It was my friend, Hub. "I'm at your house, and you're not here. I need your help, like days ago."

"I'm with the deputies searching for Harold. Actually, we just found him." I kneeled closer to Harold's body. I could still smell the alcohol as if he'd bathed in tequila. He had all his top teeth missing and I couldn't remember if that was normal. I didn't know him that well.

The deputy read my mind. "He had teeth, probably false."

"Compadre, you there?" asked Hub.

"Let me call you back. This isn't a good time." I noticed Harold's left leg bent at an odd angle. Definitely broken. A dark spot of crimson stained the leg of his Wrangler jeans.

"But, I have a missing little girl that needs your expertise. My spiritual teacher . . ."

"Hub, that sounds serious," I took in a deep breath. "But, I've got to go. Let me call you back." I pushed 'End' and slipped the cell back into my pocket. I turned to the deputy, "When's the medical examiner going to be here?"

He gazed back at me as if I'd spoken a foreign language. "Uhhh, let me call." He fumbled for his phone. "Doc Andrews from Richfield is the only one."

"He's at least an hour away," I said, more to myself than anyone.

Four more of the searchers came through the brush, stopped, and stared at Harold's dusty body. One put her fingers on his chest, looking for motion. Her face turned ashen as she lifted her hand and backed away. We waited, hoping to see his chest rise. It didn't.

I leaned closer and put my fingers on Harold's jugular, even though his stillness reeked of death. I felt a faint something. I shook my head. It was probably just the wind over the back of my hand. I grabbed his limp arm and shook it. Nothing.

Someone behind me said, "You shouldn't be doing that. Harold may be dead and drunk, but he's still one of us."

I ignored him, shook Harold again, and leaned in close to his mouth with my cheek listening for any sign of breath. Harold came to with a spasm and knocked his head into my nose.

"Harold," I said. My nose throbbed. Two more people came through the bushes.

He groaned and mumbled something. I put my ear down closer. "Where's my bottle?" he whined in a low voice.

Everyone clapped and several patted him on the side. He growled. An officer backed them off in case there were any unknown injuries. I smiled at the thought of how little Jim would react when he found out he hadn't murdered his best friend. Crazy drunks.

An ambulance arrived, and I headed on foot down Fayette River Road toward my cabin. It was only about five miles. I declined several rides offered, knowing the morning jog would clear my mind and stretch out some of the damage my second line of work involved. About halfway there, I noticed Hub's truck coming toward me. I eased over to the side of the gravel road by a neighbor's cow pasture and took morning air into my lungs.

Hub usually drove like a state employee on the clock, but this time, his truck spit gravel and dirt as the vehicle slid to a stop. He stepped out, hair wild, and eyes a touch crazy. His arms flailed in front of him as he closed the ten-foot gap between me and him. The truck door was left open.

"I've been trying to find you for an hour," he said. "Who would have thought you'd actually take your phone with you someplace. I headed up the mountain in case you went for a morning run. Nothing. Maria about bit my head off when I called her," his breath labored as he prattled on.

"What's this big problem you seem to have?" I asked.

"Juan Diego, the shaman spiritual teacher you met three years ago in Mexico. His girl is missing." Hub sucked in air through his teeth. "It's been two days and the *Federales* have found nothing. He remembered your skills and called me. I told him you'd be glad to help."

I closed my eyes and ground my teeth. "I told you I'm off for the summer. I promised Maria we'd go to California and visit her sister." I tented my fingers to my mouth. I wasn't feeling good about either option. "You know Maria."

"But you owe him."

"What?" My arms crossed my chest.

"Well," Hub backtracked, "I owe him, and you owe me. Maria will understand. Seronia is a lost little girl, Juan's only child."

He was right that Maria had a soft spot for kids, but I couldn't leave her hanging. She has little patience for people who change their promises. Especially since I'd cancelled the last four trips.

"Remember all that computer time, I spent last month for

you. Not to mention the spiritual acquisitions I obtained. Both helped you find that father."

"Yeah, I know, but . . ."

"And the help John Lennon gave us last year," his eyes pleaded. "Seronia is super-functional, but she's only seven and a non-verbal autistic. She needs our help."

Throwing an autistic young girl in the mix was a clincher, and Hub knew it. I have a soft heart for psychological problems. They are the reason I have money. What started as a chart I developed for doctor's offices to help read psychological aberrations from physical symptoms had turned into an online guide for psychiatrists, physicians, nurses, and hospitals. I had no idea it would go world-wide.

Maria might understand. I hoped.

"Let me talk to Maria, I said. "I think I can make her appreciate the situation." I cringed at the thought of her voice responding to me asking her. "I need to finish my walk and muster up the courage I'll need."

"I knew you wouldn't let me down." Hub came at me for a hug. "Oh, I booked our flight for tomorrow morning, out of Salt Lake International."

I raised my palms to Hub, warning him to step back and began jogging.